THE
LAST WINTER
OF DANI LANCING

THE
LAST WINTER
OF DANI LANCING

A NOVEL

P.D. VINER

CROWN PUBLISHERS

NEW YORK

Copyright © 2013 by P. D. Viner

All rights reserved.
Published in the United States by Crown Publishers, an imprint of the Crown Publishing Group, a division of Random House, Inc., New York.
www.crownpublishing.com

CROWN and the Crown colophon are registered trademarks of Random House, Inc.

Originally published in Great Britain, in different form, by Ebury Press, a division of Random House Group, Ltd., London.

Library of Congress Cataloging-in-Publication Data
Viner, P. D.
The Last Winter of Dani Lancing : a novel / P. D. Viner. — First American Edition.
p. cm.
1. Murder—Investigation—Fiction. 2. Murder victims' families—Fiction. 3. Psychological fiction. I. Title.
PS3622.I548L37 2013
813'.6—dc23

2013012086

ISBN 978-0-8041-3682-2
eISBN 978-0-8041-3683-9

Printed in the United States of America

Jacket design: Oliver Munday
Jacket photograph: George Baier IV
(photograph of girl: Edward Carlile Portraits)

1 3 5 7 9 10 8 6 4 2

First American Edition

For Lynne
My A-muse

PART ONE

ONE

"There's no such thing as monsters," he tells her.

The girl screws up her nose. "Look anyway. Please."

"Okay."

She hugs Hoppy Bunny tight as her dad slides sideways off the bed and onto the floor, pulling the duvet to one side and peering into the shadows.

"Nothing there."

"Are you sure?"

Even at five years old she knows that grown-ups can't be trusted with this stuff. They aren't clear about what is and isn't in the dark.

"I am absolutely, totally sure there's nothing under your bed."

"Check the wardrobe."

With an exaggerated sigh, he moves across the room and pulls the doors open quickly. Dresses and coats sway violently, like zombie hordes.

"Dad!"

"It's okay." He grabs the clothes. "Nothing to worry about." He pushes them aside and peers into the back of the wardrobe. "Just clothes, no lions or witches."

Her eyes widen. "Did you think there would be?"

"No. No . . . I was just being silly." He sits back on the edge of her bed. "There's nothing there, darling."

3

"Nothing now! What if a monster slides under the door when I'm asleep?"

"Once I kiss you good night the room is sealed, nothing can come into your bedroom in the night."

She frowns. "What about the tooth fairy?"

"Well . . ."

"Santa?"

"I meant . . ." He frowns too. "Nothing bad can come in, and Hoppy Bunny's here to keep you safe."

"How?" She looks dubiously at the small stuffed rabbit.

"Hoppy was specially trained, he only lets in good fairies or Santa."

"Hmmm."

"Don't worry, Dani. Mummy and I are downstairs. Nothing bad is going to happen. I promise." He kisses her forehead . . .

. . . and the memory starts to fade.

＊

Dani watches her younger self melt into the shadows of the night. Frozen in time, for a moment longer, is her father. The sight of him, so young and handsome, makes her smile—a sad smile. Slowly, the black hair, smooth face, elegant clothes slip away. Left behind, lying in the bed, is the older version. His hair is salt and pepper now, his face craggy and lined. He sleeps, but it's not the sleep of the just. His nights are pained by visions. More than twenty years of night terrors—and she is the cause.

She sits in the chair by the door and watches him sleep just like she does every night, watching for the shadows to take his dreams. When they come, she will sing to him. Sometimes, when he whimpers or calls out, she aches to lean forward and kiss his forehead—but she can't. Nearly forty years have passed since he banished the monsters from her room. Now it's her job—to keep him safe in the night.

She curls her arms around herself. The room is cold, though she doesn't notice, she just likes to feel arms around her. She wishes she could call the child back, see herself again from all those years ago. How old—five? So serious and confident, when had it all disappeared? But of course she knows the answer to that. "Dani . . ." he calls out in his sleep.

"Shh, sleep safe. I'm here." And softly she sings a lullaby she remembers from all those years ago.

"Care you not and go to sleep, Over you a watch I'll keep . . ."

"Not her!" He calls out in pain from the thickness of his nightmare.

"Shh, Dad." She slides off the chair to kneel by his bed.

"Dani . . ." he calls softly.

"It's okay."

"I can't find you."

He's sweating. His face is pinched and his legs begin to jerk like he's running.

"Dani!" he yells, his hands flail, jaws grind.

"I'm here, Dad," she tells him, hoping her voice might worm its way down into his dream.

He twists sharply and cries in pain. "Are you safe?"

She hesitates. "Yes, Dad, I'm safe."

He shakes, whimpering like a child. "Dani. Where are you?"

"Dad, I'm here," she whispers. "I came back."

His face contorts and he moans loudly.

"I can't see through the snow. Dani, I can't—" His body is suddenly rigid. His jaw grinds and darkness knits his brow. His back arcs—like he is having a seizure.

"Sleep, Daddy. I'm here."

He makes a low moan and, like a sudden storm, the danger passes as tension slips away from his body and he slides deep into the undertow of sleep. She watches him, listens as his breath softens until it's barely audible. He's still. He's safe. The monsters have left him alone—for tonight. He should sleep until morning.

She stretches in the chair. Her back aches and the pain in her hip cuts through her. She can't sit any longer, so lies on the floor beside him. She rocks from side to side, trying to get comfortable. It was such a long time ago, surely it shouldn't still feel like this. Phantom pains. On the ceiling, the faintest movements of shadow—grays and blacks—skirmish above her head. Slowly, the pain recedes and she sinks into the floor. She lies still, missing her night-light, wants something to eat the darkness away. She longs for dawn, for her dad to wake. She wants to talk, go for a walk, maybe see a movie? What time is it now—2 a.m.? Tiredness sweeps across her. He'll sleep—she wishes she could.

She lies still for a long time, listening to his breath rise and fall. Finally she rolls over onto all fours—stretches like a cat—and leaves. Outside his door, she pauses for a few moments, continuing to listen to his breath. One day it will end. Will she be there at that moment? Hear the body draw its final inhalation, the lungs expand and then just stop so that the air seeps away and there is nothing. Nothing. The thought scares her. The loneliness terrifies her.

She turns to her own room. Inside is her single child's bed, the same bed her father knelt under to check for monsters all those years ago. She feels a tiny shudder run through her.

"Someone walked over your grave." That's what her gran would have said.

The room is too dark, only a little moonlight spills in from the hallway. She isn't sure she can stay there. The shadows are alive sometimes.

"Be brave, Dani," she tells herself. But the old fears are strong. What would Dad do?

She bends down and looks underneath the bed. Cobwebs. No monsters—unless you're a fly. She smiles a fake smile, even though there's nobody there to see it, and she feels braver.

"Go on, Dan," she whispers, and stretches out her fingers to the wardrobe door. It swings open with a little haunted-house creak. The dresses and coats are long gone. It is totally empty. Of course it is. Real monsters don't hide in wardrobes.

TWO

Saturday, December 18, 2010

She cuts him.

His body twists. She tightens her grip on his hand as the pain draws him back from the oblivion of sedation. Eyes flicker. For a second they open: confusion, pain, fear. His palm pools with blood.

"Shh," she whispers, as if to calm a baby, squeezing his fingers tight.

He struggles one final time, but the tape she's wrapped around his body holds him securely. He drops back into the darkness.

With an unsteady hand she fumbles in her pocket for the sterile swab.

"Damn," she spits, frustrated by the delicate touch needed. With a bloodied finger she pokes her glasses, holding them in place so she can peer through the oval at the bottom. His blurred hand sharpens into focus.

She dips the bud into his palm; the cotton bloats, gorges itself. She lets his hand drop—it arcs to the floor and swings, splattering red like a child's painting, and then comes to rest, weeping onto the carpet. She's cut far deeper than was needed; bone shows through the deep trench of flesh. She doesn't care, just runs the swab across the slide, leaving a bloody smear. Done. She feels giddy. Finally she's done it. Patricia Lancing has her man. She leans forward, her mouth brushing his ear to whisper, "You are a monster."

"He needs a plaster," a small voice says.

Patty looks across at Dani, who with a shy smile holds up the toy she's squirted with ketchup.

"Hoppy Bunny needs a plaster. He's poorly."

"Oh dear, let's get him one. Maybe Doctor Duck should take a look."

"Oh yes, Mum. I'll go get him." Her daughter pads away, the memory fading.

"Danielle," Patty calls to her five-year-old daughter, but she is gone. Long gone.

She looks back to the man tied to the chair. "Why Danielle?"

The question hangs in the air between them as it has done for over twenty years, poisonous and all consuming.

"Why my daughter?"

There is no sound from him. She looks at her watch. 3:42 a.m.

She takes the slide with his blossom of blood, puts it back in its box and seals it. With reverence she walks it over to the cooler and places it inside. All is done. She hears her husband's voice slide back to her through the years: "Now what, Patty? Now what will you do?" Jim asks, but she doesn't know what to say to him, her mind too full of shadows.

She turns back to the man she has abducted. With a finger, she reaches out and tips his head. His skin is waxy, lips flecked with the drool of insensibility. She takes his eyelid and peels it back; there is nothing but a poached-egg smear. He sickens her. She raises the knife and presses it into his soft throat. It would be easy . . . so . . . she closes her eyes.

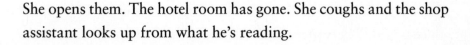

She opens them. The hotel room has gone. She coughs and the shop assistant looks up from what he's reading.

"Yeah?" He looks fourteen, all spots and surly resentment.

She points behind his head, to the serious hunting knives in the locked cabinet. He grunts, then takes a stubby key from his pocket and slides the glass away. He points to one and she nods. It's vicious, designed to slice through flesh and muscle, hack through bone. One edge a razor, the other a saw. She's come all the way across London to this little shop in Wimbledon, somewhere nobody knows her, to buy a specialist hunting knife. She carries no ID, just cash—a cover story all worked out: her husband will be hunting for the first time, big promotion up for grabs and he needs to impress. So she will have to gut, slice and cook whatever he manages to shoot. She's pleased with her invention and has topped it off with a disguise: waxed jacket and riding boots she bought from Oxfam yesterday. She's also wearing lots of make-up. Mutton dressed as mutton. She spent all morning in front of a mirror perfecting her cut-glass home-counties accent, reborn as Hilary Clifton-Hastings. Nobody can refuse to sell a hunting knife to a Clifton-Hastings.

"That will do nicely" she says and hands it back. The shop assistant peels the price sticker from the back with a fingernail that is almost pure soil.

"Thirty-five fifty."

Hilary Clifton-Hastings slides the cash across the counter; he scoops it up and scatters it in the till. No questions, barely a glance from him. She does not need her alter ego. He sizes her up in a microsecond; small, thin, gray woman in her sixties: harmless.

Harmless!

That was two days ago.

She opens her eyes. She's cold. That afternoon's snow falls on her once again. The watery sun's dipped below the horizon and the light has died. She stands, a statue, alone in the long-stay car park alongside the metal carcasses that poke from the growing carpet of snow. If anyone were watching her, they'd think she was a crazy woman. But nobody is watching, not even on CCTV. Broken yesterday and not repaired, tut-tut.

She hasn't dressed for the weather. The ferocity of the cold has surprised her: Siberia in southeast England. She knows she should go and sit in her car but everything looks so beautiful in its white coat. All around the ground is pure, unmarked, as if no living thing exists to disturb the peace. It would be terrible if she destroyed it. So she stands still and waits.

She sticks out her tongue and counts . . . one elephant, two elephants . . . a swirling snowflake lands and dissolves, wet and slightly metallic. Others fall on her eyelids and trickle away as mock tears, some alight on her skin and nuzzle into her silver hair. Each flake is perfect—an intricate and exquisite ice world—unique. Some see the hand of God in this. Not her.

❄

Fewer and fewer planes have been landing over the last few hours as the snow has got heavier. If she had her phone she could check the weather report, check the plane schedule, but she doesn't have it. She carries nothing that could identify her if . . . if things don't go to plan.

"Shall I just stand here and wait?" she thinks. "But for how long? He's already hours late, may not come at all." Does she wait until she freezes?

She watches the snow and listens for the first mutterings of an engine. She feels as if she's been placed in a magician's cabinet, waiting to be sawn in half.

Then, in the darkness some way off, she hears the chug of a

motor. She shakes a little, though not her sickness shakes. She doesn't need her medication—this is first-night nerves.

❄

All is dark. Jim flicks the light on. He stands in the doorway, holding a tea towel where the door should be. "Ladies and gentleman. I now present for your delectation and delight a master of the art of prestidigitation . . ."

"Dad!" Dani shouts from the hallway. "I'm doing magic."

"Sorry. Ladies and gentlemen, I give you the Magic of Madame Danielle Lancing."

The tea towel is pulled away with a flourish and a six-year-old Dani enters, wearing a black top hat made from an old porridge container and a paper plate. She sports a black cape that was once a towel and waves a cardboard wand that came free in a Rice Krispies packet and has been sat on quite a few times.

"I am Mystical Dani and you will be amazed," she says in as low a voice as a six-year-old can manage.

She whips the wand into the air.

"Abracadabra!" She pulls off her hat and Hoppy Bunny is on her head, dressed in a tutu.

Jim claps wildly. Dani grins, showing her missing front teeth. She waves her dad over, and once again they whisper.

Patty watches them with pleasure, and perhaps a twinge of jealousy. They're thick as thieves those two. Always have been, always . . .

"Now my beautiful assistant will help me," Dani shouts as if she were in a real theater, and Jim bows and blows kisses to the crowd, "with the Many Knives of Doom illuj-ion." She waves a plastic knife in the air.

Patty feels the weight of the hunting knife in her own hand, its edge bloody. Her husband and daughter dissolve—smoke and mirrors. They were not real, a thirty-five-year-old memory that rose to the surface; the heft of the blade in her hand is real though. What she must do with it is real. She grips it tight.

Headlights arrive, arresting the freezing flakes in mid-air. It's too big to be a car, it must be the shuttle. The excitement thaws her toes and fingers; she moves slowly toward the line of cars that will hide her from view. Finally the shuttle reaches the entrance to the car park and turns in. She feels her heart slow as the bus crawls toward her.

"Let him be on it," she speaks aloud, though the wind rips her words to shreds the moment they emerge from her mouth. The bus skids a little as the driver applies the brakes. Inside it's dark. There is no movement. She ages and dies many times before the door finally cracks open and the interior is illuminated. The driver hops down the stairs quickly, keen to get this done and get back to the warmth of the terminal. He opens one of the luggage stores under the bus and pulls out a set of golf clubs.

"How funny," she thinks as she watches him struggle with them. Shivering, the driver holds them out, as a single passenger alights. The metal whale then pulls away with a little slide of the wheels, heading back to civilization.

She watches the passenger wrestle with the golf clubs and a little pull-along suitcase. She cannot see clearly; he's too far away and in the shadows. She holds her breath while he inches toward her. From somewhere she hears:

"Mum." A voice from the dark.

"I'm nearly there, Dani. So close."

"Patty." Jim's deep voice rattles in her rib cage.

"Please don't ask me to stop, Jim."

Patty digs her gnawed fingernails into the skin of her arm—as hard and deep as she can—and the passenger stumbles closer. Face still hidden, snow billowing around him. There is a yellow pool of light and he is almost there . . . he steps into it, like an actor moving into a spotlight: Duncan Cobhurn.

He's not tall but he's stocky. He looks like a rugby player who's stopped exercising but still enjoys his food and beer. Mostly bald, just a clipped halo above his ears, black flecked with gray. His face is fleshy and pink—a mix of blood pressure and sun. He has a few days' growth of beard, which is mostly white. He's dressed in linen, a stylish white suit that might have looked great in Lisbon but is going to get ruined in the snow. He looks frozen already.

"Good," she thinks. "That will make my job easier."

The clubs are on his shoulder and swing heavily as he walks. He has to stop every few feet to clear away the little snowmen his case keeps building. As he approaches she slowly draws back into the shadows and slides toward her car.

❄

She opens her eyes. She's back in the hotel room with Duncan Cobhurn—a sedated and bleeding Duncan Cobhurn. The room is stifling. She misses the clean sterile cold of the afternoon. No snowflakes fall here; instead motes of dust dance. She remembers how Dani, when she was about five, believed they were sugarplum fairies dancing in the moonlight. The imagination of a child . . . It's just dirt and decay. This room is filthy. The walls are beige but speckled with greasy spots and chocolate-colored scabs. The ceiling was probably white once, but is now nicotine beige, and the floor . . . Christ knows what bodily secretions have seeped into it. There's a stain, just by the foot of the bed, that she thinks is the spitting image of Gandhi. Now, what would he have done? Forgiven Duncan Cobhurn? She is not Gandhi. She cuts him.

THREE

Saturday, December 18, 2010

"Wha—?" Jim Lancing wakes with a start. No idea where, frozen—panic.

"Dad." Dani is beside him in an instant.

"I'm okay, darling. Go back to your room, I'm fine. It was just a nightmare, just another nightmare."

"I should stay."

"No, no really. Please, Dani. I'm okay."

"Are you sure?"

"Please."

She nods, a little reluctantly, and leaves him.

He lies back down and concentrates on slowing his heart, pulling himself back from wherever his dream had taken him. He pictures a lake in his mind, mountains surrounding it—a calm place. Slowly the fear recedes and he is himself again. He rubs his hand, it hurts. He looks across at his bedside table. Glowing numbers read 3:42.

"Damn."

He really needs more sleep than this, but he knows that won't happen. He lies there in the dark. On his tongue there's the faintest taste, and in the air there seems to be something, tangible and smoky, but he can sense it rather than smell it. He feels sweaty from his nightmare and already the prickles of sweat are turning cold; he realizes what the taste in his mouth is: blood.

16

He rolls over onto his side and then out of bed and onto the floor. The first few steps are little more than a hobble until his creaking joints and muscles warm up. He walks down the hallway to the loo. This is the biggest show of how age has crept up on him: that he can't go through the night without the need to pee. And then, once he's there, he stands longer than ever before. Sometimes he even sits, like a girl. Tonight he sits immediately, knowing he will be in there a long time. After a couple of minutes he takes a newspaper that's folded under the sink. He looks at the Sudoku.

"I haven't got a pen," he calls out.

"Isn't there one in the medicine cabinet?"

He looks and finds a stubby pencil in with his razor.

"Got it. Thanks," he shouts to his daughter.

"Okay," she calls back. "I'll be downstairs. Waiting for you."

He finishes the Sudoku and Killer Sudoku while he's there, then cleans his teeth, trying to remove the taste of blood. He looks at himself in the mirror and isn't unhappy with the reflection. He's got pretty terrible bed-head and his eyes look saggier than usual, but generally he's not too bad for a man of sixty-four, especially at this time of night. Not gone to seed, like many others he could name—he's pretty lean. He can bend over and touch his toes without too much huffing and puffing. He would be the first to admit that his stomach isn't flat like it once was; there's a slight paunch but it's not bad, just a little loss of muscle tone to show how gravity hates the old. He rinses his mouth and then runs his wet fingers through his hair. It's still a pretty good crop, even if it has gone stone gray at the temples and the rest, once raven black, is now dusted with gray. He has always thought his features a little too pronounced, his nose too big and his mouth too wide, but he seems to have grown into them over the years.

He shivers, the chill of the morning creeping into his bones. He runs a shower, nice and hot, and steps into it. The pressure is strong—it pounds and buffets him, releasing knots.

"Jim," a voice breathes from inside the cascade of water.

"Patty?" He strains to hear—can her voice be in the water?

"Help."

He feels something deep in his heart—a tug that says something's wrong with her, his wife. A wife he has barely seen in twelve years. In the churn of the water his nightmare comes back to him.

"Are you coming down yet?" she calls up the stairs.

"Just coming," he replies, feeling guilty for not going down before now. He knows how much she longs to talk after a sleepless night, how lonely she gets during the long stretch of darkness. But right now he's too rattled by the images in his head to talk to her. He tries to push them back inside the box and paste a smile on his face.

"You need to get down here," Dani shouts.

The smile wastes away on his face. He heads downstairs. "Where are you?"

"Hide and seek" is her reply.

He finds her curled up in the big leather armchair in the room they laughingly call his den. When she was a child it had been the family dining room. But he couldn't remember the last time the house had any actual dining in it. Instead the room had become a sort of den-slash-library-slash-watching-the-world-slide-by room. It's pretty Spartan: two chairs, a small table and an old fish tank. Once, a long time ago, the tank had been home to Dani's tropical friends but now has some very creepy-looking cacti in among multicolored stones. It's the only room in the house that's allowed. to be a little untidy. Newspapers are on the floor; he only buys the Saturday *Guardian* and Sunday *Observer* each week but they certainly mount up. Books and correspondence are piled on a small coffee table. Every couple of months he forces himself to sit down and catch up with the world; he should probably do that pretty soon, he thinks.

She turns in the big chair to look up at him. Her long dark hair curling over her shoulder, pale skin flawless and her large brown eyes glittering with excitement. It shocks him a little—probably the aftermath of his nightmare—that she still looks so young. He forgets that sometimes . . . after all that has happened to her.

"You okay?" she asks with a half smile.

He nods a yes.

"Then sit down and buckle up—you are in for a treat."

She swings back in the chair to face the doors that lead to the garden. Jim sits in the other, less comfortable chair and angles it to match Dani's view. Outside it's black but he can just see someth— a light snaps on in the garden next door, bleeding across their lawn, revealing an amazing vista. Huge flakes of snow drift on the wind, buffeted and brawling like bumper cars at the fair.

"Oh my God." He's amazed by the sight.

The two of them sit watching the snow until the sensor light turns off.

"It'll go back on soon."

They sit in the dark, waiting. Jim suddenly thinks of the animals out there: Willow, Scruffy, George and others—guinea pigs, hamsters, cats and two dogs buried over the years in solemn services. He has never seen their ghosts, which he's glad about. If Scruffy came back to be stroked, like some zombie Disney cartoon, that would scare the life out of him. But he wonders where they are now. Is there an animal afterlife? Do they have souls like he does, like Dani does?

The light flips back on—catching a squirrel in mid-scurry—and Jim is once more in awe of the scene before him. The snow swirls like the Milky Way, so close he could reach out and touch it.

"Are you out there, Patty?" he thinks. "Somewhere in the snow?"

FOUR

Saturday, December 18, 2010

Tom stops to get his bearings. Peering into the dark, he can see the mouth of the bridge stretching over the Thames but by halfway across, it fades to nothing. A wall of blackness with snow rippled through it. The streets are empty but for a second he thinks he sees someone walking toward him across the bridge. It looks like . . . but then there's no one. Just snow whipped up by the wind. Who? Something scratches at his thoughts, tugging at strands of memories that just refuse to come. For a second, he knows . . . but it just fades from his mind.

He looks at his watch, it's 3:42 a.m. Everybody's asleep, except him.

He turns back to the path and kicks at the snow. For days he's been dragging a heavy heart along in a sack but now there's snow. How can anyone feel depressed when faced with this? He feels like a kid who's bunked off school to see the circus come to town, "oohing" and "ahhing" as the tufts of candyfloss parachute toward him.

"I love snow," he tells the world.

He looks over the sluggish water to the park; it could be anywhere, anywhen. The snow is already quite thick, deadening all sound, building banks and drifts. The moon's fat, nearly full, but half-hidden behind skyscrapers of cloud. He stands for a long time, a solitary figure in a snow globe, then finally turns toward the ark of glass that juts out over the river and trudges toward home.

He's left his car outside her house. He's already thinking he'll send a constable to collect it in a day or two, in case she's watching out her window.

"What a mistake," he tells the snow.

He'd known she was divorced, had two children—and that could have been fine, he's good with kids. The problem was that he'd not seen how needy she was. They'd had dinner a week ago—she'd drunk a little too much and been a little loud by the end of the evening, but he thought that was nerves. She was at least ten years younger than him, thirty, with long, deep brown hair and tall, long-limbed. That was what had attracted him to her profile. And in her picture she smiled quite beautifully—genuine, unconcerned. Just like *her* smile had been.

"And?" he asks himself. "The truth?"

Truth? He thinks. It has nothing to do with truth, or admitting anything. He knows why he'd been drawn to this woman. He knows why some women draw his eye and not others. Why he'd turned down at least two women who could have made him happy, who could have loved him. The truth was because he was in love. Still in love after all these years.

And that photo on the website had been so like her. So like Dani. He had made the date, wanting to see her smile again. Except in real life he didn't see Dani's smile. Instead there was a thin half smile, darting across her lips like an apology, and she dipped her head to hide how tall she was. Her voice had grated on him from the start too—rough sloppy diction—*you know, you know like.* But dinner had been fine. At the end they had walked to the Tube and she'd leaned into him and kissed him. He felt her small breasts push into his chest and a flick of her tongue brush his lips. She called him the next day and they had agreed to meet again. She invited him to dinner at her place. Stupid. Her place—it was obvious where that was heading. Stupid to go to bed with her. Out of her clothes she was so unlike Dani. She had tattoos, which he hated. From the start she apologized for everything. Sorry for her M&S knickers, the sheets, the children down the hall, her inexperience, how cold her hands were. "Next time it will be perfect," she whispered in his ear as he pushed himself into her.

Afterward she went to the toilet. He imagined her in there, crying for her lost life and the desperate compromises she'd been forced to make. He had to get out of the house. When she returned with minty breath, he told her he had to leave, still had a test to prepare for Year Four. He saw her flinch as he lied to her—clearly she was a woman who'd heard a lot of lies and had good radar for them—but he couldn't bear to snuggle up with her and talk about the future. It actually made it worse that she looked like Dani. Only skin-deep though. He smiles at the thought of Dani and his cheeks tighten and ache. His eyes have little frozen lakes in the corners.

It wasn't his first lie to this woman either. His profile on the dating site says he's a teacher of history at an under-performing comprehensive. He never tells anyone he's a policeman. Even those few people close enough to him to know he works for the police don't know exactly what he does. Only a few other high-ranking officers know he heads a special unit, and that he looks into the eyes of dead girls and promises them he will try to find the men responsible. And he tries. He tries. Detective Superintendent Thomas Bevans. The Sad Man.

He walks, feeling the snow give way under his feet.

"I should've put a bet on a white Christmas—the odds will be useless now," he tells the trees.

He loves the silence. Of course, at almost 4 a.m. on a Saturday morning, it is going to be pretty quiet—but the deadening effect of the snow and the low cloud has removed all trace of the world. No music of the spheres. He stops and closes his eyes. He's a boy again, remembering the first time the silence descended, a truly white Christmas. 1976.

He was eight and pretty sure he'd never seen snow before—not real snow that settles on the ground. But he remembers the rush of excitement that morning, like man had landed on Mars or something. The road outside their flat was amazing. Nothing had driven through it, not even a bike. Pure. Virgin. White. He ran out. His mum was still asleep and he ran and ran through the snow, then turned to see his tracks—the only human being on earth. Until he got to the park. And there she was. He remembers thinking, "What the bloody hell is she wearing?" She was in a white nightdress, flimsy and sheer. He could see the curves of her body beneath it— but is that just wishful remembering? No, she was fully clothed underneath, with a big sailor's jumper. She wore the nightdress over the top. She was lying in the snow waving her arms. He saw her and hid in some bushes, watching. She lay there for a while and then got up and walked away—her dark hair streaked with snow. He waited until she was out of sight and walked over to where she'd lain. There was an angel in the snow.

Christ, even at eight years old, she had done something to him. Danielle Lancing, the girl he loved. Loves.

As memories of her flit through his mind he feels a shiver run though him as if somebody is dancing on his grave. But it's just the vibration of his mobile on silent. He pulls it out and reads the short message, a missing person report. Normally he wouldn't be notified unless it was a high-profile victim. This isn't, just a Durham busi-nessman who'd been reported missing by his wife. But the name is one that he'd recently added to a high-security alert list: Duncan Cobhurn. And the memory slots into place—the woman he thought he saw in the swirling snow on the bridge, Patricia Lancing. Dani's mother. He feels lost.

"Christ."

He turns to head back the way he's come. He begins to run.

FIVE

Patty sits in the dark. She had to turn the lights out so she could no longer see him—she wants to cut his throat. She needs to get calm so she can go and check the blood, to make—

Light snaps on outside the room, headlights from a car skidding into the car park behind the hotel. The glare spills around the edges of the curtains. The blood pooled at his feet glows. Her heart somersaults. Panic. She hadn't considered the curtains; they're a cheap fabric and don't fit very well. There must be no chance someone can see inside. She grabs the gaffer tape and begins to run it across the gaps, sealing the two of them in a cube. It takes a few minutes to remove all vestiges of light seeping in from the outside world and plunge the room into pitch-black.

Dani is standing on a chair; she's eight and looking intently at the problem before her. Jim has sunk a little so that she can reach around his neck. He's wearing a rented tuxedo that's a little snug in places. Dani has the two ends of a bowtie in her hands and a slip of paper with instructions on how to tie it.

"I think . . ." Jim starts.

"Shh!" Dani holds her finger to her lips and then frowns back at the paper.

"If you . . ." he tries.

"Shh. If you want this tied properly you need to keep quiet." She reads, "Fold the left over the right . . ." She proceeds to follow the directions carefully, concentrating on the diagrams.

"Eureka!" She jumps up and down doing her happy dance. It's a little loose, but a recognizable bowtie. Dani beams broadly, proud of herself. From the door there is a wolf whistle. Jim turns to see Patty. He gives her a twirl.

"I could rent you out as a gigolo," she says huskily.

"Sorry, I'm a one-woman man. You look fantastic."

She rolls her eyes; compliments are not something she likes to hear.

"Cab will be here in five minutes."

"Will Jenny be here soon?" asks Dani.

"Any minute. She'll give you some supper, then into jammies, stories and bed. Got that?"

"Yes," says the eight-year-old with a little roll of her own eyes, as if to say: *I'm eight. I can understand simple instructions and I don't really need a babysitter anymore anyway.*

"If you win will you wake me up and show me your prize when you get home?" she asks.

"No." "Yes." Patty and Jim answer simultaneously.

"I won't win—it's just stupid." Patty shakes her head.

"Daddy says you fight for truth and justice."

"Oh does he? I just write stories in a newspaper."

"I'm going to be a superhero when I grow up," says Dani as she jumps off the chair and lands with a slam at her parents' feet.

"And what superpowers will you have?" Patty asks her. Dani thinks for a moment.

"To make people be nice."

Patty snaps the light back on in the room. She checks the tape again. His mouth's totally covered, but just to make sure, she pulls his head back to rest on the chair and wraps layer after layer of tape around and around. He can't possibly move now. There is no dignity. He's wet himself; it drips down the chair and onto the floor, joining his blood. The smell is rank. It looks as if he's melting, like the Wicked Witch of the West.

When she's finished with the tape, she turns her attention to the room. A double bed dominates. She has lain on it; it's lumpy. She didn't pull back the sheets, sure they wouldn't be clean and not wishing to leave any evidence. She wears gloves, has done each time she's entered the room. She also wears a shower cap and plastic pinafore, as if she works in a meat-pie factory. There's a bedside table with alarm and telephone, a chair by the window, a wardrobe that contains a mini-safe and an ironing board. She looks down. The blood will be difficult to get out of the carpet.

"Maybe when I'm finally done with this room I'll leave a pile of money for the poor cleaner who finds all of this . . . If all goes well," she thinks.

According to the plan, she should return in less than eight hours to find nothing disturbed and her prisoner still unconscious. If not . . . then she must leave no trace. She checks all the drawers, they're empty; not even the Gideons see any point in coming here.

She moves to the bathroom: cracked white tile and a faint smell of bleach over damp and mustiness. The shower curtain has mildew along the bottom. She brought no toiletries with her, has not touched the two small plastic beakers, nor the two small bottles of shampoo and body wash. There's a hand towel. She wonders if she used it and decides to take it with her just in case. She stuffs it into her bag.

"Better safe than prison," she thinks.

She turns to leave and catches sight of herself in the mirror. Blood is smeared on her glasses and arcs over her cheek, sweeping across her right eye. She draws back from her reflection, horrified for a second and then . . . exhilarated. Fiery eyes blaze through a red cowl of his blood. She smiles at her bloody twin. She likes it, would like to keep it forever, a red badge of courage. Nemesis—the Red Revenger. But she's no superhero. She wipes the blood away with a wet-wipe she pockets after. In the mirror is a crone once more. She gives the bathroom one final look and heads back to the bedroom. Everything is clean. She looks at her watch: 5:30 a.m. Time to go. She checks she has the room key and then switches the light off and plunges the room once more into darkness.

From somewhere far-off she hears Jim ask her: "Patty, what would your superpower be?"

She whispers into the dark. "To bring back the dead."

SIX

Saturday, December 18, 2010

Tom sits at his desk. He should get moving—he doesn't have much time—but he can't move. For the last ten minutes he has read from a small purple book. The same page over and over. On the cover, written in bold black letters: PRIVATE—DO NOT OPEN. He takes the diary and slides it back into the safe in his desk. Inside there are two other diaries and a small photo album, full of pictures of Dani. He locks the safe and slides the desk drawer closed, then locks that too. No one knows he has a small safe in his desk; he fitted it himself one weekend.

Tom goes through his checklist one last time. He'd signed in twenty minutes ago, chatting to old Charlie on the desk for a while, asking about his daughter just as he always did. Then he took the lift up to his office on the third floor. He'd unlocked it and turned his computer on, logging in at 5:22 a.m. and started an e-mail. Now it is 5:36 a.m. Time to go. He heads into the corridor and takes the stairs down to the first floor, the main ops room for Operation Ares.

It's a large room with floor-to-ceiling glass composing one wall. Almost every other inch of wall space is taken up with whiteboards covered with lists of names, photos of victims, schedules of surveillance, reports and statements. Seen from eye level it's a mess, a Rorschach test in three dimensions. Yet from above it resembles a hive city with maze-like avenues created from dozens and dozens of dividers forming little rooms or corridors where desks can congregate. Everywhere, everywhere is paper. Great, towering skyscrapers of paper. In some places they are still intact, in others smashed down or mashed into other towers as if Godzilla has rampaged through central Tokyo. Some of the paper skyscrapers spill onto the floor like a river that's burst its banks. In other spots, reams and reams are scrunched into balls and lie under desks or scattered around empty bins. A sorry testament to the lack of basketball skills in Britain.

At this time of the morning, before natural light begins to spill through the glass, it feels oppressive. A city of paper, dark and shadowy. Except for one desk that blazes in the very center of the web. This is where the graveyard shift works, or more likely dozes, while they wait for information on breaking crime. Mostly they file reports for later attention by the day shift, but sometimes they need some poor bugger woken up and dispatched to some drafty wasteland to look at a body. Tonight they had just passed on a run-of-the-mill missing person's report . . . but that had made Tom head directly there, not passing go and not collecting £200.

Tom looks at his watch: 5:38. In under an hour the graveyard shift will be over and the morning staff will start to arrive—he has to move. He can feel his stomach spasm; he's the boss, he should be beyond reproach. What he's about to do is misconduct at best. He vowed to himself, twenty years ago, that he would be straight, that his conduct would be whiter than white, that he would never do anything that he knew was wrong. Not again. Not since . . . That was why he was the youngest special-operations superintendent in the Metropolitan Police; that was why he had the loyalty of his team. And will he jeopardize that now—for her? For Dani? Of course he will.

He takes a deep breath and swings the door open, making straight for the only officer—Eddie Matthews. Fat Eddie. As he walks toward Eddie, Tom can see from the way he slumps sideways that he's asleep. He comes level without disturbing him, then slaps him hard on the shoulder. The big man jumps like he's been electrocuted.

"What the fu— Guv? What are you doin' 'ere?"

"No peace for the wicked, Eddie." With a Cheshire cat smile, Tom sits on the desk and looks the big man up and down. "Honestly, Eddie, have you got a shirt that isn't covered in Pot Noodle and tomato sauce? You look like you're bloody homeless."

"Sorry, guv, I'll—" Eddie looks like he might cry for a second and then hauls himself out of his chair and shambles off toward the gents.

Tom watches him go and feels a pang of guilt. It was a cruel thing to say. The reason Matthews had been given the graveyard shift was because his wife had kicked him out and he actually was homeless. A WPC had found him sleeping rough one night and called Tom rather than move him on or arrest him. Now Matthews had a rollaway bed under his desk, a corner of the gents had his suitcase in it and a mug with a razor and toothbrush. As long as no one had to see him with his shirt off and he didn't smell, everyone was pretty pleased to have an officer permanently on nights.

Tom watches the big frame amble into the gents and then quickly pulls out Eddie's chair and sits at the desk. Any tracing request needs to come from Matthews's computer; that would make everything look normal. If Tom did anything from his own computer or accessed any of the Serious Crime Squad's PCs there would be trouble. Of course, he's the boss and he knows Matthews's username, Fat Eddie. But he doesn't have his password. It takes just one guess. Rachel. Eddie's wife's name, poor bastard.

It takes a few seconds to open up all the information on Duncan Cobhurn, then he copies it into the management pensions file on another server—a report so boring nobody has accessed it in six months—closes down the file and logs out.

He slides the chair back and swings himself onto the desk. Then he waits for the gents door to open. It takes about a minute, then, as Eddie appears, Tom opens his desk and takes out a Picnic bar.

"Guv!" Eddie wails.

Tom smiles broadly and takes a big bite.

"That's me last one."

"I'm saving you from yourself, Eddie."

"I don't need saving." Eddie approaches his desk, sullenly reaches into another drawer and pulls out a Snickers.

"Last one?"

"Last bloody Picnic, I love those. I've still got Snickers, Mars and a couple of Lion bars."

Tom shakes his head. "See ya, Eddie."

Tom starts to walk off but Eddie asks, "Didn't ya want something, guv?"

He calls back over his shoulder, "Just some sugar, Eddie. Cheers."

***

Back in his own office Tom opens the pension file and cuts the missing person report from it. He excises any trace of it and saves it in his personal documents on his desktop. Then he opens it and reads quickly but carefully.

Missing person: Duncan Cobhurn.

Date of report: Friday, December 17, 2010, 11:45 p.m.

Reported by: Audrey Cobhurn. Wife.

Called wife at 4:20 p.m. to say he had arrived and would see her in three hours.

Landed at Heathrow from Lisbon. Flight BA147

Arrival confirmed by BA at 4 p.m.

Additional notes:

Cobhurn car found in long-term car park. Tires slashed. Snow has obliterated any signs of potential struggle. Bags missing.

House keys discovered in glovebox of car.

Status of investigation:

Potential abduction enquiry.

"Christ!" Tom's face drains of all color as he reads the report. Something was happening after all this time. He needs to see them again, Jim and Patty. They will have to talk about what happened twenty years ago.

Tom opens his drawer, then the safe, and fishes the diary out once again. He reads, though he probably could recite the page from memory.

October 3, 1985

Tom said today he is applying for Cambridge too. Probably King's to read literature. I'm sure we'll both get the results we need, but is he going there because of me? I don't know. I love him, of course I do—he's brilliant. My best friend and he's been so amazing the last year. There is no way I would have held it together without him but . . . what if he suggests we get a flat together? In one sense it would be great but in another, I don't know. He wants more. What do I want? I wish I could ask Dad about it but really I think his head would explode if I talk love and sex. I'll ask Izzy, but she has a bit of a blind spot when it comes to Tom. I know he's the best friend in the world, but . . .

SEVEN

Saturday, December 18, 2010

It's 6 a.m. Still a couple of hours before the sun will be up and even then it will probably be pathetic, wishy-washy gray light like dishwater. They have been watching snow swirl for a while and playing games. I Spy fizzled out quickly, but naming films and books with heavy snow scenes lasted quite some time.

"I need a coffee," Jim finally tells his daughter.

She starts to lift herself out of the chair.

"No, stay here and watch the snow." He turns away before he can see her face. He just feels like he needs some time on his own.

Three measured spoons into the grinder, top on, a triple tap on the side to make sure all the beans are in the center and then he presses the button and counts to thirty before the beans are ground. It's all a little OCD. He tips the coffee into the pot, the roasted scent swirling around the room. He pours the almost boiling water on (starting the little timer on the fridge) and watches the black mass fizz and bubble as a creamy skin forms on top. He slowly stirs the pot with a chopstick. Why is Patty back in his thoughts? From somewhere deep down in his body he feels a sense of dread start to build again, to . . . The beep of the timer pulls him back to earth and he plunges the coffee. He pours and sips. The black tar catches in his throat, acrid and syrupy, and sits uneasily on his empty stomach. Maybe a piece of toast would make him feel better. He slices himself a thick piece and puts it under the grill. The echo of her voice plays through his head. Urgent, desperate and needy. His heart begins to race and his chest tightens.

"Dad." Dani is next to him. "Just breathe."

He immediately starts to calm. Dani has always been able to cheer him and calm him. That's why he needs her. Why they need each other.

"Dad. Dad, the toast's on fire."

"Oh hell." He pulls the grill pan out and dumps the blazing slice into the sink. Dani doubles up laughing.

"It's not funny."

"It is, it so is."

He turns the taps on full and the blackened bread disintegrates and washes down the plughole.

"Bit of luck the smoke alarms don't work anymore."

The kitchen smells bitter and smoky. It reminds Jim of a Bonfire Night from many years ago. He closes his eyes and can see Dani— she must be about six or seven. That night he nailed Catherine wheels all along the outside wall and made a big production out of lighting the first one, which spun and shot vicious sparks everywhere. He'd made a mistake; the fireworks were much too close, the sparks from the first hit the next and the next. Suddenly they were all alight. Spinning, squealing and roaring until one of them shot off the wall and landed in the bin, setting it ablaze. The next-door neighbors called the fire brigade, thinking it might spread. Of course, by the time the firemen arrived it was out and they were pretty annoyed at being called to something so minor on the busiest night of the year. He was really embarrassed but Dani sat there in silence, her face illuminated first by the sparks and flames, then by the flashing blue lights of the fire engine, all the time smiling so broadly. When it had all finished and the grumbling firemen had left, she said, "Do it again, Daddy."

"Do you ever talk to your mother?" he asks. It suddenly seems such an obvious question but he's never asked it before.

Dani scowls. For a second he's scared she doesn't know who he's talking about—has she forgotten her mother? Then she shakes her head. "No," she answers sadly. "You miss her?"

Jim can only nod. Miss is such a plain little word to describe how he feels. And after his nightmare he can't shake the sense that something awful has happened.

EIGHT

Saturday, December 18, 2010

As soundlessly as possible, Patty opens the door and cranes her head out, first left and then right. Empty. She steps out into the hallway, pulls the door closed and slips the DO NOT DISTURB sign onto the handle. She peels off the gloves and slips them inside her bag, then the shower cap. She hopes she looks normal once again. She draws a deep breath into her lungs and holds it there. She will succeed. She releases the breath and walks to the service lift. She almost uses her bare finger to call the lift, but stops herself just in time.

"Think, Patty. Think."

She pulls a rolled-up glove from the bag and pokes the button through it. The lift arrives quickly and she takes it down to the lower depths.

The door opens and she strides out, trying to look as confident and non-kidnapperry as possible. The effect is immediately ruined as she jumps out of her skin at the explosion of sound her heels make on the concrete.

"Christ." She stands shaking for a full minute before she can pull herself together again.

She's lucky. There is no one to hear or see her. The car park has no CCTV; this was one of the factors that made her choose this particular hotel. She slips off her shoes and walks to her car.

She opens the driver's door and slides in. Then she locks herself inside. It's not something she would normally do, but this morning it makes her feel safer. She turns the engine over, wincing a little at how loud it seems, and then she slowly drives up the ramp and out into the street.

Slide.

"Fuck."

She loses control. The top of the ramp is sheet ice, the wheels slew to the left and the brake does nothing. The nose of the car hits the wall and she hears the crack of glass. She turns the wheel slowly and bites down on the accelerator. The wheels spin but don't catch.

"Fuck." She floors the accelerator, the car pitches forward, she brakes hard and the car slides into the street completely out of control and veers sideways into a parked car. She closes her eyes tight as metal crunches into metal.

She sits for a few seconds while her racing heart slows a little. She tries the clutch again, slowly, until it bites and the car creeps forward. Okay. She slowly pulls into the middle of the road and . . . there's a snowman. Where the hell did it come from? It has a carrot for a nose and lumps of coal for eyes. Where did someone get coal?

Past Frosty, illuminated in small pools of yellow streetlight, she can see bank after bank of snow—it looks like Narnia. There's no moon, just oppressive cloud covering the sky. This was never part of the plan. She slowly lets the clutch bite and pushes forward, nudging the snowman in the tummy and then collapsing him. The head lands with a bump on the bonnet of the car and looks at her sadly, before it rolls off as the car swings . . . steer, steer . . . the wheels won't do what she wants and again she lurches into the curb. Crunch.

From somewhere she can hear the clatter of grit being shot at high speed, pinging off metal and concrete. She feels panic building.

"Shit shit shit shit oh shit. Patricia, breathe."

She has driven this route three times over the last six weeks, each time obeying the speed limit, and it has taken her forty minutes. But today?

"Do not have a panic attack, Patricia. Do not. You have time, you have hours."

She has no idea if the streets are passable. All she can hear echoing in her head is Dustin Hoffman whining, "I'm an excellent driver."

She pulls out into the street once more, and immediately feels the car slipping as the wheels slur away from her.

"Steer into the spin, not away." She remembers that from some TV show or something. "I am an excellent driver, dammit," she says through gritted teeth.

She gains some control and pulls away again, creeping forward at about two miles an hour. "I have planned this meticulously. I have driven this route; I know it like the back of my hand," her voice is level but intense. "I have change for the parking meter in a Ziploc bag and I have his blood. I am not letting this fucking weather stop me."

She winds slowly through the streets. Everywhere there are cars skidded, crashed and abandoned. Some have run into other cars, some into brick walls. She thinks once or twice that she sees heads slumped against windows as drivers sleep in their cars. There will be many, many war stories for people to tell their loved ones when day breaks. In the distance sirens and car alarms wail like babies. Instead of forty minutes it takes two hours to drive the distance to the lab. While she drives the snow falls around her.

She remembers the first time her parents took her into Central London—maybe she was six—to see the Christmas lights shining all the way down Oxford Street. Someone famous turned them on, a singer. She can't remember his name all these years later, but she does recall how magical it all was.

"I declare these lights . . ." Flick—from nothing to great beauty, all in a split second. After that, her parents took her for dinner somewhere swanky, or at least to her it felt like a palace. They ordered her spaghetti—it was the first time she'd ever had pasta and it seemed so exotic. Then the biggest treat—the London Palladium to see *Peter Pan*. When the pirates were on she remembers squirming in her mother's arms and watching through her fingers, ready to close them tight when it all got too scary. But more than anything she remembers Tinker Bell. She can still feel the tears of her six-year-old self as they run down her cheeks when the fairy drinks poison.

"Save her, Peter!" six-year-old Patricia screams, along with about two thousand other girls.

"We can all save her," Peter Pan shouts, "if you believe in fairies."

"I believe, I believe!" Patricia screams, everyone screams and the air is full of fairies, dancing, flying . . . just like the snowflakes.

Patty brakes, softly at first until she feels the wheels skid and glide. Then she pumps her foot hard. The wheels bite, the car slows and slides until the curb stops it with a little jerk. She looks at her watch. It's 7:38 a.m. She's parked directly opposite the main entrance to the testing labs. On previous trips at this time, even before the doors were opened, there were lights on inside, preparation for the day ahead. Now, however, inside it's black—no glimmer of light.

Snow still falls, a fresh blanket to cover the ground. She doubts the Tube will run, maybe some buses. But will any of the lab staff make it to work?

"I need to breathe," she thinks and slips out of the car into the icy air. On one of her reconnaissance trips she had gone to an all-night cafe for a mug of tea. It was very close by, so she turns to head for it. As she walks away from the car she feels a slight tug—his blood seems to call her.

NINE

Saturday, December 18, 2010

Jim stands by the phone, which sits on the arm of a chair in the living room. He looks at his watch. Almost 9 a.m. He was brought up never to phone anyone before 9 a.m. or after 8 p.m.—that was just how it was.

"What about a movie?" Dani calls from another room.

Jim looks out through the windows as the snow still swirls in the gray light—banked up against the garden fence and the door.

"I can't see any cinemas being open today. Maybe tonight," he calls back.

"What about a soup kitchen?"

"To help the homeless?"

"No, I thought you might need some soup, old man," she says with a smile as she walks in. "I know how hard those dang-fangled ring pulls are to open."

"You cheeky—"

The phone rings. Jim grabs at it.

"Patty?" He turns his back on Dani.

There is only the sound of someone breathing.

"Patty?" Jim's desperation oozes into his voice. "Patty?"

"No. No, it isn't Patty, Jim. It's Tom. Tom Bevans."

"Tom?"

"Tom," Dani echoes his name, though Jim cannot hear her anymore.

"Long time, Jim." His voice seems to come from far away.

"Has something happened to Patty?"

"Dad." Dani tries to get his attention, but her voice is suddenly so small. She feels giddy—unreal, like she weighs nothing, is nothing. She starts to feel a little scared.

"No, no, that isn't why I'm calling."

"Then why? I don't underst—"

"We need to talk about Dani. About what happened."

"I—" Jim's head pounds.

"Did Patty tell you I saw her?" Tom asks.

"You've seen Patty, when?"

"She told me she'd tell you."

"Tell me what?"

Tom pauses, annoyed—unsure how to proceed. "Dani's case is being looked at again, potential new evidence but—"

"What are you talking about?"

"That can wait, something else has happened and I need to see y—"

"Dad." Her voice is so tiny, but Jim hears the fear in it. He turns.

"Oh my God." He drops the phone.

"Help me, Dad," she pleads.

His twenty-one-year-old daughter looks as if she has aged a thousand years in seconds.

"I need a hug." She stretches out her arms.

"You know I can't."

"I need you to hold me, Dad."

"I want to but—"

"I'm begging, Dad."

"Dani."

She moves to him, but he pulls away.

"Dad," she says, with such hurt, and turns her back on him.

"Jim . . . Jim . . ." the phone is calling from the floor. Tom desperate to know what has happened. Jim puts the phone back on its cradle and then pulls the little clip out of the socket so the phone is dead. He looks for his daughter—she is gone.

"Dani?"

No reply.

He finds her standing in the garden, her head down. He walks out to join her, bracing himself against the intensity of the wind.

"Come back inside, darling."

She looks up at him. Her face pale and beautiful again.

"I need someone to hold me—to feel something." She lifts her arms for snowflakes to fall on them; she longs to feel the bite of cold as the crystals strike and melt.

"I want to feel life again."

"I'm sorry" is all a father can say to his daughter.

The snowflakes drift through her to strike the ground. They cannot touch her.

"Dani—"

"What is wrong with me, Dad?"

"Nothing, Dani. There's nothing wrong with you," he tells his dead daughter.

She looks at the ground, sees his footprints alone in the snow.

INTERMISSION ONE

Tuesday, February 14, 1989

Jim hears them enter the street and walks outside to meet them. He watches the horse-drawn carriage arrive. Black and sleek, the horses shake their heads and flick their tails. The youngest of the funeral directors has a pocket of carrots and Polo mints to keep them in line.

"Say goodbye in style," the funeral arranger had said, as if there was something to celebrate. So Jim had booked horses. As a girl Dani had loved them; they'd gone to Devon when she was six and she'd ridden a big brown carthorse. She squealed with delight the whole time. So why not get horses? Because he hadn't thought about the size of them, the smell of them, the rank deposit one of them would make outside the house while they wait. There is no "style" in saying goodbye to Dani.

The funeral director's mouth moves, but Jim hears nothing. He feels sick, but there's nothing in there to come out. For the last few days, all he's taken into his body has been a little water, a few cups of tea and a bottle and a half of cheap Scotch. At six that morning it was just dry heaves.

His back hurts. He spent last night in Dani's bed. He'd never realized how soft the mattress was. It had seemed a good idea that evening, even though Jacks had warned him. He thought it would be time to say goodbye. Instead he had lain awake all night, hearing her voice, sensing her every time sleep seemed about to claim him. He misses her. He misses his daughter so very much.

The funeral director repeats his words. "It's time, Mr. Lancing," he says, waving his plump hands.

Jim goes back into the house. Patricia's still on the sofa, slumped even further against Tom. She's so heavily sedated she doesn't know up from down. Maybe that made it a little easier now, but what would they pay for all this in the end?

In the kitchen Jacks and Ed, their oldest friends, finish the washing up. They'd been there last night. Jacks had slept next to Patty and Ed was on the couch. Thank Christ for friends.

For a second, just for a second, he wishes his mum was there, that she could hold his head in her arms and coo to him like she did when he was a boy. But there's no one to coo. She's dead and gone as well. His life has always been about women, his women: Dani, Patty, his mum and long ago his gran—Nanny Lily. He'd always been a mother's boy; Patty had often taunted him with that but . . . he liked it. And she did too, really. Patty wasn't interested in machismo. But as much as he misses his mum, he knows that she's lucky to be gone. His mum had been mad about Dani and she had adored her gran. If he believed . . . but he didn't. He could fantasize about his daughter being greeted into paradise by his mum but that was all it was, fantasy.

"Just get through today. Just today," he thinks.

He feels Ed's hand on his shoulder and a whisper in his ear. "Time to go, Jim-boy."

He nods, thankful for the darkness to be blown away, even for a few moments. Glad to have his best friend there, though anxious about what will happen once Ed and Jacks have gone. Jim and Patty have so few people in their lives. Their parents have gone. No brothers or sisters to lean on, no nieces and nephews to get caught up with. Jim and Patty are only children who had an only child. Why had that happened?

They could all have fitted in one car, but the funeral directors sent two. So Ed and Jacks travel in one long black car and Jim, Patty and Tom in the other. The trinity of the pained. Jim likes the speed the horses move at, slower than slow. He sees drivers fume all around, dying to honk and swerve round the cortège—but unable to cross that Rubicon of disrespect.

The three of them sit in their snail of a car, watching the horses draw the casket forward. All is silent, except for raspy breaths from Patty, a side effect of the sedatives. Jim sneaks a sidelong look at his wife. Her eyes are glassy, her mind trapped somewhere in an amber of Valium and God-knows-what. This fact makes his stomach lurch and anger fizz deep in his empty belly. She was meant to have been off the strongest drugs for today, the doctors had promised him that she would be awake. But this morning there had been "an episode." That was what the nurse had called it. She'd shot Patty up with something "to calm her." Zombify her, more like.

"She will hate me for this," he thinks. He already hates himself. But he doesn't have the strength to tell everyone to go home. He needs today to break the pressure of the storm that's built over them. He needs to see others who loved her, Dani's friends. So many of them have called, written and even knocked on the door. That has moved him so much. And, most important, Jim needs to remember the girl he raised and loved above all others, to remember her how she was. Not as the lifeless, defiled body he saw in the morgue.

When they arrive Reverend Chapman is waiting for them. He has the whitest teeth Jim ever remembers seeing. Jim dislikes him intensely. Reverend Chapman never knew Dani, feels no real sympathy but there aren't many places where you can bury someone and seat two hundred mourners.

"Hypocrite fuck," Jim whispers to himself.

He knows Patty would never have let God anywhere near their Dani. But she's out of it and he had to make the decision. Alone.

Jim gets out of the car. Tom holds Patty until Jim's ready, then between the two of them, they manhandle her out. Jim shakes the vicar's hand.

"This is my wife, Patricia."

"I am so sorry for your loss." He holds her arm for a second, squeezing—then he lets her go.

"This is Police Constable Thomas Bevans." Jim pauses for a second. "He was Dani's boyfriend."

It's a kind lie. Tom feels his gut clench and his eyes turn gritty. He takes the clergyman's hand.

"I am so sorry." The white teeth gleam.

They walk through the vestry. The walls are covered in photos, snapshots of Dani. Notes pinned to them, flowers and jewelry scattered all over.

"Your daughter was loved."

Jim nods. Love. He thinks of his mother.

On an easel outside the chapel Jim sees his mother's photograph, and underneath it reads: GRACE LANCING, 1901–1976. Eight-year-old Dani stands in front of it frowning and asks "Who's that lady?"

"That's Gran," Jim answers.

She looks at him crossly and shakes her head. "That isn't Gran, we're at the wrong funeral. That's some other lady. She isn't old enough to die."

Jim looks closely at the photo. It had been taken before he was born—his mother as a young woman, between the wars. She'd been picking hops in the country with her sister. Even in black and white he could see how healthy and fit she looked. Happy.

"It is Gran, just a long time ago, when she was young."

"Oh. Olden times." Dani nods sagely. "How old is she there?"

"Nineteen or twenty, I think."

"Oh yes. That's much too young to be dead."

Reverend Chapman leads them out of the vestry and into the church. He nods across to the organist who strikes up "Nearer My God to Thee." Jim looks across at him angrily; he'd said no hymns, no church music. Chapman does not meet his gaze, instead he leads them into the center aisle and the four of them process toward the front pew.

They walk slowly, like the horses, and Jim looks out at the sea of faces. Students from Dani's university have come by coach from Durham, organized by the students' union. They sit together in a group. Already tears stream down faces and pretty blonde girls lean against each other, clutching hands and promising to stay in touch their whole lives, no matter what. Jim smiles at them even though he recognizes only two or three. In another group, closer to the front he recognizes most of the sixth form from Dani's school and in another pew is the entire running team. He's so deeply proud that Dani had been so popular. He can see them, there in the pews, sharing anecdotes and memories, tears and even some laughter. Halfway down, Jim suddenly realizes he will never lead his daughter down the aisle to be married. He stops dead.

Chapman sees Jim freeze, the color drain from his face and his legs start to shake. He immediately steps back and kindly but firmly takes his arm and leads the three of them down to the front. He deposits them there, in the place of honor, then walks to center stage. He lets his eyes move across the congregation as the final lines of the hymn fall away. Then he walks across and lightly touches the casket, directly above where the head lies. It's a small ritual of his—a final blessing for those he is about to deliver from this earth. It's subtle but the families always like it: a little bit of theater that gives them permission to go up and touch the casket later, to say goodbye to the girl they loved. He knows how important that is, to release the grief and to stop any thought of the body inside—of the tests, the prodding and indignities that come with violent death. With rape and murder.

He looks down the aisles and sees the row after row of pretty young women whose thoughts must be so conflicted this morning. Anger, fear, grief and some guilt. Some part of them all must think—it wasn't me, thank God it wasn't me. But it was their friend. Toward the back there are men in uniform. Policemen of all rank from low to high. Some are there to support their colleague who has lost his young love. Others are there to be seen, a public act of contrition for their failure to find those responsible. Chapman finds it distasteful—the motives of these men are tainted. They are there for the press not the family. Then behind the uniformed men are the press. Again, a few are there to support a colleague and the mother of the murdered girl, yet most of the others are beasts full of the scent of blood. A photogenic, middle-class "good" girl missing for three weeks and found raped and murdered. Tabloid gold. He hopes they will behave—in church, at least. He looks back to the school friends, and then slowly onto the family.

It will be an emotional service and Chapman's prepared. Large boxes of tissues have been placed at the end of every aisle and there are four professional grief counselors on hand for free advice after the funeral—he's pulled out all the stops to make this one work. After all, the press are here and so is the archbishop. This is bigger than the jockey and the serial bigamist combined. Showtime.

Reverend Chapman waves to someone at the back, and the sound of Siouxsie and the Banshees sweeps out from the speakers above the pulpit.

In the front pew Jim bows his head and pulls Patty close to him. Beside them, Tom Bevans's heart breaks.

At the back of the church, someone slips in and stands behind a stone pillar, unseen by other mourners. Tears slide down his face. He knows he should not be there but can't help himself—the pull is too strong.

"I am so sorry, Dani. I never meant . . ." His words are swept up in the howl of the Banshees.

TEN

Jim makes hot chocolate, piping-hot milk with heaps of dark cocoa. He pours two mugs and sets one on the table in front of her. The curling steam circles her face and seems to shift the lines, smudging her cheeks, turning her features to air.

"I think I can smell it." She turns her face up to him, a huge smile.

"That's great." Jim beams back, though he knows it can't be true. Maybe she's remembering the scent—drawing on happy childhood winters or perhaps it's just wishful thinking. He sips his own, it's bitter with too much chocolate. He watches her—lost in thought somewhere.

Finally she snaps back. "How's yours?" she asks.

"Oh it's good. Really good. Especially on a day like today."

She nods.

"How about we go for a walk in the park?"

She seems not to hear him at first, then responds slowly. "I'd like that."

"Great."

They sit together in silence, until his mug is empty and hers is stone-cold.

"I'll run up and get something warmer." He tells her, and heads upstairs.

He doesn't exactly remember when he first saw Dani—Dani like she is now. For a while, after her death, she seemed to be always there in the corner of his eye, but when he turned to find her she was gone, melted away or morphed into another face. But that flash of her was enough to keep him going somehow.

But there came a point, maybe a year after her death, when it wasn't just a glimpse. One day, soon after he'd resigned his job, he saw her straight on. She was on a train he'd just left. For some reason he turned back as it was about to leave the station, and there she was. She winked at him. A week or so later she waved from a taxi. She looked as she had that last time he saw her alive: dark brown shoulder-length hair held off her face by a clip, freckles dotting her nose and upper cheeks like they did even in winter. She wore no make-up and looked healthy. Looked happy. He never told Patty he saw her. He knew what she'd say: "You are cracking up, my friend, you need to see someone."

That was pretty much what she said to him most days back then. He hated it when she called him *"my friend"* and of course she knew it made him crazy. And, in part, it was why she said it. She knew long before she left him that she would, and a part of her wanted to make him hate her, make him glad she was gone instead of just feeling abandoned. Of course that plan was futile. Without Dani, Jim held on to Patty harder than ever. He knew deep down it stifled her, pushed her away, but he couldn't help himself. The fear of being alone was too deep, but that very fear made it inevitable. The man who loved women but who was left by them all.

It took Patty eight years to leave him. Eight years after Dani died to feed the resentment and build the courage to leave the man she loved. When she did, Jim fell apart. He called for her, howled for her, and for Dani. Then when Jim hit rock bottom, about a week after Patty left, Dani came back to him. He'd been in the living room and he thought he heard the front door. He rushed out, like a dog desperate to see its owner.

"Patty?" he shouted.

The hallway was empty. He just stood there, staring at the front door, his brief moment of optimism deflated like a ruptured balloon. The sun was going down and the glass of the door was flaring with the last few rays. It was actually quite beautiful, reminded him for a moment of Notre Dame at dusk. Then, within the shimmering orange-gold light, a shape seemed to coalesce. The sun slipped away and Dani stood there. She was wearing a red duffel coat and held a beaten-up suitcase.

"I thought you might want some company," she said with a smile. "Can I come in?"

He nodded and she walked past him into the living room. Not floating, not see-through. She left the suitcase in the hall. Later he noticed it was gone. That night he asked her to take her old room and she did. He asked where she had been, what she remembered. She said there was nothing. He accepted it, though he liked to imagine she'd been traveling—seen the world like she'd always planned. Once she'd graduated. Had she lived.

"It's so quiet."

Jim nods.

Father and daughter walk together toward Greenwich Park. Jim steers them on a slightly longer route than normal; yesterday he saw a poster on a tree: missing cat. He knows to avoid it. The streets are empty. It's not even 10 a.m. but the grayness feels like dusk. Snowflakes still fall but not so thickly; the wind has died so they gracefully drift toward the earth, turning slowly.

As they approach the park, they begin to hear the first sounds of the day—whooping and yelling. They enter the park at the top of the hill leading down to the Thames and the sprawling vista of London. Today the skyscrapers stand like gray mountains in among the clouds. The two of them stop to view the scene. Jim feels the cold in his chest, watches his breath billow like a dragon's smoke. But when he turns to Dani there's nothing.

"What's going on in your head?" he asks her softly.

She turns her back on him and walks away. He watches her for a moment and then follows.

"Dani!" he calls to her and she turns.

She is just twenty-one, frozen in that state forever and . . . her face is shattered, a snowball punches through it.

"Be more bloody careful," Jim screams at the kid.

"It weren't anywhere near you," the kid shouts back.

"You hit my daught—" He stops. Looks at Dani, her face is back to normal—and she bursts into laughter.

"Sorry, kid," he calls back and starts to laugh himself.

"Your face." She points, still laughing.

"Your face."

And they walk to the observatory—like they've done a hundred times over the years.

❄

"Do you remember anything?" he asks.

The day she came back to him he asked the same question, and he kept asking for months but she always shook her head. He could see the pain, so he stopped. But after his nightmare, and the call from Tom—he feels like something is coming.

"I . . . Dad, I don't know."

"It's okay."

"Is it?"

Her face pinches, mouth becomes hard.

"You said you came back for me."

"I did. You called me."

"Where were you?"

"I don't know."

They're both silent. They sit on the wall of the closed observatory and watch children sledge down the hill.

"In my day we used a *Rupert* annual," Jim says, pointing at the sleek blue sled that a small flame-haired boy is dragging up the hill. The snow has started to fall a little heavier again. Jim watches it settle on the wall beside him. The spot where he can see Dani sitting. Suddenly he jumps up and runs toward the flame-haired kid who has finally got the sled to the top of the hill.

Dani watches him pull something from his pocket and gesture wildly to the boy. Then he turns and with the broadest smile, waves at Dani and motions her to come. He hands something to the child and takes the sled. He sits on it and waits for Dani to scramble onto the back. Then kicks off.

"Whhhheeheehehheheheeeeeeeeeeee . . ."

The sled shoots off down the hill. Dani screams. Jim puts his arms in the air—the wind biting his face, his hair billowing out—and wipes out. The snow shoots up his shirt, down his neck, in his mouth and down his pants. The cold hits him like an electric shock, and he rolls and rolls until the hill runs out.

He lies there, wet and cold but most of all scared. Dani stands over him. She is twenty-one years old, beautiful. He is petrified he is going to lose her again. That was his nightmare—that is always his nightmare—being alone.

"Are you okay?" she asks.

He can't answer, doesn't trust his voice. He feels the weight of twenty years bear down on him.

We need to talk about Dani. About what happened. Tom's words echo through his mind.

At the top of the hill, directly above Jim, stands DS Tom Bevans. He had planned to talk to Jim, had walked a long way through the snow, but seeing him like this—having fun like a child—he can't. Instead he turns his back on the older man and trudges back the way he came. In his pocket the diary feels heavy. He should have returned it to Jim and Patty years ago—but it's too late. Everything feels too late.

Saturday, September 27, 1986

This will be my last entry in this diary. Tomorrow I'm packing everything up and on Monday I will be gone. This feels a little like the journal of a child. Time to grow up. I hope when I come back to read this in years' and years' time—maybe when I've got a child of my own going off to university—that I'm not too embarrassed by my immaturity. Anyway, this is the end of an era, the end of a life. I won't be like Mum, though. When she went to uni she never went home again. I know she never saw Gramps after she left and Nanny had to get the coach to us if she wanted to visit even when she was dying—I won't be like that, couldn't cut Dad out of my life. But . . . I do have to push Tom back a little. I shouldn't have said he could come up on Monday—I don't know how to let him down easy. I hope he'll find some pretty policewoman soon. I need to start the page again, reinvent myself. A new Dani Lancing.
Finis

PART TWO

ELEVEN

Sunday, December 31, 1989

S-E-B M-E-R-C-H-A-N-T

She writes his name in her tiny, precise hand on a yellow Post-it note. In a zip-like motion she sticks it to the wall below the word BOYFRIEND? Above TORTURE. Her eyes flick across the wall—layers of photos, press clippings, witness statements, police reports—hundreds of documents pinned and stapled, all covered in questions on yellow notes. Always questions—why, how, who— almost a year of questions. She has stood before this board for months, adding nothing but dead ends, theories—nothing concrete. Ahab, standing at the wheel, scouring the infinity of the ocean for a sign. But today the whale has been sighted: Seb Merchant is found. She steps back, knocking a pile of frames that are on the floor. She kicks them further into the corner, hearing glass splinter. They used to hang in front of her—two diplomas and three awards for journalism. They had once been her proudest achievements, now they have no place on the walls.

She feels the broil in her stomach; this will end soon. She's a little light-headed—she should probably eat something, can't remember the last time she had, and she will need her strength for later. From downstairs she hears a clatter. They're still here, she'll wait for them to go before venturing out.

She falls into her old office chair, it tips back like an astronaut

63

waiting for the kick of G-force. The wall fills her vision, making her feel . . . she looks down. With a bent paper clip she digs into the quick of her fingernail. She watches the little bead of blood she's teased from her finger, imagines it swimming with life, and then brings it up to her mouth and sucks it away. The taste makes her want to heave. Downstairs she hears another thud and crash—Christ, he is so obvious, she knows what he wants and she feels so tired of disappointing him, so tired of seeing his pain. He has no idea what she needs, what they need.

"Help. Professional help," he had said with his big sad cow eyes, adding the killer blow: "Dani would have wanted this."

She agreed and they went to see Alice Bell, for thirty-four minutes.

"Bereavement counselor. Fucking joke. Fucking joke, Jim," Patty snapped at him afterward. "BACP, UKRCP. They aren't real qualifications, might as well include the fifty meters backstroke."

She remembers the pain in his face as she spat out her poison. It shames her now, remembering the vitriol. It was almost six months ago but the memory feels fresh. His pain feels so fresh.

"Fucking joke. And did you see that photograph?" she snorted.

He had seen it, the only personal item on her desk. It showed Alice Bell, maybe ten years younger, though you can clearly see it was her, with arms around a child in a wheelchair—they both beam with happiness.

"What the fuck does she think she's saying with that? 'I know pain too, I know what you are going through, but it isn't all bad'? Bitch." She spits out the final "bitch." She sees Jim cringe at the coarseness of her language; he's never heard his wife speak like this before. Jim didn't sit on the news desk and watch her trade crude insults night after night with leery old men who hated working with her but wanted to fuck her anyway. She used to keep work and family life separate: Jim and Dani were like oxygen for her—

she needed them to live—but her career was food, the nutrients for a healthy Patricia. Now she had neither. Her editor himself had said she lacked focus, had lost her journalistic balance. He smiled, of course, offered a leave of absence. She told him to stuff it. She knew her "balance" wasn't coming back. Not until she had revenge. That was what kept her going now.

She knew Jim had liked this Alice Bell, had found her calm voice and kind eyes comforting. Patricia had seen only danger in those eyes, the kind that could lull you into trust. Trust could kill them. She knew Alice Bell's kind of help was not what she needed.

"To come to terms with Dani's death—"

"Dani's multiple rape and murder," Patty interrupts her, bearing witness to the truth of it, the horror of it. She sees the blood drain from Jim's face, a sadness creep across the professional Ms. Bell.

"Your loss is terrible . . ."

Patty hears the first few words and then drifts away—it's all blah blah blah. She isn't looking to come to terms with Dani's death. She's looking for vengeance and justice. Only then might there be peace.

❄

Jim treads carefully up the stairs, virtually silent. As he reaches the top stair he can see Patty through the slats, sitting at her desk and staring at the wall. He hates that wall. He knows it's totally irrational, how can you hate a wall? But he hates it. Hates the curled and flapping paper covered in questions, hates the lists, the accusations, the anger spewed over every surface. But worst of all are the photos—the room she was found in and two taken of her after. When there was no more Dani, just a husk that looked like his daughter but had none of her life. They make him die inside.

He needs to ask Patty one last time if she'll come with them. He already knows the answer, knows she'll say no just as she has done at least half a dozen times over the last twenty-four hours, but he'll give it one last try. He'd be so happy if she would go with them.

"Patty," he calls. Then waits. "Tom and I are going. Please come with us."

She tilts her head, the tiniest movement, so she can look at him and then, without answering, kicks the door so it swings closed.

"Okay," he says to no one in particular and walks back down to Tom, who is waiting in the kitchen.

"No?"

Jim shakes his head sadly. Tom nods to show he understands, then picks up his overcoat and they head out into the bitter cold.

It's only ten in the morning but the sky is gunmetal gray. They drive to the crematorium. It's the same route they took for the funeral but now they move faster. The heater's on full blast to keep the windscreen from icing over. Nothing is said.

At the crematorium they park and get out. Tom slams the door, which echoes through the cemetery like a gunshot. The trees stand skeletal, waving fingers in the sky. Everywhere you look an angel stands sentinel over a fallen loved one. Tom pulls his overcoat closer to his throat, breath streams from his mouth. Jim carries a bouquet of yellow roses. Tom can't imagine where he got them on a day like this. Tom carries nothing but inside his breast pocket he has a slim volume of poetry—Keats. He will read one and then leave the book for her.

They walk in silence, both knowing where they are going, neither knowing that the other has made this walk twenty or thirty times already—alone. In the garden of remembrance there is a small plaque, chosen together in those first few days.

DANI, LOVED DEARLY AND MISSED DEEPLY

They stand close to it, her men, Dani's men. Slowly Jim moves forward and places the flowers on a ledge just below the plaque. He whispers something to the air and then steps back while Tom draws out the slim volume and reads.

"Bright star, would I were steadfast as thou art."

As the front door closes Patty gives an involuntary shudder. It's time. She's excited but there are other emotions too. Darker ones, that she holds just below the skin, willing them down until the time is right. She opens her bag one final time and checks the contents. Tickets, notebook, keys, whistle and pepper spray just in case. She feels the weight of the small canister in her palm and wonders if she will use it today. A big part of her hopes she will.

She's not told Jim her plans. Not told him she's going to Durham or that she's done something the police couldn't do: track down the elusive Seb Merchant, Dani's ex-boyfriend. Secret ex-boyfriend that her parents never met, never heard her mention once. Patty only knows about their relationship from fellow students. His name has come up time and time again. Most of them say he's trouble.

He was missed by the police in the initial trawl for statements, as he wasn't a student with Dani—he'd been a student five years before but had dropped out halfway through his second year. He stayed in Durham, and each year he made noises as if he'd start his degree again but he never returned to college. No one knew how he made his money; a few suggested he was independently wealthy. The police had finally put him on the list of people to talk to but they couldn't find him. Patty has.

She feels something tingle, deep down. This is the break-through—she knows it. He has something, something to tell her that will reveal the truth at last. And. And. There is a possibility he is Dani's killer. And . . . and . . .

"What would you do?" asks Alice Bell near the end of that thirty-four minutes.

"I don't understand," Patty says coldly.

"You say you are investigating Dani's death."

"Murder."

"Dani's murder. You are looking for her killer, yes?"

"Yes."

"So what would you do if you found him?"

Patty is impassive. She watches the woman before her, the soft kind eyes and mouth that twitches a little—sharing the pain. Patty will not answer her, instead they will let the final minutes drain away into nothingness. But she knows her reply.

I will find him. I will kill him by cutting his heart out. I swear.

"Should be a bloody florist," the young man says, cocking his head toward the pile of bedraggled bouquets swept into a corner of the garden. Jim looks at his own yellow roses lying by her plaque. He will leave them here and they will rot and turn to mush. Who de-cided flowers were a suitable tribute for the dead?

"Instead of a copper?" Jim asks.

Tom kicks at the gravel, sending a shower pinging against the fountain in the center of the garden.

"More public respect, more useful, better hours."

"Really." Jim shakes his head. "No florist is going to find who killed Dani."

Tom feels himself flush with shame. "No. Not likely."

The two men stand in silence. Tom knows what Jim wants—some assurance that Dani's killer will be found. He wishes he were anything but a policeman right now. Both men stand and think of Dani. At some point tears come for them both. They lose all feeling in their feet from the cold, yet neither wants to be the one to suggest leaving. Any connection with the girl they love is better than none.

Finally it's Jim who makes the move.

"A drink, maybe a bite to eat?" Tom asks, hoping to keep the link alive.

"Maybe another day. I think I should get back to Patty."

" 'Course. Yeah." Tom nods and starts to wiggle the toes he knows are in his shoes somewhere. He wonders if this is the last time he'll see Jim. Then together they walk to the car, hobbling slightly on their frozen feet.

"Patty," Jim calls as he walks through the front door. He's bought an extra large portion of chips from the Sung Lee and two giant pickles. He imagines them sousing them in malt vinegar, sprinkle of salt and then Heinz poured all over. Maybe they could eat on the sofa, in front of the TV—see the New Year in together. A new start, maybe. They could hold each other. Make love in their bed. Wake up in the morning and talk about Dani and love each other again.

"Patty?"

But there's no reply. He finds a note on the kitchen table.

Gone. Back later. P.

No little x of a kiss. Jim wonders for the thousandth time if his wife can bear to be with him any longer.

"Will you stop staring at me, I feel like I'm on fucking suicide watch," she'd said just yesterday.

He makes himself a coffee, and sits at the kitchen table, staring deeply into the patina of the wood until it swims before his eyes. He loves this table. He and Patty found it in a junk shop in Chichester soon after they were married. It was a beautiful shape but scuffed and scratched, a piece hacked out of the middle. They bought it for next to nothing and restored it, the two of them, a shared project. They found a piece of wood that was as close as close, its twin, and joined them together. Jim traces his fingertips across the top, following the grain with his hand. Even though he knows where to look for the piece they grafted in, he can barely see it. The scar has healed and the wood bonded.

He remembers how happy they'd been working together, sanding and planing. It's a beautiful memory and he allows it to wander through his head and warm his thoughts. Then it passes and the cold invades his mind once more.

There is a light knock on the door.

"Are you okay?" a woman calls out.

Patty can't answer. She sits on the toilet and sobs as the train sways beneath her. In the bowl her bile and small flecks of the little she ate this afternoon swill about and will not flush away. Tears flow freely, splattering down into her lap as she leans forward. It had taken her all this time to find him, months. Sending letters, pestering his family, putting posters around, all to find this Seb Merchant and . . . and it was such a fucking waste of time and now there is no lead, there is no suspect, there is no hope.

She sits there, on the foul-smelling toilet, and lets the grief and frustration bubble up and die. She's lost. She's used up every last favor and dried up the last reserves of goodwill. She knew it was coming, has seen how old colleagues shy away from her or run the other way when they see her. How the Durham students take a step back from her when she tries to question them, thinking they've told her every last thing they knew about Dani. She knows how she's pestered them, but she thought something would give, someone would crack, and allow her a glint of hope. But what happens now?

"Are you okay? I'll get the guard," the voice calls through the door once more. Concern mixed with more than a little annoyance.

"I'm . . ." Patricia begins. "I don't need the guard."

She hears the woman grumble and walk off, possibly searching for another toilet. Patricia tries to stand but the nausea sweeps across her once more and she drops back feeling everything unravel. She is so scared, scared that nothing of Dani will remain, even her face is fading in her thoughts. In her bag she keeps a photo. She stares at it every day but she knows that more and more it is the photograph she remembers and not Dani. She can do nothing for her now, all those years of feeding, washing, dressing, encouraging and loving—loving, always loving. But at the end it was all shit, all such shit, all arguments and disappointments and all fucked up. With no goodbye, no time to prepare. That Christmas. Oh God, the Christmas—last Christmas.

"I forced her away." Patty cramps at the memory. Dani was

meant to stay for a week and it was just two days. They argued so bitterly.

"That was what I left her with. She hated me." The tears will not stop.

"It will get better, time heals all wounds," Jim had said. Fucking liar. The only thing that will ease the pain is to find the man who did this and . . .

"How do I do that?" she shouts. "How do I find him?"

The train rattles on.

Finally the river runs dry and she can clean herself up and leave the small cubicle. She sits in the first empty seat she finds where she can be alone. Then she closes down.

It's dark when Jim looks about him. He must have fallen asleep, curled up in his chair. Again.

"Christ . . . arrgh." His leg's asleep. Pins and needles dance along the sole of his foot and march up his leg. He feels scrunched up, a tall man forced into a box and— the phone. It's ringing and that's what's woken him. He launches himself out of the chair and limps into the hall.

"Hello?" he tries to keep the urgency out of his voice.

"Have you been watching it all? Dancing on the Berlin Wall, the crumbling ripped-down bloody Berlin Wall, who would have thought it? We won. We're giving peace a chance." It isn't Patty but Ed, sounding a little boozy.

"It's good to hear from you," Jim replies. It really is good to hear from his oldest friend. Ed and Jacks have done so much over the last year.

"Well, I watched the moon landing with you, I think this is the next big thing. And it was pretty obvious you'd be at home while the rest of the world celebrates the end of nuclear war. Greenham Pat must be wetting herself."

Despite himself, Jim smiles at his wife's old nickname.

"She isn't here." He thinks for a second. "I have no idea where she is. What's the time?"

"It's ten o'clock. If you're on your own, get the fuck over here and get drunk with us and forget, just for one night, about this fucking awful year."

New Year's Eve, he'd forgotten. He cradles the phone between chin and ear and pulls his sleeve away from his watch. He squints in the near dark. It's ten past ten. On the table the unopened chip packet has gone cold and soggy. There will be no new start with Patty tonight.

"So come. Jacks wants you to." In the background there is a snort. "And there's twenty or so people here that don't know you're the most miserable fuck in the world and—"

"I can't. Patty might be back in time."

"In time to do what? Give you a kiss to ring in 1990, say, 'It'll all be fine next year'? I love . . ." Ed pauses, thinking he might have gone too far. "Oh, Jim. I'll come over and get you."

Jim hears Jacks in the background saying that Ed's too drunk to drive.

"Thanks, Ed, but I can't," Jim cuts in.

"Leave her a note and drive over. You can make it by midnight. Don't be by yourself. Not tonight."

"Thanks, Ed. Love to Jacks."

"You fuc—"

Jim misses the rest as he puts the phone down. The silence in the room seems so profound all of a sudden. He appreciates Ed's try at getting him over, but he can't betray Patty. Betrayal? What a strange idea. He just needs to be there for when she needs him, that's all. Isn't that love?

He closes his eyes tight and indulges himself in a happy memory: the first time he saw Patricia.

She was looking down reading a story as he walked into the university newspaper offices. He was going there to see Connie Tunstall. She had kept telling him he ought to contribute and he always said he was too busy. But that night he and Connie had arranged to meet to go and see a film and he was half an hour early, so he decided to pick her up at the newspaper office.

So, he walked in. The editor's office was at the back, overlooking everything, but at that exact moment Patricia was standing at a desk by the door looking over some boy's shoulder, reading his text. As Jim walked in she looked up for a second and caught him full blast with these eyes. Kapow! "Come to bed eyes" is how he described them to Ed the next day. Hazel with flecks of gold, languid like they couldn't be bothered to look at you, sexy as hell. And then there was her mouth. Full, soft—perfect. He fell in love with that mouth there and then. He may even have drooled a little. He was immediately drawn into her orbit like a love-struck moon. She was the editor, in her second year reading politics, and by all accounts had turned an unloved, barely read monthly into a must-read weekly and was advising other universities on what to do with their crumbling old titles. As he watched her advising and guiding the cub reporter through his story, he was immediately struck by how she took charge with such a deft touch, getting the best out of him not by domineering but by persuading and suggesting. Jim had already fallen a little in love with her that first night, before he even got to her desk and offered his services as cartoonist.

He flicks on the overhead light, which seems too bright somehow. He hears some thumping music from somewhere close, maybe two doors down. The sounds of the party make him feel even more alone. He wishes he could have a drink but there's no alcohol in the house. He indulged a little too much in the months after Dani's death and cut himself off. Maybe for New Year's Eve . . . but he doesn't want to go out in case Patty calls. So the best he can do for a treat is a squashed Quality Street from the back of the sofa.

He turns on the TV but keeps the sound off. The cameras keep flipping between countries where fresh-faced young people smile and dance and look so hopeful. 1990 really is going to be a new world for them all to live in. But how will he live in a world without Dani?

At five minutes to 1990 he switches on the sound and watches while the world calls in to show what an amazing decade the nineties will be. It can't be worse than the eighties, surely.

Finally it's time to countdown from Trafalgar Square as Big Ben winds up for the momentous dongs.

The crowd begins its chant.

Ten

The phone rings. Jim grabs it.

"Patty?"

Nine

"Jim," she sobs.

Eight

"Where are you?"

Seven

"I thought I had him, Jim. Thought I'd found him."

Six

"Who, Patty?"

Five

"The killer, Dani's killer."

Four

"But it wasn't him?"

Three

"I can't find him, Jim. I can't find him."

Two

"Let's just let . . . I love you, Patty."

One

The crowd roars. Otherwise there is only silence.

INTERMISSION TWO

Monday, June 14, 1982

He cannot take his eyes off her, this lovesick, pale boy. For about another minute that will be fine, watching her is acceptable while she runs. But soon she'll finish the race, and then he'll have to stop, peel his eyes off her skin and look elsewhere. She's coming into the final stretch, miles ahead of the competition, she runs fluidly, seemingly with little effort.

He's watched her for a long time—years—since they started school together at five years old. His first real recollection of her was as Mary, mother of our Lord. She was chosen to lead the nativity and for a glorious day and a half he was to be her husband, Joseph. Mr. Chinns explained the story to them, and Tom tried to imagine what living with Dani and their child would be like. On the run on a donkey: romance, tragedy and adventure. This was the first time his creative imagination had swung into gear and it flipped a switch in him. They were bonded, and it was strong; a desire to protect and love Danielle Lancing was etched on Thomas Bevans's young heart.

It was only a day and a half of married bliss. There wasn't even a rehearsal, so they never got to stand next to each other as husband and wife. Instead, he began to itch, and broke out in red welts that were diagnosed as chicken pox. He missed three weeks of school, had a pretty miserable Christmas, and it was all over. He was lucky—there wasn't a single scar from the pox. At least, none on the outside. Inside, it felt like there was a tiny little arrow embedded that cut every time he thought about or saw Danielle Lancing.

Despite the dig of pain, he watched her whenever he could. In the eight years following their doomed nativity they barely spoke, even though they continued to be in the same class all the way through primary and into secondary school. Tom was too shy, Dani too popular.

Then at the start of this school year, when they were both assessed and found to be in the top twenty percent of the population in terms of intelligence, they were placed in English Literature One. Together, at the same desk, they were forced to talk about love. John Keats.

She breaks the tape, no one anywhere near her. He claps, watching her swing around the extra bend as she slows, her limbs powering down. He must stop gazing now . . . now . . . now! He pulls his head away with some effort, and looks across the stand. Her father's there; he's still watching her and clapping hard. He seems not to know the decorum of school sports day. A few other parents look at him with some distaste. They believe he's gloating, although Tom thinks he's merely a man visibly filled with pride. For a second he wonders what it would be like to have such a father. Then the man, still clapping, looks sideways and sees the boy staring at him. For a second their eyes lock and then the boy holds up both of his thumbs signaling he too is in the Dani Lancing fan club. The man smiles, then turns back to admire his daughter once more. The boy can feel himself turn red. Even at fourteen he knows the double thumbs is juvenile (for a short while Arthur Fonzarelli had made it fashionable, but anybody actually cool knew that time had long gone).

He picks up the briefcase his mother insists he uses, even though he is mocked for it, and walks down the line of seats toward the exit. He'll not look back at her. He knows that by now she will be surrounded by handsome athletes. He walks away. There's a kiosk nearby that sells ice cream, cake and drinks. He doesn't feel like going home just yet, so he heads over and buys a Zoom. He sits on a bench overlooking the bowling green and bites into the cold. He replays the race in his head, watching Dani stretch and—

"Excuse me," a voice calls out from a little way off.

The boy does not look up, assuming someone else is being called.

"Excuse me . . . Mr. Briefcase."

Tom looks up and sees it's Dani Lancing's father calling him. The man half-waves, then walks across the bowling green toward him.

"I'm sorry, sorry to shout. I don't know your name so, Briefcase. Nice case by the way. My grandfather had one just like it." The older man reaches the younger one and stops. "Jim. Jim Lancing. I'm Danielle's father."

"Tom," the boy says, not standing. Jim holds out his hand and awkwardly they shake.

Though it is still a pretty warm afternoon, Tom can't help but feel a chill run down his back. Is it obvious, can this man see how Tom feels about his daughter?

"How can I help?" Tom asks.

"You seemed to know Dani."

"A little. We're in English Lit together."

"Well, have you any idea where she might have gone? I was meant to be taking her home, at least I thought I was but . . ."

There was a party for the sporty and attractive kids, something Tom would never be invited to. He was about to tell her father the address but some alarm bell went off in his head.

"No. No, sorry, I don't know where she is," he lied.

"Okay." They both just stand there. Tom feels his Zoom begin to drip. Finally the older man says, "Well, thanks."

Jim Lancing walks off, a little unsure about where to go and what to do. Tom watches until he disappears. Then he picks up his case and heads toward Islington and the party. Obviously he wasn't invited, but now he bears a message. That is his ticket to get in and get close to her. It's slight, he knows that, but maybe it's just enough to allow him entrance to the inner sanctum.

TWELVE

Saturday, December 18, 2010

Patty walks to the cafe, all the while feeling the pull of his blood. There is only one customer, a cab driver, sitting alone in the far corner. Patty looks him over. People-watching is still one of her favorite ways to pass the time and she can't resist trying to unpick his life story. They make eye contact for a moment. He has a haunted look, like a man who is pushed or pushes himself very hard. Does he need the money to fund some addiction? Or does he just need to keep moving, keep awake like a shark, desperate just to keep going, no time to think? And what might he see in her—does she stink of desperation? Can he tell that she has lived and breathed revenge—has stayed alive for one purpose: to catch the man who took Dani's life and pitched them all into this everlasting, ferocious winter of grief and loss?

From behind the counter a figure emerges. A bleary-eyed young man, dark and handsome.

"Tea, please."

"Ereogo?"

"I don't understand."

He mimes, pointing at the seats or out the door.

"Oh, yes, of course. I . . ."

She would like to sit there and drink the hot tea, cradle the ceramic bowl in her hands and let the heat seep through into her icy fingers. But the blood is in the car and what if someone tries to steal it?

"Take-away, please."

He takes a Styrofoam cup and fills it from the urn, then splashes a little milk into it before sealing it with a white plastic cap. Patty takes it from him with a mumble of thanks and drops two coins onto the counter. She turns on her heel and walks back to the door, immediately sorry for her decision to opt for take-away as the heat is dampened by the foam of the cup and her fingers stay cold. Outside, on the street, she pours some of the tea directly onto her skin and it turns a bright and angry red, but she can't feel it.

Patty perches in the doorway of the lab, waiting for the staff to struggle in, the blood cradled in her arms. Her anxiety is building but she tries to keep it in check.

"Just wait," she tells herself. And she can wait. She is the queen of waiting. It seems like all she has done for the longest time. Finally, her patience pays off. The first staff member arrives. He looks at her nervously.

"Can you stand back?" he asks.

"Oh, of course. Yes."

Patty steps away from the stairs and the keypad. The staff member taps in his code and then edges in, keeping his eyes glued to Patty. It's only once he's inside that Patty realizes he thought she might try and force her way in to get drugs or start begging for something. When the next staff member arrives, Patty moves away and immediately launches into her best Hilary Clifton-Hastings, non-threatening cheery voice.

"Hello. Just waiting to have someone run some tests. That's all."

They look at her like she's crazy. That may be better than fearing she's an axe-wielding junkie.

Finally the door is open to the public and she can walk inside. Roberta is there, the woman she'd met with the week before. At that meeting, she had given Patty the slide and refrigerated box as well as instructions on how to take the sample. There were two options, she had said. The easiest was with a swab inside the cheeks, Invasive but did not hurt in any way. The other option was a blood sample—a prick was all that was needed. Patty had decided on blood, but a little more than just a prick. Patty hands her the box with the slide of blood. Roberta checks it is sealed correctly.

"Please take a seat." She motions to two chairs in the corner and then she punches digits into a keypad and disappears into the main part of the lab. Patty can't sit. She stands. After about twenty minutes Roberta returns.

"The sample is well collected and seems clean. It can be matched with the sample you brought in before. We will have the result tomorrow."

"I'm sorry." Patty tries to keep the scream out of her voice. "We had agreed a four-hour test time."

"I know. Normally that is possible but we are understaffed today, the sn—"

"I understand there may need to be an extra fee for expediting the result. Needless to say I will be happy to pay it." Patty smiles.

"I see." Roberta nods. "Four hours. And the expedited rate is an extra fifty percent." She smiles a snake-like smile.

"I'll come back for the result."

※

She begins to retrace her steps to the cafe, following the breadcrumbs of memory, but finds a modern coffee shop open on the way. It's a corpo-chain shop but all the better for anonymity. Plus it offers bagel and baguette breakfasts, as well as superskinnysoy-moccacinolattes. Patty orders and pays. The staff do not make eye contact, they have no interest in her life story, why she is there, what she wants. Perfect. She sits and closes her eyes. Immediately tiredness sweeps over her. She's exhausted but must not sleep. Soon she will be able to. Then she can catch up on more than twenty years of sleep. She sips her coffee and feels her mind slip back twenty years—that last Christmas won't stay out of her thoughts.

* * *

"Dad." Dani hugs him tight. Father and daughter seem to become a single being for a few seconds, and then release.

"I'll take your bag in." He lifts the backpack over a shoulder and walks it inside.

"Mum." Dani embraces Patty, but it doesn't have the same warmth or urgency. Patty can't help but feel that old jealousy. They break their embrace, or is it that Dani tries to break free but Patty holds on? She looks her daughter in the face. Dani looks tired around the eyes and her face is fuller. Patty can tell her daughter has completely given up on training, less lean than she has been for years, even a little tummy forming. Student diet is a killer.

"I am so looking forward to bread sauce," Dani says with a huge grin. She firmly twists from her mother's grip and heads inside.

* * *

"Do you remember this?" Dani holds up the treasure she has unearthed.

"Do I?" says Patty, laughing. "That's Hoppy Bunny. I bought her for you when I was pregnant. I'd only just found out. We were living in Clapham and I went to Arding and Hobbs. Three shillings she was." Patty smiles, thinking she's finally connecting with her daughter, that whatever is going on with Dani will come out. Instead, she watches a cloud sweep across her daughter's face as she closes off once more. Patty watches her go through the old boxes for a while longer and then leaves her to get on with it. In the kitchen she makes coffee and wonders for the millionth time what is up with her. She'd been home two days and was so morose. Even Tom and Izzy coming over hadn't cheered her up. Patty lights a cigarette, opens a window a crack and blows the smoke out.

She remembers the absolute joy she had felt when she bought Hoppy, her first real acknowledgment that a life was growing inside her. And she can remember so clearly how Dani's eyes had lit up the first time she saw it and how she squirmed as Patty bounced the bunny on her tummy.

"Hoppy loves Dani, hop, hop, hop."

As a child Dani had loved her mother best of all but the older she got the closer she and Jim became, until one day Patty felt an outsider in her own family. Maybe it was puberty; the teen years were tough. She finishes the cigarette and flicks the butt out of the open window, staring out into . . .

"Mum."

"Christ." Patty jumps at her daughter's voice. "I didn't hear you come in."

"I'm not going back to uni. A year—"

"Don't be stupid."

And the row strikes like a tsunami.

❄

"It's Christmas Eve," Jim pleads with them, but he knows it's futile. They're both too stubborn to back down now.

"I'm going." Dani is adamant.

"Stay till after Christmas Day at least," he asks.

"Let her go. She can think about how stupid she's being," Patty almost spits.

"Don't worry, I'm not staying here."

"Dani, please, sweethe—"

"I'm sorry, Dad. Bye."

There was no goodbye for Patty.

That was the last time they saw her.

Alive.

INTERMISSION THREE

Tuesday, February 14, 1984

Dani and Tom sit back-to-back, leaning against each other. He has the cigarette, takes an amateur pull on it, does not inhale and passes it back to her. She takes it from him like a precious relic and in a gracious sweep brings it to her mouth. She drags the smoke deep into her lungs, holds it there and then, with a practiced pucker, releases a perfect smoke ring. It sails away, slowly breaking down until it dissolves. She wonders if she could blow a smoke ring over an erect penis. She takes another deep draw on the cigarette and aims at an imaginary erection.

"Good smoke ring," Tom says looking round. She doesn't tell him what she was aiming at.

He casually drops his eyes to his watch. "I think we need to get back, Dani." He stands, making sure she doesn't tip backward.

She looks down at the cigarette, knowing he's right but feeling resentful. Geography and chemistry will never be as useful to her, in real-life situations, as being able to smoke with style. She imagines she's Julie Christie as she takes the cigarette up to her mouth and draws softly but intensely on the tip, the end glowing powerfully red. She rolls the smoke around her mouth like she's seen her dad do with wine, then pushes the smoke out through her nose, a perfect dragon drag. Satisfied, she flicks the butt into the corner. It bounces underneath the spare pommel horse.

Inside their corrugated metal smokehouse it was dry, but outside the air is damp—as close to rain as you can get without it actually raining. Both feel their hair start to curl slightly at the ends and their school uniforms dampen. They walk back to the main building in an uneasy silence. He's dying for her to mention the card—the one he delivered to her house at five o'clock that morning. He hadn't signed it, of course, but desperately wanted to hear about it from her. Was she excited? Who could her mysterious admirer be? How did she feel about what was inside the card—a ticket for Siouxsie and the Banshees at the Apollo the following week. E4, upper circle.

Dani was thinking about the card. Of course she knew it was from Tom, just like she knew he had the ticket next to hers. If he'd said, "Let's go see the Banshees," she would have gone, probably would have let him buy her ticket. But this romantic bullshit made her feel uneasy. She should never have kissed him. He'd caught her a little upset, more than a little drunk, on the rebound and easy prey. It had been stupid. She didn't want to lose him, he was her best friend, but she'd let him imagine something he couldn't have. He wasn't someone she could have fun with—at least, not just fun. With the athletes and sporty-boys it was easier; they didn't ask any searching questions and had no real feelings to hurt. She could talk to Tom; they both had issues with their mothers and had dreams of the future. Tom was cool . . . but not cool enough. Not for a boyfriend. And he wasn't sexy, and Dani was starting to appreciate sexy.

"Are you training later?" he asks. She doesn't respond right away. The answer's "no," but that didn't mean she was free to hang out. Instead, she was going to take the Tube into town and mooch around the pub opposite Goldsmiths in the hope that she'd see *him* again. She knew very little about him; they called him Bix and he did something with Lego and dog shit. He was tall and arrogantly, jaw-droppingly handsome. He was a friend of Toni's brother and they had all met up on Saturday. Bix hadn't talked to Dani directly, but she'd watched him as he dominated the group, talking with passion about art and sculpture as he drank cider and smoked his short, stubby roll-ups, which he made look fucking sexy. In part, this was why she was smoking at lunchtime—to get good enough to smoke with him. The other part was that she wanted to get stoned very soon, and knew you had to be a smoker or it didn't work.

"Yes, I'm training. My sprinting needs some work," she says into the air, not catching his eye. She hates lying to Tom. If it had been anything else she'd have told him. In the last year he'd become her closest friend, even listening as she droned on about her mum and bloody Greenham Common. Not even her dad was so attentive, but she knows Tom wants boyfriend/girlfriend. No matter how selfish her mum says she is, she will not screw Tom over and make him listen to her moaning about love stuff.

"We could get together after training."

"No. No idea how long I'll be." She keeps her eyes ahead, trying not to blush at the lie.

He nods like he agrees, but feels disappointed. He had wanted this to be their first Valentine's together. They carry on, walking in silence, until the school gates come into view.

"The careers fair is on Friday. Ha—"

She groans. "God, Tom, I have no idea what I want to be when I'm a grown-up. Not dead and not a journalist, that's about it."

"Okay," he says, trying to sound upbeat.

They reach the school gates and push inside. This is where they part. He knows she's off to geography. He has her timetable memorized.

"Tomorrow, seven thirty at the bus stop?" she asks.

He nods. She squeezes his arm and walks off. He watches her cross the playground. His stomach tightens when she finally disappears. He knows something is happening, changing. Over the last six months he's seen how she's slipped out of her training regime, started to wear make-up and think about what she's wearing, but he doesn't know what it means. In his pocket the Siouxsie and the Banshees ticket burns a hole. They often spend their evenings together, sometimes studying but mostly just talking, but there is nothing about these evenings that could be called "romantic" and he wants a real date. He can still feel the adrenaline of their kiss, even after more than two weeks. It's like some super battery, revving him up. He wants more, wants everything. He wants Dani. From inside the closest building he can hear the bell ring. He runs to class.

THIRTEEN

Saturday, December 18, 2010

"Maybe we should go to her house," Dani suggests.

Jim shakes his head. "If she was there she'd answer the phone."

"Unless . . ." Dani realizes her mistake and stops. Jim switches the radio on and they listen, but can only bear it for a few minutes. Everything is closed, cut off, trapped, lost, buried, worst since records began. The end is nigh. He's called Patty five times over the last few hours, and of course he's imagined her lying on the floor unconscious but . . . deep down he knows his fear isn't really about Patty being hurt.

"I need to get in touch. Tom might . . ." But he's afraid to call Tom. For some reason he needs to talk to Patty first. And . . .

"The Lost Soul." He suddenly realizes there is someone who might know where Patty is, or at least have a mobile phone number for her. Jim runs upstairs.

"Dad?" Dani calls after him.

"I'll be down in a minute."

He stands before her door. He hasn't been in there since the day she left. He puts his hand to the door and . . . push. A rush of stagnant air, the slight sweetness of damp hits him. The room is empty. The wall is gone. The pictures and endless reports, the questions—all gone. The desk is empty but he hopes he'll find a leaflet in the drawer. Yes.

"But it's miles, Dad."

"I can do it. I know the short cuts."

"But she might not even be there."

"I know, but I have to do something." Jim smiles at Dani and heads out. He knows she's right, it's a long way and the news says there's no trains or buses—but it's the only thing he can think to do. He's tried calling but just gets an answering machine. He has to try to see Karan Noble. As he walks, he tries to remember Karan's story.

Karan Noble had twin girls, Emma and Tamsin. At the age of eleven they disappeared. It was 1976, the hottest summer for decades, and the girls had been playing in the garden in an inflatable paddling pool they'd been given for their birthday. Karan had called them in for dinner at about six o'clock and there was no reply. No girls. Nobody was sure when they could remember seeing them last. There was lots of media interest initially, pretty girl twins, photogenic and newspaper-selling. But that died away as the reporters came up against a brick wall with the family. Karan shut herself away from the world and left it all to the husband who was a cold fish. With little media attention, the police found the trail quickly became cold. With no prodding from the family, it just all dropped. It was a mystery for seven years. Then, an accident in their street led the gas board to dig up most of the road and some gardens behind the houses. The twins' bodies were found in the garden of Karan's next-door neighbors, Ken and Sarah. For Karan, who had almost got her life back together, it was like losing them all over again. Maybe worse—now she knew there was no hope. And she had trusted Ken.

He had been the first person she had called when she found the girls missing. He had led the search around the neighborhood.

"We won't give up, we'll find them, Karan. Have faith," he had said to her on the third day and she had wept in his arms. That memory, after her children's bodies had been discovered, had made her physically sick.

He was arrested and pleaded guilty. He said he had invited them in for a cold drink and put on a film, a film of men having sex with teenage girls. When they tried to leave he stopped them. The police searched the house and discovered an entire cupboard filled with films and photographs of children being abused. There were photographs of Emma and Tamsin. He was convicted of their murders. Karan's marriage had lasted just a few months after the girls went missing. By the time their bodies were found, their father was remarried, living in France with a four-year-old son. About a year after the neighbor was convicted, Karan Noble set up the charity Lost Souls. Its agenda was the campaign for stiffer penalties for endangering, harming and killing children, no matter the circumstance. As a secondary goal, it tried to fight for state funding to provide counseling for grieving parents, their extended family and friends.

Karan had passion for her cause, but no real knowledge of how that message could be put across to politicians and the press. Then she met Patty about six months after Dani was killed. In many ways they were made for each other. Patty was both a journalist and activist. She knew how to get stories in the papers and who to harangue. Oh, she could harangue. Karan was someone who could organize and structure. Patty was never someone who was going to build a charity from the ground up, but she could help to shape someone else's cause. So Karan took on Patty as a kind of manager, to shape policy. Under Patty, Lost Souls became a lobbying group, a powerful mouthpiece for anyone who had lost a loved one to violent crime. And of course it was Patty who became the public face of Lost Souls. When children went missing or were murdered, she was one of the first to be called by the press or TV for comment. Jim had hated that; he hadn't liked the friendship that had developed between Patty and Karan. To him it didn't seem based in support for each other but in a shared spite and pain. It hadn't surprised him at all when Patty had confided in him, about a year after joining the charity, that Karan regularly paid money to see that the man who killed her children was beaten and abused in prison.

Jim walks without pausing until he reaches the South Bank, directly opposite St. Paul's Cathedral, snow scattered over its dome like icing sugar. There he stops and leans on the railings. The beauty of it makes his heart soar.

"It's lovely."

He turns to see his daughter. He smiles, pleased to see her.

"Do you rem—" he starts.

"I remember you boring me witless talking about Wren and the dome and the flying buttresses."

He laughs.

"Happy days." She grins.

Silently the two of them stand by the river and watch London, a thousand years reflected in the shimmer of water.

"Shall we go?" Jim says as the cold sneaks into his fingers.

They push on, cold breath billowing from his mouth like steam. They walk past the National Theatre, toward Big Ben and Parliament. Then over the Thames, as the snow begins to fall once more, hard and heavy as the afternoon light dies.

They stand before the slate-gray building on the edge of Dryden Street and look up at its darkened windows. There might be a faint glow coming from the very top floor, it's hard to tell. He looks at the run of intercom buttons down the right side of the door; the top two are for Lost Souls. He pushes them both, one after the other. There is a long wait before a weirdly crackling and rather irritated voice asks, "The office is closed. Who is it?"

"It's Jim Lancing. You might remem—"

The intercom buzzes and the door pops open slightly. He pushes it forward, holding it wide as he turns back to Dani.

"I think it best if you stay down here."

"Good, I'll window shop." She sounds quite excited.

"Okay. I don't suppose I'll be that long—an hour at most."

"Rendezvous back here at seventeen hundred hours?" she asks.

"Fine."

Dani smiles and turns away to walk toward the heart of Covent Garden.

He climbs three flights of a very steep circular staircase to get to the Lost Souls office. Theater posters adorn the walls of the first two flights. The second floor seems to be home to theatrical agents, though judging by the posters they seem to represent only second-rate ventriloquists, mesmerists, the runner-up in some ancient talent show and a fizzy blonde dance troupe that have had ten years airbrushed off them.

The top floor opens out onto an area that resembles a private dentist's waiting room. There's no one there, but there is a sign, propped on a small table. It reads: PLEASE TAKE A SEAT.

There's an old leather sofa and three less comfortable-looking chairs. At the far end is a small receptionist's desk. He chooses the sofa and sinks comfortably into it. There's a coffee table, but all it contains are the glossy flyers and annual reports of Lost Souls. He doesn't pick one up. He's seen them many times before and knows that on page four there is a picture of a stricken Patty holding up a photograph of Dani. He'd argued against its inclusion but Patty insisted. "Jim, the charity needs a public face. You need to poke people and show them the reality: loss and grief. Loss and grief sells."

"Charities aren't selling anything."

"What century are you in?" She laughed. "Charities need to sell harder than anyone."

Of course, deep down, Jim knew Patty was right. But he deeply resented their grief being used like that.

It takes Karan Noble about ten minutes, but finally she appears from a small door Jim hadn't noticed. She's a tall, slim woman, somewhere in her late sixties. Her hair is up, which gives her a sense of elegance. This is further enhanced by her plain silver jewelry, which highlights the silver in her hair. Jim has met her twice before. Both times he had felt she didn't like him, didn't trust him. Her eyes told him that he was judged. Now he sees something new in her eyes. She's wary and looks a little afraid. He wonders what's changed. She walks to the desk and stands behind it, as if it affords some protection to her.

"Mr. Lancing."

"Mrs. Noble. I was hoping you might—"

"I really can't help you. I don't have any information I could share with you. Even if I had, I wouldn't."

Jim looks surprised. "I . . . it's Patty."

"Patty has made her own choice. She needed to act and she has done so."

"What, hang on, what choice?" Jim stands and Karan Noble steps back. "I just want to know about Patty. I've tried to call and can't reach her. I thought you might know something."

She pauses. Karan Noble knows, she knows everything. She had watched Patty lose hope over the years, watched her anger die. She had even thought it a blessing; no one could live with that much rage. Then suddenly the fire burned again. Patty said nothing but Karan knew only one thing could make the anger return: the chance to catch him. The chance to kill him. She would never betray her friend.

"I don't. I know nothing, Mr. Lancing."

"A mobile number, an e-mail she might check."

She pulls her arms tight around her defensively. "Nothing."

"Please. Somewhere she might be?"

"I can't. I would like you to leave."

"I'm worried about Patty. I'm sure—"

Karan's face clouds over. "My understanding is that Patty hasn't seen you for years. That doesn't sound like a man who cares."

"That's not right. I mean, it is years, but . . . I just . . ." He feels a headache begin. "This will sound crazy. Out of the blue I suddenly started thinking about her and I've been worrying about her ever since. I can't get her out of my mind."

Karan snorts a little and starts to shake her head.

Jim continues. "Something is happening and . . . and I think you know what it might be."

She raises her eyebrow and then a wry smile creeps across her face. "My husband, ex-husband, had a heart attack two months ago. Not fatal, but serious."

"I'm sorry."

"Don't be, it's more than thirty years since he meant anything to me. I mention it because there was a time when I thought that if anything happened to him—anything at all—that I would know, some intuition or something. But . . ."

"But everything changes when a partner moves on," says Jim softly and Karan meets his gaze properly for the first time. She nods.

"I can't help you, Mr. Lancing."

"Can't or won't?"

She smiles. "Can't, won't—they're the same thing. Now, please leave."

Jim feels the blood pound at his temples. He opens his mouth to argue with her but at that second there is the slam of metal and brick from somewhere close by. A car alarm immediately sounds and various voices begin to shout. Jim and Karan both move to the window, three or four figures can be seen scurrying around the corner, heading to something. Jim looks down. Dani is in the middle of the road waving manically. From that distance he can't really see her expression, it's more like a smudge, but he knows something is very wrong.

He turns to Karan Noble "I have—" He doesn't finish, but rushes out of the room.

"What the hell?" Karan Noble shouts after him but he's gone.

He takes the stairs two at a time, bouncing off the walls of the narrow staircase until he hits the bottom. He tumbles out into the cold evening air. Dani runs to him, so panicked she runs through a parked car.

"Dad!" She looks scared, so pale—even for a ghost.

"What? What's happened?"

"Dad, this way . . ."

She turns and runs into the road; Jim follows.

"Watch it!" the driver screams, as Jim swerves at the last moment to avoid being hit by the only car on the street. Dani runs around the corner. As he gets into Drury Lane, Jim sees a group gathered around a man lying in the middle of the road. A car has crashed into a wall to the left of them—the driver has got out of the car and is swaying slightly—he looks both dazed and angry. Jim slows and comes to a halt next to Dani, who watches the group.

"I should help."

"No need, he's dead," she tells him in a small voice.

"How . . . ?"

"I saw it." She turns to Jim. "He collapsed right in front of me, but . . ."

"What?"

"He . . . his body fell but another part of him stayed up, standing there. Like his flesh just fell away and his spirit was still upright. He looked right at me—could see me. He looked shocked, confused . . . he looked down and saw his body and then . . ."

She screws her face up, the memory cutting into her.

"Then he just seemed to freeze. The spirit part of him that was standing opened its mouth. I think he was going to say something to me. Ask what had happened, but he just suddenly seemed to shake—like a huge current was running through him and he lit up like the sun—and then . . ." She struggles to express it. "He turned to steam, or something like smoke, and was gone."

She closes her eyes, replaying in her mind what she'd seen.

"I don't understand, Dani," Jim tells her.

"He was gone, Dad. Gone."

"What?"

"Not like I can—he was gone. Nowhere. His spirit just went."

"Dani . . ."

"Then the car came—the driver saw the body in the road at the last second and steered away, hit the wall. Lucky he was moving so slowly."

"Oh" is all Jim can say.

They stand silent while the wail of the ambulance builds around them. It trundles through the still treacherous streets. As soon as it arrives two paramedics jump out. Dani finally lifts up her face to meet her father's gaze. Her eyes seem to dance with a firelight Jim has never seen before.

"I don't remember it, Dad. I don't remember my death. I don't know why I'm here. Why didn't I go like he just did? What . . . ?" She can't complete the sentence. Instead she turns and starts to walk away.

"Dani," Jim calls to her. "Please don't go." But she fades from sight.

He waits for a while, hoping she will come back, but after half an hour his fingers and feet are frozen. Full of questions he trudges back to the Lost Souls building. Now it looks totally dark. He knows Karan Noble would never let him back in. But she had confirmed something was going on—"Patty has made her own choice. She needed to act and she has done so"—that was what she'd said, but what did it mean?

He sighs heavily. He's no closer to finding Patty, and is even more worried than he was that morning. With a heavy heart, Jim heads slowly up Dryden Street toward home.

❄

Patty suddenly sits up like a marionette, her strings jerked—ready to perform. She has no idea where she is for a second, the sound and images so alien—then it all rushes back: the knife, the blood, the drive through the snow, handing the sample over, the end to her long, long wait.

On the table the superskinnysoymoccacinolatte is cold, a film formed over the top. Her hand reaches up to her lip and she feels drool. She reaches into her bag and pulls out a packet of tissues to mop her lips. She looks at her watch—11:30. The four hours are almost up. It's time to go back to the lab.

She feels like she's moving through mud; the air is sodden with the weight of loss: lost laughter, lost moments, lost . . . She moves slowly through the streets, almost like a bride moving down the aisle, she feels like she is about to shed her old life and become someone new.

She climbs the stairs to the lab. She asks for Roberta, again trying to smile and affect the cheery Home Counties voice.

Roberta enters. She is all frowns, but as she sees Patty she smiles. "It is good news, I think."

Patty imagines the blade in her hand, sees herself slide it into him, spit in his face. She cries her tears that splash down upon him as his life slimes away. The blood and tears mingle, bloodred pain and crystal joy. Both will free her.

Roberta, still smiling, tells her the result. Her lips move but the sound is distorted. Patty starts to sway; she looks down at her hand covered in his gore. Blood spews onto the floor like broken waters as a baby squirms in the dirt, fighting for breath. She tumbles forward. All is black for Patricia Lancing.

INTERMISSION FOUR

Monday, February 8, 1999

She stands on the threshold. The train station behind her, looking down the path that winds into the middle of town. She's made this walk so often—dozens of times over the last ten years—but today her legs feel like jelly. She has come to despise this city and its occupants, maybe not all but certainly the young ones, with their long limbs, super-white teeth and clear skin. They strut around like they own the place—she hates it—the arrogance of the young and privileged. Even the student selling the *Socialist Worker* sounds like a refugee from the House of Lords.

She pushes herself forward and starts to trundle down the path. It's five months since she was last here, then it was the start of the new university year. She had quizzed the staff for the thousandth time—nothing. Very few remain from Dani's day, a couple of secretaries, two senior masters and no students; they have masters and PhDs now and are scattered all over the planet. The police gave up on Dani long ago, even Tom has moved on. And Jim . . . Patty suddenly stops and grabs hold of the metal rail. Behind her a Japanese student with a large trundling suitcase has to make an emergency stop.

"Excuse me."

Patty takes no notice. The path ahead swims, she sits down—feeling damp from the ground seep into her jeans. The diminutive Japanese student swears under her breath as she manhandles the enormous suitcase around the madwoman sitting in everyone's way. There is no way forward—that is the only thought in Patty's head. Ten years. There are no leads, no evidence, no chance. She feels sick. Tired and sick. She hates Durham. Before Dani came here Patty knew nothing about the city. No, that isn't quite true—she had known one girl from Durham, a prostitute who worked out of a slum in King's Cross. Tina. Tina? When Patty first met her she was still pretty, only twenty, slight but not addict thin. She'd arrived from Durham a few weeks before—running from someone or something. Running to the big smoke where the streets were paved with gold. Stupid girl. She had a son who was in care—she swore she'd get him back. She begged Patty to help. What a fucking joke, he was better off without her. Fucking Durham.

Patty sits on the step and lets the day slide away from her. At some point her stomach grumbles so loudly that she gets up and walks down the path to find something to eat. In a greasy spoon she orders a cheese sandwich and glass of milk. There's a phone box outside and she considers calling Karan. She wants someone who might understand. Might appreciate what ten years of death feels like . . . but she doesn't ring her. Truth is there is no one who can know what she has gone through, feel the frustration of her failure to find Dani's killer, know the guilt she feels about those first few days when she was drugged up to the eyeballs and no help. She feels the shame nuzzle her heart even now, gnaw at her: "You fell apart when you were most needed. Ninety percent of all crimes are solved in the first twenty-four hours and you were no use—you might as well have killed her." That is what her head tells her. The milk seems to curdle in her mouth. She takes one bite of the sandwich but can't force it down. She spits it into a napkin. Why did she come here? She envies Karan Noble. She lost her daughters but at least she knows who to blame, who to hate. She has the pleasure of knowing his life is being made a hell in prison—that she pays for him to be beaten and worse every week. That is something. Something.

"Really. Would that make you happy, Patty? To have a man raped and beaten for your pleasure?" Jim-in-her-head asks.

"Yes."

"Are you so lost?"

"You have no idea who I am these days."

"I am so sorry for you."

Patty gets up and pays the bill. Outside it is quite dark. The day is lost. She stands there stuck. She could go to a hotel and start early in the morning. Maybe the local paper has . . . but instead she turns toward the path back to the station. The chance to avenge Dani has gone. There is no revenge for her. This has been a long way to come for a bite of cheese sandwich.

"Sorry," the man says as he hits her shoulder, walking the other way.

"Watch where you're going," she calls back to him.

He goes a few steps more and looks back. He recognizes her immediately from the church. Ten years—but it's her mother. His chest tightens as he watches her walk up the hill. He feels a force, like a rubber band stretched between them. He follows her, keeping his distance as she heads up the hill.

In the station she turns to the platform heading south, and he walks to the opposite platform and sits, watching her across the tracks. She has a thin jacket on; she looks frozen but seems oblivious to the cold. She's lost a lot of weight since he last saw her; she looks lean now, like a runner. She looks more like Dani—how Dani might have looked when . . . if . . . he feels a tear breach his defenses and roll down his cheek.

Patty looks across the train tracks and sees a man crying. He reminds her of Jim for a second—so close to tears all the time. She wonders why he's crying . . . and then the London train rattles into the station wiping the image from her sight. Was the man real—or just Jim-in-her-head? She will not admit to missing him. Not allow the loneliness to flood back in. She had to leave him; the closeness was killing them both.

She rises slowly and walks to the train. She will not make this journey again. There are people she can help through Lost Souls, there are men she can punish, laws to change and young women like Dani to protect. Maybe she could even write again . . . maybe . . .

He walks to the edge of the track and tries to catch a glimpse of her on the train. A part of him wants to run through the tunnel to the steps and get on the London train. Maybe he could sit opposite her and . . . what? Say sorry. Say sorry for the pain, sorry for his part in Dani's— From nowhere a hand grabs his arm and pulls him back as a train rushes past his nose.

"You need to be careful," a voice tells him.

"Yes. Yes, thank you. Thank you."

From the air, a disembodied voice announces the London train is about to depart. The man stands there and watches as it pulls out of the station. Then he heads back to the twisting path that leads to his wife and daughter.

PART THREE

FOURTEEN

Monday, October 4, 2010

Tom stands on the doorstep, frozen. His arm raised, finger pointing toward the doorbell, yet he cannot move. It's a cool autumn day, but his hairline is beaded with sweat. His eyes are wet with tears that threaten to stream. He lowers his arm and pulls at his jacket, which is a little too snug along his back. The insignia on his chest and shoulders pronounces him Detective Superintendent in the Metropolitan Police; inside the uniform he feels like a child, knocking on the door to ask if his friend can come out to play. He breathes and steadies himself once more. This should be easy, it isn't like he's calling to tell someone their loved one has been killed. Not this time.

Inside the house, a body lies on the floor. She looks dead, but not at peace, her brow puckered, her mouth pinched. The doorbell rings, the body doesn't move. The doorbell sounds a second time and the face creases with annoyance. Patty opens her eyes, they swim, unfocused for a second and then fix on the world. She had been lost inside her head somewhere in a fog. Her stomach growls, she has no idea when she last ate. The doorbell rings again.

"Go away!" she shouts. She doesn't open the door these days. She doesn't answer the phone either. It's never anybody real anymore.

The doorbell sounds three times in quick succession.

"Christ," she mutters and rolls over onto all fours, then pulls herself upright and walks to the door. She doesn't know why; it was just that the three quick rings reminded her of something.

On the doorstep, Tom braces himself.

"What the hell is it?" Patty glares at him angrily for a moment and then softens as she recognizes . . .

"Pup," she whispers. She takes a step forward and her hand reaches out to trace the lines around his eyes.

"Hello, Patty," he manages to squeeze the words past the lump in his throat. Her fingertip is suddenly wet and she pulls her hand away, embarrassed.

"Tom. It's good—a surprise—but good to see you. Come in." She steps back and he follows her in.

She takes him into the lounge. It's quite Spartan—there are two chairs and a small table covered with leaflets. She says something but he can't quite sync her mouth with the sound. It looks like Dani's mouth, which is odd because it never used to. It had been very full, soft and inviting. He remembered Jim telling him one day—one drunken night really—how it had been Patty's mouth he had fallen for that first night, the greatest mouth he had ever seen. Now it was thinner and tighter. Tom wondered if it ever laughed anymore.

"I am so sorry. I have no tea or coffee or anything really." Her stomach growls again and she hopes he can't hear it. "Water?"

"No, I'm fine."

She stares at him, not knowing what to do—it's years since she had to entertain. He stands awkwardly, waiting for her to offer him a seat, until he realizes she never will.

"Can I sit down?"

"Yes, yes, of course. Where are my manners? I don't have any tea . . ." she trails off knowing she's said that already. She flushes with embarrassment.

"You look good."

"Liar." She sits opposite him and studies his face—so hard to see the boy in there now. She remembers how he had aged suddenly after Dani . . . after Dani. But now he doesn't just look merely old but craggy, weathered—it suits him. Suits his position, he has authority about him. She likes it, and yet, feels a stab of pain.

"It is good to see you," she says, and means it.

"I was sorry about you and Jim."

She waves her hand as if she were swatting a fly—wiping away the past.

"It's twelve years. Too long to care about." She wonders for a moment if they still see each other—Tom and Jim. They used to go for drinks, after they'd been to the garden of remembrance. Remember what? The good old times.

"You've done well for yourself. I've seen your name in the news over the years."

He ducks his head. "Luck."

"Don't be silly. Intelligence and a good heart—that will get you high in the police. So few of them have it."

"Well," he starts, but doesn't know what to say. He remembers Dani yelling at him, "Don't join the police, for God's sake! Mum, Mum tell him." And Patty shot him a look that was so full of disappointment he almost gave in.

"Where are you at the moment?" Patty asks. "You were family liaison weren't you?"

"Yes, I was always the one called in to tell the bad news."

She nods. She knows what they used to call him: the Sad Man.

"Now I head up a special operations unit, small but . . ." he trails off again.

"What does the unit do?"

He looks at her. He can feel his face crumble a little. "We investigate sexually aggravated murders, usually multiple victims."

She nods. The irony is not lost on her.

"Children?"

"No, the Child Protection Unit deals with under eighteens."

"No, sorry . . . I meant: do you have any? Are you married?"

His face is blank for a second. "No."

From nowhere, a thought hits her that takes her breath away: "Why is Tom here, in uniform?" Numbness spreads across Patty's chest, her stomach starts to churn. Tom is the harbinger of death—it's Jim . . . A tremor begins, a bad one.

"I'm sorry I . . . I . . . could you . . ." Patty stammers, hands already shaking. She stands and makes her way over to the mantelpiece with intense effort. There is a bottle of pills there. Tom strides over and tries to help, but she brushes him away. She takes two of the small pills and swallows them down without water.

"Patty?" Tom asks with obvious concern.

"I'm fine." Patty can hear how sick her voice sounds; it embarrasses her. She sounds like an old woman. She pulls herself together.

"Tom, is it Jim? Is he . . . ?"

"Oh no, sorry, no. Patty, no, no. This isn't a bad news visit. Christ, I'm sorry."

He takes her hand and leads her back to the chair.

"Could you get me a glass of water?" She points toward the kitchen and he rushes off.

He returns with a full glass and hands it to her. She drinks greedily; it triggers more growls from her stomach.

"Good. Thank you." Patty closes her eyes. She breathes into the tremor—feeling it lessen and finally ripple away.

Tom stands waiting until she finishes the water. He takes the empty glass and sits back down, a little shocked.

"Why?" she asks breathlessly. "Why are you here?"

What does he say? He feels lost.

"Is it an official visit?"

No nods, he tries to speak but his voice seems a long way off. It's stupid, he has done this a thousand times.

"There is a chance . . ." He stops and starts again. "Patty, there have been breakthroughs, scientific breakthroughs in forensic technology, DNA matching and profiling over the last few years. Pretty amazing steps forward—you probably know this already."

"I haven't kept up with the technology lately, I . . ." she trails off.

"Okay, well there's been a revolution in forensic analysis, and it's meant that cold cases all over the country are being reviewed. There's a series of teams looking at every unsolved murder case. Families are being contacted and . . ."

The penny floats in the air and then drops like a hand grenade. "Dani? Will they review Dani's case?"

He pauses, a little scared by the small flame he has seen ignite in her eye.

"Yes. Dani's case is on the list. They would have sent an officer round from family liaison but . . ."

"You volunteered."

He nods. He could add: "I wanted to see your face when you got the news, I wanted to manage your expectations—not to get your hopes up." But he doesn't. He can't.

They sit silently together for quite some time. Patty's mind is whirring. She used to keep up with the changes in procedure and testing; it had been part of her job. She remembers sitting in the British Library reading the *Journal of Forensic Science*, but when did she do that last? She was at a conference in Berne on DNA profiling. When was that? 2000? 2001? Ten years ago? When did she stop looking? When did she give up on Dani? She shakes her head, trying to clear the brain fog, feeling the cogs start to engage once again.

"What do you mean by forensic analysis?" she asks.

"It's an evidence-based review. They'll go through the file and look at whether any of the recent technical advances can be used to develop DNA matches, looking at samples taken at the time to consider if they can be tested."

"Samples?"

She remembers the cold and damp of the room. Spider webs that not only have spread into the corners but seem to creep over the ceiling, and down onto the metal struts of the shelves, knitting the darkness together. She can't imagine this room ever having been cleaned, the must of decaying paper and mold making her sneeze again and again.

She waits while the man who manages the evidence store tracks down the files she needs. He moves slowly, far more slowly than she has patience for.

"Really, I could find it myself."

"No. No, sorry to say I couldn't allow that, my dear—authorized personnel only." His voice has a sibilant hiss; his skin looks mottled with mildew. Maybe all the years down there have turned him into a half-man. Certainly looks like it.

Finally he emerges with a green file. She knows that means an open case. Open but cold.

"Now, miss, you understand I am doing this as a favor to PC Bevans, up there in Greenwich."

Patty nods.

"Officially, you are not here."

"I understand."

He nods over at a desk and chair. "You can sit over there."

"Can I make any copies?"

"No. You can make notes and sketches. No photographs and you can't leave this room with any of the papers. Want a cuppa?"

She nods and accepts this kindness from a stranger. He walks off and she prepares herself. She slips her hand down her leg and into her boot, removing the tiny Leica camera. She quickly photographs each page. She can only hope she has got the exposure right; the head photographer on the paper had given her lessons, though she hadn't told him what she planned.

She hears Tom's warning echo through her head. "Careful, Patty. Take care of yourself."

She knew what the warning meant. It wasn't merely "Don't get caught"; it was "Don't be disappointed." He had told her many times that the file had nothing—no leads. But the file held photographs.

"From after she was found . . . in that room," Tom told her with a shaking voice.

"I understand." And of course she had understood; she'd seen crime-scene photos and autopsy photos many times. She could handle it. She had to see everything. Tom had nodded, looking defeated and a little worried.

"I'll arrange it."

She photographs each page methodically and quickly with the little spy camera, but does not read anything, barely glances at the content. Not until she has finished and stowed away the camera does she begin to read the file.

Patty shakes those memories away; she needs to concentrate on Tom now, not twenty years ago.

"What forensic testing . . . of what evidence, Tom? I saw the files back then and there were no DNA samples taken." She tries to remember the exact wording. She's sure it said: "Samples collected for storage: none."

"I haven't seen the original report. Perhaps they weren't classified as samples because by the standards of twenty years ago they weren't." Tom tries to make it sound like he isn't guessing.

"But today? Today these tests . . ."

"Minute traces can be tested today whereas twenty years ago you needed so much more. And samples can be taken from so many more surfaces and materials."

"And does the file have—"

"Patty, I don't know. Maybe, but . . ."

He feels out of control. Normally he wouldn't give the family any technical detail, just be calm and reassuring without getting anyone's hopes up. But this is Patty.

Tom continues. "They sent me a scan of the log sheet—it's a one-page summary on the front of the file. It says there were fluid samples taken and clothing samples retained."

Patty feels tears break through the levee and begin to run down her cheeks. She thought she'd cried every tear her body was capable of years ago; she'd become desiccated through so much sobbing, but they still come. Tom stands and moves forward slowly, like a trainer with a wild animal. He puts his arms around her shoulders, and . . . Flashback to twenty years ago and he is breaking the news to her and she begins to scream and scream, he holds her tight. The same woman twenty years later . . . He can feel a fury build in his own chest but he holds it down.

Later, when he is alone, he will scream Dani's name until his lungs feel like they will burst. Then he will cry for her and her mother. He will cry for them all. Now, he and his love's mother are wrapped together before the last sob wracks Patty and she pulls herself away from him. She gets up and goes in search of some tissues. All she can find is a roll of toilet paper.

"Patty, you have to know that the chances are slim. Really slim that anything is even usable, let alone could provide evidence."

"But possible?"

He should say "no." He can see her hopes rise. He should say "no" to save her more torment, but he can't. "Yes, it's possible."

Possible. The word seems to burrow into her, letting the fog out. Her heaviness falls away, like one of Salome's veils dropping to the floor revealing the shape of something indistinct, a tease, but something is there. Patty feels alert, for the first time in years.

"Do you have any idea about the timescale? When will Dani's murder be reviewed?"

Tom hesitates. "Forty-eight months," he tells her, deeply embarrassed. "Probably about forty-eight months. I'm very, very sorry."

"Oh, Tom" is all she can say.

They sit together for a while longer, though there is not much more to be said. Tom gives her a web address and tells her that a letter will arrive soon restating pretty much what he has just told her.

"Jim will be informed too," Tom tells her.

"I can tell him," Patty offers.

"Or I can."

"It would be better if I told him."

"Fine." Tom nods.

In her heart, Patty knows she won't tell him and thinks it better if he doesn't know. Not for a while at least. Finally Tom moves to leave and Patty shows him to the door.

"Oh. Wait," and she runs off.

Tom stands at the door awkwardly as time ticks by. She is gone for at least five minutes, before she finally returns.

"There is this. I thought you might . . . I don't know why I have it. I have almost nothing else but . . ." She hands him a small metal cup on a fake marble plinth. On the front is a gold-colored plaque that reads:

14 June 1982
800m Champion
Danielle Lancing

He smiles as he runs his finger along the rim of the trophy. He remembers the day as if it were yesterday, not almost thirty years ago. She broke the school record that day, and that night was the first he talked to her, talked to her properly, just the two of them.

"Tom. Isn't there something you can do to bump her up the list? Surely there must be."

He looks at her as the memories crash around him. Patty was good. She had ambushed him at his most vulnerable.

"There is nothing I can do," he manages in a small voice.

"That can't be tr—"

"Cold cases are looked at by another unit. I can't ask for preferential treatment, and they wouldn't give it. Besides, I think the chance any review will uncover something is so small. Really, Patty, I don't want you to have false hope."

He holds out his hand to her, but she pulls away. He can see her harden before his very eyes. He hears it in her voice too. The ice queen.

"Don't worry about me," she tells him and opens the door. "Bye, Tom."

"Patty."

He walks away from the house. Darkness has fallen while he was inside and the night air is chill. He hopes he made the right decision, to see her himself rather than have a junior FLO deliver the news. He doesn't know what four years of waiting will mean to her. He remembers all too vividly those first few months, that first year or two. She was like a hunting dog, pulling apart everything. He didn't know how Jim could stand it back then, watching the obsession grind her down and waste her away. He desperately hopes this will not rekindle that madness. There is no chance that the samples will provide the evidence to find the killer—this isn't TV. There is never going to be an answer to who killed Dani.

※

Patty watches him walk down the road, away from the house. As he retreats, she feels the tremor begin. She rides the crest, surfing the crashing wave out . . . out . . . out . . . It takes a long time for her to come back to her body. She has found over the years that the tremors are like ripples made by a stone thrown into a lake. A small splash and there's just a gentle undulation that carries you outward until calm returns. A big stone and it's a roller coaster. And this? Well, this was no small stone, this was Atlantis, sliding under the churning ocean creating waves that could last for all time.

FIFTEEN

Tuesday, October 5, 2010

The dead leaves crunch underfoot as Patty runs. She knows it's some kind of addiction—she craves the endorphins her body ekes out like some crack-dealing Scrooge. She runs every day, has done for the last six or seven years. Sometimes only a few miles but often fifteen or more. Always alone. It depends on how much thinking she has to do, or how desperate she feels. On desperate days she runs the furthest and fastest.

It's cold. Autumn is really biting, but the sky is clear and there's some watery sun that shines through the brown papyrus of the leaves. She can see her breath.

Still less than a day since Tom's visit. It feels like she's been struck by lightning. "She's alive, she's alive!" She imagines some mad scientist howls at the moon in glee that Patty Lancing is reanimated.

"When did I die?" she asks herself.

"When you gave up hope," he echoes through her head.

"Oh, are you back in my head, Jim?"

"I never left, just waited for you."

Patty speeds up, trying to outpace the truth. Because, of course, she had given up. She had looked under every rock, tried to dig out every secret surrounding her daughter's death, but there was nothing. She hit brick wall after brick wall as if someone were blocking her at every stage. But she still went around the maze time and time again. Month after month and then year after year. And then—she can't pinpoint the time or the place, but she started to slow down. Then she fell to her knees and crawled and finally she lay down and died. That was probably when she started to run. Her body still worked, but inside there was nobody home. When was the last time she shed a tear, the last time before yesterday? Years. Years and years. Silent and cold, dead but running. Until now. Bolt from the blue and . . . her case will be reviewed. Something to live for. But four years? She runs faster.

❄

Her lungs burn, and finally force her to stop. She has lost all sense of time; it's dark and she has no idea where she is. The temperature's dropped, suddenly it's freezing. She looks up to the moon and to the side sees the Pole Star. She could wish on it. The thought makes her smile.

"Star light, star bright, first star I see tonight. I wish I may, I wish I might . . ."

But what does she wish for? She closes her eyes and a face she had almost forgotten fills her mind.

SIXTEEN

Friday, October 8, 2010

The *bizness 4 U* building had been launched, with great fanfare, by a government minister five years before—all slick and shiny. Two hundred subsidized luxury offices to boost London's entrepreneurial spirit. Today, half are empty, the other half full of massage therapists, women baking organic flapjacks and media start-ups. Patty arrives on level four and peers out from the lift. It looks exactly the same as levels two and three, both of which she has walked around for the last twenty minutes. The carpet is luxuriant, but hideously turquoise. Large plants in pots have been placed every ten feet, real plants, but the lack of light has caused them to brown at the edges and curl like old toast. At least half of the lightbulbs are blown and a large pink penis has been drawn in the lift. This is the last floor she will look at, she decides, and heads out. Nothing, nothing, nothing . . . But then the final door reads MARCUS KEYSON INVESTIGATIONS. She feels a little sick.

She has spent the last four days, since Tom's visit, in the British Library reading the *Journal of Forensic Science*. She realizes now just what an explosion there's been in criminal investigations in the last four or five years. The uses of DNA matching and profiling have boomed over this time and she had sleepwalked through it. For four days she has read voraciously, yet after all that, she has no greater insight into Dani's case. She does not know if her killer can be found. What she does know, however, is that she needs to find out what samples the police gathered in 1989. Then she can discover what can be done with that evidence and see where it might lead.

She knocks. The door is opened by a stunning young woman, petite with auburn hair cut into a bob and, refreshingly, no make-up. She smiles. "Mrs. Lancing?"

Patty nods. Doesn't correct her, not trusting her own voice.

"Please take a seat. Dr. Keyson will be with you soon."

She indicates a row of four chairs with a wave, then turns to walk back to her desk. Her hip drops, as if she has been hit, then rights itself and she drags her foot forward. It is the worst limp Patty has ever seen—she immediately feels sympathy for her—then catches herself. "Stupid," she thinks. "She doesn't need sympathy from the likes of me."

Patty walks to the seat furthest from the receptionist and scans the room. It is nothing like she'd expected; it looks more like a high-end psychiatrist's office. Two pieces of large expressionist art dominate the room as well as four smaller contemporary sculptures. In front of the chairs is a low-slung coffee table, which, thankfully, does not have nine-month-old gossip magazines resting on it. Instead there are gallery catalogues, most in English, but some in Spanish and French. In the corner is a crate full of children's toys. Patty wonders who brings a child to an appointment like this. Apart from the entrance, there are two other doors. On the walls there are a few small, delicate drawings and a series of framed diplomas, which mostly hang above the pretty girl's desk, highlighting that Marcus Keyson is indeed an accomplished doctor of forensic sciences. She wonders why he is here, in this run-down building. She had seen his name mentioned in two or three of the articles in the journals she has been devouring. In each one he was lashing out at the police, saying that they missed too much evidence, that they did not have the proper training needed to keep a crime scene clean. She had googled him. It was obvious that he had been a shining star in the firmament of forensic investigation, but something had happened and, like Icarus, he had tumbled down to earth. She couldn't find what but did discover that he acted as an independent investigator on forensic assessment of evidence and DNA. His website said he had strong links to the Metropolitan Police and that total privacy was assured. Free initial consultation. So she had called.

"Can I get you a tea? Or coffee?" the receptionist asks.

"No. No, thanks . . . actually, yes, yes, I would like a tea. Black, black, please."

"Of course."

The girl leaves her desk and limps toward one of the mystery doors. It must be a kitchen, or at least a room with a kettle. Patty doesn't really want the tea, but she needs something to do with her hands, to quell the tremor that is beginning to build. In her pocket she feels the weight of her medication. She could take two small white pills, which would control the shaking but it would dull her too. And that is not acceptable; she needs to be sharp.

After a few minutes the girl returns with a tray. On it are three mugs, a small dish of sugar sachets and a plate of biscuits, fancy ones coated in Belgian chocolate. Two of the mugs are stylish Pantone designs, the third is a beaten-up old thing, its surface pitted by a thousand buffets in a dishwasher. But you can still see the faded legend: WORLD'S FAVORITE DAD. The girl puts the tray down and takes one biscuit and the DAD mug and walks to the third door and knocks. There is a muffled response and she enters. Patty takes the mug of black tea into her hands and holds it. It's been made from real tea and not a bag; a few specks of leaf swirl in the depths as the undertow forces them to the top, only to drag them down once more. Her shakes are almost under control. She closes her eyes and visualizes them fading. "I am not solid; I am not rigid. I am liquid; I am air. I am—"

The door opens and the receptionist limps out. "Dr. Keyson can see you now."

"—I am blood."

Patty rises from the chair and walks slowly, keeping herself steady. The pretty receptionist smiles and touches her arm, just for a second.

Marcus Keyson is sitting on the edge of his desk, his coffee mug wrapped in a bear paw of a hand. He smiles and stands to greet Patty. He's tall, about six foot five. Late thirties, early forties, which Patty finds amazing, given the diplomas liberally covering the walls in the outer office. He has strawberry-blond hair, very expensively styled, with eyebrows that seem almost white. His skin is tanned and slightly ruddy. He wears white linen suit trousers and a long shirt with a granddad collar. No tie. No jacket. No shoes. He has bare feet. He has bare feet. Patty stops dead, thinking she's come to the wrong place—this is some new-age therapist who's gonna yin her yang.

"I think there might be some mistake," Patty starts.

"Marcus Keyson. Forensic investigations. This is the right place, Mrs. Lancing." He stretches out a hand to her and with it, guides her, like they're dancing, to a chair. Then he sits back on the corner of his desk and looks questioningly at her. He says nothing.

"Dr. Keyson—"

"Marcus." He smiles, then nods for her to continue.

"Dr. Keyson, your website details a specialism in forensic assessment."

"That's right. How's your tea?" he asks with an open smile and sympathetic eyes.

"Erm. Okay."

There is silence. Patty can feel a cold invade her chest. She needs to get out and starts to rise. But he's quicker. He puts his hand gently on her shoulder and presses her down firmly.

"Would you like to tell me about your . . . ?"

"Dr. Keyson." She closes her eyes. She has stood and looked into the chasm so often . . . she leaps.

"My daughter was kidnapped, raped and murdered." Just facts, headlines, nothing of Dani. He remains silent. "Good," she thinks, "there's no poor you." She has been hollowed out by poor you. He stays silent, his eyes coolly assessing her.

"When did this happen?"

"She was found in February 1989. She had been missing for three weeks. There were no leads and no one was ever arrested."

"I'm sorry, there is nothing I can do for you. 1989." He says the date like it is the dark ages.

"I fully understand the—"

"1989." He stands, dismissing her. She does not catch his eye; instead she begins her story.

"I was visited by the police a few days ago. My daughter's case falls into some criteria for reopening her file."

He flicks his eyes to the clock behind her head, makes some internal calculation and nods slowly. "Yes, cold cases are being reviewed systematically." He stops and looks like he's choosing his words carefully. "It's purely evidence-based, so that would indicate that there was some kind of sample taken at the time."

"Exactly." She fishes in her pocket, pulls out a notebook and reads from it: "Fluid samples taken and clothing samples retained." She closes the book again. "That's what he said, but it

made no sense. I saw the notes, back then, and I was sure there
were no—"

"A police officer told you all this?"

She nods.

"I'm surprised they were so . . . candid."

"I was insistent."

He looks at her, and his brow furrows. "Not a good sign,"
Patty thinks.

"I still don't think I can be of any help, Mrs. Lancing."

Patty can feel the shake. A vibration runs through her and down
the chair to the floor. She clenches her hands and feels the nails cut
into her palm, but they are too bitten-down to draw blood.

"Could I have a glass of water, please?"

He looks as if he is about to say no, then nods and leaves the
room. Her head swims as though she might pass out. She takes one
of the pills from her bag and places it on her tongue. He returns
with a glass of water. It has ice and a slice of lemon; she almost
laughs. She manages a polite "Thank you." He looks concerned.
Patty knows she must have turned white, like a ghost.

"Are you?"

"Fine. I'm fine. Please."

"To be honest, Mrs. Lancing, the samples taken in the eighties
will be no good now for any kind of analysis. Procedure back then
was . . ." He whistles through his teeth. "Neanderthal."

"But there have been successes, with Low Copy Number analysis. Some of those samples date as far back as 1981."

"You?"

"I did some research."

She doesn't tell him she has barely slept in four days, reading
and rereading a hundred case studies.

"Hmm." He nods, drumming his fingers on the desk. "That's

true but . . ." He pauses. "In 1989 you really needed to have had a forward-thinking officer at the crime scene for any samples to be viable today. Twenty years . . ."

"But it's possible?" She is strong, not needy or desperate.

"It isn't beyond the realms of possibility," he says carefully. "It's not inconceivable that a DNA profile could be produced from the sample." He frowns. "If—and I cannot stress strongly enough—*if* it were cleanly taken and well stored."

"Then it could be matched on the police DNA database?"

"Potentially, *potentially* it could be matched with DNA previously taken." He shakes his head. "But there are big *ifs* in the mix."

"I see." She closes her eyes. "I must not get my hopes up," she thinks.

"But hope is the only thing keeping you alive." Jim-in-the-head says.

Keyson pulls a small notebook from a desk drawer and takes a pen from his pocket. "Were you given any kind of timeline on the review?"

Patty nods slowly. "He said it could be four years."

Keyson stabs the pen into the notebook. "Okay, so it's a grade two case."

"Grade two?"

"Grade two or priority two cases. Firstly, there's no one being held in custody for a crime, so there's no potential miscarriage of justice to address. Secondly, there's no indication of a link to another murder or serious crime—those cases are priority one. Otherwise, where there's the potential to solve a cold case, those are graded priority two."

He smiles and knocks back the last mouthful of his tea.

"So my daughter's killer could be identified?"

"Without access to the case notes I couldn't comment."

"But a sample exists, a sample of DNA that could identify her murderer?"

"Patricia, can I call you Patricia?" He doesn't wait for her reply. "I cannot, in all my experience, hold out any hope that a sample taken from your daughter would shed any light upon the identity of her killer. In 1989 no police investigation could analyze a forensic sample and cross-match it with a DNA database. Now they can. It's an enormous advance. And yet . . ." He sees the hope in her. "Perhaps, in another four years . . ."

"Dr. Keyson, I don't have four years. I'm dying. I have cancer." She had not rehearsed the lie. She hadn't even consciously decided she would lie. But she realizes she will do anything. "I can't wait for the police. I have waited over twenty years already and cannot continue. I will not be here in four years."

"I'm . . ."

"DS Bevans made it seem—"

"Tom Bevans?"

"Yes. You know him?"

"He's a senior officer. The head of Operation Ares."

"Yes."

"He personally gave you this information?"

"Yes. He has been involved from the start—with Dani's murder."

"Dani?"

"My daughter. Danielle."

"Your daughter is Dani—and she was murdered in London."

"No. No, she was killed in Durham. She was a student there."

"Durham." Patty can see the cogs churn in his head. Then he swings himself off the desk and walks behind it. Something in him has changed, his eyes no longer sympathetic, instead they burn with intelligence.

"Let's start from the beginning."

INTERMISSION FIVE

Monday, February 20, 1984

Downstairs is a heaving mass of bodies, writhing like worms in mud. Dry ice, cigarette smoke and sweat curl up and fill the air. Upstairs, the seating makes it more organized but still bodies bounce and jerk to the pounding rhythm. All is dark except for dim green exit signs and the strobe lights on stage, which catch the band in frozen image after image. Tom feels carsick. Nic Fiend wails into the darkness.

The sea of sound is overpowering. Tom feels it in his body, working him like a marionette, pulling him this way and that as the band crashes, guitar and drums pitched at incredible decibels. To compete, the singer has to screech ever higher and louder. They don't play like a team but like competitors racing to the finish. Exhilarating—but his head hurts.

Tom would rather be outside away from the smoke but he has to be in his seat: E5. It's the only place he knows for sure she'll be. The Banshees won't be on for ages. Alien Sex Fiend has just started and there are another two support bands he's never heard of. To be honest, he doesn't know much about Siouxsie Sioux—just that Dani loves her. And he loves Dani.

He would have preferred to have taken her to a movie. *Footloose* or *Police Academy*—they both sounded good. In a cinema they could hold hands and share popcorn while they watch. And after he could lean over and kiss her.

Yeah, right! Like that was going to appeal to Dani Lancing. No, Dani will love seeing the Banshees, and he will bask in that.

A final screech of guitar and vocal cord end their biggest number and the crowd screams and claps. He joins in, though his applause is a little lackluster. As the band launches into another song, Tom turns round to scan the doors once more. She probably won't come until the first chord Robert Smith plays, but he can't help himself. He knows he should feign nonchalance, get caught up in the music. He should watch the bands. Even after she arrives and sits next to him, he should pretend not to know she's there until a song ends and he calmly notices her.

"Oh, hi, Dani. This is cool."

Except, even he knows that saying anything's cool would be romantic suicide. Maybe he should keep quiet. And not dance. Christ, it's really difficult—especially when his heart's flailing like Keith Moon on a bender.

Under the chair he has a hip flask for them, well, mostly for her, filled with vodka he's nicked from his mum's stash under the bed. When she arrives he should say nothing, just hand her the flask and go back to the music. That is wha—

Someone moves in next to him, into Dani's seat.

"No, that's ta—"

"Hi, Tom," the girl shouts, smiling broadly.

"Tash?"

She leans across and pecks him on the cheek, then smiles a little flirtatiously. She's a girl from their class, not someone he knows well. She's pretty with a very sharp nose. He's only ever seen her in glasses before, but she must be wearing contact lenses. Her hair seems glittery too. She has a lot of lipstick on; he thinks he must have a little kiss tattoo from her peck on his cheek.

"Good to see you, Tash. Someone else will be here in a minute though, that's her seat."

"No. It's mine." She waves the ticket stub at him. "I bought it this afternoon off Dani Lancing."

"Oh!"

"She said you'd be here. Said you'd look after me." She smiles broadly. He pulls the hip flask from under his chair and passes it to her. She takes a chug from the flask, cut short as she coughs and splutters from the bite of the alcohol in her throat.

She laughs. "Shit, Tom."

Later he walks her home. His eardrums still throb and hum. Tash had loved the night. She'd danced, screamed and drunk the whole hip flask. Her face is deeply flushed and she walks with a pronounced sway. She hadn't been bad company, but Tom was deeply disappointed by the evening. He would have liked to have gone straight home to bed, pulled the covers up over his head and escaped into sleep. Not an option. He couldn't leave Tash to get home alone, could he? But he was a bit worried about her parents chasing him down the road, screaming that he'd got their darling daughter drunk.

They barely speak on the walk home. Tash doesn't mind; in fact it helps to build the mystique of this pale thin boy. She has just had one of the best nights of her life and is thinking this edgy young man has earned himself a reward. Just before they get to her road, she stops by a house with a large hedge. The house is dark and the closest streetlight is broken. It's almost black in that little part of London. She takes Tom's hand and pulls him toward her. She leans over and plants her mouth on his, her tongue pushing forward through his closed lips and into his mouth.

He kisses her back, eyes closed, imagining it's Dani. She tastes like vodka. Tash takes his hand and brings it up to her shirt. He cups her breast.

"Nice," she says and kisses harder, her teeth nipping his lip. The little dab of pain breaks the spell—it isn't Dani. Tom takes his hand away from her breast and gently ends the kiss.

"We need to get you home," he says and draws her out of the shadows, the way you might lead a toddler, and walks her home.

In a small grubby flat above a kebab shop on Streatham High Street, Dani lies on a sofa. There isn't much light in the flat. What there is shows the walls are covered in drawings, like some primitive cave. The smells of greasy roasting flesh fill the room, mingling cloyingly with a sweet incense of vanilla and sandalwood, both scents fighting against the heavy fug of dope smoke.

Dani tries to get up, off the sofa, but her body doesn't respond like it normally does. It's as if she's floating in treacle. Everything is disjointed. She tries to speak, but slurs, she understands nothing she hears. She feels the joint back at her lips, but she no longer has the ability to suck the smoke into her lungs. There is music from somewhere, plaintive and soulful, but she can't make out the lyrics.

Her beautiful art student takes a final draw on the joint and holds it there, looking down at the young woman almost comatose on his sofa. Then he leans forward, opens her mouth with thumb and finger, and blows the smoke in, watching it billow around her lips and then up into the air.

She feels the tug but is not sure what it is. Her jeans are pulled down and taken off. Then her knickers. She falls asleep.

SEVENTEEN

A cheeseburger waddles past, waving a handful of flyers.

"Happy Meal?" it asks.

Patty looks blankly at it.

"Okay, have a good day." It shrugs and ambles away to accost a large group of tourists. Patty turns to the restaurant and peers through the glass; she can see very little evidence of anyone inside feeling any joy. She pushes the door and goes in. The traffic sounds die behind her, to be replaced by the hubbub of twenty different languages fighting to be heard over the noise of deep-fat frying.

She spots Keyson immediately. He sits in the corner. Somehow he's folded his large frame into a garishly colored booth that seems designed for toddlers. He looks like a giant in a fairy tale, made all the more surreal as he's surrounded by a group of yelping Japanese exchange students who crowd the tables around him. Patty takes a deep breath, as if about to dive underwater, then she steps forward.

There is ketchup in the corner of his mouth, making him look a little like a vampire—eyes glazed over, sated by his gorging. Then he sees her and a genuine smile creases his face. She crosses the room, avoiding the mustard and BBQ landmines. He pulls his coat from the seat opposite and she slides into it.

"No trouble finding the place?" he asks.

"I used to work close by."

"I'm giving evidence at the Old Bailey later, so it was a good option to meet here." He slurps the last of his shake and dabs at his large mouth with a tiny serviette.

Then something shifts and a cloud crosses his face as he slips awkwardly into professional mode. He starts to say something but it's obliterated by a sudden cackle of Japanese. "Where the hell is Godzilla when you need him?" Patty thinks.

"I missed that, can you repeat what you said?" she asks with annoyance and leans toward him close enough to smell the tang of gherkin and special sauce.

"There was a prime suspect in your daughter's case, did you know that?"

The world becomes silent. Around her, mouths from across the globe chew the cud of news from home: latest fashions, crazes, diets or plain who-fancies-who and what they did or didn't do. The world goes on around her, but nothing touches her consciousness. Nothing but Keyson's words.

"Prime suspect . . . no."

Keyson nods sagely as if confirming some ground-breaking theory. "The detective at the time seemed to feel there was a strong case. I'm reading between the lines, of course, but there was a partial print from your daughter's left hand on the boot of this man's car."

He punches her hard, the lip is ripped by the teeth, blood vessels burst bleeding into soft tissue, the bruise blossoms like poppies on her cheek. The blow spins her, balance shifts and she falls sideways—her hand strikes the car just before her hip does. Slam! She is lifted off her feet for a fraction of a second as her head snaps back. Even six years of ballet can't keep her on her feet as she begins to fall. Her arms start to wave, trying to regain balance but it is too late, she is past the point of no return as she falls. In a second he is on her, punching her chest, face, shoulder, forehead—until all goes black.

"Patricia?" Keyson waves his hand in front of her face, bringing her back.

"Yes, yes, I'm . . . please, tell me the rest."

He hesitates, seeming to be unsure of what to say next. "There is also a sample of . . ." He stops and looks down to his notes.

"Tell me." She holds her breath.

He coughs and, in a monotone, continues. "Semen was recovered postmortem. It may be adequate for testing."

Patty gulps in air. "That's wonderf—"

"But . . ." he cuts her dead, "there is no sample from any suspect."

"I don't fully understand what—"

"It means that when the police get around to your daughter's case they can profile the DNA and check it against the national database."

"And that's over five million people."

"Exactly. And you might be lucky and find that the killer is in there."

"But . . ."

"The *but* is that your prime suspect may not be in the database—won't be, unless he's had a DNA sample taken for another reason."

Patty nods. She feels the hopelessness spreading around her like ink in water.

"And . . ." He shakes his head. "I spoke to someone at the DNA database. Your man was right—it will be at least four years before your daughter's case is opened. I even told them you might be dead before then. They didn't care."

Patty wants to roll into a ball. Tom was right: she shouldn't have got her hopes up. "Is there anything we can do?"

"Well . . ." He leans in closer to her. "I have a contact." He stops and chews his lip.

The penny drops; now she understands why they've met here and not at Keyson's office. She's seen men act like this many times, when they had information to sell to the newsroom. This is about a bribe.

His voice drops as low as it can possibly go. "I can get your daughter's case file. That would include all samples."

"But . . ."

"You're right, there is a big but. Two big buts. The first is that I would need a pretty hefty amount of money to secure this."

"How much?"

"Ten thousand pounds. That's for my contact, you understand."

She nods. "The second but?"

"Do this—get the evidence illegally—and it will destroy any case against the killer."

"But if the sample matches?"

"Doesn't matter. If the evidence is out of police control, even for a second, it's useless."

"But with the DNA match I could prove it was him, show the results to the news."

"You could. But he'd still have to give a DNA sample voluntarily. And the publicity would mean he could never be charged. Any legal case would be impossible. You'd never get justice through the courts."

"Justice . . ." She wants to laugh at such an outmoded concept. Funny guy. "I'll get you the money, Dr. Keyson. Thank you."

She stands and holds out her hand, like shaking on the promise of a new job or the price of a house.

"I'll be in touch," he tells her.

"Soon," she says. "Soon I hope." She turns and leaves.

He watches her walk to the door. She is swallowed up by the maelstrom of London life. Then he smiles.

INTERMISSION SIX

Dani holds Tom's hand tight, almost crushing it. He doesn't mind. They don't speak, there's nothing to say. It was all said last night when she lay on his bed and told him the story.

"I can't tell them, I can't, Tom. They'll be so disappointed in me—I am so fucking stupid."

"Dan—"

"Don't, Tom. I'm an idiot, a comedy stereotype: teenage and pregnant. A fucking joke . . . a joke." She finishes with a tiny voice, then lies her head back on his pillow and sobs.

The injustice burns in Tom's stomach like poison. He's never felt anger like this, sulfuric in his veins. He wants to run out into the night and kill him, to beat him to a pulp. Except he needs to stay here, with her, to hold her and tell her it will be okay. Tell her that he loves her. But he does neither. Instead, he sits and watches as the girl he loves falls apart on his bed.

Even as Dani lies there crying, she knows it's unfair on poor Tom; she feels so ashamed of how she has treated him. She can't tell him that it happened on the night she should have been with him at the concert. Of course, had she have been there, she would never have been in this state. She feels so lost, alone and stupid. She loves her parents, but could never tell them what she has done. They would help her, of course. They would love her, of course, but they would always look at her with such disappointment. Her mum would hold it over her—in some weird way Dani thought Patty might be pleased. It would prove forever that her daughter doesn't have the strength, the moral purpose, the drive that she had. And her dad . . . oh, her dad. He adores her and she could not bear to watch the disappointment, even pity, spread across his face for the first time in her life. She could not, would not, be less than the perfect daughter for them.

"So will you come with me tomorrow?" she asks Tom.

"Of course. I'll always be there when you need me."

"Thank you," she says as she takes his hand and squeezes it.

The appointment was made through rape crisis to make sure her parents would not find out the truth.

When they first arrive at the clinic they are led into a private room. The nurse asks Dani to come in alone but she refuses, wanting Tom to be allowed in. The nurse eyes him with distrust. She obviously wants to make sure this is not coerced; she assumes Tom is the father . . . father? Hardly a father. Inseminator, perhaps?

Tom blushes under her gaze. He is not the man who has done this—but inside, to his shame, he can't help but think that he would give anything to have been the one who had begun a life inside Danielle Lancing. And he hopes that one day he will, when they are married.

After Dani gives her details she's examined. This time Tom stays the other side of the curtain. Then they are both asked to wait.

They sit with four other pregnant teens—two of them are obviously with their mothers, all tearful. One teen sits alone, her back rigid, her head held high. The last has fourteen-month-old twins, who play with Legos on the floor. She looks like the devil is at her heels.

They wait for two hours until Dani is called. She smiles weakly at Tom when finally it's her turn.

"I'll be here when you come round," he says.

"I know you will. You're my Galahad," and she kisses him on the cheek. There is no passion, but for Tom it's the best kiss of his life: there will never be another to beat it. Then she turns and follows the nurse.

An hour later he's called to see her in the recovery room. She sits up in bed wearing one of those awful gowns that no one can be glamorous in. Dani sits drinking tea that is so sweet it makes her grimace with every sip. She looks incredibly pale. Tom thinks her more beautiful than anything he has ever seen.

"I can go any time. I just need to get my clothes on."

He nods. "I'll go and call a cab."

"I can get the bus."

He shakes his head, taking charge, possibly for the first time in his life.

"No. You get dressed and I'll get a cab."

She holds on to his arm as they walk down the front steps. The cab sits there, the diesel engine chugging, ticking the clock round. Tom had raided his room—the large Roses chocolate jar and his Star Wars pencil case had been full of change. Now about thirty pounds in coins weighs down his backpack. He hopes the cabby won't make a scene about being paid in shrapnel.

They get inside and Tom reels off Dani's address but she corrects him and instead gives Tom's. She looks at him, her eyes pleading. He nods. Then the cab wheels away.

They sit on the backseat and Dani slides sideways and lays her head on his lap. Tom watches the cabby tilt his mirror down so he can see if any funny business is going on in the back. Tom strokes her hair and tries not to get an erection.

At the end of the journey he pays the fare. He gives a decent tip to stop any complaint.

Then Dani laces her arms around him and he helps her up to his room. He puts her into his bed, fully clothed, and she falls asleep. He sits in a chair and watches her.

At about 9 p.m. she wakes and asks for water. Then she gets up and uses the phone, calling home to tell them she's staying the night with a friend. Her dad answers, he wants more details, but she tells him all is fine, that she's tired and is going straight to bed. He isn't pleased but says "okay." Then she goes back to Tom's room, strips to her underwear, gets into his bed and sleeps for another eighteen hours.

When she finally awakes she finds him sitting in an armchair by the bed, watching over her. She holds her hand out to him and pulls him onto the bed with her. They spoon together though she is under the sheets and he on top of them.

"Thank you," she says softly to the back of his head. He tries to turn but she stops him. She likes him to be close but doesn't want him to see her.

"I want to say something . . . not to you, exactly, maybe like a New Year's resolution. I think I just have to say it to get it out there."

"Okay."

"I won't ever do that again."

He stays silent, waiting to hear if there's more.

"I don't know how I feel about kids, I . . . I'm not sure my mum's the best role model for balancing a career and motherhood. But I didn't take care of myself and . . . and look at the mess I got myself in. I need to look out, think—not just jump at things for the challenge, to see what happens."

Tom nods but doesn't really understand. His own desire is so focused on Dani that it skews his natural inquisitiveness. He notices other women, especially their breasts and bums, but always in comparison with Dani. For him there is no one else.

"I need to get my shit together," she says, forcing a smile that's more like a grimace.

They lie there for a while and then Dani sighs, gives him a last squeeze and gets up to face the world again.

EIGHTEEN

Thursday, October 21, 2010

The next few days Patty spends in some kind of limbo. Waiting. Waiting for news from Keyson. Waiting for the name of her daughter's murderer and, of course, considering how she might end another human being's life. Planning a killing. Really anticipating, imagining and relishing the taking of his final breath. Both in her waking life and in sleep, she is consumed by a bloodlust that has lain coiled around her heart for twenty years and is now ready to strike.

She has become an early riser. Not because she goes to bed early—she doesn't—but because she's weaned herself from the need for sleep. Four hours is all she's needed for many years. Even that seems a luxury now, as she rises at five o'clock after just three hours of sleep. But she wakes refreshed, buzzing with adrenaline. She's moved the telephone next to her bed and during the day walks around the house with it in her pocket, desperate not to miss the call from Keyson. She still leaves the house to run but she's gone for only an hour and takes her mobile. When she returns, she checks the answering machine and calls the talking clock to make sure the phone has no fault. She waits.

She waits for four days and three hours. Then the phone rings. They speak for a few seconds. That afternoon, she goes to her bank and withdraws the money. She is surprised at how small ten thousand pounds is, just a paper bag about the size of a sandwich.

Friday, October 22, 2010

Patty drives into the NCP car park and all the way to the top level. That high, it's almost totally empty. She parks in the outer rows looking out over the Thames. It's a crisp autumn day with barely a cloud in the sky. The sun is bright, but not warm. She stands on the edge of the parapet and looks out. If she leans forward and cranes her neck out, she can see down the river to St. Paul's. The majesty of it takes her breath away and for a moment makes her forget why she's there—what she will soon do—but just for a second.

She watches boats motor along the Thames, mostly tourists boarding in the shadow of Parliament and going downriver. So many years since she has done anything like that—enjoyed the city she had once loved so much. She and Jim used . . . Oh, what good will that do? The past is buried, burned black, and should not be dug up. Instead, she thinks once again about how his filth can be examined on a cellular level. How each cell bears his signature; his blood and piss and seed all spell his name and will prove his guilt. Then, once it is proven beyond doubt, she will kill him.

She wades in her daydreams for about ten minutes before another car drives up the ramp. Keyson is at the wheel. He's alone. She feels inside her coat once again to make sure the money's still there. She realizes she's enjoying the cloak-and-dagger aspect. Keyson parks his car and gets out; he wears a World War Two–style trench coat, slightly turned up at the neck. In his hands is a metal box.

"Mrs. Lancing." He nods in greeting, then tips his head to indicate the box. "This is the sample." He holds it gingerly. He hands it to her as if it might explode. She takes it with her fingertips. He hands her a wad of paper.

"These are the instructions on how to store the sample. You need to get it home and in your freezer quickly. Did you prepare it like I said?"

She nods. "I did everything like you said."

She had stripped all the food out and taken it to a soup kitchen rather than throw it away. Then she'd bleached the interior and lowered the temperature to minus eight degrees.

"Good. That's good." He puts an envelope on top of the sample box in her hands, then reaches into his inside coat pocket and pulls out a file folded in half. "These are the case notes."

He places those on the box too. Then he grins at her. "It's a beautiful day and hopefully we'll have a really nice week. Anything planned for the weekend?"

She ignores the question. Instead she walks to her car and carefully places the box on the passenger seat. From her pocket she takes the brown paper bag and hands it to him.

"Thank you. I hope you find what you're looking for," he says, offering his enormous hand for her to shake. She reaches up to him and lets him squeeze her fingers once. She watches him drive away and then she collapses.

She wakes some time later, freezing. She can feel foam fleck her lips. She has rolled herself half under her car, probably had a small seizure. She slowly rolls onto her side and then gets up, her joints straining and her teeth beginning to chatter. Her vision swims slightly, her focus shifting, not too much but enough to worry her. She has barely eaten in three days.

"Get your bloody act together, Patricia," she hisses to herself. She gets into the car and starts it up. No heat yet.

＊

In her kitchen she stands by the sink and eats a packet of biscuits from her almost bare cupboard. She finishes them and forces herself to drink a large glass of water. Then she turns to the box. She tears the security tape from around it and takes out one small, squat jar. There is a label on the outside; the ink is faded and the paper dried-out from twenty years in a fridge. The faded and stained label around the jar reads: CASE HTR234Y678D: DANIELLE LANCING. MULTIPLE RAPE AND MURDER. 7 FEBRUARY 1989. SAMPLE: SEMEN FROM VAGINA RECOVERED POSTMORTEM.

She places the jar in the freezer and closes the door.

＊

Patty switches on the lights and settles into an armchair, unfolds the document wallet and, as if curling up to read a good book, she begins. After half an hour she stops. Her heart is beating triple time. He had been right, Dr. Keyson. The officer in charge had felt there was a very strong case against this man, this prime suspect. He had been a client at the health club Dani had temped at in the summer after her first year at university. He'd been linked to her during a routine questioning of her colleagues. One of them had said that he'd given Dani a lift home once. He'd denied this, but his car was checked and hair, which seemed to match hers, was found on a jacket on the backseat and a partial print was found on the boot. That had been enough to question him but no further link could be made. He'd argued that she could have just been walking through the car park and touched his car, and her hair was similar to his own daughter's and it was probably hers. No charge could be brought. He was top of the suspect list for months and eventually the investigation petered out.

She reads the report again and again, at first becoming angry that the investigation had failed to make the final link: they let the bastard go. But soon the anger seeps away and is replaced by a steely calm as she settles into the knowledge of what will happen now. His name is here in black and white: Duncan Cobhurn.

When Patty finally looks at her watch, it is 3 a.m. She should sleep, but sleep's for the dead. Now it's time to plan.

Saturday, October 22, 2010

Patty finds him online. She ignores an actor Duncan Cobhurn, who's a Winston Churchill look-alike, and there's a guy who values property for some huge investment bank but he's too young. She also disregards the evangelical preacher from Arkansas who believes God will produce a fireball that will purge the Earth of all homosexuals in 2020. But there's a story from 2008 in the *Durham Chronicle*: LOCAL BUSINESSMAN RUNS FOR MAYOR.

She clicks on it. Sixty-three-year-old Duncan Cobhurn, owner of the successful Porto Pronto chain of Mediterranean furniture design shops, is running for office. Blah blah blah . . . it's him. Must be. A later story shows he lost the election; some kind of smear campaign was blamed. Another story about him has a picture; she clicks on it. The grain makes it hard to see details, but that is her Duncan Cobhurn. He's shaking some teenager's hand and handing over a check, blood money probably. He reminds Patty a little of Bob Hoskins and . . . Jim. A short, squat Jim.

She finds another photo from election night. He's with his wife, Audrey, and their daughter, Lorraine. Patty examines the daughter—she doesn't look a bit like Dani, but they must be about the same age. If Dani had been allowed to live, they would be about the same age. Patty can feel the blood around her heart boil. She googles Porto Pronto and finds the website. They open at nine. She calls at 8:50 a.m. and lets the phone ring a long time before a slightly distracted receptionist answers.

"Por—"

"Is Duncan there?" she asks in as friendly and girly a voice as she can manage.

"Sorry, no, we don't actually open till—"

"Do you have the authority to book me an appointment with him?"

"I—"

"We're old friends. I'm just in from Seville. My time is pretty limited. I'm about to jump on a train, I only have a minute or so."

"Okay. Erm, let me see. Could you see him . . . ? This week is pretty bad, he's in Lisbon . . ."

"Oh, is he already there?" Patty asks as nonchalantly as she can.

"No, he's in London today. He flies out from Heathrow Monday morning. So you could see him next Monday, maybe?"

"I'm gone then. Oh dear . . . I really wanted to see him, it's been absolutely ages . . . well, it will have to be next time. Or maybe . . . Lisbon, does he fly there often? I have a holiday home there, you see."

"Well . . ." The receptionist hesitates.

"Maybe I'll call Audrey instead and try to see her." Patty tries to make it casual, but planting the wife's name works a treat.

"Well, he flies to Lisbon every month, mostly the last Monday so . . ."

"Oh, you have been so helpful. Tell me, sweetheart, what's your name, I must tell Duncan how wonderful you've been."

"Greta, it's Greta."

       ❄

She calls back at 12:20, recognizes Greta's voice immediately and hangs up. At 1:10, however, there's another receptionist.

"Greta, please." Patty tries to sound her most authoritative.

"Greta's on lunch. Can I help?"

"Oh hell. Well, I bloody hope you can help. It's Monarch Travel. Our computer's gone mental and I know your boss is flying Monday morning out of Heathrow."

"That's right. Lisbon."

"Well, we've got no records available so I've no idea if he needs a cab . . ."

"No, he's driving himself. He leaves it in the long-term there."

She rolls the dice. "And it's the 9:20 a.m. BA flight?"

"That's the one, and back on Friday morning."

Patty quickly scans the BA printout of flights to Lisbon. "The 11:40 coming back."

"That's it."

"Lovely, my darling. All right, let's hope the IT department can get their fingers out of their arses long enough to get us back online."

"Good luck," she says, which makes Patty smile.

       ❄

Monday, October 25, 2010

Patty gets up at 4 a.m. and grabs a bucket of mud from the garden. She smears it all over the car, making sure to obscure the number plate. Then she gets dressed in clothes from the back of her wardrobe that she hasn't worn in years. They come from an era when she had curves and filled them—perfectly, according to Jim. Now they hang like tents. She should have given them to charity but they have a sentimental pull. The old life.

She completes the ensemble with a scarf, hat and sunglasses. In the mirror she cannot recognize herself. Then she drives to Heathrow.

She arrives at 6:30 a.m. and parks in the long-stay car park. She reasons that if he uses it often he must know exactly where the shuttle picks up passengers, so parks close to that. The spot is directly below a CCTV camera, which she hopes will make it harder to view her. It's all automated so there is no actual person in the car park to notice that she's just waiting. Only cameras, like so much of England now.

She gets out of the car and goes into a dumbshow, looking angrily at the car and then opening the bonnet. She swears, stamps her foot and then calls someone on her phone. If a security guard shows up she'll tell them she's broken down and is waiting for the RAC.

Then she gets back inside and settles down to wait for Duncan Cobhurn.

She has almost given up hope when, finally, at 7:45 he arrives. He speeds into a spot and leaps out looking flustered. He grabs a pull-along suitcase from the backseat and runs to the shuttle stop. Her heart is pounding. She hasn't thought about what to do now. She can see the shuttle come through the gate and make its way slowly to the stop. Should she get on the shuttle too? She's paralyzed. She watches him jump on the little bus, which then trundles away to the terminal. Once it's out of sight, she opens her car door, swings her head out and vomits violently.

Thursday–Friday, December 16–17, 2010

She takes a train out to a town she's never been to before. She carries only cash with her; no cards, no ID. She doesn't use her Oyster card. In charity shops she buys two outfits. She also gets a pair of large sunglasses, a hat and a wig. In a pharmacy she buys a bright lipstick, a shade she would not normally be seen dead in. At a hardware store she adds two rolls of gaffer tape and a small rubber ball.

She finds a park that has a public toilet that's reasonably clean and has no attendant. Inside she changes into one of the suits and, in the cracked mirror, applies the lipstick. The sunglasses and hat complete her transformation. She rides a bus out to an address she'd found the previous day in *Loot*. There, from a very friendly but highly suspect man called Dave, she buys a car for cash. No log book—no questions. She drives the car home and parks it in her garage. Her own car is parked on the street. She does the trick with the mud again until it is impossible to see even the make of car. Then she showers and dresses in the second outfit. She takes the Tube out to Amersham, reasonably close to the airport but not right there. She walks to the hotel she's chosen. She has stayed there three times already, each time checking in as Joyce Adams and paying the bill with cash. She pays for three nights, telling the bored clerk she's on business and is eight time zones out—she does not want anyone disturbing her so she can sleep. No room service, no cleaning. She needs nothing.

In the room she sits and watches TV for two hours. After that she turns off the TV and leaves the room as quietly as possible. She places the DO NOT DISTURB sign on the door and takes the lift down to the parking area. She saunters through as if her car is just at the end of the row . . . but walks all the way out to the street.

She sees no one. From there she walks back to the Tube station and retraces her steps home. She gets back at midnight as Friday slides into being. Today is the day. She does not sleep.

At 8 a.m. it is time for her to get ready. She dresses in the second outfit she bought yesterday. She puts on the wig and threads the sunglasses into it, then applies the unnaturally bright lipstick and looks in the mirror. A stranger stares out. She logs onto the Heathrow site to see the flight arriving from Lisbon at 11:40 a.m. It's in the air but the weather report is poor and deteriorating. She opens her bag and checks the contents: money in Ziploc bag, the hypodermic and drug vial, the tape, the ball, a long knife. In the hall is a folded wheelchair to put in the car. It is time to go.

It cost £500 to have the CCTV put out of action in the long-term car park. That had been Patty's main concern right from that first morning she watched Cobhurn get on the shuttle. She had known then that, with luck, the long-term parking was where she would kidnap him from. She had to put herself in the mind of the police. Once Cobhurn was reported missing they would retrace his steps. They would find that he landed and took the shuttle, and they were bound to look at CCTV footage from the car park. She called someone on a London paper; she'd known him years before when he was just a cub reporter. Now he runs the crime desk. She asked him for a snitch, pretended to be working on a book of true crime. He gave her a name and that name gave her another. After five degrees of separation Patty had some kid who had twelve ASBOs ranging from tagging his school gym to exploding garden gnomes in the local shopping mall. She left his money and instructions in a

Hello Kitty bag on a park swing, a few days before she planned to kidnap Cobhurn. At 10 p.m. on Thursday, December 16, he shot the head off every camera in the car park. Money well spent.

She arrives at 10:30 a.m. and as she waits the first snow begins. She watches the flakes—their beauty mesmerizes her and yet she curses them. As the storm thickens she realizes that very few planes are landing. She had not factored in God.

After two hours of sitting she cannot stay in the car any longer and gets out, feeling the snow crunch beneath her feet.

"There is something very Zen about watching snowflakes tumble through space as you turn to ice yourself," she thinks, slowly accepting the idea that he will not be arriving—that his plane had been grounded somewhere or redirected to another airport.

"If I have to wait I will." She knows she must get him. And something keeps her there, in that cold parking lot, until the sounds of the shuttle break the dead silence.

She sees him alight and struggle forward with his golf clubs and little pull-along case. She steals back to her car; it must be timed perfectly. He waddles forward, dragging his case and bouncing the club bag. Finally he gets to his car and throws his bags down in anger as he realizes what has happened. She must time this just right. She knows that. She eases out of her parking space and slowly moves toward him just pulling alongside as he gets out his phone. She winds her window down and shouts:

"Are you okay?"

He looks over at her; she can see he's shaking with cold and anger. "Some fuckers have slashed my tires."

"Bastards. Kids today see something they want—a beautiful car—and they just have to wreck it." She nods sadly.

"If I could get my hands on 'em, I'd wring their fucking necks."

Patty smiles. "Do you want a lift back to the terminal? You could get security to call a repair truck or something."

He starts to shake his head but stops. Wind whisks freezing flakes into his face and he looks down at what he's wearing.

"Yeah." He nods. "Thank you. Yeah."

Patty gives him her most dazzling smile, then flips open the boot. He walks around to it and throws his bag and clubs in.

"Be careful of the wheelchair," she shouts back to him.

He closes the boot and gets in beside her.

"I really do ap—"

"Seat belt, please," she interrupts.

And as he reaches over to find it, she slides the hypodermic into his neck. He jerks away, but not far enough and she manages to push the plunger all the way home. He looks at her, incredulous, his lips try to form a word, an expletive—*fuckers*—but the syllables crumble, soundless, and then he does too.

She shoves him back in the seat and clips the belt. Done.

Her first stop is a dumpster she'd noticed on the drive there. She puts gloves on and then pulls out his case and clubs and throws them inside. She slides him out of his jacket and throws that in too, including his wallet and ID. Then she drives directly to the hotel, parking in the deepest recess of the underground car park. There is nobody else about. She walks to the back of the car and takes out the wheelchair. She unfolds it, and then, with every ounce of her strength, manages to maneuver his body into it and strap him in. She wheels him to the service lift and they go up to level two. Her room is close to the lift. She has the key ready. Luck is with her; there is no one around. She opens the door and wheels him in.

She looks around at the room. It is exactly as she left it the night before. No one has been in. She turns on the TV and then turns to the man in the wheelchair. The man she has abducted.

From her bag she pulls one of the thick rolls of gaffer tape. She pulls at it and it makes a sound like fabric ripping—she loves that sound. Then she begins to wind the tape around him, like a snake coiling its prey.

She knows what she is about to do. She will restrain him so that there is no chance he can escape or call out. Then she will take a sample of his blood. She has already delivered the semen sample from the killer to a private lab in the city. Once she has his blood sample they will compare the two and when they match them—proving his guilt—she will return to this hotel room and then will cause him pain before she takes his life. After that there is probably nothing. Finally, after more than twenty years of waiting, Patricia Lancing takes a knife and cuts his flesh.

INTERMISSION SEVEN

Friday, January 9, 1981

Patty looks at her watch: 5 a.m. Christ, she's bored. She sits alone in her battered green Cortina with just her nan's old Thermos, Trebor mints, a Zippo and two packs of B&H for company. She tries to stretch, but it's a little car. She'd like to get out and walk around but she's on surveillance and it's really not good to get spotted by a nosy neighbor. Instead she lights a cigarette and smokes it like her granddad showed her—wrapped inside his hand like he did in the trenches. She can't open the window and so the small car fills with smoke, nice.

She wonders, for the thousandth time, if this is all a waste. An anonymous tip-off to the crime desk and she beats five boozy hacks, who all think the story should be theirs, and scuttles up to Leeds. This isn't how it should happen. This is not investigative journalism—it's a fucking feeding frenzy. Journalists calling in favors, throwing out backhanders, threatening pimps, pressuring whores—anything and everything to get an angle on him—and Patty is raking through shit with the best of them. She is the best of them, she knows she is. It just pisses her off that she has to work so hard to get those bastards to see it, and that she has to keep proving it. But this one would set it in stone—that she is the equal of any man. The Holy Grail of blood and murder, Sonia Sutcliffe. The police had taken her into protective custody at first, but they let her go, to "be with relatives" a couple of days later and—gone. No statement, nothing. Nobody knows where she is or who she is, this woman who married a monster, who might be a monster. That's why Patty's sitting, desperate for a pee, in a cramped smoky car all night. The thought of interviewing a female killer—multiple killer of women, a modern-day Bonnie Parker—well, it makes her heart soar. This was what she went into crime reporting for: to cut open the belly and see the filth and shit. To shine a spotlight into the corners and watch the spiders and cockroaches run. That is the only way she can see it getting better.

"This is such a mind-numbing waste of time," she thinks, just as the front door shoots open. Three men come out, walking quickly—they're huge. A fourth figure emerges, much smaller—a woman. The men form a rugby scrum around her. From somewhere, behind Patty, there's the sound of an engine turning over.

"Fuck." She's out of her car in a second, running to the house. She'd parked across the street but they must have known she was there.

The three goons walk quickly and are at the gate just seconds after Patty—the front two stretch out enormous hands. The third, comically, is trying to throw a blanket over the woman in the center, who shoves it back at him.

"I have no camera," Patty shouts, holding her hands up in the air like it's a robbery.

The blanket is thrown to the ground as the front two men separate, revealing Sonia Sutcliffe.

"Sonia," Patty calls. "I'm on my own. I just want to talk; hear your side."

Sonia steps out onto the pavement and Patty moves to bar her way. The front two men hesitate, unsure how to treat a woman reporter with no camera.

"Your words, Sonia, not some hatchet job. That's all, I promise. My name's Patricia Lancing." Patty holds out her hand.

Sonia looks down at the outstretched fingers—then up into her face. For a moment she thinks she sees Sonia's eyes soften—but there is no trust. Patty sees a woman who has heard too many promises that turned out to be lies. Sonia breaks the contact, turns and moves forward. A car screeches into the curb. Patty tries to follow but a giant hand holds her shoulder.

"There's big money in it, for your story," Patty shouts after her—desperate to keep her there. Sonia doesn't look back. The car door opens and she gets in, followed by the three men.

"Sonia, please tell me. How could you not know? Sonia, how do you live with a monster? How do you live with yourself?"

The car speeds off. It had all taken no more than a minute.

"Bollocks."

She stands there, feeling the cold creep into her bones. Finally she gets back into her Cortina to finish the Thermos of lukewarm coffee and have a cigarette. She sits in the driver's seat and goes over the encounter again and again. There was no interview, no story—but there was something. Sonia could have gone out the back way and avoided any confrontation, but she didn't. She wanted to walk tall, not skulk away. That said a lot about her, but was that a story? It certainly wasn't news. Patty finishes the cigarette and then has two more while she thinks. She should drive home. She could be there for the afternoon—but that makes the trip a waste and she wants a story.

She drives to the hotel she'd booked. The room's basic—it smells of stale smoke and dust. The overhead light doesn't work; she has to turn on the bathroom light and use a shoe to hold the door open. The only window is painted shut. The saving grace is that the water is scalding hot. She runs a deep steamy bath and lies there for over an hour, smoking the rest of the pack and turning into a giant prune. The towel looks disgusting, so she drips dry on the carpet. She pulls back the sheets—they look okay. She falls into the bed naked and grabs a few hours' sleep.

✶

It's 11 a.m. when she wakes. She has to be out of the room in an hour so she dresses quickly and goes down to the breakfast room. There's no food but she does manage to get a black coffee out of a young Italian girl. Deep in her notebook she finds a phone number she jotted down some months before. A Bradford number. It's the home phone of the mother of one of the victims. No reply for quite some time but Patty is patient. She lets it ring and ring. Finally a woman answers dozily and agrees to meet.

✶

"Hello. Hello. We spoke on the telephone earlier," Patty shouts through the letterbox. There is no reply. Patty waits a minute before trying again.

"You said I should come. Patricia, my name's Patricia Lancing."

She can't see anything inside the flat but she can wait. She stands back from the door and turns to look out over the balcony. She's on the third floor of a block of flats where four identical squat blocks face each other with a courtyard below. To one side there is an area of grass and some rotating clothes dryers but they're naked, much too cold and wet for clothes to dry. The sky is gray, one of those English days where it won't ever get properly light, merely go from dark to gray to dark again. Kids are running about in the courtyard.

✶

It takes two cigarettes and another round of pounding on the door before a bolt snaps back, a chain scrapes and the door opens. The woman doesn't step out onto the balcony, merely beckons Patty inside with a wave of the hand. As she walks in, Patty can feel eyes on her from all directions. Patty follows the hand into the living room and it points to the sofa.

"Tea?" the woman asks over her shoulder as she walks into the kitchen.

"I'd love some," Patty replies, even though she hates the industrial-strength tea they always serve in the north.

While the woman makes a pot, Patty looks around the room. It's pretty bare. On the walls she can see the telltale signs of pictures having been removed. Every family picture has been taken down. Destroyed, or stored away for a time when seeing them won't cause such pain?

The woman enters with a small tray—two mugs of tea and a little plate of biscuits. She pulls out a table from a nest and puts Patty's tea and the biscuits next to her, before sitting in an armchair across the room, cradling her tea in her hands. Patty's notes say this woman is forty-seven but she looks sixty-five. Her hair has fallen out in clumps all over her head. Her fingertips are speckled with dried blood where the nails have been shredded.

"Thank you for agreeing to see me." Patty smiles.

The mother says nothing but their eyes meet. All Patty can see in them is helplessness. The air swims with pine air freshener and Patty feels a little light-headed.

"I'm not here to drag up awful memories."

"Me memories ain't bad. They're all I've got now," the mother says in a voice that seems both raw and soft at the same time.

"Tell me something wonderful, a great memory of the two of you."

The woman closes her eyes for a second, her forehead wrinkles.

"She weren't a bad girl. I know some a me neighbors'll say different, but I had owt trouble. She were only seventeen." Her eyes glisten.

"Her father?"

The woman frowns, as if she doesn't understand the question at first.

"Gone. Long gone. They're all gone." She gazes into her tea. "Tap." She says suddenly.

Patty shakes her head, not understanding.

"She loved tap. Gene Kelly and Fred Astaire. Whenever there were one o' them films on we'd watch it. She 'ad the shoes. I got 'em for 'er—sixth birthday, I think. She 'ad tap every Saturday morning. I loved to watch 'er . . . that were a special time."

Patty nods. She keeps nodding as the woman talks about her daughter, unfolds her box of memories. The mother talks for an hour.

"I 'ave to go to church now. I go every day. Will youse come too?"

They leave the council flat and walk down the stairs and across the courtyard, both silent. In the air are the sounds of a baby crying, and from somewhere far-off, a dog howling. The estate is only about twenty years old, but it already looks shabby and unloved. They walk through the courtyard and into a small alleyway, which Patty knows she would not walk down alone after dark. The alleyway leads into an identical courtyard, which leads to another scary alleyway. Through that they come to a small modern church, built as part of the estate.

Inside, the church is Spartan. There are pews that look more like the kind of stackable chairs you'd find in a school. No stained glass; in fact, there are only three small windows—mounted quite high so very little light can enter. The only decorations are tapestries that look machine woven, depicting the twelve stages of the cross. One is particularly harrowing—Jesus being stabbed by a centurion. It's in front of that image the two women stop. Patty stands, uncomfortable, while the grieving mother bows and crosses herself. Then she kneels and prays for her seventeen-year-old Lamb of God, slaughtered by Peter William Sutcliffe. Patty sits next to her, feeling like a fraud in the house of prayer.

They sit in silence for twenty minutes and then it's time to leave. Patty follows the mother out. While they were inside the light died; it's turned dark and bitterly cold.

"Thank you," the mother says, throwing her arms around Patty, pulling her close, making Patty feel very claustrophobic. She lays her head on Patty's shoulder and a great sob convulses her.

"I am sorry for your—" Patty pauses. "For your daughter. I'm sorry."

The mother smiles a watery half smile before wearily heading back toward her flat. Patty stands outside the church for a while. She lights a cigarette, smokes it greedily all the way to the butt, and then heads back to her car for the long drive.

It's after midnight when she finally arrives home. Soon, after she left Bradford, she had felt a great pull, a real need to get back to Jim and Dani. Especially Dani. She realizes with shame that she never did call her today, she really had meant to, but . . .

The house is quiet and dark. Once inside, she goes directly to Dani's room and pushes the door open. There her daughter lies, asleep on her side. Not dead, not lost, but at home with them. As soon as she sees her, Patty realizes she has been nervous all the way home—scared she would not be there when she got back. She watches Dani sleep for a long time before she can tear herself away.

In the dark of their bedroom she puts her pajamas on. Jim lies on her side of the bed but as she pulls back the covers he rolls over into the cold half, leaving her to snuggle into the warmth he'd just left.

"Did you speak to her?" he asks, his voice a little slurry from sleep.

"No, just a glimpse. She had three thugs. Spoke to the mother of one of the girls, though. Poor fucking woman. Heartbreaking."

"I'm sure." He rolls over to face her, blinking some of the sleepiness away.

"What about here, how'd it go?" Patty asks.

"I cooked a big lunch."

"Love-struck pup come?"

"Of course Tom came. Good too, he does the dishes."

"You don't think he seems a bit too interested?" She pauses. "You know what I mean."

"They're just friends."

"He's here an awful lot."

"I don't think he likes to go home. He likes Dani."

"That's the problem."

"Why's that a problem?"

Patty doesn't answer, not sure she can explain what she means. She worries that Dani has no sense of proportion. She's got a dad who puts her on a pedestal, and some love-struck kid who would do anything for her.

"Just that she might be a bit big-headed."

"Well, you keep her grounded," he says, and Patty can't tell if that's barbed or not.

"So did she like it?" Patty asks.

"Oh, yes, she was really happy with it. After school we took it over to the lane and tried it out."

"Did you have cake?"

"She said she was too old for cake. We had fish and chips and a semi-frozen cheesecake from over the road. I put a candle on her cod. Thirteen wouldn't fit."

"Rubbish portions over there. Was it just you two?"

"And Izzy. We missed you."

"Yeah, well. Now she's a teen she's meant to hate me."

"Do something nice for her in the morning."

She shakes her head. "I need to be in the office at the crack of dawn if I'm gonna get anywhere with the story."

"Okay," he says without a hint of reproach. He kisses her softly on the forehead. He means it as a loving gesture but Patty finds it annoying. Within seconds he is asleep. Patty lies there wide awake. She can't smoke in bed anymore, not since setting fire to the duvet, but she feels desperate for some nicotine goodness. For a long time her mind whirrs, thinking about Sonia and the grieving mother, about how both their lives have just been turned upside down. Then her thoughts drift back thirteen years, to when she is in hospital cradling her newborn daughter. At the time, the world seemed to offer everything, nothing scared her. Dani could grow up to be anything she wanted—and she would be safe and protected. Patty would never let any harm come to her—she would keep men like her own father from hurting Dani. And she would have the kind of relationship with her own daughter that had been impossible with her mother. Where had that gone wrong? How were they drifting apart as Dani got older?

"Where do we go from here?" Patty asks the night.

PART FOUR

NINETEEN

Sunday, December 19, 2010

Patty tries to open her eyes but they're glued together. Panic starts to rise. She can hear something, some snatches of speech, but none of it makes sense. She's cold, naked from the waist down. Panic spikes, out of control.

"Christ, w-w-w-where . . ."

Her throat is so dry, she tries to claw at it. She pulls at her arm but it doesn't respond. Panic surges. She pulls and twists. There's something holding her. Her arm hurts, a scratch and tug as she struggles.

"Oh, Christ, he's got me." A scream builds in her chest, billows up her body. She doesn't want to die. She doesn't want to die now.

Hands hit her shoulders, push her back.

"No! Help!" She can feel his hands slide around her throat. "Jim, help me!"

"Quiet, sweetheart." A lilting voice, insistent but not threatening, envelops her. The hands are firm. They push her back down. "Careful now, darling, that there tube's for your own good. You need that for water and nutrients. I'll get someone to put it back."

The hands push Patty back down onto the bed, her head sinking into the pillow. Then the sound of soft footsteps. Patty shakes, every muscle in her body burns. Her eyes feel stitched shut. She forces them apart—they crack and tear. Light flickers in, like flame scorching. A faint shape. She can't focus, all just a charcoal smudge. More footsteps, different this time, heavier. Someone is moving her arm, pinching her really hard and there's a burning.

"You gave us quite a scare you know. There we go . . ."

The burning stops. The voice is a woman's, older than the first.

"I'm going to call a doctor. Tell them you're awake."

She leaves, heels clicking on the hard floor. Patty feels her stomach tighten. A doctor? Where the hell is she? She tries to sit up but everything swims and black bleeds in.

"Hello there. I'm Dr. Frobisher."

There is a light, white hot. Just for a second, but it burns itself into Patty's sight and floats there like a storm cloud. Water pours from her eyes. There is some spray, a cloth.

"Your eyes have been weeping and are swollen shut. This should make you feel better and the swelling should calm. Try to open them very slowly." With the cloth he wipes under her eyes and around her mouth. She can feel her lips are cracked. She tries to suck on the cloth. With a "tut" he pulls it away.

"You have an intravenous drip in your right arm. Do you understand what I mean by that?"

She nods. She'd like to tell him that she isn't a bloody idiot, but her throat won't cooperate.

"I had the sister tape down the tubes so they stayed in while you were unconscious. But I've moved them so you can sit up . . . can you try for me? We do have a lift we can use at the back."

Patty slowly sits up and an arm snakes behind her to help. Under normal circumstances she would recoil from the forced intimacy of the touch. Under normal circumstances, but she's too weak and so she allows the unseen arm to sit her upright. She can see down her body. She's dressed in a hospital gown, hence the lack of underwear and basic dignity. The doctor continues to prod and poke her like a cow being valued for a quick sale.

"You're a bit of a mystery, you know," he says as he lifts first one foot then the other and pinches her toes. "We don't even know your name. Could you tell us your name?"

Patty looks blankly at him.

"You had no form of identification on you, no bag, no purse, nothing. Were you robbed?"

Blank.

"Not sure? You had a fall, there's a bang to your head—nothing serious. We were more worried by how dehydrated and undernourished you were. So we sedated you and we've been feeding you by drip and line. Do you understand?"

Blank.

"Now you're awake, we would like you to start eating. We need to build your strength up."

"How lon—"

"I can't hear you," he tells her gruffly. She motions to a water jug and glass on the cabinet. He pours a little water for her and hands it over. She rolls the water around her mouth. It feels better but she can't swallow and has to spit back into the cup. Dr. Frobisher grimaces.

"How long was I sedated?"

"Twenty-four hours—just over, maybe."

"Twen—" Her throat fills with the bile of a scream. Weight bears down on her chest. A day lost. They'll have found him and . . .

"No. Naaaaaa . . ." She remembers Roberta's words. Her wail fills the ward.

"Now, I—" Dr. Frobisher starts to panic in the face of raw emotion. "I'll get . . ." He runs off to find help. The inhuman sound gets even louder. Two women in their nineties begin to cry, both believing a bombing raid is about to start. One whimpers with fear; the other sobs for the man she loved and lost so long ago.

The ward sister rushes over. "What the hell is going on?" The sister grabs hold of Patty and shakes her. "What? What's the matter?"

"It wasn't him."

"Who?"

"It . . ." Patty's eyes are wild, snapping back and forth. "The killer, he was . . ." she feels the ward sister draw away . . .

"Killer?"

. . . and that snaps Patty back. "Can't get caught now—the killer is still out there. I kidnapped the wrong man," she thinks.

"It . . . it was a bad dream. I had a bad . . . please excuse me."

"I don't understand." The sister eyes her patient with some suspicion. "You're okay? Are you in pain?"

"No. No pain."

"Okay, then please lie down, I'll go and prise our Dr. Frobisher out of the toilets and we can see about getting you something to stabilize you. Maybe get some meat on the bones, eh?" She smiles. "Okay?"

Patty nods. The sister leaves and Patty lies back, feeling her heart pulse—reliving Roberta's words—the mouth moving and the air suddenly becoming hot and toxic. "Not a match." Not. It wasn't him. Duncan Cobhurn didn't kill Dani.

"Oh, Christ." She allows the dam to break and the tears to flow free. She sobs for ten minutes and then, with an absolute force of will, pushes the wall of self-pity away and starts to drag herself up from the pit.

When she is almost herself, she begins to look around and plan her next step. To her side there is a locker. She leans awkwardly over and pulls the door open. No clothes—but her glasses are there—she puts them on and the world becomes slightly less blurred. She can see a ward of maybe eight beds. Old people. Bloody old people. It's the ward her mother-in-law died in.

"I am not old," she croaks, but nobody acknowledges her. She pulls off the covers; she needs to get away. She tries to swing her leg out, but the tubing pulls and pain burrows deep. She has a catheter.

At some point a woman, possibly the first voice she heard, approaches with a mug of tea and places it on the tray next to her. Patty takes it. It's sweet but very refreshing. She closes her eyes again and listens to the staff as they patrol the ward. She begins to distinguish the voices, gets an understanding of who's in control. What they do there. Twenty-four hours. "So it's Sunday—morning or night?" she thinks to herself. She looks at her wrist and then in the locker, no watch—she wore no jewelry. Even the bifocals were an off-the-peg pair from the chemist's. No prescription, nothing that could be used to trace her. Except her, of course. Except for the fact that she's lying down like a fucking dog waiting to be found. Obviously Duncan Cobhurn will be free—when? He would have woken up at some point on Saturday afternoon. If she was lucky he would have slept until the evening, but as soon as he'd woken he would have started making a lot of noise. Enough to wake the dead. So he'd have been found at some point last night—the best she could hope for would be this morning. Then what? She tries to rifle through the filing cabinets of her mind for all the cases she's reported on over the years. How long does it take to take a statement? Make a photofit? He saw her for only a minute and she was in disguise—what would the police have? Nothing more than a general description: woman in her mid-sixties, tall and thin. But they're not idiots. At some point they will work out what the cut in his hand was for. Maybe it was good that she cut so deep—it isn't obvious that it was for a blood sample. But they will realize it quickly, and then they'll check all testing facilities. The lab will be discreet, but an ambulance was called from there for a tall, thin woman in her sixties who had collapsed. Christ, the trail leads directly to her. It is only a matter of time.

"Nur . . ." Patty croaks and looks up, and sees not just a nurse walking at the end of the ward but a man too. A policeman. Patty feels a tremor start to build.

"Oh fuck. Calm. Calm, Patty." She lies back and closes her eyes, trying to keep the shakes away.

"I understand she's awake," a male voice says.

"She was, but now she's resting."

"Well, I'm happy to wait."

Patty opens her eye a crack to see him.

"Ah, there she is."

"Ahh!" Patty screams and rolls her head, kicks her legs, looks terrified.

"Officer, move back." The sister dives in, shoving the policeman back and grabbing Patty's hand. She writhes and screams—not sure herself what part is real and what an act.

"It's okay, he's leaving. Don't worry," the sister says, trying to reassure her.

"I'm sorry, love, didn't mean to frighten you." But he doesn't back off.

"Ahh!" Patty screams again and thrashes harder.

"That's it. Out." The sister shoves him back.

He holds his ground. "Just a few words."

"Now." The nurse uses her body and literally bumps him back. He looks angrily at her but can tell she won't budge. "Out, Officer. Come back tomorrow morning," she says with an edge of threat to her voice.

He nods and walks away slowly from the ward.

Patty starts to calm as he retreats. What does he know? Will she be arrested in the morning or does she have time? Time, what the hell is the time . . . ? So Cobhurn wasn't the killer?

The ward sister returns and sits on Patty's bed. "Well, you're quite the enigma, aren't you?"

"What's the time?" Patty asks softly.

"Six twenty."

"Sunday . . . morning?"

"Night. It's pitch-black out. Do you need to know the month too?"

"I know the month, and I know who's prime minister."

"Then you know more than most people here. But do you know your name? Your address? Do you remember anything about what happened?"

Patty shakes her head.

"Are you on any regular medication? If you are then you should be taking it. Warfarin, maybe?"

"I . . ." She almost tells her that she takes 9 mg of Ropinirole, but can't let even a crack of her real self open. "Nothing. I'm tired," Patty tells her, noticing her own voice for the first time. It sounds empty and hollow, like her grandmother's before she died.

"Okay." The sister leans over her and pulls the bedclothes up and tucks them in tight. Patty notices her breath is Tic-Tac sweet. She must be covering something. Smoking perhaps, or booze.

"I'm going home soon. But I'll ask the night shift to look after you, and I'll see you in the morning before the police get here." She pauses. "If you have anything you need to tell, to anyone, I urge you to speak soon. The police are quite unsympathetic when they have to do all the work." And with that, she walks away. Patty listens to the click of her heels as she walks as far as the nurses' station and then talks to one of the newly arrived night staff. Patty strains her ears to hear.

"Bed three . . . malnourished . . . quite possible she's had a mini-stroke . . . what caused her to collapse . . . seems not to have directly affected her speech . . . recall has been degraded . . . possibly. She may be faking that, or at least making it appear worse than it seems. Not sure why, but she seems afraid. We need to keep a close eye on her." Then the ward sister leaves.

Patty lies there for some time as the staff change over and medicines and cups of tea are brought round. All the time, she's thinking she needs to get out before morning. The fact that they sent a constable means they don't know exactly who she is or what she did. The ward sister wouldn't be around for the night; she has her suspicions that something is wrong, but didn't convey that directly to the night staff. They just think she needs extra care. Maybe Patty can work that to her advantage. She looks around the ward and quickly sees what she needs. A mobile phone sits on the short wardrobe between one of the sobbing old women and a skeletal woman who has not moved. She can make this work; she knows she can. In fact, she feels more confident, stronger than she has in a long time. Maybe she needed a day in hospital. But no more.

At 10 p.m. they turn down the lights. Patricia has no intention of sleeping, which she thinks is lucky because the last place that encourages sleep is a hospital. She continues to watch the nurses buzz around, waking the poor old dears every damn hour to stick something in them or make them swallow this and that or just fiddle. Because they can. But she learns quickly about the routines on the ward and which nurses will bend the rules if you annoy them enough.

She waits until midnight, when things start to slow. She props herself up in the bed and looks around. Everyone seems to be asleep in the ward. Her bed is halfway down the room, too far from the light switches. Above her bed is a large, extending lamp. She can't reach up to it, but there is a cane hanging from the handle of the chest of drawers to her right. She reaches over to it and loops the leather cord at the end around her wrist. Then she takes aim and swings the cane violently at the light. She means to turn it on. Instead the cane swings like an executioner's axe and lops the head of the lamp off, flinging it out into the center of the ward where it crashes to the ground with an explosion of metal and glass.

"Nurse! Nurse!" someone screams. Lights flare on and nurses run. There is pandemonium. It is time for Patty to go to work. She has her target in her sights. Nurse Lucy, who has texted her boyfriend forty-seven times in the last two hours and given at least two old women the wrong medicine. As Nurse Lucy rushes past Patty grabs at her.

"Nurse!" she barks.

"I can't . . ."

"I need to go to the toilet."

"You don't need it; you got a thingy. You don't need to get up."

"My dear girl, I am Hilary Clifton-Hastings and I have been taking myself to the toilet for sixty years. Please remove this catheter."

"I can't."

"I would appreciate being left with my dignity." She almost shouts the word dignity and can feel all the other old dears in the ward nodding their agreement.

"Really I—"

"Please. Dignity." Patty knew that would push the nurse's buttons. It's all about dignity these days—can't keep old dears on their backs, drugged up, peeing and pooping with nothing to do until MRSA and bedsores get them.

"Honestly, it's dead busy . . ."

"Then who is the senior consultant on call? I might well know them from the Rotary club?"

She sees Lucy stiffen. She hates to bully the girl but she has to get out of there.

"Okay." Nurse Lucy pulls the bedclothes back and with a snap of surgical tape and a tug—she removes the catheter. "You'll need a walking frame. Your legs'll be a bit wobbly. Wait here."

Patty watches Nurse Lucy grab a Zimmer frame from by the door. She wants to yell out, "I'm not old! I don't need that," but she thinks better of it. Better to play along and act like some frail old fool.

"Here ya go. Hold on to the bar and hoist your—"

Patty grabs the bar with disdain and pulls. Her legs give way, they're jelly. She collapses back onto the bed.

"Marta!" Lucy calls out to a colleague.

"Christ," thinks Patty. "I am an old fool. Jelly on a plate, jelly on a plate, wibble-wobble, wibble-wobble, old crone in a state."

Patty needs both nurses to hold her up while she does the latest St. Vitus dance craze.

"Back to bed," says Marta. "You need the catheter still."

"No. I will use the toilet myself—like a normal person." And Patty takes a step. She doesn't tumble, the momentum takes all three women forward. She has to keep them going. Together the nurses and Patty weave drunkenly to the toilet, propelled by the sheer force of Patty's will.

The nurses want to take her inside, but she refuses.

"My legs are fine now. Please let me do my business in privacy, I am not an animal."

"Okay," says Lucy and Marta walks off. "I'll wait right here, and you must leave the door open in case I need to come in and help."

"Of course, my dear," Patty agrees through tight lips.

As soon as she is inside the lavatory, Patty curses the situation. She's got herself free of the catheter but that won't help if her damn legs won't work or if the nurse hangs around all the time. She punches at her legs.

When she can't punch anymore she leans over the sink and runs a basin of cold water to dunk her face in. The water feels good. She looks at herself in the mirror.

"Look at you—old, old woman. What a bloody mess," she tells herself. "Christ. Did a mouse die in my mouth?" she thinks, running her tongue around her dry mouth. She hobbles back to the door and looks out. The younger nurse is still there, hovering, waiting for her.

"Clean teeth, I must clean my teeth!" And she exhales in the young woman's face.

The nurse recoils. "Okay. Wait here. I'll be back in a sec." She trots off to find a toothbrush and toothpaste. Patty eyes the journey back to the bed and beyond, to the bed by the window and the mobile phone.

"I can do it."

She pushes off with the frame and begins to walk, tottering and swaying like a marionette with half her strings cut. Jelly legs flying everywhere. Her eyes start to stream; she bites at her lip. She is falling to one side.

"Come on, you silly old cow." She pulls up on the frame.

The distance is narrowing; she is almost there. She makes it to her bed and stops to rest. She listens hard: is someone coming? No. Geronimo! She is off again. Step after step, her legs almost useless, her arms trembling with the exertion. The phone, she can see the phone.

"Think about prison," she hisses to herself as she crosses the final yards to the phone. She grabs at it and nearly tips over. The old woman next to her whimpers and turns over. The skeleton merely lies there. Patty flips the phone open, praying to a non-existent God for some battery power.

"Yes!" The time flickers at her. 12:57 a.m. She dials a number she has not called in many, many years, but will never forget. It rings.

"Come on come on come on come on come on come on come . . ."

"Hello?" His voice is sleepy.

The years stretch into eternity.

"Hello? Is somebody there?"

Patty finds she's mute. She had no idea what a profound shock it would be to hear his voice again, really hear him, not just the constant echo of him in her head.

"Hello?" he repeats. "I'm going to hang up now."

"Jim," she says in a voice that sounds a thousand years old.

There is silence, just his breath. Patty thinks she would have been happy to have listened to that breath for a year and a day, but her toothpaste will be here any moment.

"I'm in trouble. I need your help. Please go to my house; there is a spare key taped inside the blue recycling bin in the alley, to the left of the front door. I need you to go in and get me a change of clothes, including underwear and shoes. Bring them, in a bag, to the Royal. I'll meet you by the toilets next to X-ray; remember where they took your mum when she broke her hip. Meet me there at exactly three a.m. Don't park in the car park, park in a side street. Then take me home. I'll explain it all, I have to go now."

She flips the phone closed and sets it back down on the cabinet. No one seems to have heard her. There is no alarm, no pointing finger, no searchlight. She spins the Zimmer round and heads off back to the toilets, faster than before. Her legs are hers again. As she gets to her own bed, the nurse returns.

"Oh. I thought you were going to wait for me in the loo," she says, a little peeved.

Patty snatches the brush and paste from her and charges for the toilet, this time slamming the door and locking it. The nurse is shocked for a second and then runs to the toilet and bangs on the door.

"Let me in. Right this second, or I'll call security to take the door off."

"I will be out in one minute but I want some privacy," Patty screams through the door. She angrily brushes her teeth until her gums bleed. Then she sits on the toilet seat and weeps.

TWENTY

Monday, December 20, 2010

Jim slides the key into the lock as if he owns the place and pushes the door open—he quickly steps inside. Behind him, Dani hesitates.

"Come in quick," he hisses.

"Do you think it's okay—can I come in?"

"You're not a vampire. Get in quickly, we don't want a nosy neighbor calling the police."

"But . . ."

"Sorry." He closes the door on her. He pulls a torch from his pocket—he flicks it on and the beam falls on a small mountain of pizza flyers and minicab cards, as well as three days' worth of newspapers. Jim scoops them up as Dani walks through the door.

"That was rude," she says, waving the torch away from her face.

"We looked suspicious and a bit crazy, plus we don't have much time. We need to get your mum in less than an hour."

"It was still rude to slam the door in my face."

"I didn't slam it. I closed it."

"Thanks for the apology." She walks off to explore downstairs.

Jim takes the pile of junk mail and newspapers into the lounge where he drops them on a small table. He shines the torch around the room, trying to keep the beam away from the windows. The room is almost bare. One chair and the small table.

"Nunnery chic," Dani says walking in.

"She seems quite minimalist," Jim agrees. "Not much to show for a lifetime," he thinks.

"I'm going upstairs to find some of her clothes."

"I can be fashion consultant."

"No, you wait here—I'll be quick."

He walks upstairs, holding the light down to the floor. He has no idea where her bedroom is, so pushes randomly at a closed door and it slides open. He raises the torch and the light hits . . .

"God." The air is knocked out of him. His hand shakes. The torchlight skitters across the wall. *The wall*—in all its glory, re-created just as it had been in their house all those years ago. Though now it's even bigger, with more Post-it notes and more pictures. The day Dani arrived at Durham—so happy. Home at Christmas, her birthday . . . then those other pictures of her, his child defiled. Dead. So pale and yet beautiful. The same as she is now—the same as she is downstairs. Full of life. He feels sick, doubles over.

"Dad?" she calls.

"Dani, don't come up here," he shouts back, his stomach cramping. "Don't come . . ."

"What are you going to do? Slam the door in my face again?" She floats through the door. "I can go anywhere. I'm the Ghost of—" She sees the photos, sees herself: her hands tied, her body bare, the bruises covering her arms and legs. Post-it notes scream "torture," "multiple rape," "feces and urine." Around her the air seems to turn tar black.

"Dani . . ." Jim reaches out to her, he tries to scoop her into his arms—if only he could hug her—but she dissolves. The torch blinks out, there is only black—the shadows seem to suck all life from the air.

"Dani, Dani, please come back." But there is nothing. The torch flickers once again—the beam catches her image one last time. Dead.

Jim takes a final look at the hateful wall. "Oh, Christ, Patty." He walks backward out of the door, closing it gingerly, as if there's an unexploded bomb inside. He pauses for a moment, unsure of what to do. Then slowly he moves to the next room, her bedroom.

Inside there is just an unmade bed, a tatty old wardrobe and a few boxes. The bed makes him feel sad. Sad and old. It all feels intrusive and voyeuristic, especially going through her clothes to put together a bag for her, but he does as she asked. He is also saddened by the fact that he recognizes every item of clothing. Hasn't she shopped in twelve years? With the bag ready, he closes the door and goes back down.

Dani sits in the living room. He would have missed her but for the slightest sigh as he passed the doorway. He strains into the darkness and makes out her faint shape.

"I'm sorry, darling."

"Not your fault. You did warn me." She pauses. "Why don't I remember?"

"Did seeing the pictures . . . ?"

"No. Maybe. I can see flashes."

"Faces?"

"I . . . yes."

"Do you recognize them?"

She opens her mouth to speak, but it all seems too unclear. She closes it again.

"Can you describe them?"

"No. No, it's all deformed, hazy—like I'm seeing everything underwater."

"Maybe . . . maybe that's best."

She shakes her head slowly. "All I remember clearly is hearing your voice far-off, and then opening my eyes and I was me, but not myself anymore, not whole. I felt scared and so alone."

"Never alone."

"Really?" She shakes her head sadly. She feels alone so often.

"Let's go and get your mum," he says softly.

"Okay."

He drives to the hospital. He remembers not to park in the hospital car park but doesn't trust the side streets. Instead he pulls over on the main road close to a bus stop. There won't be any buses tonight. The drive had been more than a little scary for him; Dani had loved it. From the moment she'd yelled "shotgun" to the final skid into the curb, it had been like a roller-coaster ride. He would not have gone out in those conditions for anyone else.

"I'll go in alone."

"Dad!"

"Wait at the car, please." He turns on the radio for her and gets out into the icy wind. He walks toward the hospital slowly, a little like a penguin as the snow shifts under his feet. He feels guilty about asking Dani to stay in the car, but he doesn't want her with him while he confronts Patty. He's starting to get worried about why she's in the hospital—in his mind he visualizes *the wall* once again. Is Patty still obsessed with finding Dani's killer after more than twenty years? What might she have done? The snow begins to fall once more. He can't move.

"Are you okay?" Dani calls from the car. Jim turns and waves to her, though he doesn't trust his voice. "Shout if you need me," his daughter calls out.

His mouth feels like black pepper has been ground into it as he walks slowly inside. Right inside the door is a desk that, during the day, is manned by volunteers. Of course, at this time of the morning it's empty. Lying on the top is a pile of maps with a handwritten sign saying: PLEASE TAKE. On the board behind the desk is a list of the departments and the buildings they occupy. Jim looks for the department of psychiatry. He's relieved to see there's no unit or secure ward listed. He remembers waking from the nightmare—how scared he was for her. Have faith, he thinks, and heads toward the X-ray department. He knows the way—he has been to this hospital many times over the years. His mother died here, he had his prostate poked here. Now what?

X-ray reception is closed when he arrives. The air seems to fizz with the smell of bleach and the ageing institutional lino floors seem tacky as he walks on them. He sits in the central bank of chairs, probably the only time he's ever managed to get a seat here. Normally patients stand three or four deep waiting for their close-ups. To complete the zombie-movie aesthetic, the strip light above him flickers. He checks his watch: 3:02.

"Maybe it's a joke," he thinks with no conviction. Then he hears footsteps from behind and turns. He doesn't recognize her for a second. She's thin—marathon runner thin. It shocks him a little.

"The clothes, Jim, for Christ's sake, we don't have much time. Is that it?" She snatches up the bag and heads for the women's toilet in the next corridor.

Jim watches her go. Only a few seconds—but he knows she isn't mad. She's Patty—she looks older, leaner but . . . "Christ." The intelligence flares in her eyes. She's illuminated from within. He realizes that, after all this time, he desperately wants to hold her.

Patty storms out of the toilets after a minute. She throws the bag, Jim isn't sure if it's to him or at him. She looks angry.

"What the hell were you thinking?" She indicates her body.

Jim looks down at her and blushes. The clothes he picked out make her look like a clown.

"You . . ." He wants to say: "You used to be taller, fuller, more . . ." but he dries up. She is thin and bird-like, angular and pointy . . . and amazing. And angry.

She walks toward him and her head leans as if to kiss, but instead she hisses, "Go out the Warren Street exit and I will meet you on the corner by Wimpy."

"Patty . . ." he starts but she's already heading away. Jim watches her stride purposefully away toward the main exit. She walks quickly but erratically, correcting herself as she veers slightly from one side to the next. Then she turns the corner and is gone. Jim feels like he's in a dream. He looks at the sign above him; the Warren Street exit is on the other side of the hospital. He needs to head into the belly of the beast—Accident and Emergency. He gets up and goes forward. Corridors wind and turn like in a maze, then suddenly the corridor opens out onto a full room of men clutching arms and heads, girlfriends with hands covered in gore and children asleep on laps. Except for the red flash of blood, all is pallid and miserable under the glare of strip lights. Everywhere, people seem to huddle and wait for help. That's what hospital emergency departments are at night: a sodium-lit purgatory.

As he walks through, hollow eyes look up, pleading with Jim to diagnose, advise and administer drugs so they can get home to bed. Everyone looks so desperate. But all Jim can do is shrug apologetically and try to avoid stepping in the fresh drops of blood. They look like scattered breadcrumbs leading the lost back home. Jim looks around—why is there no one with a mop at this time of the night?

Close to the exit Jim sees a man with green skin, eyes that are a huge black void, hair matted with blood, kicking a vending machine.

"Where is my fucking Coke?" the man repeats over and over. Each time the searching question is underlined by a thump to the Perspex cover. "The hospital is a place for philosophers," Jim thinks. "Where indeed are our fucking Cokes?" Jim stops and gently hits A11 on the machine. The mechanical arm moves, trundles across and delicately plucks a red-and-white can from the shelf and drops it into the chute. Jim nods. He can't heal anyone but he can at least deliver some succor. The automatic door slides open and he walks out into the night. The door slides back and he can just hear the man.

"I wanted Diet Coke."

The street is empty and cold, still snow-spewed as it continues to fall. The car is on the other side of the hospital—Jim hopes Dani is okay, he wishes she were with him now. He crosses the treacherous street and can see the restaurant. He approaches the Wimpy with caution. He can't remember the last time he saw one; he thought they'd gone out of business years ago. They seem to be something from a bygone age—before the Whoppers and Big Macs came and swept them away. He assumes Patty will be in the doorway, but as he gets level, it's empty. No one inside; just enormous close-ups of meat. It reminds him of the hospital. The mixed grill looks like pictures he's seen of men eviscerated in war and they make him feel a little queasy. Where is she?

Then he sees her pushed into the doorway of an off-license. She's rocking slightly on her heels, back and forth, looking tightly wound. He opens his mouth to shout but stops. Instead he moves slowly, his hands outstretched, showing he has nothing in them, as if he's approaching a dangerous animal. Patty catches sight of the movement and instinctively pulls into the shadows.

"It's okay, it's me."

She relaxes a little and steps forward.

"What's up?"

"It's good to see you, Jim." Her voice is husky with intense tiredness. She smiles and he feels like he's twenty again. "What took you so long?" The years melt away. She'd said those exact words the first time he kissed her. He'd been gathering his courage for weeks. Finally the dam had burst and he had launched himself at her in the clumsiest way. Instead of a clean kiss they had bumped chins and clattered teeth.

"If we're going to do it, then let's do it properly," she had said and grabbed his jacket, pulling him to her and . . . fireworks.

"Patty . . ."

"Can we get to the car? I'm cold and you didn't exactly bring me winter clothes." She sounds exhausted but her prickliness has melted away.

"I'm parked a little way away. Have my coat." Jim peels off the jacket and holds it open so she can slide inside. He feels her move against him—brittle, bird-like. A memory hits him hard—that first night—the curves and full breasts, the weight of her as she lowered herself onto him with her hands on his chest—taking his breath away. He can't help himself as he puts the jacket around her—he pulls her into him and closes his arms around her like he did all those years ago. Then, she melted into him like syrup—tonight she pulls away and her face is a mix of rage and fear.

"I . . . Sorry. I was just . . ."

She doesn't make any reply, just shudders a little from the cold. Jim motions with his hand toward where the car is parked and she moves off. Nothing is said as they walk. Clouds roll by, mostly unseen in the dark night until the moon is revealed just for a few seconds. Jim slides back through the years: he is walking with Dani, right on the spot where he is now. They are crossing this same tarmac strip. How old is she? Eight? They have just visited her gran, who is dying. They walk in silence. Her small, warm hand in his. She's deeply thoughtful, then she looks up to him and asks: "Where do we go after we die, Daddy?"

"The next right," he shouts to Patty, who is ahead of him. His hand seems a little warm, clammy as if it has held a small, sticky little mitt. The moon disappears once more as the clouds roll by. Ahead, Patricia strides forward.

"Just there, on the left. Red Saab."

The moon skids back and Jim can see Dani sitting on the bonnet of the car. She smiles broadly and waves, happy to see him. He waves back to her, not thinking. Patty turns and sees him; she jumps.

"I've got this bad shoulder. I was just stretching it." It's a terrible lie. On the car Dani laughs.

"I'll open it." He pulls out the little leather fob and for a second it feels like a small hand rests in his.

Where do we go after we die, Daddy? The air seems to carry the echo through the decades.

Dani slides off the bonnet and walks over to her mother, looks directly into her face, but Patty sees nothing and climbs into the passenger seat. The clouds scud past once more and the moon is so bright, it feels like daytime for a second, then it fades to black as the clouds roll past again.

Jim climbs into the driver's seat. He can see Dani in the rear-view mirror, leaning forward on the backseat, her face blank. Jim wonders what she's thinking, the three of them together after all these years. In the backseat Dani sighs and then yawns. Patty silently stares out of the window. Jim pulls away from the curb, the wheels skid but he slowly moves forward, heading to Patty's house. The roads are clear of traffic and the main roads are pretty well gritted. After ten minutes he allows himself a sideways look at his wife. She's closed her eyes, might be asleep.

"Do you remember Monty?" Dani asks from the backseat.

"Of course," he says softly. Monty had been Dani's dog. One day, it must have been her last term or so of A levels, Dani came home with him. Patty was fine about it and Jim loved dogs, so Monty stayed. Of course, when Dani went off to university she couldn't take him, so he stayed with them. Jim had thought that he would end up being the main carer for the big lump, but when it came to it, Patty had been the one to replace Dani in terms of walking and feeding. Jim hadn't minded; he thought it was good for her and gave Patty and Dani something to talk about. In some ways it was a little bit of a bribe for Dani: don't just come back to see us but to see Monty too. He'd been a great dog, adored Dani, so happy to see her when she came home. Until she didn't, of course.

Patty withdrew her love then. It was almost as if Dani's death burned all affection out of her. She didn't show anybody or anything any love. Maybe a cat could have survived the loss of love, but not Monty. He would literally howl into the wilderness that was Patty's face, trying to get her to see him, to respond to him, but there was nothing. Jim thinks it broke the poor dog's heart. They gave him to some friends about three months after Dani's death. Within a year he had developed cancer and was put down.

Jim never told Patty. By that time, he thought, the capacity for grief had left her.

"I remember Monty." Jim flicks his eyes to the rearview mirror but cannot see Dani's face in the murk of the backseat.

Where do we go after we die, Daddy?

Jim tries to recall his exact words to his poor little girl who was losing her beloved gran.

"Mrs. Henson said heaven was where Gran would go. Will she go to heaven, Daddy?" she asked him.

Jim feels shame. He could have planted the seed of hope in his daughter. Let her believe that, no matter what terrible things happen to us in life, that death honored the just, good and blameless lives of ordinary people. But he didn't.

"Dani, I really don't know. I think that Gran will have no pain anymore, which will be really good, but probably there is just nothing when you die, darling. Nothing."

Nothing? Had he really believed that? The man who lives with his daughter's ghost? "I am such a bloody hypocrite," he thinks.

The moon slides behind the clouds once more and is finally gone. He sneaks another peek across at his wife. The closeness of her makes his chest burn a little. He has been so lonely. The worse loneliness had been in those between years—when Patty supposedly was still with him and yet she was so distant. Then he had no one. During that time he left his work—he even volunteered for the Red Cross. For a year he drove trucks of medicine and aid, usually flying to the nearest safe haven and then driving truckload after truckload of life and hope and aid to desolated areas. He delivered food and medicine to Sri Lanka, Turkey and Haiti. He saw so much destruction—but it hardly affected him. Whenever his truck had rolled into town, a group of children would follow. He always kept his pockets stuffed with energy bars so that when they caught up with him, he could hand them out. There were never enough. In those moments he didn't feel powerful, no Santa or Jesus—not even some low-rent Robin Hood. Instead he felt needy, desperate to buy some love, to show himself he could do good in this shitty world. Just for a moment to see pain turn to a smile. That was what he failed to do in the years with Patty, after Dani died. To turn off the darkness inside his wife, just for a second. Even with those poor kids, he could do nothing. After a year of volunteering he stopped. Instead he drove a minicab in London. He liked to keep moving— he thought he might die if he stopped. Then Patty left him and . . . but tonight, when she needed someone, she called him. If it weren't nearly four in the morning, and he hadn't just broken someone out of hospital, he'd feel heartened by it. Maybe tomorrow he would. Right now tiredness was starting to sweep through him and make him feel nauseous. His introspection is broken by the sound of snoring. He glances across at Patty and allows himself a chuckle.

Jim finally pulls up outside Patty's house at 4 a.m. and cuts the engine. Next to him Patty breathes softly, lost deep inside some inner world. He opens his door and slides out of the car, his back crunchy from sitting. He slams the car door; it does the trick and wakes Patty. She drifts for a second in some calm waters and then, as memories flood back in, she tenses once more.

Jim opens her door and bends down. "You're home."

"Do you have the spare key?" she asks, her speech thick with tiredness.

"Of course." He hands it to her and watches as she walks into the house. She wobbles slightly as she walks, as if she's on too-high heels. At the door she fumbles with the key, pushing and scratching, until finally the metal slides into its sheath and she goes inside. She leaves the front door open.

"Dad," Dani calls from the car.

"Yes, darling."

"She's left the front door open."

He nods.

"You need to go and close it."

"True."

"I'll wait. Don't worry about me."

He nods to her and walks over to the house. He holds the door, feeling the heft of the wood in his hand. He could shut it and leave; deep down he thinks this would be best. But instead he follows Patty inside and shuts the door behind him.

The house is dark. Jim tries to remember the layout from his brief visit earlier. Suddenly there is a cry, a scream of pain. Primal, animal, intense pain. In the darkness Jim is enveloped by the scream, the pain. It tears into him; he knows what it is. He rushes forward, unsure where to go. He sees a bar of light under a door and hits the wood. The scream rises in force, hitting him in the chest and ripping the years away from him. Patty is on the floor in the lounge. In her hand is one of the newspapers and she waves it around, then claws at the front page. She screams again, then rolls into a ball. She is having a fit—some kind of seizure—just like when she'd heard Dani was dead. A scream of pure pain. The intensity of loss, the hunger of despair—it cuts right through him.

"Patty. Patty. Look at me, calm down."

He tries to put his arms around her and hold her, calm her, but she lashes out—forcing him back. Her body arches; she looks as if she could snap in two. He lunges again, trying to grab her arms, but she beats at him. The scream rises even higher.

"Patty, Patty, calm down."

She writhes and twists. Jim holds on for dear life like a cowboy at a rodeo. She butts him in the face—so much pain. His lip is cut and there's blood.

"Mine or hers?" he thinks, frightened and not knowing whether to call the hospital or the police or to try and ride the roller-coaster to the end. He grabs her shoulders and pulls her closer, tighter.

"Patty, we love you," he moans into her hair. Then he starts to rock her, tiny movements he has not made since Dani was a baby. And he sings, barely audible, but he sings for her soul. Finally she starts to slow. Her screams collapse into shakes as her entire body vibrates. Slowly the muscles start to unwind, and she softens and curls into his arms from choice. She wraps her arms around his neck pulling herself into him, almost crushing his chest. Her sobs start to calm and she fades to black.

They are still for half an hour. She lies curled in his arms while he breathes in the perfume of her hair and her skin. Then suddenly, as if a momentous decision had finally been reached, Jim lifts her, supporting her head as he would a child, and carries her upstairs. He lays her down on her bed. She rolls onto her side and curls. She is so thin, so small. He searches, first under the bed and then in the wardrobe. He discovers a large duvet and spreads it over her. He feels like forty-five years of his life have melted away—it is that first night once again. She is so beautiful. Her skin is aglow and her hair ripples down her back in cascading waves. She is once again his pre-Raphaelite queen on a bower. He cannot help himself, but leans forward and kisses her head, then strokes her hair. Then he lies down on the bed. He does not plan to sleep, just to lie there in case she wakes, just a few inches between them. He closes his eyes.

Patty wakes, and for one blissful moment, floats above the world like a newborn, innocent. Aware of the press of another body against her, she feels the warmth of contact and is drawn into that gravity, yearning for embrace, her arms folding around the other figure. Then the memories flood back, swamping her, stealing her breath as they have done every morning for more than twenty years, grinding her under their heel. She begins to shake.

Jim feels the tremor beside him. Through the sticky curtain of sleep he holds out his hand and she grabs at it; they grip hard, harder. Just like they had done with her morning sickness. "Squeeze. Tighter, Jim, squeeze tighter."

He did, with all his might. And if it didn't work, then he held the hair away from her face while she retched . . . then wiped her vomity mouth for her.

"Oh, that's disgusting, Jim. You don't have to do that," she'd say.

"I don't care." He didn't.

He wakes. The pressure on his hand and the allure of the past draw him from sleep. For one terrible moment he is lost, buried, at the bottom of a hole as it fills with sand and he is running, scrambling, trying to climb out. Then the hand holding his own calms him. He remembers where he is. Their hands squeeze together, they roll face to face. Scared, needy, hungry and as old as the earth. Patty reaches out to his face and strokes it, feels the stubble, the gray stalks of hair forcing their way though his toughened skin. She could never have described it to another person, could not even have formed the words to tell herself about his face, his cheek. Yet she knows every contour of his face and body. A lifetime melts away, she does not see him now, not the sixty-four-year-old Jim, but he's a boy in her bed. So fine, so fine.

He opens his arms and she rolls into them, they hug so tightly. She feels so different in his arms, there is no curve and heft—now she is air and breath. Her once alabaster skin ravaged by loss, grief and despair. And yet.

"You are so beautiful," he whispers.

"You bloody idiot."

He looks into her face. Her smile dazzles him like the sun and her lips caress his. He can taste the salt of tears.

"I love you, Patty. I love you," he breathes into her, overwhelmed by the rush of emotion and desire that he finds in his heart and mind and body.

She leans into him, snuggles her mouth into his hair and whispers.

"Jim. I killed a man."

REPORT OF SURVEILLANCE

Monday, December 20, 2010

3:58 a.m.: Car arrives outside residence. Red Saab. License plate: SD54 GRD

3:59 a.m.: James Lancing (positive identification from photos) exits car and opens passenger seat. Helps woman out of car, she is incapacitated, appears drunk. (Positive identification of Patricia Lancing.)

Img007/008/009 Three photos taken of couple.

4:02 a.m.: Sounds of commotion, screams, etc., from suspect's house. Next-door neighbor's lights on for a few minutes. Lasted duration of 2–3 mins.

Log end.

Parked almost directly opposite Patty's house is a white van with tinted windows. Inside, invisible to anyone in the street, is Grant Ronson. He sits in the driver's seat writing up his log.

It is now almost 4:30 a.m. and there has been nothing since the screaming. The house is quiet and dark. The young man is bored again. He had thought this job afforded some glamour, even danger, but it is mostly bloody boring. On the seat next to him he has yesterday's *News of the World*, an iPod and a well-thumbed copy of *Escort*.

There is a rubber tube coiled off the seat and onto the floor, which snakes back behind him into a large jug that is almost completely full of his urine. It's starting to smell. He has another two hours until his shift is over and the day shift arrives. He yawns. He picks up the paper again and scans the front page.

The headline reads: MURDERED MAN IDENTIFIED.

He reads the article:

The body discovered on Sunday at the Thursdowne Hotel close to Heathrow has been identified as Duncan Cobhurn, a businessman from Durham, owner of the Mediterranean furniture company Porto Pronto. He had been missing since Friday when he was due to return home via Heathrow from a business trip to Lisbon. Police have speculated that this was a kidnapping that had gone disastrously wrong. Police insiders have said they think that the perpetrators used too great a dose of narcotic and bound Mr. Cobhurn too heavily, resulting in death from asphyxiation before ransom demands could be made. There is, however, evidence of torture which has also prompted comparison with the Soviet spy Alexander Litvinenko who was poisoned in London in 2006 . . .

Ronson throws the paper down, bored. He yawns. If nothing happens soon he's going to have to masturbate again. At least that will kill some time. Janet from Edinburgh deserves more attention. He sits for a few minutes and then unzips his trousers.

PART FIVE

TWENTY-ONE

Tuesday, February 13, 2007

"Two dog walkers found the body on the allotment," DI Thorsen explains to Tom as they half-slide, half-drag themselves through the glossy mud. "They called it in at about 6:20 a.m. A local response officer was here in about ten minu— careful!" Thorsen grabs his arm as he slips sideways down an oozing incline. She steadies him. She's got Wellington boots on. He wears black Oxford brogues. They both know which of them is the more stylish—and who's ruined their shoes.

"Luckily the kid was bright enough to radio it in as Operation Ares."

Tom nods. He walks with knees bent and feet splayed. They reach the bottom of the treacherous hill. Tom looks across the mud—rain falling a little heavier now. He sees a shoe lying alone, an evidence marker pushed into the mud alongside it. It's the size of a child's shoe—but the heel shows it was made for a woman. A shoe to dance in, have fun in. Not die in. It seems so alone, sitting there in the rain.

Around them, officers buzz like flies, taping off areas, erecting tables—making an island of hi-tech in the mud. Over the body is a makeshift tent, not much better than the kind Tom had made as a kid, though then he'd used blankets and dining chairs and now it was plastic sheets and metal struts. Over to one side three officers stand, puzzling over a laminated manual, trying to build a tent wide enough to cover the body and surrounding area. Tom watches them slowly turn the manual 180 degrees, scratch their heads and slowly turn it back the other way. Christ, they're idiots.

"Could you?" he asks his efficient DI and points to the three stooges. She shrugs and trudges over to them, already barking orders. Tom knows she'll get it built.

He closes his eyes for a second and the world around him slows and disjoints, moves out of focus. Then he moves to the covered body—there is only the victim. He pulls aside the plastic sheet . . . a dead young woman. The latest in a litany of lifeless young women into whose eyes he has gazed. Another young woman he will silently promise to avenge. He looks at her face—her eyes are open—staring. Gray-blue eyes and the palest skin. In life she may have been ruddy, healthy, but now her lifeblood was a part of the mud that lapped at her face.

"Guv," Thorsen calls to him and he looks up to see the full tent ready to slide over the body. He nods and steps back, thinking it doesn't matter much anyway—this rain has almost certainly washed away any really helpful DNA evidence. He sighs, watching his breath spiral up. It will be another long day. The SOCO team will start to gather evidence. Take photos, bag the clothes, take samples from the victim—trim her nails, swab her mouth, vagina, anus—nothing is private. Not today. And at the end of all this, Tom doesn't expect there to be much more learned than he saw from a casual glance.

The body is Sarah Penn's. She's been missing for three days. He recognized her from photos. Her mum and dad brought the snapshots in the day she was reported missing. Holiday photos from Ibiza last year, though death has wiped away her smile, and the rain has uncurled the bounce of her hair and left it smeared across the ground.

She's naked—her clothes thrown all around. She has been beaten and sexually assaulted. She is without most of the skull above her left eye. Claw hammer is Tom's opinion, based on twenty years of seeing death and on having seen the same injuries twice before—Heather Spall and Tracy Mason. Sarah Penn is victim number three.

"Guv?" DI Thorsen calls to him, miming a drink. He nods and she grabs a Thermos. He turns back to the body.

"I'm sorry, Sarah."

He remembers thinking when he saw her photos, "what a pretty girl." A tear runs down his cheek for all the pretty dead girls. It melts into the rain. Within an hour or two, he'll be standing at the front door of her parents' house about to tell them the news they've dreaded for the last three days, if not the last sixteen years. He knows there'll be tears, maybe screams, denial, blame. All the while he will be there to share their pain. To show them that the police care about their loss, the country cares. That is what he does. He tells families they have lost someone they loved. He is the Sad Man.

Thorsen holds out the metal cup. He takes it from her with a nod.

"Same MO as Spall and Mason?"

He nods.

"I'll send a FLO."

"No. I'll go."

He doesn't think of himself as much of a policeman; there are no *little gray cells*, no deductions and last-minute reveals. But what he is good at—what he is best at—is winning trust. Opening a dialogue with witnesses, family, their friends, and teasing out information. People look at him and trust him, especially the damaged and needy. They see a kindred spirit in Tom. They see someone else in pain and they open their hearts to him. No family liaison officer has ever opened up partners, kids, parents or friends like he does. That's why he's the Sad Man and why he runs Operation Ares. He named the unit himself—Ares the destroyer, the god of fruitless violence, a coward who kills for the sake of killing.

Suddenly the tempo of the rain changes: more aggressive, faster and harder. Hailstones. The seventh plague of Egypt. Big chunks of ice slam into the plastic sheets. The officers buzz around more quickly. More plastic is stretched, arced over skeletons of metal. DI Thorsen yells, points—then men run for cover. Tom looks around the allotment. Any early buds are going to be smashed and splintered. Luckily there are no fruits yet, no tomatoes to crush, no strawberries to mash. Tom should get under cover too but he can't leave Sarah. Something more than hailstones rained down on her. She deserves more than this, so much more than this. Little girl lost. Found in body, but forever lost. Tom waits out the storm, feels the ice bounce off his cap and splash mud over him, but he stands sentry over Sarah until the hail thins and is gone. Now it's just rain.

"Bevans," a loud voice booms out.

Tom looks up to see an idiot juggling a trowel, a watering can and a packet of seeds. It's impressive juggling but it all makes Tom feel so tired. Were it one of his team he would scream at them to have some respect. Instead he waves a tired hand at his friend and pulls his shoe up out of the mud. It squelches satisfyingly, like a movie sound effect.

"You're meant to set an example," Tom hisses to the tall pathologist when he gets over to him.

"I am. This is work-life balance. See?" He throws the items even higher, catching the can and seeds, but the trowel spins out of control and shoots into the ground. It sticks in the mud, pointing straight up like an arrow, sending a billow of muddy water up Tom's leg.

"Whoops." The pathologist laughs.

"Grow up, Dr. Keyson."

Tom walks away, frustrated by the man who, he believes, doesn't comprehend the concept of the chain of command. He seems to have no respect for authority. Tom wonders for a thousandth time if his new friend is autistic to some degree; brilliant people often are. And there's no denying that Marcus Keyson is special; highly intelligent and charming, he's the youngest pathologist working with the Met by ten years, but there is something a little odd about him, something cold and calculating, something that disconnects him from everyone else.

"Or is that just paranoia?" Tom asks himself. Or maybe even a little jealousy? Or is it just remorse? After being closed off for so many years, Tom had finally opened up a little to someone, and now he wished he hadn't. It was stupid. Drunk stupid. Lonely stupid. Tom knows he shouldn't drink, but his loneliness had got the better of him. He should have bought a hamster, not tried to have a friend. He'd gone so many years without one—why had he tried now? But of course that was the point, wasn't it? It had been February 6—the anniversary.

❄

"Why?" Keyson asked.

"No one is meant to drink alcohol on police premises."

"They all do."

"I don't care about that. I'm the boss and I need to be beyond reproach, or at least look like I'm following the rules."

With a shrug, the tall man pops the top off the bottle and takes a swig.

"Christ, Marcus."

The pathologist pops another bottle and hands it to Tom, who takes it furtively and then sits at his desk and pulls out two mugs from the bottom drawer. He hands one to Keyson that reads KEEP 'EM PEELED. The second he keeps for himself. They pour their bottles into the mugs, then Tom puts the empty bottles into his drawer.

"World's Greatest Dad?" Keyson points at Tom's mug.

"I. It . . . My . . ." Tom stammers.

"Nobody expects the Freudian Inquisition?" jokes Keyson.

Against his better judgment, Tom laughs. "Okay, Siggy. I bought it for my dad, when he was still with us. I was about twelve. Big fucking joke."

"You kept it. Waste not, want not?"

Tom nods but it isn't the case. He kept it to act more like a warning, something he would see everyday. Be careful who you raise to the level of a god.

Tom sits at his desk, Keyson opposite him in the bollock chair, so named as you only sat in it if you were getting a bollocking. The two men raise their mugs and drink in silence. As they drink, a tear runs down Tom's cheek.

"Is this why they call you the Sad Man?" Keyson asks, pointing to the tear.

"Jesus." Tom pulls a box of tissues out of his desk. He takes one and wipes his face.

"Sorry," Marcus Keyson manages to make an apology sound more like an accusation.

"I have no control of my eyes. I just tear up . . ." Tom doesn't finish the thought—"I tear up when I think of anything sad." Tom knows full well what everyone calls him; he even thinks of himself as the Sad Man, but no one says it to his face. That's the problem with Marcus Keyson—no off switch, no self-censor. Tom picks up the beer and drinks the whole mug down in one go. The genie is out of the bottle.

"How old do you think I am?" Tom asks.

Keyson knows the answer, but remembers how surprised he'd been when he discovered it. He mimes supreme concentration. "Forty-eight?"

Tom smiles. "I'm thirty-nine."

Tom knows that forty-eight is a kind guess. Most people say early fifties. And that's now—even when he was thirty, people guessed he was fifty. The first three times he tried online dating he was accused of lying about his age on the form. Once it led to a stand-up row in a Pizza Express. After that he started putting down forty-eight. He didn't change the age he wanted, twenty-five to thirty-five, and was amazed that he got more responses when women thought he was nearing his fifties.

Beer number seven slides down. Now, both men are lying on the floor, heads almost touching. The time is uncertain; all they know is that the building is mostly dark and out of the seventh-floor window there is nothing to see. No stars and no moon, all hid by brooding clouds. Tomorrow it will rain. And the next day.

"Don't look that way. The wind'll change and you'll get stuck like that."

Tom laughs, more a schoolboy snigger, really. The beer has taken twenty years off him. "My mum would always tell me that. I thought it was just more of her crap—but it turned out to be true. Dani died, I cried, and all the fun was over. I got stuck like this." He laughs a touch hysterically, but truthfully. It feels good to tell someone.

"When?" Keyson asks.

"1989. She was twenty-one."

"You loved her?"

The tears run sideways and pool in his ears. He can only nod.

"And that's what made you join the police? You wanted to win justice for her?"

"No." He feels the guilt rise in him. "I'd already joined." He can hear them: his mum, teachers, Dani asking him, "Why, why?"

"Why?" She wasn't angry; she just didn't understand it. Dani could not comprehend why he wasn't going to take the place at Cambridge.

"Explain it to me," she asked. But he couldn't.

"I left school and joined. It was for her, though—it was for justice. For Dani. Somebody had hurt her and—"

Tom holds the pint glass. It feels awkward in his hand. The alley smells of urine. It's dark and he can't see much except for the pub over the road, which throws rectangles of light into the black street. He's in the perfect position to see the front door, see when it swings open and *he* leaves. Tom knows the man is in there; he checked it out. Bix was there. Lego-and-dogshit Bix.

Tom had walked into the pub, bought himself a pint, taken a few sips, then left with the glass and crossed over to the alley. He'd tipped the beer down a drain and settled down to wait. At 10:50 he heard the last-orders bell clang. Soon. He stretched his stiff legs. A few minutes later a group of lanky men came out, five of them all looking the same as each other. Floppy hair, black T-shirts and jeans, leather jackets, canvas bags slung over a shoulder. Individuality—three cheers for that. They slapped backs, arms or palms before each one peeled off, heading in a different direction. Tom nearly set out to follow the wrong man, but at the last minute one of them shouted.

"Tomorrow, Bix!"

"Right," Bix replied, and Tom saw his mistake; he should be following the other lanky, arty bastard. He switched to following him. He slammed the glass against the wall and it sheared in half leaving a jagged edge, a nasty-looking weapon. In ten minutes it would cut through the young man's face. Ending his pretty boy looks forever.

The room is swimming a little. Tom thinks Marcus might have fallen asleep. He knows he should get up soon; his bladder feels distended, but it all seems like such an effort. The glass slices into skin, flesh—then grinds on bone. There is blood and a scream.

"I did something awful," Tom's voice slurs a little, part alcohol and part melancholy. "I did it for her, Dani. For her. To defend her. She'd been hurt and I knew he'd do it again, hurt more women. I stopped that."

That is what he has told himself for years. In front of Marcus Keyson, however, it sounds a little thin.

"I thought about it a lot afterward. I did my A levels—even applied to university with Dani. But I couldn't stop thinking about what I'd done. I joined the police," he says in little more than a whisper.

He would like to tell Keyson what he did, that he *glassed* a man. But he cannot. It still shocks him today. And he avoids the obvious question: would he do it again? He hears the scream. The warmth of the blood. The bile rising in his throat. He knows the answer is yes.

"So, the love of your life was murdered?" Keyson's voice sounds warm and surprisingly sober.

Tom is pulled from the nauseating memory. "Yes. Her last year at university. When she graduated we would have been married, but . . ." The air above him feels heavy as he lies alongside his confidant, looking up at the ceiling.

"Durham. She was reading classics. I hate Durham."

"Really?" Keyson sounds a little wistful, enough that Tom rolls his head slightly to look at his friend. "I love it."

"All surface. It looks beautiful but underneath . . . there are maggots."

The two men are quiet for a few minutes, each lost in his own memories. Tom hears his new friend sigh and looks across to see tears running down his cheeks toward the floor.

"Are you . . . ?"

"I was at boarding school," Keyson begins. "I'd gone from the age of five. I was the sad child with big eyes who waves goodbye to all his friends at holiday time and spends a boring break with the sadistic form master and kindly matron."

"Your parents?"

"Gone."

That single word is all he says on the subject of his parents. There is a minute of silence as the two men reflect on this new level of intimacy between them.

"One year, maybe I was nine, I was invited home for Christmas by one of the other boys. We weren't even that close and I thought it was a cruel joke at first, but at the end of term a car came and collected both of us and our trunks and we went to his home for the holiday."

"Durham?"

"Yes. The boy's father had spoken to the headmaster. It had begun a little selfishly, really. The boy had lost his mother and his father was concerned for him. He thought that if he had a friend to play with, that Christmas would be . . . tolerable." He pauses and lets that word fill the air around them. Tom knows how keeping busy makes life tolerable.

"Anyway, it was the best two weeks of my whole life. Sad?"

"No . . . no."

"I went home with Paul every holiday after that. His father bought us bunk beds and, well, they were my family. My father and brother."

"You still see them?"

The pause tells Tom everything he needed to know. "I'm really sorry."

"I loved them both. Gerald, Paul's father, inspired me—he was the coroner there, the most dedicated man I ever met."

"In Durham?" Tom feels ice shift in his chest.

"I followed him into the work, something to prove, I suppose. Oh . . ." Both men suddenly feel a weight push down on them. "Christ, Tom, your girl died in Durham."

Simultaneously both men imagine Gerald's scalpel cutting deep into a young woman's chest. Marcus Keyson reaches out and puts his hand on Tom Bevans's arm. Such a little gesture but Tom could not remember the last time anyone showed him such kindness. Tom feels his own hand begin to stretch and, with the lightest of touches, he rests his hand on the other man's arm. Together, swimming in the memories of those they once loved, they lie and stare at the ceiling.

TWENTY-TWO

Tuesday, February 7, 1989

There is a strange crackling from the body on the bench. It happens three times before the figure moves, rolling slightly to free a hand from the black cocoon. It pulls out a squat brick with an antenna, and holds it close to what must be a mouth.

"PC Bevans" is all it says, in a voice syrupy with tiredness.

There's a long pause. Tom pushes himself up on his park-bench bed, keeping the sleeping bag pulled up to his neck. His shoulders are killing him and his lower back feels compressed, as if he'd been carrying a rock uphill for the longest time. He waits for the voice in the machine to tell him the news.

"They . . . found 'er." The voice just peeks through the static. "Call just came in from Durham CID."

Tom knows the news is not good. He shakes his head free of the last cobwebs of fatigue.

"She's dead?"

The silence says it all.

"Mate, I am so sorry," Sarge finally manages.

"How can they be sure?" Tom asks, deadpan—dead.

"An anonymous tip-off just before midnight. A male. He said they'd find Dani Lancing at a private address in Durham. A car went straight there and found the body, the first officer on the scene called it in."

Tom's stomach pitches.

"But are they sure it's her?"

"The first OS had taken the file—all the missing-persons photos. He said he was sure it was her but they called the flatmate over anyway. She made the positive at about one this morning."

From somewhere an owl hoots. Tom's mouth feels rank. He spits into the grass.

"How had . . . ? What's the cause of death?"

"Don't know. There'll be an autopsy later."

Silence. Chill.

"Had she been . . . ?" Tom tries to ask.

"Oh, mate. I don't know." Sarge sounds like he might cry; he hates breaking bad news. It was part of the reason he'd taken the desk job in the first place—so he didn't have to deliver the worst news to people and watch as they disintegrated before his eyes. But he owes something to this young policeman. He grits his teeth.

"She was tied up when they found her . . . Tom, I'm sorry. That's all I know, the full report will be in later. Sorry."

"What about her mum and dad?" Tom's voice barely registers.

Sarge twists the volume dial and asks him to repeat.

"Her mum and dad, who's going to tell them?"

"Durham CID are sending someone down. They wanted one of their own to see her parents and talk to the papers—you know, with everything that's gone on."

"Oh yeah. The reporters."

They had been like flies on shit the last couple of weeks, plastering Dani's picture all over the front page. Hounding them, wanting anything, everything. And that bastard from the *News of the Screws*—he'd been the worst—disgusting. Well, at least he wouldn't be bothering them again.

"When will the Durham team be here?"

"Hour, maybe two. They're going to meet the DS at some cafe on the way. Get a quick briefing, then the pair of them will drive in together. I think the plan is to get there at about six. I think they're gonna ask the parents to do a secondary ID of the . . . of Dani. But they're dealing with it as a known victim."

"Thanks, Sarge. Over."

Tom feels frozen. He puts the radio down on the bench and swings his legs off. He puts them tentatively on the ground—pins and needles run up and down like electric charges. He feels like a zombie, dragging around a dead body because he's too stupid or too cowardly to lie down. The radio squawks once more.

"I'm re-jigging the rota. Don't come in till Thursday night," Sarge says through the static.

Three days to recover from the loss of your one true love.

"I need to bring the radio back."

"Thursday's fine. Go home, Tom."

"Sarge."

Tom takes his thumb off the radio and lets the silence engulf him.

He sits for about forty-five minutes, not really thinking, not really doing anything. It's still dark. Last night the moon had been so bright, but it's gone now and Greenwich Park is purple and navy. Tom can just about make out shapes. He hobbles over to a bush and pees into it. He hopes none of it is splashing onto his boots, but really, what does that matter? Once again he's slept in the park like a tramp. He had the idea after Dani had been missing for six days, to keep a walkie-talkie with him at all times. He talked to Sarge about it and he agreed that whoever was on duty would let Tom know any news that came in. The first few nights he'd been at home but he couldn't sleep, worrying that if a call had come in he couldn't get there quickly enough. He wanted to be at the Lancings' the second there was news. So he started to take a sleeping bag onto the heath, only a five-minute walk from their house. It was cold, but nothing that the four-season Everest sleeping bag couldn't deal with.

He used his uniform as a pillow, wrapped up in a soft waterproof, and he always remembered to take a change of underwear and a sponge bag. If he was on duty, he'd wash at the station house; if not, then there were public loos that opened at 7 a.m. on the other side of the bridleway. Normally that was fine, but this morning it isn't good enough. His teeth need a good clean and his chin's scratchy with a lot more than Mickey Rourke stubble. In the dark he can't see that the hairs poking through his skin are pure white, like those spreading out from his temples.

Maybe three weeks ago. Maybe then, he would still have been described as a boy: the pale, skinny boy. Of course, nobody who knew him would say it to his face, but he heard it. Old ladies would see the uniform, stop him in the street and then argue with him, insisting he was a tall child dressing up. One even threatened to call the *real* police. He'd tried to grow a beard, but it had been a disaster. He had been thinking about ordering a pair of glasses with clear glass to see if they made him look older . . . That was three weeks ago. This morning, no person on earth would mistake him for a boy.

He looks toward the old, old tree, where the woods seem to curve down to the horizon. There, that's where the sky will start to glow soon. In all seasons and all different daybreaks, he always knows when it's about to start—when that first barely perceptible change will come. It's no innate skill in him; it's the birds. No matter what month it is, the birds will begin their chorus two minutes before he sees the first ray. He doesn't know if they sense the change or if their eyes are just that much more sophisticated than his, but something alerts them and they sing the new day into being.

For the past nine days, except for two shifts of night duty, he has lain on this bench and slept at least part of the night here before waking for the miracle of dawn. He'd never slept here before Dani went missing, but he had sat in this spot and watched the dawn arrive. He'd done it some two dozen times over the last five years, and always the same thought had been in his head and heart: is this the day I can persuade Dani Lancing to love me?

The first time it had been Valentine's Day 1984. He'd delivered a card to her house—anonymous of course, and then had run out to the park, amazed by his daring and full of excitement and expectation. He'd not planned to watch the dawn break; in fact it had surprised him. It was an accident—he'd been looking directly at the spot where the sun rose and . . . He was amazed by the beauty of it. A golden-orange light exploded in the grass and rose to form a miasma around the trees, for a short while making them look like angels; at least they did to a romantic teenager, who had just delivered his first declaration of love.

"Is this an omen of good luck?" he thought. Of course it was not the day Dani Lancing fell for him . . . in fact, it had been a bit of a disaster, but a love of watching the daybreak from this spot had been born in him. Today, once again, he will watch the dawn from this bench.

The birds begin the overture and there . . . ta-da. Raspberry ripple smudged into the dusky gray of the sky. It's morning: February 7, 1989. The worst day of his life. The weather forecast predicted a dry warmish day. Not the weather for this news. It should be raining. Storming. Torrential rain to batter and destroy—thunder and lightning. Drama.

She's dead.

He doesn't actively think, "I'll break my orders," but he looks at his watch at 5:30 a.m. and is aware that he should be telling Patty and Jim that Dani is gone. He pulls the walkie-talkie out of his pocket and slides the button down. He croaks into it.

"Sarge?"

"Bevans?"

"I'm heading over to the Lancings'."

"Oh fuck, Tom, don't do that. The brass'll be there in half an hour or so. Let them deal with it."

"Sorry, Sarge. I'm not in uniform, I'm off-duty and a family friend. I won't say anything about hearing the news from you. Sarge . . . Jack, I am very grateful." Tom drops his finger off the call button.

"Bevans. Bevans . . . Fuck."

Tom turns the volume down low and puts it in the bag with his uniform. He knows his sarge is right, but this is his duty. The DS from Durham can deal with the shit from the press. Tom can't think about that, all he knows is that two people are in pain. And, it strikes him only now, that it's two people he loves. Sort of, certainly two people he has become close with, cares about. Is that love? He stands and swings his bag onto his shoulder. Then he heads out.

"What the hell are you doing? Do you know what they call you? 'The pup.' Stupid love-struck pup. She says you follow me around drooling like some lost dog." He hears Dani's voice in his head.

It had been his third visit to her in Durham, the third term of her first year. He'd gone for the weekend and right from the start she'd been eager to pick a fight. He'd said something about Patricia—

something nice—and Dani had blown up. Tom hadn't risen to the bait; he could see what was going on. A lot of their friendship had been born out of each of them moaning about their mothers. Dani liked to riff on her absent, career-obsessed mother and Tom would tell stories of his mother's drinking, offensive boyfriends and the beatings. Then his mum died.

It was the middle of Dani's second term, that first year. Dani hadn't come to the funeral. He had hoped she would, had asked her to, but she was busy and had tests. It was a dismal turnout. An aunt he barely knew. A woman who said she knew her from bingo and three drinking mates who sat in the back row and raised cans of Special Brew to their lips as a parting toast.

Tom sat alone, in the front row. He wore his uniform. He wasn't sure why but it helped keep him strong—it was unseemly for a copper to blub in public. He sat there waiting for the vicar, wishing for the day just to be over. Then someone slipped in beside him and a hand gripped his. He looked over and it was Patricia. She didn't say anything, just winked at him.

After the funeral they walked together, around the cemetery. There was no wake. No sandwiches starting to curl in the back room of a pub somewhere. Instead, the young policeman and the mother of his love walked and talked. Well, she smoked and he talked. He talked of his mother—but it wasn't the complaints and horror stories he might have told Dani. Instead it was tales of laughs, fun and shared happiness: the time when this happened, that broke, they got lost going there, she used salt instead of sugar . . . good times. And under the outstretched wings of a stone angel, in a field of the fallen, Patricia folded Tom into her arms and stroked his head while he cried.

"Poor pup," she had said, comfortingly.

Of course, the minute he'd heard that Dani was missing, he had gone to them. "What can I do? What do you need?" Patricia and Jim appreciated it. They weren't being taken seriously in Durham, they said. They wanted him to check out the progress from inside the force. That was his mission—if he chose to accept it. He did.

After Dani had been missing for seven days, Tom was at the Lancings' every evening for an update. On his days off he went to Durham and talked to the police there. He went alone, even though he knew Patricia was going too—sometimes with Jim, but other times alone. He liked spending time with Jim, but often Patricia scared him. He had no idea what drugs the doctors had prescribed for her, but he thought no human being should be that tightly wound. Her grief scared him. It felt like a violent cloud that hung over anyone that came close to her. In her presence he felt frustrated—like a child furious at the injustice of the world and yet unable to do anything to change it. At least with Jim he could put a hand on his shoulder, connect at some level. With Patricia, she was inside some private bubble, waiting and waiting and waiting for her daughter to come home.

"Oh, Jesus." A sob convulses him. She isn't coming home. Not for them and not for him.

"Dani!" he howls, filling the park with pain.

For a second he's outside his body looking in, watching some old, old man weep for his lost love. The pain screws his face until it shatters like fine porcelain in a fire. Then the wind changes and he's stuck like it. The Sad Man is born.

Jim stands in Dani's bedroom and looks out at the encroaching day. He likes to be in there; it still smells of her: coconut shampoo and menthol cigarettes. She'd been home for just two disastrous days at Christmas. They had rowed and . . . they hadn't had enough time. They hadn't even spoken to her on her birthday. The first time . . . but he mustn't think like that. She'd be back soon and the room— her room, was ready. He'd changed the bedding only a few days before and bought a new toothbrush and the toothpaste she likes. When she's found, she'll need to be looked after, be in comfort and safety. That's their job, their only . . . Through the window he sees Tom enter their road, walk a little way and stop on the corner. Jim feels his stomach churn. He can see the young man batting at his face, like a wasp is buzzing around. Then he realizes Tom is crying.

Jim's throat closes up; he finds it hard to breathe.

"Patty." He thinks of his wife next door, asleep for the first time in days—even if it is purely due to sedation. Tom will be here, will knock in about a minute. Why is he crying?

Jim is out of the front door as quietly as he can. He's in the street before he realizes he's still in his pajamas. He looks down the road—Tom's still where Jim last saw him—was that good news? He walks toward Tom, each step becomes a wish, a prayer. "Let her be alive. Found alive. Found alive." Hope.

Tom sees him approach and tries to pull himself together. He remembers the first time they ever spoke, after they both watched Dani run. He even remembers the stupid thumbs-up he gave him that day. The pain spasms the policeman. Jim sees the pain and slows. There is no good news. There is no hope. Their eyes lock like two gunslingers facing off at dawn. Tom shakes his head and the tears stream. With a cry, like he's been shot, the pajama-clad man falls to the ground.

TWENTY-THREE

Friday, October 8, 2010

Marcus Keyson sees the way her hand shakes. After a while he discounts nervous energy and decides she has Parkinson's, probably early stages, and isn't fully managing her medication yet. While she talks he watches her. She looks like a runner, very thin but muscular, powerful. She could have been a looker when she was young; she has the bone structure for it. Her eyes are the real point of attraction, they actually seem to burn as she talks about her daughter. Though, truth be told, he's pretty much zoned out of her story, just the odd nod here and there. Something she said early on sent his mind spinning.

Finally she stops talking and looks at him expectantly, like a puppy. He nods slowly; that always seems to put people at their ease.

"Mrs. Lancing, I will need to look into this further. I have ex-colleagues I can talk to, I have a relationship with the Durham coroner's office. But just to recap, you mentioned Detective Inspector Tom Bevans—he's an old friend—was he involved with the original investigation?"

"No, not really, just by . . . he . . . he was Dani's friend."

"Friend?"

"He . . . does it matter?"

"I don't know. Maybe."

"He was . . . he loved her."

"She loved him?"

She pauses. "No, not in that way."

Bingo.

After she leaves, he googles her. Award-winning crime journalist, first with the *Northern Echo* and then the *Independent*. There are dozens of articles she'd written over the years. Two books, one titled *Wives of the Killers*, which seems to be a series of interviews, and *The Ugly Man*. Both have great reviews and the second won two prestigious awards. There are also press releases and news stories linking her to Lost Souls, a charity campaigning for victims' rights. Next he googles images of her and there are many: one of her accepting an *Evening Standard* prize, a National Journalism Award for an interview with Sonia Sutcliffe, another of her on a demo and a few at Greenham Common. The best is one of her haranguing Margaret Thatcher. He was right: she had been quite a looker back then. He feels excited, his whole body tingles. The long-dead girl and Tom Bevans. And . . . something else is pulling at threads in the back of his mind. A long-ago tragedy. He struggles to remember—a note he had seen twenty years before. A suicide note. It spoke of shame, corruption and . . . lance. Was that it? Lancing? He shakes his head—the thread will not unravel. Instead he turns back to the job in hand and flicks the intercom.

"Can you come in here please, Lauren?" he asks.

A few seconds later his assistant limps in.

"I need you to find me an investigator in Durham. They're to find out names and addresses for anyone involved in the investigation of a murder. Danielle Lancing, February 1989."

Lauren starts to make notes.

"I want to know the name and current address of every copper on the murder team back then. I also want to know who was writing up the notes, and where any samples and evidence are kept. Okay?"

She smiles. Everything is okay as far as she's concerned.

"And . . ." He pauses. "Gerald Spurling. I think you'll find he was the coroner on the case. I'd like to see his reports from the public record."

"Okay." She nods.

"And can you check on the state of forensic review with Durham CID, make it sound general but I need to know about this girl, Dani Lancing. Why is her case coming up now, is it just luck or did someone request a review?"

"Will do." She smiles.

"And call Ronson and ask him to come and see me ASAP. Oh, and I want all the murder team members cross-referenced with a London officer—DS Tom Bevans. He was a PC back then."

Lauren stops making notes.

"He's the one who—"

"Yes. Yes, he is, so do a thorough job. Okay?"

She smiles and moves to walk around to the back of his chair; she stretches her fingers as she walks and reaches out for the back of his neck.

"Not now."

She blushes at the rebuff. "Of course," and she leaves.

Marcus Keyson sits back in his chair and dares to dream—of revenge. A chance to get back at the man who made all this happen—who destroyed his career, tarnished his reputation and betrayed him. His Judas. Maybe all this could be turned to some financial advantage as well. Tom Bevans should pay. Maybe Patricia Lancing should pay too; he could do with clearing some of the debts—even get away from this awful place.

"This is so good. So good."

TWENTY-FOUR

Monday, October 11, 2010

Keyson pushes the heavy doors open and stands on the threshold of bedlam. He whistles "The lunatics have taken over the asylum" as he steps inside the special ops room for Operation Ares. As he does so, he slips the ID card from around his neck and drops it into his pocket. It's a fake, of course, and impersonating a police officer is a serious offense. He smiles.

For all the chaos, it's the sound that really makes an impact. Officers howl into their phones, each having to project over the din of colleagues and the incessant squawking of dozens of unanswered phones demanding attention. Added to that are the slams of filing cabinets, the squeals of felt-tip markers and the pacing of a lot of nicotine-deprived, overweight men.

The air is sticky with testosterone and cheap aftershave, knock-off Calvin Klein from Petticoat Lane market. Keyson had forgotten its pungency. He takes a deep breath and heads for the center of the web. This had never been his office but he'd spent so much time here it had almost been home—once. For three years, unless he was actually scrutinizing a cadaver, he had been here, among the living. He'd believed he'd made friends. For a while, he thought Detective Inspector Jane Thorsen might be the one. Not a long while, though. He reaches the heart of the operations room, unnoticed, and stands there waiting.

He watches his ex-colleagues and imagines them all dead. Violent, blood-splattered deaths, and he's the man brought in to solve their murders. It cheers him enormously. Finally he's noticed. A nod, a shake of the head, a whistle, someone pointing and then the wall of sound deadens and flatlines. Close by there is a chorus of "I'll call you back." Phones are replaced on their receivers. The room is quiet.

"What the fuck do you want, Keyson?"

He turns. Of course, it's Clark. Clark, who used to call him "Marcus." Who had invited him to both his stag night and his wedding. Clark, who had once vomited on his shoes—suede shoes—and told him he'd never loved his mother and now she was dying of cancer and what could he do? Clark, who had practically offered him his own sister once, but who had spat in his face after the tribunal. The two men square up. Keyson would be only too glad to fight Clark.

"Clark," Thorsen barks through a megaphone. The sound echoes off the walls filling the room. "If you lay a hand on a civilian, you'll be on a fucking charge so fast."

"But—"

"Get back to work. Stay where you are, Keyson."

Grumbling, the crowd dissipates back to desks and phones. The noise level builds again and all is back as it had been. Thorsen waits to make sure everyone has obeyed, then walks over to Keyson. As she approaches him, she notes the small changes. He is still well groomed, always spent freely on his hair and skin, but his clothes are a little shabbier than before. The coat is the same he had three years ago and his shoes are worn. There is a shine to the knees of his suit—not worn-out, but the old Marcus Keyson replaced his wardrobe every year. Interesting—life in the independent sector not quite so sparkling for God's gift to forensic science.

He is still bloody handsome, though, she thinks as she stops in front of him.

"Why the hell are you here, Marcus?"

"Good to see you too, Jane," Keyson says, with what he believes is a winning smile.

Thorsen crosses her arms and glares at him. Keyson notes how she hides her chest, breast reduction in her late teens due to backache. In bed he had kissed the tracery of fine scars. He never told anyone, not even after she'd maced him. That should have earned him something, shouldn't it? He'd even met her mother.

From behind DI Thorsen, a small, bespectacled man emerges, looking a little mole-like: DI Jenkins.

"I think, unless you need something, that you should turn around and get out, Dr. Keyson." Jenkins—the voice of reason. The only one who didn't turn against him after the tribunal. How he hates Jenkins.

"I'm here to see the Sad Man," Keyson says to Jane, ignoring Jenkins altogether.

"I'm sure the guvnor has no desire to see you again," she says, her voice level but full of fury at the disrespectful use of Tom's nickname.

Keyson nods, then takes a pad and pen off an adjacent desk and quickly scrawls a note. He folds it in half and hands it to Thorsen.

"Please give him this. Tell him I'll be over the road in Munchies. I'll get him a tea. Four sugars, if I remember correctly."

He turns on his heel and walks back toward the door. He feels the daggers in his back from all quarters, but he's pleased with how it went. If he can avoid food poisoning in Munchies, this will be a good day.

DI Thorsen stops for a second outside Tom's office; she's shaking a little. She feels so angry at the ex-pathologist that she needs to pause. Marcus Keyson betrayed them both, but in a funny way it's Tom who has been more deeply affected. She was the one who'd slept with him, had even taken him to meet her super-judgmental mother—and annoyingly her mum had been thoroughly charmed by him—but she has other friends, real friends. She's been on a lot of dates since, slept with a number of men, and it's water under the bridge as far as she's concerned. But Tom doesn't make friends, at least none that she knows of, certainly none in the force. That was why it had seemed so strange that he and Keyson had become close. She knows better than anyone how seductive Marcus Keyson can be—clever, funny and a great listener. She remembers that Tom and Marcus had even talked about holiday plans, a long weekend in Copenhagen for some conference. Didn't happen in the end. Instead, Professional Standards took Keyson into custody one afternoon and closed the unit down for three days while they investigated accusations of gross professional misconduct. They had all been questioned. The entire department had fallen under suspicion, especially Detective Inspector Jane Thorsen, the idiot who had been dumb enough to sleep with him, and Detective Superintendent Tom Bevans—his friend. Detectives from DPS had been through both of their files and their personal lives with fine-tooth combs. It took months, but eventually the only person reprimanded was Keyson, though there remained a stain on the reputation of the whole Serious Crimes Unit and Operation Ares in particular.

It was hushed up, of course. No press got wind of it. They discharged Keyson with no pension, but there were no criminal charges. She still doesn't know how the slimy bastard managed it. That had been three years ago. Since then she had barely thought of Marcus Keyson. He had no lasting power over her life, though she feels that Tom is still hurt by the loss of his friend. So, how would he react now? There is only one way to find out. She knocks.

"Come in," he calls.

Tom Bevans stands by the window looking out onto the street outside. The gray December light makes him look even paler than normal; his silver-white hair shines a little. He turns toward her, his face seeming to contain both a little boy and an old man simultaneously. Though he is her superior officer, she wants to hug him to her and make him eat some soup.

She holds up the note. "Marcus Keyson just slimed in."

"Keyson. Why?"

"He asked me to give you this." She waves the note. "And to tell you he'd be in Munchies and would get you a tea."

He walks over and takes the note.

"Cheeky bastard, well, he can go—" He unfolds the paper and dries up.

"Guv? Guv, are you okay?" She thinks he's seen a ghost.

"You said he's there, now?"

"He came in, gave me the note and left."

"Well, how the fuck did he get in here? He doesn't have clearance."

"I don't know, sir." He had never shouted at her before; she feels herself contract a little, like when her father had come home.

"Okay." He sees her flinch from him and immediately feels guilty. "I'm sorry, Jane. Thanks, thanks for bringing this up to me. You go back to work, I'll . . . you go back."

She nods and walks toward the door, feeling the tension in the air. She can see he wants her gone. She'd like to offer help, but she leaves instead.

Tom waits until Thorsen has gone and then calls down to security for them check the log. There's no Dr. Marcus Keyson entered.

"Well, he was just here," Tom tells them angrily. "Read me the names of everyone admitted into this building in the last half hour—I don't care how fucking busy you are."

The sixteenth name strikes a bell: Lewis Mason. There'd been a detective about ten years ago with that name but he'd transferred to Cardiff and then left the force. He'd become a hypnotherapist, specializing in helping the gullible and weak give up smoking and lose weight.

"Check Mason right now," he ordered. Security checked— Lewis Mason's level one clearance was still operative; it had never been rescinded.

"Well, bloody do it now!" barked Tom. "Then, start going through all existing access and check that the officers are alive and still work here . . . I don't care how long it'll take. We just had someone break into the Ares op room; he could have been a suicide bomber."

Tom slams the handset down. In all likelihood this was probably worse than a suicide bomber. Damn Keyson. The scrap of paper Jane had handed him was still lying on his desk. He picks it up and opens it again. Two words, but they make the pit of his stomach lurch.

Danielle Lancing.

TWENTY-FIVE

Monday, October 11, 2010

From somewhere a trumpet plays "Joy to the World," but plaintively, as if performed by a heartbroken elf.

"It's only mid-October," Tom grumbles under his breath as he stands under a grocer's awning and scans the road. The rain is falling harder now and the street ahead's a wind tunnel, threatening to slice anyone salami-thin if they venture into it. Tom's hand slides through his white hair. He should have brought an umbrella. From where he stands he can get to Munchies in about two minutes—but he will arrive looking like a drowned rat. Normally he wouldn't mind—he's not a vain man—but Marcus Keyson brings out the worst in him.

"Come on, calm down for a couple of minutes," he tells the rain. Of course, it gets harder instead. "Typical."

He can't delay this much longer. It's already forty-five minutes since Thorsen gave him the note. After checking security, he quickly scanned the last six weeks of crime digest—an online summary of crime. He filtered it using as many keywords as he could think of: Keyson, Lancing, Durham University, Durham gang, Merchant and Cobhurn—nothing came up.

Then he washed in the gents—used Fat Eddy's deodorant and razor—and put on the spare shirt and tie he kept for snap inspections. Waste of time. The new shirt is now completely soaked and he already smells a bit.

"Over the top," he sighs, and makes a dash for it. He hits a paving stone and it rears up, shooting mucky brown water up his leg and into his crotch. He remembers his old religious education teacher, Vicar Tim, standing in front of them intoning in his deep somber voice: "With pestilence and with blood, I will rain down upon him."

"What shit has Dr. Marcus Keyson come to rain down on this sinner's head?" Tom wonders. Then he catches himself and realizes he's in full-on apocalypse mode. "Really, Tom. Really—Bible quotations now? You need to get out more. And you need to stop thinking about yourself in the third person."

He walks on, waddling like a duck as the muddy water soaks through his crotch.

Finally he reaches the cafe, but stops short of the door. Rain runs off him in little waterfalls, his socks are wet and his underpants squelch. He wants to shake like a dog but where's the dignity in that? Instead he squeegees his hair with his hand and composes himself. At least there are unlikely to be any of his colleagues inside the cafe. *Real* coppers went to Fred's—a large greasy spoon just around the corner. Fred's is cheap, decidedly cheerful, and gives you the kind of home comfort that most coppers don't get at home. Unpredictable hours, and the fact that most of the women they know work long hours too, means most male coppers defrost and microwave their own suppers in front of the telly or computer. Or they eat at Fred's and flirt with his two plump daughters. The women coppers are similar; they either go home and heat up ready-meals for their husbands and kids—who are jealous of the time they spend on the job—or they eat a super-food salad from M&S on their own, knock back three or four vodkas and fall asleep in their clothes. This is modern policing.

While the worst of the storm drips off him, Tom reads the specials board through the window: sunblush tomato and feta quiche, balsamic roasted parsnip soup, halloumi and couscous salad. Was this a date?

Below the board, sitting in the far corner, he sees Keyson, whose table is littered with empty cups and a teapot. Stone-cold, thinks Tom. As if he knows he's being watched, Keyson slowly turns and looks straight at Tom. He waves.

Tom pushes the door open and steps inside. A very pretty waitress waves him toward a table by the door, but he shakes his head and indicates Keyson's table.

"He's my plus-one—finally," Keyson calls to her. Both he and the waitress laugh. Tom grimaces. He takes off his coat and hangs it by the door, on a rack that is supposed to look like deer antlers. Keyson stands as Tom approaches and holds out his hand. Tom ignores the gesture and pulls out the other chair at the table—but as he does so he looks down. Scattered across the table are papers and photographs: Dani, Patricia, Jim and a face he barely recognizes—but it's circled in red ink. Ben Bradman.

Tom reels. "I . . . I'll be just a second."

"Gents is over there." Keyson points with a smile.

Tom heads off.

TWENTY-SIX

Monday, January 30, 1989

"Peace, man." The reporter flashes a two-finger salute as he opens the door and sees a uniformed police constable standing there.

"Mr. Bradman?" asks PC Tom Bevans, controlling a desire to punch him.

"That's me, Mr. Policeman." He smiles.

"I wonder if I could come in and ask you a few questions, Mr. Bradman?" Tom asks in a level and friendly voice.

"Well, now, I am not at all sure about that. I would have to make clear I was in no way waiving my rights and not agreeing to my premises being searched or—"

"This is not about you directly, Mr. Bradman. Let me assure you I am not interested in what might be in your flat. I just want to ask you a few questions concerning the disappearance of Danielle Lancing. In your article this weekend you seem to hint at information you may have obtained—"

"Whoa, whoa there, Officer. A reporter's source is sacrosanct. When he talks to me, that is like a priest hearing confession."

Tom has trouble seeing Ben Bradman as any kind of priest, but he tries to keep the incredulity out of his face and voice. "Mr. Bradman, I have no desire to shatter the integrity of your relationship with your source. But I would like to ask about the information itself, and I do not think your hallway is the place to do this."

Bradman thinks for a second. "Okay, but wait here."

He closes the door behind him and goes into his flat. Tom stands stock-still. He assumes Bradman's hiding his dope stash. Even through the door he can smell the oppressive fug of cannabis. He waits about two minutes and Bradman reappears. He nods and Tom follows him in, closing the front door. As he walks over the threshold, Tom slips his hand into his pocket and fingers a brass knuckleduster taken from the evidence room. He slips it on his hand. He follows Bradman into the living room. The curtains are closed.

"Anyone else here?" he asks.

"In a flat this size? You're jo—"

Tom swings hard and fast; he feels a snap and hears the crack of cheekbone and his own knuckle pop out of its socket.

"Fuck!" both men shout together. Bradman drops to the floor, his hand to his face—blood showing through his fingers. It reminds Tom of how a torch glows red through your hand when you cup it. Tom pulls off the knuckleduster and pops his finger back into its socket.

"Jesus shit. Shit." Bradman keeps repeating.

"Stay down or I will hit you again," Tom says, in his best hard-man voice. He really hopes Bradman does stay down. His hand hurts so much he doesn't think he could hit him again.

"Franco will get his fucking money. I just need another day or two." Bradman is almost hysterical.

"I'm not from Franco."

"What?"

"I'm not from Franco."

"Then . . ." His brain reels: who is this guy if he's not from Franco? "So, what do you want?" he asks, starting to get angry.

"I told you. I want to talk about the story you wrote on Dani Lancing."

"You are shitting me." He starts to get up.

Tom kicks at his knee, smacking him back down to the floor. Bradman grunts and grabs at the knee, smearing blood all over his jeans, which are filthy already. Tom unfolds a sheet of newsprint from his pocket.

" 'Dani Lancing has been painted as a promising student, sports star and much loved daughter—a good girl. However the truth may be very different. There is evidence to suggest Dani was involved with drugs in her first year at Durham University and was selling them to finance her lavish lifestyle—' "

"Freedom of spee—" Bradman interrupts.

"You fucking liar!" Tom shouts, kicking wildly at Bradman's leg.

"I reported fairly," Bradman whines.

Tom kicks at his leg again, this time just hitting into the thigh. "*Fair*, you don't know the meaning of the word. You smeared a poor sweet—"

"Oh please. I read all that shit in the *Independent* and *Echo*. I heard stuff about Snow White."

"What?" Tom drops to the floor, making Bradman squeal a little. "What did you hear?"

"She . . . she used to be the bitch of the campus pusher: king of the uni smackheads."

Tom feels his stomach freeze. "You liar." His voice is a little uncertain.

Bradman seizes on that; he continues, more brazen now. "She got turned. Happens to students all the time. She's probably drying out somewhere—or stuffed to the tits on junk."

Tom punches hard, into the floor by Bradman's head. He hears his knuckle pop again but doesn't feel it—his body is awash with adrenaline.

"I love her!" Tom screams into his face.

All color drains from Bradman's face, finally understanding what has happened. "I . . . I'm sorry."

"Sorry? Sorry?" Tom barks.

"You're right, right of course. It's not true. I embroidered, embellished. You gotta understand, there's a pressure . . ."

"Pressure?" asks Tom, in a small voice.

"I can see what I've done now." He laughs a nervous, edgy laugh. "I've tried to shoehorn two stories together: student druggies and your missing girlfriend. I'm sorry. We can do a big story—get the public looking under every rock and stone. Telling them how brave she is, about how amazing her parents are . . ."

"What did you hear?" Tom almost whispers into the reporter's ear.

"Look. We can—"

"What did you hear?" Just a breath.

"Probably nothing, I—"

Tom swings again—the knuckleduster connects with chin—blood in the mouth.

"Fuck, fuck . . . I heard rumors. Okay, just rumors."

"Who from?"

"I can't—"

"Give me a name." Tom takes the knuckleduster and drives it into the reporter's hand, crushing it into the floor. He screams.

"A jazz guy, trumpet player in Durham. Diamond earring in his right ear, shaved head. I don't know his name. Honest."

Tom pulls the brass knuckleduster off his hand. Bradman pulls his fingers into his chest and rolls from side to side, tears rolling down his face.

"Thank you for your help, Mr. Bradman." Tom stands up—it's over.

Bradman lies there and watches the policeman rise. He suddenly realizes it's done, just a hurt hand and knee—that's all this is. He laughs. Then he opens his arms as if to embrace humanity, his face sad—what can you do? Life.

It was the gesture Tom hated: supplicant and weak—a victim. It reminded him of all the ponces he'd arrested, the women he'd seen battered, his own fucking father after he'd beaten his own son and he opened his arms as if to say "It was your fault after all, but I forgive you." Tom sees red. He grabs the knuckleduster and punches—once hard. There is a crack—metal on bone, a pistol shot. Bradman lies unmoving.

Was it premeditated? That's what Tom has asked himself so many times over the years. Ben Bradman and Bix Lego-dogshit.

He looks down at the body in front of him. Feels for a pulse—weak, but there. He isn't dead. Tom runs into the bathroom and throws up. When he's finished he cleans the bowl and bleaches it thoroughly. Whether Tom had planned to knock him out or not, he hadn't planned what to do next, but it came to him in a rush. He started to search the flat; he knew Bradman had hidden something. He found it quickly but it was very disappointing, a small bag of dope—not enough.

"Think, Tom," he tells himself. He needs Bradman out of the picture for a while. He can't have him investigating Tom and Dani again.

Bradman's keys are in the back of the front door; he'd used them to open up when Tom arrived. He checks Bradman's pulse again. He'll be out for a while.

"Okay." He grabs the keys and leaves the flat, locking the door behind him. He runs down the three flights of stairs to the street and out into the night. It's almost ten o'clock but where he's going, that's like morning. Bradman had given him the answer to the problem himself. Franco.

It isn't far. He's only been there once before, as extra support if a riot occurred. Franco ran drug distribution for almost the whole of East London. Pretty amazing, considering he is eighteen years old. Tom runs the whole way there. The base of Franco's empire is a four-story block of ex-council flats sold off by Thatcher in the mid-eighties. Now it is equipped with armed guards on the roof, a helipad and the most sophisticated set-up of surveillance cameras in London—including those around MI5. As soon as Tom gets to the forecourt of the block, he can feel eyes on him. He knows at least one rifle will be trained on his head. He stops at the entranceway. It's dark, but he knows how misleading that is. Blackout curtains mask the fact that most of the flats are being used to manufacture crack, PCP, amphetamines and a wide variety of mood enhancers and brain-cell killers. Tom doesn't care.

He stands on the threshold of the enemy kingdom and looks up. He's wearing his uniform, which was great for getting into Bradman's flat, but makes him a terrible target now.

"Into the valley of death rides the idiot. Cannon to left of him . . ." Tom holds his hands up, showing his palms.

"I want to see Franco," he shouts.

There is nothing for a while and then a booming voice calls out, "Strip." And from all around there are the deep, throaty laughs of bored men.

In ultra-slow motion Tom slides out of his jacket, then unbuttons his shirt and removes it. Then he undoes his belt and trousers—they fall to the floor. He slides his hands into the waistband of his . . .

"Leave the underpants on. We don't wanna see your skanky white cock," a voice calls out.

"I need to see Franco," Tom shouts back to the unseen voice.

"We's thought you were auditioning for the Chippendales." A whole gang of voices laugh and there are the slaps of high-fives.

"I have a proposition for Franco."

"Some naked white guy gonna propose to Franco!" another voice shouts and a peal of laughter echoes around the block.

"Come on up, Officer Dribble!" shouts the first voice and Tom walks out of his trousers and heads up into the jaws of Franco's headquarters.

The stairs smell of piss and weed. He takes them two at a time, starting to feel pretty cold.

Once he gets to the top floor, there is a group of armed men waiting for him. Even though he is near-enough naked they still frisk him for weapons. One of them cups his balls and grips his penis.

"This is no time to get an erection," he tells himself. Thankfully it's cold and the frisk only lasts a few seconds.

"You can see I don't have anything. No weapon, no wire, nothing. I'm not here as a copper but as a regular citizen. I need a favor from Franco," Tom tells the assorted men, none of whom seem to be in charge. A nod seems to run around the group and one of them disappears inside.

"Nice night," Tom says, trying to be friendly.

The gunmen laugh and then melt into the shadows leaving him seemingly alone. He stands shivering for ten minutes before the door opens again and he is motioned inside. Once over the threshold he is frisked again by a giant of a man before being led into a large room.

"Wait here," he's told, and the giant leaves.

The room is empty, except for a huge sofa. On one end is a beautiful young woman, maybe eighteen, with flawless cinnamon-colored skin. She wears a silk sarong that looks like the sun, it's so bright. She is as high as a kite. Her eyes are rolled back in her head and she sways to music only she can hear. Occasionally she giggles. Tom sits at the other end of the sofa, as far from the girl as he can be.

"I really need to see Franco quickly," Tom says to the air, assuming a hidden camera somewhere. Bradman will wake up within an hour or two and time is short. "Ben Bradman owes Franco a lot of money. I am here to buy that debt from him . . . as well as something else."

Tom hears a click from somewhere.

A minute later the giant reappears and ushers Tom from the room and into another. This room is even larger. Tom wonders how it's possible—the entire story of the block must have been knocked through into one flat. In this room there's a full-size snooker table. Franco is playing a long red. He pots it expertly and straightens up. He's a tall and imposing figure; the story Tom had heard was that his bloodline was ancient African royalty, and the young man holds himself ramrod straight. Franco turns toward Tom and for a second seems so young, a gawky teen with a slightly cheeky smile and swagger. Tom feels a smile start to break, then recalls a body he saw a month or two ago. A mutilated corpse, punished by Franco, and his smile fades. The story goes that Franco inherited this empire from his uncle, who had built it up over twenty years using a mixture of loyalty, brutality, fear and clever pricing models. The uncle had been known to be cruel and heartless. Franco was said to be worse. Tom looks to the other player. He recognizes him off the telly—an up-and-coming snooker star.

"Police Constable Bevans, do you play?" Franco asks as he eyes up another long pot.

"There's a table in the station house. I've played a few times," Tom replies, trying to keep his voice level. Of course his uniform is downstairs with his warrant number on it, someone must have linked the number to the name. Still, it was quick work to get a name.

Franco nods and folds himself back over the cue. He wears sunglasses, which he pushes down his nose so that he can look over the top. He pulls the cue back and shoots the white ball down the table. It clatters into the black, which dances in the jaws of the pocket before spilling back onto the table.

"Bad luck there, Franco. Do you want another try?" says the professional. Tom can hear the fear in his voice.

"No," Franco says, sounding a bit brittle. "I'm done." The professional looks like he wants to cry. "Fuck off, pool boy."

The giant reappears and leads the snooker player out.

Franco walks off, through another door. Tom looks around and then follows him. The new room is even larger. Pinball machines line one wall and a large office table sits in the middle. Covering one wall is a huge noticeboard, breaking up East London into the areas led by its chief distributor. Shit, this is gold dust for the anti-drugs unit, Tom thinks, but he looks away. He isn't here as a policeman. A rolled-up dressing gown hits him in the face.

"Please put that on, PC Bevans."

Tom does as he's asked. It is a flaming red and yellow kimono— a dragon.

"Looks good on you. Very Hendrix. Keep it as a gift."

"Thank you."

Franco sits down at his desk, feet up on it. He pushes the sunglasses back on his head. Even though he's tall, the desk dwarfs him—Tom cannot help but think he looks like a child playing businessman. Tom is left to stand.

"So what do you want, Mr. Policeman?"

"Ben Bradman, reporter with the *News of the World*."

"A filthy rag. A friend?"

"He is no friend."

"I am pleased to hear it. The man is scum."

"He owes you money. I will buy that debt from you."

Franco raises an eyebrow. "Why would you do that, Mr. Policeman?"

"That's my business, Mr. Franco."

Franco smiles. "He owes me four thousand pounds. I will sell that debt to you for eight thousand."

"Agreed." Tom doesn't stop to think where he could possibly find the money. "Of course you can see I do not have the money on me."

"When we shake on the deal, you will have two days to deliver the money."

"Fine." Tom pauses. "There is something else I would like to ask of you. Something . . . more unusual."

"More unusual than buying this debt?" asks Franco, intrigued.

"I think you will find it so." He pauses to concentrate his courage. "Heroin, Mr. Franco. I want a large amount of heroin. Enough so that when it's found by the police, it will result in the person in possession being sent to prison for a long time. But I do not want to buy the heroin, I want to borrow it and return it. Probably in three months' time."

For a few seconds there is nothing, then Franco's throat erupts with a deep laugh. "You are right, Mr. Policeman, that is indeed most unusual." He laughs again. "You are a strange man, PC Bevans."

"Call me Tom."

Franco reacts like he's been slapped. He is up and across the room in an instant. In one fluid motion he grabs Tom by the throat, kicks his legs out from under him; he falls with a crack to his knees. Franco jabs a small blunt-nosed gun into Tom's neck.

"Tell me, friend Tom, why do you do this?"

Tom feels the cold metal press harder into his throat. "You wouldn't understand."

"Try."

A pause.

"My . . . a woman is missing. She is my best friend and Ben Bradman told the dirtiest lies about her."

Franco lets him go, almost like Tom burns him, and turns away.

"I am sorry." He pauses. "Tom."

Tom stands, the gun is gone. Franco returns to his desk, though this time he does not put his feet up on it.

"Okay, I will give you half a kilo of dirty heroin. It's cut with bathroom cleaner; it is likely that any conviction for supplying contaminated H would result in the judge throwing away the key. Would that suit your purposes?"

"Yes." Tom feels shame for a second, then remembers Bradman's words and his story in the newspaper.

"I do not require the heroin back. I do not sell dangerous product. It was cut by a business associate. An ex-business associate."

Tom remembers the mutilated body—was that his crime? "Thank you. I will also need some . . . other evidence."

Franco nods. "I can supply that also. I suggest you will need to administer at least one dose of genuine product to Mr. Bradman to complete the frame. You may also have that free and gratis. I do not like this man, you understand."

Tom nods.

"Do you know how to administer such an injection?"

Tom creases his brow. "I saw a police training film at Hendon."

Franco grimaces. "I know that film—it is useless. Come with me."

Franco walks Tom back through the snooker room and into the sofa room. The beautiful woman is asleep.

"Wait here." Franco leaves for a minute or so and returns with a carrier bag, which he hands to Tom. Then he leans forward and pulls open the woman's sarong.

"Lovely, yes?"

Tom doesn't reply, but he cannot help but think she is exquisite, flawless, except for her shoulder where there is a sore red welt. It is a brand that has been burned upon her, a single F. She is the property of Franco.

Then Franco pulls her legs apart and Tom sees she has a line of tracks spreading along her inner thigh. Some are pinpricks, others little scabs, and two are little open mouths. They spread from her like a butterfly emblazoned on her body.

"Here." Franco takes a syringe out of the bag and pushes the lever up. A drop of liquid is pushed out of the needle. "You will have seen this on TV—there must be no air in the syringe. Use it to create a number of pinpricks on Mr. Bradman's arm, then do the final one into a vein. Tie this around his arm. We do not need to protect Mr. Bradman's pretty arms."

He shows Tom how to tie a rubber tube around the girl's arm, then he flicks her forearm to show the vein.

"You see?"

Tom nods. She stays asleep through all this. Somehow it makes it worse. From somewhere the giant reappears with a bag marked HOMEPRIDE FLOUR.

"Here is all you need."

"Thank you."

Franco holds out his hand. Tom looks at it nervously for a second and then extends his own. Franco's grip is like a vice. He holds Tom's hand and does not let go.

"Tom, do you know how I happen to run this business?" asks Franco.

"I understand that you inherited the business from your uncle."

"True. And do you know what happened to him?"

"I do not."

"I slit his throat and drank his blood. That is, by tradition, how we transfer power in my tribe. When the old ruler became too weak he would choose a successor. That man would then drink his life and his strength. Her name?"

"Danielle."

"And for her?"

"I would drink a man's blood."

He nods. "Two days, Mr. Policeman," and releases his hand. "This act of faith, of trust from me, will be repaid. You understand?"

Tom nods.

"One day, friend Tom, one day I will ask something of you."

Downstairs Tom puts his clothes back on. They are cold and wet—he doesn't like to think about what the wet could be. He returns to Bradman's flat. It had all taken a little more than an hour. The reporter is still unconscious. Tom thinks of the beautiful human pincushion back at Franco's. He feels sick, but rolls up the reporter's sleeve, takes the needle and presses it into his arm.

Later, Franco tells his men that he will be alone with the cinnamon-colored beauty. There are sniggers and winks—each man knows why he wants to be alone with her. He tells them not to disturb him under any circumstance, and closes the doors to her room. She lies on the sofa in a drug-induced sleep. He sits beside her and draws her toward him, her head down to rest on his lap. He smoothes her hair and strokes her face. She means nothing to him. He would not kill for her, would not lift a finger for her. There is no one in the world he would risk himself for, no one for him to care if they live or die. With that thought in his head, he sheds a tear. The first since he was four years old.

TWENTY-SEVEN

Monday, October 11, 2010

Tom walks back into the cafe—at least he's dry now, after nearly twenty minutes of wringing out his clothes and keeping the air dryer going. He walks over to Keyson's table and sits down. The table is still strewn with photos and newspaper cuttings dating back to Dani's disappearance. He's seen all of the photos of Dani except one: her at some swanky party. She looks all dressed up. It's folded, he reaches out to it open it.

"No—no." Keyson puts his finger on it and slaps Tom's hand away. "Tea's cold, Tom. I'll get you another." He waves at the waitress who quickly comes over.

"Another tea for my friend and I'll have a black Americano. Candy—what biscuits do you have?"

"Rich tea, Bourbons, custard creams, Garibaldi . . ."

"That's it. Garibaldi—a plate of those, please."

The waitress skips off, eager to please.

As soon as she is out of earshot, Tom growls, "What's this about?"

"Oh, Tom, can't two old friends get together and chat?"

"We are not old friends. If that's all this is, then I'm off." He kicks his chair back with a squeal like fingernails on blackboard.

"Please sit down, Detective Superintendent Bevans, and you will learn something very much to your advantage."

He remains standing. "Just spit it out, Ke—" He dries up as Candy skips back with the plate of biscuits.

"Thank you, Candy," Keyson says with his night-time DJ voice. Candy oohs a bit, then leaves.

"I did not come here to watch you flirt with waitresses."

"No, but you did come." He smiles, knowing he has all the aces. "I have been retained by Patricia Lancing. You do know Patricia Lancing, don't you, Tom?"

Tom feels the skin tighten on his scalp. He sits back down.

"Her daughter was murdered and . . . well, you know all that, don't you?"

Tom remembers the two of them lying on the floor next to each other, heads almost touching. He remembers how good it felt to finally tell someone about Dani.

"You told me the story of your one true love—do you remember?"

Tom is silent. He looks coldly into the other man's eyes.

"The night, I believed, we became real friends." His eyes flash a deep anger. "If I recall correctly—she studied at Durham. Classics, wasn't it?"

"You know it was."

"You never told me her surname but . . . fancy her mother coming to me to look into her death. To help solve the twenty-year-old mystery."

"Marcus . . ."

"Of course, it could have been a coincidence, there may be many murdered Danis—but I told her I'd look into the case and I did. I went to Durham."

Tom's eyes widen. "You were there as a child. The coroner . . ."

"Yes. I shared that with you, didn't I? My mentor, my second father."

Tom breaks eye contact.

"I hadn't been back since his death. More than ten years but I still had contacts—he had been much respected. It wasn't difficult to get to see the case notes."

"Those are sealed—active officers only."

"Your name appears all over her case notes." He pulls a folder from the pile, Tom snatches it and leafs through. He recognizes his handwriting on most pages.

"I could charge you for having these."

"Possibly. You're probably right. I shouldn't have them."

"Here we are at last. These'll warm you up." Candy reappears with the drinks and places them down on the table. She seems not to notice the bubbling tension between the two men. She has unbuttoned her blouse a little.

"You are a treasure, Candy." Keyson winks.

She blushes and walks off.

"Excellent." Keyson picks up a biscuit and dunks it into his coffee. "Named after Giuseppe Garibaldi, you know."

"The man who unified Italy in the nineteenth century—I know."

"Tom—"

"Detective Superintendent Bevans, if you don't mind."

"Okay. Fine. Detective Superintendent. I have been retained by Patricia Lancing to help expose the killer of her daughter, Danielle Lancing, in February 1989. I have ascertained this is the same Dani you claimed to have loved—"

"Damn you, Marcus."

"Claimed would have married you—which was news to her mother."

Tom just catches himself in time—his fist balls and he wants, so much, to send it into this man's face. This . . . Calm, he must stay calm.

"Patricia Lancing has entrusted me with photos, newspaper

clippings and authorized me to access her daughter's case notes. I also have the coroner's report . . ." He pauses theatrically, relishing the flames of unease that lick across Tom Bevans's face. "And his examination notes. His personal examination notes."

"Where the hell did you get those?" Tom asks, angry to be so wrong-footed by Keyson.

"Oh, Tom, and you're one of the bright ones. I don't think that's actually important—what is crucial in finding the man responsible for your Dani's murder is discovering why the final report and the initial notes vary so much." He dunks another biscuit. "Because the funny thing—and it genuinely is a funny thing—is that these notes are full of inconsistencies, inaccuracies and blatant mistruths."

Tom sits there feeling himself shrink, little by little. He wants to say something but his mouth is parched and no words form.

"I have been able to piece together some of the story, the true story. I spoke to a retired sergeant, Ray Stone. You knew him a little, I believe. He ran the Durham evidence store back in 1989. Fascinating man; he has throat cancer and talks out of his neck with a stick. He said to say 'hello.' "

"Don't remember him."

"Tom!" Keyson wags a finger as if at a naughty schoolboy. "You have got to work on your poker face. How did you get where you are today?" He grins.

Tom gulps, he thinks the same sometimes.

"So you don't remember Sergeant Stone? Well, he remembers you."

"That's nice. If you have his address I'll add him to my Christmas card list."

"Oh good idea—then you'll need more stamps—I have another name to add. Journalist. Ben Bradman. Ring a bell?"

"Bradman," Tom whispers.

With a single finger Keyson slides one of the newspaper clippings around to face Tom. He recognizes it immediately as Bradman's *News of the World* story. Out of Tom's left eye slides a single tear.

"We talked for quite a while, he and I. He had a lot to say about you, Detective Superintendent Bevans, none of it complimentary. You know he didn't do well in prison, don't you?"

Tom says nothing. He knows that Bradman was sentenced to seven years and spent four years and eight months in prison before he was paroled. He knows, from reading the governor's reports, that he'd been beaten and sexually abused there. Tom lowers his eyes, not wanting Keyson to see the shame burning in them.

"I know nothing about him. I only met him the once."

"Quite a meeting, though. I should think every one of his nightmares ever since features you. I wouldn't have thought you had it in you, Tom. You devil."

Tom feels bile rise in his throat. "You know nothing about me, Keyson."

"But we were such good friends," he says with a frosty smile.

Tom wants to deny it and yet . . . and yet. "You betrayed that friendship."

"Me?" Keyson's face turns scarlet. "I betrayed you? Liar—you destroyed me. You dragged me through the mud and had me fired."

Tom stands quickly, pushes himself away from the table, scared.

"You threw away your career, Marcus, you did it to yourself."

With a squeal, Keyson pushes the table away so nothing stands between the two men—he reaches out to grab him by the throat.

"Is everything okay?" Candy is by Keyson's shoulder looking concerned. "Do you need . . . ?" She places her long fingers on his arm. Keyson pulls his arm away like it's been burned and turns— snarling at the interruption.

"Get the fuck back to—" He pulls his arm up to swat her away. Candy screams and shrinks back afraid.

"I'm sorry. So sorry. I—" He is immediately a civilized man again, but too late—she scampers back to the kitchen. A second later the chef emerges, a cleaver in his hand in case of trouble.

"Misunderstanding, nothing more. Sorry about that. We'll leave immediately. Maybe the bill?" He smiles his most winning smile. The chef grunts and walks back into the kitchen. Keyson swings back to Tom.

"No more time for niceties. Patricia Lancing, the mother of your one true love, came to me to help find her daughter's killer."

Tom nods. "Changes in DNA profiling. The potential for matching samples with—"

"Oh drop it, Tom. DNA technology—don't make me laugh. I don't need a fucking microscope to solve this mystery. I just need to look past the cover-up."

"What do you—"

"I've done it, Tom. I've found the killer of Danielle Lancing."

The blood drains from Tom Bevans's face.

Marcus Keyson smiles. "You killed her, Tom."

PART SIX

TWENTY-EIGHT

Monday, December 20, 2010

She watches them sleep. Her parents. It probably crosses a line, to sneak into the bedroom and watch them—Dani isn't sure her moral compass is so accurate these days. She sighs. They're both fully clothed. Her mother is wrapped in a blanket. She's drawn her legs up into her stomach, like a baby in the womb. Her father lies on the outer edge, almost falling off the bed, but his legs curl against Patty's and they hold hands.

"Did you know that otters sleep holding hands?" Dani remembers telling her parents that fact one day when she was five or six. For a long time afterward, at bedtime, she was an otter and her dad would hold her hand while she fell asleep.

She reaches out to their entwined hands—maybe she could. She holds her hand just above theirs—it looks as if the three hands are joined—but they aren't. She cannot grasp them and her hand slips through . . . she pulls it back. She can't feel, can't touch. Just watch. She knows she should be happy—if her parents could be together again, it would make her dad so happy. But what would it mean for her? Would he need her? He is her only link to the world—would she fade for him? Might she be completely alone? The thought fills her with dread. It's hard enough at night, being alone while he sleeps and having nothing to do but watch over him and blow the cobwebs of fear from him when the nightmares come. If he turns his back on her she will have nothing. Will she even exist with no anchor to life?

She looks out of the window. Snowflakes turn in the air once more. It will be dawn again soon—a new day. She closes her eyes and stretches out her hand to the glass; it slides through. She rises on her toes and leans—leans—leans forward and . . . she is through the glass and outside, in the air, falling? No, floating. Slowly she turns in the air like the snowflakes, twisting down, gravity has no effect on her, nor does the icy wind. She floats softly in the sky. A shooting star. There is a flash in her head—an explosion. She feels arms on her, holding her down—feels immense weight on her hips—something snaps. She hears a scream of pain—it must be her own voice. Hands squirm all over her, sharp pain in her arms—her wrists—smells of sweat, beer, sick. Her flesh is twisted, mouths bite her, suckle from her—a tongue forces into her mouth. White-hot, searing pain. She is violated. She falls through the air. The snow catches her. Her limbs and joints scream out—she burns. She opens her eyes. A face, a form.

"Tom?"

But he isn't there. Just a memory.

***

"Jim. I killed a man."

Patty's words ricochet around his head. Alongside him she sleeps. It took a while to fall under after her confession. She wept, she curled in his arms and wept. He feels guilty but it made him happy. To hold her again.

He has no idea what the time is, but can see a dim light seep through the crack of the curtains. His body would appreciate more sleep but his mind is doing star-jumps. Patty killed a man.

He heads downstairs. In the kitchen he opens cupboard after

cupboard—desperate for coffee. It's a kitchen with a lot of storage, but it's mostly empty. There isn't even any salt or pepper.

"Oh, thank you, Saint Java," he exclaims when he finally strikes gold. In a scrunched up carrier bag, stuck down the back of the sink, he finds an old, half-empty jar of Nescafé. It's nestled in the bag alongside a pile of individually wrapped plastic cutlery, a mound of sugar sachets and about twenty little ketchup pots and a mayonnaise dip with a sell-by date that passed three years ago. He pulls out the coffee jar and, with some effort, unscrews the lid. Inside the granules are congealed into a solid lump. He tries to hack some out with a plastic knife but it just snaps. So he boils some water—in a saucepan—and pours it into the jar. The granules start to dissolve and he pours them into a cup. He sips at the coffee—it's disgusting, but he still drinks it.

"Jim. I killed a man."

"Slow down, Patty. Tell me slowly."

"Tom came to see me."

"Tom . . . Tom Bevans?"

"He told me that Dani's case would be reviewed—that there was a new way of analyzing evidence samples."

"Hang on, Tom told you. Was he talking as a policeman, was it an official visit?"

"Yes, it was official. He said he wanted to do it himself rather than send some family officer."

"So . . ." Jim's head reels. "What did he say?"

"That a team, a dead case team, in Durham will investigate."

"That's wond—"

"Jim, he said it could be years. Another four years."

"It's already been twenty."

"I can't do another four years. I won't."

"So . . . what did . . . ?"

"I hired someone. An ex–police pathologist named Keyson. He knew who to talk to and who to bribe."

There is silence while the last piece of information sinks in.

"And?" Jim asks—suspecting that he doesn't want to know the answer.

"He found a suspect, a prime suspect, someone the police had thought could be the murderer. They had been almost sure but there wasn't enough evidence. But they had samples from Dani. Samples that were useless back then, but now—now could prove his guilt. They could catch him. I could . . . I could . . ." Silent tears flow.

"Patty." He reaches out to her but she pulls away.

"It wasn't him."

"We can look ag—"

"You don't understand. His photo—it's on the cover of every Sunday paper."

"Why?"

"He's dead. Jim, I killed him."

Jim feels cold in his bones as he cradles the coffee. He isn't going to drink any more, he just wants the warmth. He stands in the kitchen unraveling last night's conversation. She'd kidnapped a man and killed him. That was what triggered her seizure. He feels scared all of a sudden. He heads to the living room, he needs to see the man who threatens to take his wife away again.

The floor is strewn with shredded newspaper. He bends down and pulls out yesterday's *Sunday Times*. Only the headline is legible: HEATHROW TORTURE MAN IDENTIFIED.

"Christ, Patty."

Under that is the *Observer*. The front page is also obliterated, but on page three there's a photograph. A man in his early six-ties, close-cropped hair, bullet-shaped head. His name is Duncan Cobhurn.

"Oh my God." Jim recognizes the face, knows the man. He wants to be sick; he needs air. He pulls open the curtains and—there's a body lying in the snow outside.

"Dani!" Jim runs to the front door and out, around the side of the house and into the garden.

"Dani." He stands over her. Her lips are blue, eyes closed—skin pale. She looks like she did in the morgue. That awful day when he—

"Dad." She opens her eyes, they brim with fear. "I saw them. They hurt me, they hurt me so much."

"Dani." He desperately wants to hold her.

"They laughed, Dad, they held me and wouldn't stop and . . . Tom. I saw him too."

"What? When?"

But Dani's eyes are taken by the scrunched-up paper Jim still holds. She sees the photo and her eyes widen.

"Dad, why—why is there a picture of Duncan in the—"

Jim pulls it away but she's seen the caption.

"Murdered? Duncan murdered?"

"She—" Jim clams up.

"She? Christ! What happened, Dad?"

TWENTY-NINE

Friday, September 30, 1988

Jim has a key; the landlord sent it after he called. The van he's borrowed is parked downstairs. Inside there's a ladder, dustsheets, two tool kits, filler and plaster, primer and paint—lots of paint. He loads himself up with as much as he can possibly carry and takes them up—clanking all the way like the Tin Man. He only wants a heart. He manages to juggle it all at the front door, and he slides the key home and pushes the door open.

He only gets a few steps inside when the bedroom door flies open and a blur rushes out: a man, naked except for a towel that he's still tucking round himself.

"Who the fuck are you?" he shouts at Jim.

"I . . . I'm sorry, this was meant to be—" he starts to explain when another figure appears from the bedroom, wrapping a sheet around her. It's Dani. Jim sees red.

"Dad, don't!" Dani screams.

"Dad?" the man says, as Jim drops the paint and pulls back a fist.

The naked man responds by holding his hands up in surrender—his towel falls off. He stands there naked and smiling. Jim hits him in the face—a knockdown.

"Dad!" Dani shouts and drops down next to the naked man. "I'm sorry, darling," she says to the naked man, using the corner of the sheet to wipe a stripe of blood from his lip.

"Dani. What th—" starts Jim.

"Dad, just go."

"But—"

"Now."

Jim doesn't move. He looks down at the man he's punched. He's at least forty years old. He's shorter than Jim, squatter but more toned with muscular legs, like a rugby player. His hair is short, graying and there's the beginning of a bald patch at the back.

"Bloody cavemen," Dani tells them both, talking to them like naughty children. She helps the fallen man to his feet. He wraps the towel back around himself and holds it securely.

"This is my father, Jim Lancing. Dad, this is Duncan. Duncan Cobhurn."

Duncan holds out his free hand to shake—Jim keeps his hands by his side.

"Okay, so we're going to play that game." Dani bites at her lip. "Dad, please go over the road. There's a cafe there—the Grange. It's okay, nice eggs. We'll be over in twenty minutes."

"Just you, not . . . him. I'd like to talk to you."

She pauses.

"That sounds like a good idea." The naked man squeezes her hand. She gives him a small nod, then turns back to Jim.

"Just me. I'll be over soon."

Jim grunts something and leaves.

❄

In the kitchen of the Grange Cafe is a tall, skinny man. Serving out front is a bubbly young woman who gives Jim a big smile when he walks in. He sits at a table; in the middle is a laminated hand-written menu propped up between two globes, red ketchup and brown sauce. He picks up the menu but can't read it; his brains are scrambled. The waitress gives him a minute before coming over, notepad in hand.

"What can I get for you?"

"Coffee."

"No food?" She looks very disappointed.

"I'm waiting for my daughter."

She trots off, leaving Jim to stew.

Twenty minutes later Dani arrives. Jim's pleased to see she's alone. She sits down opposite him. He looks over to the waitress and for a second can see a strange look flick across her face. Confusion? Had she seen his daughter in here with an older man before? Had she thought they were father and daughter? The look is replaced, almost instantaneously, by a smile. They both order a cheese and onion omelette with chips.

"The omelettes are good here," Dani tells him once the waitress has retreated.

"Good."

"You came to decorate. A surprise for me. That was really nice of you."

He shrugs. "I thought you were in the Isle of Wight."

"My plans changed. I should have let you know."

"You . . . no. No, you weren't to know. That's why they call them surprises."

"And the surprise was on you," she tries to joke. It falls flat.

They sit in silence. The waitress brings Dani a herbal tea.

"You look . . . you look well," Jim finally tells her. And she does. He can see that her hair has been cut recently, her fingernails aren't bitten down like they have been the last few times he'd seen her. She's even put on weight—she actually looks a little cuddly rather than being lanky and gazelle-like. He likes it—makes her look more like Patty. All her life people have said Dani looks like Jim, and she does, but he can see Patty there too. He likes this new look.

She smiles. "I'm happy, Dad."

"Dani, I really don't mean to pry or anything, but—"

"Shut up, Dad." She doesn't say it with any malice or anger. "Please let me say some things."

Jim zips his lips, like he used to when she was a girl. It makes her smile.

"You think I'm being stupid, don't you?"

"Dan—"

"Listen, Dad. Look, I know how awful all that shit with Seb was—I will never forget what you did for me then. You saved me, but that's over. I've grown up so much in the las—"

The waitress walks over with the omelettes. Dani stops talking while she waits for her to leave.

"I know he's older than me—he's forty-four."

"He's my bloody age."

"Dad. His name's Duncan. He imports furniture, rugs and tapestries from the Mediterranean. He's really successful. Don't look like that, Dad."

"Forty-four?"

"Don't you trust me?"

Jim sucks air in through his teeth. Reluctantly he nods.

"He loves me, Dad. I love him. He's proposed."

"Oh, Dani." Jim throws his cutlery down. The clatter echoes through the cafe, causing the waitress and cook to look over.

"Butterfingers," he says loudly, waving the digits. The waitress smiles and she and the cook go back to reading magazines.

"Don't you want me to be happy?" Dani asks in little more than a whisper.

"That isn't fair, darling."

"It is. It's all about trust, Dad. This isn't like with Seb."

"I should bloody hope not—you swore to me that would never happen again."

"And it won't, Dad. I am not the same person I was then. You helped me so much when I needed you. But Duncan has too. He knows all about it, all about how awful it was and he's kept me sane and . . . I love him, Dad. He loves me."

"And he said he wants to marry you."

She nods and then drops her eyes again.

"What? Dani, what?"

She doesn't reply. Instead she holds up her left hand and wiggles the ring finger.

"You are joking? Oh, Dani."

Father and daughter eat their omelettes in silence.

***

"The chips were good," Jim says finally, when both plates are licked clean.

"Tony's the cook and owner," she points at the tall, skinny man. "He double cooks them for crispiness. His lasagne's great too."

"With chips?"

"Of course—what else do you eat with lasagne?" She smiles.

"I told your mum I'd be gone till Friday. The plan was to do repairs today, then paint tomorrow and touch up any last-minute things Friday morning before going home."

"Duncan's gone. I told him I'd call tomorrow . . . maybe we could . . ."

"Decorate together?"

She nods and smiles.

He remembers the fun they had. There was no more talk of Duncan and there was no more talk of Seb Merchant. They listened to the radio and worked. Mostly Radio 1, but they switched to local stations to avoid Dave Lee Travis. When they were tired, they went out for food and beers, and in the evening they listened to John Peel. It was the last of the good times. After that, there was only that awful Christmas and then . . .

THIRTY

"Dani. Please, let's go inside. I'm freezing."

"Not until you tell me what happened to Duncan."

"He . . ." Jim shakes his head. "Could he have been responsible for your death?"

"No." Her eyes flash. Jim has not seen her angry once in the last twelve years—but she is now. The paleness of her skin is burned away as the anger rises.

"He wanted to marry me, Dad. You know that."

Jim feels sick to his stomach. So many secrets, so much unsaid. "I never told your mum about him. I hoped it would end, that you'd realize he was too old for you."

"I loved him."

"He . . ." Jim feels shame creep in on top of the cold. "He was the prime suspect in your murder."

"He wouldn't . . ."

"The police didn't realize you were . . . lovers."

The snow starts again, falling into Jim's hair—the flakes drift through Dani.

"Samples were taken—when you died."

"From me?"

"Yes. The man left . . . anyway, they couldn't test the samples then. They can now."

"The man who . . ."

" . . . could be found. Yes. That's what your mum was trying to do. She bribed a man to get the samples and then . . ." Jim stops. He is shaking. "She needed to test them against the prime suspect."

"Duncan?"

"She tied him up . . ." He doesn't need to finish—Dani can see where he's headed.

"Oh my God!"

"Dani."

"Mum killed him."

"She was doing it for you."

"Mum killed him."

"She didn't know . . ."

"She didn't know he wanted to marry me," Dani says in the smallest voice. She looks at her father, so full of sadness. Then she fades.

"Dani," he calls, "Dani, don't go. Please come back. Dani!" But he knows it's futile. "Dani."

She looks at herself in the mirror, remembering the excitement she felt seeing his blood smeared over her face—like a mask, a super-hero's mask. The Red Revenger—when was that, two days ago? Now there is none of that hope, none of that energy. She flew too close to the sun and fell. She has failed.

In the bedroom she stands and watches him sleep. Jim, the white knight who came to save her. What mess has she gotten him into now? What further misery will she pile on his head? She'd like to lie back down, snuggle into him, let him protect her, just for a day. Or two. But no. He looks so innocent lying there. He looks like Dani. She has failed them both. She slides down the wall, her legs suddenly jelly-like. It should all be over now. Roberta was supposed to confirm his guilt and then—armed with that proof—she was to take her revenge. End his life as he ended Dani's. And then . . . then Patty was to leave his stinking corpse, go home, finish the letter on her computer—the story of his crime and punishment. Then . . . then . . . then . . . she can't even say it to herself. But now? Oh Christ—it breaks on her like a tsunami—she has killed an innocent man. She is as bad as Dani's killer. She knows there is only one thing she can do, but . . . Dani will never be revenged. Never.

"Jim. Jim." A hand shakes his shoulder. "It's five in the afternoon. I thought I'd better wake you."

He rolls over, opens his eyes—it's all a bit blurry and dark.

"Five?" He can't believe what she said. Something's wrong—and then he realizes the problem: he slept well. No nightmare.

"When did you fall asleep?" she asks.

"I . . . I don't know. I went downstairs to look for coffee."

"Did you find any?"

"None that was fit for human consumption."

"Oh well, if you're going to be picky . . ." She leaves the room.

He remembers the morning: finding the newspaper, seeing Duncan Cobhurn's picture. Dani's pain. He rolls over and walks downstairs.

He finds her in the lounge—she is staring out the window. "Is this the man you killed?" He holds the newspaper—the same photograph Dani saw.

Patty nods. "An innocent man." Her eyes hollow out with the memory of his death—bound and gagged, blood oozing from his hand.

Jim shakes his head. "Maybe he wasn't so innocent."

"I had his DNA matched with the killer's—not the same." She crosses her arms across her chest. "Last night you were great, when I needed you . . ." She stops. He can see how hard she's trying to keep herself together.

"Patty, we can—"

"I'm a murderer. I need to call the police and confess."

"Patty?"

"Jim. He has a wife. Can you imagine how our lives would be different if the police had found the man who killed Dani? If we hadn't had all that worry—not knowing why. All that time I searched . . ."

"Dani's death wasn't an accident—this was."

"Was it?" Patty asks, looking frightened. "I almost slit his throat there in the chair. I tied him, cut him and left him with no water or food—pumped up to the gills with horse tranquilizer. How does that sound like an accident?"

"I . . ." The brutality of Patty's words stops him short. "I don't know. I don't care. I just don't want to lose you again."

"Jim." Her eyes flare. She wants to tell him he lost her twenty years ago. Last night was just an echo of something long dead.

"Patty, don't decide now. Just spend the day with me."

She can't say no, it's what she wants more than anything in the world.

Jim showers first, then Patty. She stays in that stream until the hot water is exhausted. How can a person feel so happy and so sad, all in the same moment? She loves Jim, she has throughout the last forty years, and she can have him back. But at what cost?

When she gets downstairs, Jim is in the kitchen and the room is filled with mouth-watering smells. He's run out to the shops, bought a pile of newspapers, fresh coffee and a coffee maker, eggs, bread and cheese. There are these tiny little tomatoes and olives with a box of salad leaves, plus little pre-cooked potatoes with basil. It all looks very year-in-Provence-y. He has the plates warming in the oven like Patty's mum always did when entertaining guests. Posh.

"Can I do something?"

He shakes his head. "Just sit down."

"Where? I don't have a dining table."

She goes to her bookcase and pulls out two large coffee-table books, *A Pictorial Journey Around the Galapagos Islands* and *The Bloody Monks.*

"We can use these as trays."

Patty watches as he efficiently pulls plates from the oven, flips an omelette and slices it in two. Molten cheese oozes from the wound. He scatters some leaves on the plate and spoons quartered tomatoes, olives and pesto-covered potatoes on the leaves.

"That looks like a painting," she says, a little awed. "My stomach is growling."

He shrugs. "Let's hope it tastes okay."

As soon as the plate is in Patty's hands, she tears into the food. She eats ravenously.

Jim watches, amazed. "There's no more, but I could knock some up quickly."

"Toast. I really want some toast. Is there any butter?"

He nods and starts to rise.

"No, eat yours. I can make toast." But even as she says it, she wonders if she actually can. She hasn't made it in more than twenty years, but surely it's something you don't forget.

She walks into the kitchen and stops dead. She has no idea if she has a toaster. She assumes she doesn't but looks around, just in case. There's a sliced loaf on the side, another of Jim's purchases, and she pulls out two slices and puts them under the grill. The oven came with the house and she has barely used it—just the hob. For years she has literally lived on tea and sandwiches or soup bought from Marks and Spencer. She can't remember the last time she was hungry—really hungry—craving sustenance. Jim walks into the kitchen to see her finish her fourth round of toast and popping two more under the grill.

"I can't stop." She laughs, as tears run down her cheeks. "I can taste it too," she says with astonishment. "It tastes good. Better than good. It tastes, I don't remember the last time I actually tasted something."

He says nothing, but pours himself more coffee and returns to the living room. She eats four more rounds of toast before leaving the kitchen to find him. He sits there, sipping coffee and scouring the newspapers for news of Duncan Cobhurn's murder.

Patty pulls the paper from his hands and slips onto his lap. She takes his head in her hands—there is a symmetry between this and Duncan Cobhurn—she held his head like this, but then his glassy eyes didn't look back. Now Jim's eyes brim with hope and love and sadness and . . . and . . . she kisses him.

***

"Jim, the funeral is next Tuesday. I need to go."

"No. Please, it's crazy."

"A whole week away. I'll see her, see his friends and family and . . . decide."

Decide whether to confess. It means she loses all this. Loses Jim, and any chance of justice for Dani.

"Patty . . ."

"Jim, let's have Christmas. We can have a week without any mention of Duncan Cobhurn or his family or—anything. Just us. Then we can talk about this and plan what will happen on Tuesday. But let's just have Christmas. You can love me like it's 1979."

THIRTY-ONE

Saturday, December 25, 2010

They walk hand-in-hand through Greenwich Park at dawn. There's still snow under the trees and frozen leaves crack underfoot. They have had five days together. They went to the zoo, up in the London Eye at twilight and walked the length and breadth of the National Gallery, Tate Modern and St. Paul's. They've eaten Vietnamese and Thai food and, after so many years apart, they made love. They have not spoken once about Duncan Cobhurn—in fact, they have not talked about the last twenty years at all. They have talked about their friends at university, especially Ed and Jacks. They've laughed, sung, and people-watched. They agreed not to buy presents for each other, though both have a little something tucked away at home for after breakfast. The last two nights they've spent back at the family home, the home they bought together some thirty-five years before. Now they walk. There is nothing to say—they both just bask in the other's presence.

At the crest of the hill they stop and look out over the sweep of London. They have always loved this spot, this view over the park into the heart of the city. He feels her hand slip from his, but he is lost in thought. He is thinking about Duncan Cobhurn—about him and Dani. Jim still has not told Patty about those days decorating with Dani. He wishes now that he had told her the truth all those years ago, but then it was Dani's secret. Just like the trouble with Seb Merchant had been their shared secret. He had not wanted Patty to worry, either time. But knowledge of both worry him. He needs to tell . . .

"Aaaaah!" His face is wet and freezing. Patty scoops up another handful of snow and shoves it right in his face.

"Patty!"

"No. You were being maudlin. It's Christmas."

"You sound like Noddy Holder."

"Do not take his name in vain."

They both laugh. Patty scoops up another handful and cups it—pressing the snow into a ball.

"You dare!"

It hits him in the chest. "Oh, you asked for it." He starts to gather his own snowball. It's war.

An hour later they reach home. Both are frozen, covered in snow and happy.

"Go get changed," he tells her. "I'll make hot chocolate."

Patty goes upstairs and Jim walks into the kitchen. He stands there, quietly, listening. He whispers to the air: "Dani? Where are you?"

He has not seen his daughter since he told her of Duncan Cobhurn's death. He misses her. Cannot bear the memory of the sadness on her face. It reminds him of one other time, soon after she came to live with him.

"Can you tell me?" he had asked.

She thought for a second, her nose crinkling with concentration.

"I don't know what to say, Dad. I don't remember what it felt like. It just all changed, slipped away and . . . I think I just winked out from one way of being and then there was something else. I just wasn't alive anymore."

He had nodded at her words, but doesn't really understand them.

"I used to see you, just catch a glimpse of you in a crowd."

"I kept my eye on you."

"Why?"

"I was worried. You seemed so sad."

"Did you watch your mum?"

"Not really. She was stronger."

"It was her that fell apart when you died."

"Yes. That surprised me, really."

"Then you came back properly. After your mum and I . . ." He paused, the pain of that time shifting in his chest once more. "Why did you come back to me?"

"You called me."

"Did I?"

She nodded.

"I needed you." He sighed then looked sadly at his daughter. "Was there pain?"

"Oh, Dad, you keep asking that. If there was I don't remember, and it doesn't make any difference now."

"And the man who . . ."

"Dad!" She dropped her head. They had agreed he would not ask that again. "I told you I don't know. I can't remember." She kept her head down for a while then raised it and smiled at him— that beautiful open smile.

The memory of her fades and Jim is alone in the kitchen once more. "Where are you, Dani? Have you remembered more?" he asks the air. There is no answer.

It's 11 p.m., Christmas night. One hour left of their holiday from life and responsibility. Tomorrow reality will wash back in. Today they have made love, watched twenty minutes of *The Great Escape* on TV and made a roast dinner. Now, they are back in the park, where the day started. The sky is black, yet the scene is ablaze with lights and the occasional firework that arcs into the darkness above the cityscape. Jim and Patty came prepared for the cold. They have a Thermos of hot coffee and several blankets. Jim puts a bin-bag on the bench and then a blanket. They sit and pile the other blankets on top of themselves.

"Tomorrow . . ." Patty starts.

"Shh. No tomorrow, just tonight."

They snuggle together and watch the city lights wink at them until the cold finally sneaks into their bones. Then Jim pulls a bag from under the bench.

"I was wondering what you had in there."

"I hope it still works."

Jim pulls out a black case, which he flips open to reveal a little portable record player.

"Oh my God. The Dansette Transit. You kept it?"

"I kept everything. Here." He pulls out a cloth bag and places it alongside the record player, then pulls out a small, shiny vinyl disc.

"You haven't—"

"1963, 'Heatwave' by Martha and the Vandellas."

"You romantic bastard."

"Birmingham University dance hall. You were all Peter, Paul and Mary."

She laughs. "And you were all Johnny Cash, Man in Black."

"But we danced to Martha and the Vandellas. Our first dance."

She shakes her head. "You're crazy."

"And Elvis, the Beatles."

"Even Cliff Richard." She makes a gagging face.

He puts the needle on the record, and through the hiss and crackle, the song starts.

"Dance with me?" he asks and holds out his hand. Patty nods and takes his hand, melting into him. In the cold of the wee small hours, they dance.

When the song ends, Patty lifts the needle and starts it again. They dance six times to the same song, before Jim suddenly stops and pulls out his phone.

"Who are you calling?"

Jim holds his hand up to quieten her as he listens to the phone ring for ages before it's answered.

"Hello. Who's that?" a sleepy voice asks.

"Listen to this." Jim puts the needle back on and places the phone close to the little speaker.

"Is that you, Martha?" the voice on the other end croaks.

"What's going on?" a second voice, more distant, and very sleepy, comes from the phone.

"Do you remember, Ed, November 1963, Birmingham University?"

"I remember an old friend from those days who must be fucking dead because he hasn't called me in years."

"Merry Christmas, Ed. Love to Jacks."

"I think you owe us at least eight birthdays and Christmases."

"It's almost midnight," Jacks says, with sleepy annoyance, in the background.

"Is there a point to this call, Jim?" says Ed. "We could have a pint next week or have you got some horrible terminal disease and you're running down memory lane before you snuff it tomorrow?"

"I'm in Greenwich Park, dancing in the dark with my wife."

"Remarried—good for you. I hope she's a looker." He whispers to Jacks, "New wife."

"Congratulations. Now let us get back to sleep!" shouts Jacks.

Patty grabs the phone. "No, still the same old wife."

At home in Dorset, Ed and Jacks jump up in bed like they've been electrocuted.

"Patty?"

"I think the object of this call is to ask you to dance with us again," she says.

"It's almost bloody midnight. I'm sixty-five," Ed says in disbelief.

"We all are," says Patty. "Isn't it great?"

She puts the phone back down by the Dansette and lifts the needle again. She drops it on the first groove and takes her husband in her arms to dance.

In a bedroom 134 miles away, a couple who have not danced together in a long, long time, get out of bed. They put on the speakerphone and dance with their oldest friends.

When the song ends, both couples kiss and Ed takes the phone.

"We love you. Let's get together soon. I think we have both really missed you. But now bugger off so we can get some sleep."

"We love you too," Jim tells them before he ends the call. He stands there for a while, silent, thinking about his oldest friend.

"What else do you have?" Patty asks.

Jim opens the bag and looks through. "Carole King, Four Tops, Diana Ross, Donovan . . ."

"Anything. You decide. I need to pee." Patty runs off behind a bush. Jim continues to fish through the bag until he finds something that makes his heart skip a beat. He pulls it out and looks at it in the moonlight.

"I remember that from my first party."

Jim turns to see his daughter standing there.

"Good to see you," he tells her.

"Do you remember? I danced to it with . . ."

"Gary, Gary Rohr. Buck teeth."

"My first kiss." She smiles, remembering such an innocent time. Behind her there is a flare of firework from somewhere behind Canary Wharf.

"Come up and see me . . ." he starts.

" . . . make me smile," she finishes.

He puts it on. Steve Harley's unmistakable voice cuts through the air. Jim holds his hand out and the ghost drifts over. Without touching the two of them move and spin together.

They dance until Patty returns and steps through her daughter's image, making it shatter into a million fragments, to take her husband's hands and dance with him.

"This was . . ." she starts.

" . . . Dani's favorite," he finishes her sentence.

THIRTY-TWO

Sunday, December 26, 2010

They danced in the park and watched the stars until four that morning before they went home. Now, at 2 p.m., they sit surrounded by newspapers and with a laptop open. They are back in the rushing of time that is real life. Patty sits at the table, head down over her laptop, searching, intently scrolling and noting down things in a small Moleskine notebook. Jim stands to the side, alternating his gaze from the road outside to the side of his wife's head, his mind in an absolute turmoil.

"What are you looking for?" he asks. "What are you hoping to find?"

"I don't know," she tells him, though she knows full well what she's searching for. She wants to see photographs of the wife . . . widow. Ideally two photos: before and after; happy and sad—the eternal opposites.

The first would be the couple, together and happy. The second would be of her alone, after his death. Patty wants to see her grief.

"Bloody hell, that sounds sick," she thinks. "Why do I need to see that?" But she knows the answer: because she wants to judge her sorrow.

In her own wallet she has two photographs of herself. She never leaves home without them, though she hasn't looked at them for a very long time. She just needs to know they're there. The first shows her happy . . . no, not happy, that is far too bland a word. She is absolutely ecstatic—caught in a moment of rapture with her husband and her child. She is whooping, whooping with delight. Her perfect child has just won the English prize at school and Patty dreams she will follow her into writing, noble writing for great causes, something to make her so very proud. Patty can close her eyes and see that photo in every detail. It is taken in the grand hall of her school. Dani is about twelve and is standing on the stage holding a cup aloft—her prize. Slightly behind her are Jim and Patty. Jim stoops slightly to make sure his head is in the picture. His hair is still a brilliant black, he's dressed like a cut-price Steve McQueen—he looks great. Patty has long hair—probably the longest she ever wore it. It suits her, spilling over her shoulders. She wears a clingy dress—a floral pattern that shows off her fuller figure; hourglass many people called it. Patty knows it's her and yet she barely recognizes herself.

It's the woman in the second photograph, the *after* image, taken maybe three years ago and thirty years after the first, who she recognizes in the mirror today. Sat alongside the first photo, it reminds her of some champion slimmer standing next to the cardboard cutout of their former giant self. The contrast between the two Pattys, especially in the face, scares her a little—showing how the acid of loss strips away the flesh, etches the lines of pain and rage into the body. This is how she judges pain and loss. And that is why she must see Audrey Cobhurn. To weigh up her loss like a butcher judging a cut of meat. But the search yields nothing. There is only a half-turned shot of her from her husband's failed election bid. It tells Patty nothing.

"I've got to go to the funeral," she says.

"You won't do anything stupid though, will you?" he asks nervously. "You won't confess without talking to me first?"

"No," she lies.

In the middle of the night Patty wakes. Jim is curled into her, as if they are one body. His body heat keeping her warm.

"I must remember this, all this. If nothing else, I must never let this memory go," she tells herself.

She can see what it means to him—he sees it as the continuation of a forty-year love affair. He's the romantic one. For Patty it's new and exciting, a final fling before everything rusts away or falls off; something that can live away from the burden of their previous life together. Could she ever be that Patricia again?

She slips out of the bed, as quietly as she can. As her flesh pulls away from his, she feels the separation—the pop of the skin disengaging. It makes her heart dip.

She walks downstairs as quietly as she can and makes her way to the den. The curtains are not drawn here, and moonlight illuminates the room. What she sees most in the room—in the whole house—are the missing things. Once upon a time this room had been filled with photographs, certificates, diplomas and trophies. Dani had been a winner. If she ever sees this room again she will replace those pictures. The time for grieving is long gone. They should remember their beautiful girl and sing her praises to the heavens—not hide her away like they're ashamed of her.

She walks over to the fish tank—well, ex-fish tank. Dani used to keep her beautiful little friends in here. Jet-propelled flashes of neon that would fascinate her for hours and hours. That was before running became her big passion. At some point, when she was about twelve, they stopped replacing the ones that died. After about a year they were all gone and the tank was drained. No one wanted to get rid of it and so the bottom was spread with soil and brightly colored stones. Then exotic cacti were planted—the kinds that would be all right after you left them for months with no care.

Patty pushes her long, slim fingers down inside the tank. Through the stones and into the soil, the dry soil. She moves her fingers like worms through the crumbling bed until she finds the buried treasure. She had placed it there many years before. The memory of that day shames her.

She had been sitting at the kitchen table. It was early; she had barely slept—again. She was smoking—again. She had promised Jim she wouldn't smoke in the house but . . . but what? She had thought: "Fuck him and his stupid rules."

He had come down and seen her sitting there, wreathed in smoke. He hadn't said a word, just looked at her, a pained expression on his face like a fucking martyr. She took the cigarette and ground it out in her own hand. It hurt. She had wanted a reaction, wanted him to scream at her: "You idiot, you stupid self-obsessed cow, you weak, feeble woman. If you want to harm yourself then do it properly, kill yourself and do the world a favor."

He hadn't screamed. He had said nothing like that. Instead he cleaned the wound, slathered it in antiseptic cream and bound it in a bandage. All the while looking at Patty with love and compassion. It was then that she knew she had to leave him. When he left the house that morning she packed a small bag, wrote a note and, lastly, walked over to the cacti tank.

She blows on the treasure, removing the little bits of soil attached to it. It's still a little grubby but seems fine. She slips it back onto the second finger of her left hand. Perhaps she could try to be that Patty again.

THIRTY-THREE

Tuesday, December 28, 2010

She drives to Durham. She leaves plenty of time and so arrives early at the churchyard. She stands outside and waits. She's well insulated against the cold, but still finds herself hopping from foot to foot and clapping to keep the blood circulating. She sucks in the chill air and feels it burn her throat a little.

The church itself is impressive, flint and cobble hewn from the earth and tamed into a house of worship. The churchyard looks ancient; the headstones are a little like medieval teeth and tree roots have burrowed beneath them forcing them to stick out at odd angles. It is a dramatic place to be laid to rest; a dramatic place to be unmasked as a murderer too.

Patty has a story all worked out if anybody asks who she is, or why she's there. She'll be Carol, Carol Plimpton, née Hawkins. She worked with Duncan a long time ago, before he set up on his own. She carries no identification and, once again, all her clothes are from a charity shop, except the underwear.

It's a long time since she's walked inside a church, years, and much longer since an event of joy beckoned her in. In her twenties and thirties it was weddings, then christenings; now it's funerals. She's stopped attending obsequies though, now she sends condolences, in a few instances a tasteful floral tribute, but she can't attend in person. There were two or three funerals of contemporaries from university; she went but found she had to fake compassion, pretend some sadness; it made her face ache and stomach churn. Of course, there was another reason: she was avoiding Jim. The last funeral she attended was seven or eight years ago. Poor Connie Tunstall, the woman who was responsible for Patty and Jim meeting, though of course Patty knew Connie kicked herself for that. Connie had always had a thing for Jim. And of course Jim had been there too and . . . she had hated seeing him then. Why? She smiles. These last few days things have begun to get clearer—clearer than they've been for twenty years. She did not want to see him for fear he would cheer her up. How idiotic, to be so married to grief.

"Christ, am I going to be cursed with epiphanies now that I'm a murderer?" she laughs to herself. Then she remembers Audrey Cobhurn and feels ashamed by her flippancy. Her head swims a little and she walks further into the churchyard, all the way to the wall that separates the church from the farm. She looks out and sees beauty all around. She sniffs the air; it's tinged with that scorched leaf smell she remembers from childhood and knows that somewhere there must be a bonfire. She remembers that there used to be a man at the end of the street who roasted chestnuts on a brazier. The smell drove the kids wild, but Patty remembers that when she finally tried some they were disappointing. The hot, sweet nuts were not as tasty as the smell they gave off. In her mind that man was always there, in the street, ringing his bell and yelling through all seasons, but it can only have been December and maybe January too. In summertime it was Tonibell ice cream.

Duncan Cobhurn is being interred in the earth. Patty finds that surprising. She thought everyone was burned nowadays, that there was no room left for the brittle dust of mortal remains. But she does understand it. The thing about burial is that there's somewhere to visit, a plot to tend and make beautiful. She would have liked to have had Dani buried so there was somewhere to go . . . but she was *unavailable* for the funeral planning. Jim made the decisions. Now, each year on Dani's birthday, Patty goes to a park, always alone. She knows that Jim goes to a garden of remembrance where Dani's ashes were scattered but Patty doesn't want to go with him. Especially not to somewhere that celebrates her death. Instead, Patty goes to a park, the closest point she can get to where Dani was born. The hospital itself was pulled down years ago and is now a supermarket. She went in there once. Worked out that Dani was born in the deli section. It could have been worse; feminine hygiene and incontinence were close by. Patty bought some cold cuts, salami, breaded ham and a baguette. She thought about eating them there and then, but it seemed a little crass. Instead she walked outside and wandered around the area, until she found a little park.

She sat in there, that first time, and ate and thought of Dani. She went back a week later—this time she had a sapling with her, in a plastic bag. The man at the garden center said it was really sturdy and would grow quickly. She also bought a little spade plus that stuff like chicken wire you see around baby trees. She dug a hole, popped the tree in, then pushed the soil back and put the coil of wire around it. There's no plaque or anything, but Patty know it's hers. It has thrived over the years and now gives enough shade in the summer to allow her to picnic underneath.

Cars begin to arrive, a fleet of them sweeping in formation like geese headed for home. Black. Traditional. The first setting the speed, slow and dignified. One by one they sweep in and park.

Only when all the cars stop, does a tall, silver-haired man with military bearing walk forward and open a door. Patty can see why he became a funeral director. She immediately trusts him; maybe she should tell him she's the murderer and get it all over and done with.

"Christ, Patty, that's not funny," Jim's voice-in-her-head tells her.

From the phalanx of cars there is now a steady pouring of black suits into the courtyard around the church. Some walk straight in, others take the opportunity for one last cigarette before they receive the reminder of their mortality. Patty insinuates herself into a clump of middle-aged mourners and they file in.

"Just look at her if you have to, but please, please, do not try and speak to her. Please," Jim had asked her that morning.

"Okay, fine," she had said without meaning it.

The church interior is just as impressive as the outside, with delicate stained glass and tapestries that shimmer across the walls. The pews are ornate and each one has a series of hand-embroidered cushions on them depicting a Bible scene.

"Hope I get Sodom and Gomorrah," Patty thinks.

The most impressive part of the church, however, is the carved Jesus which towers over the congregation, his face a bloody mask of pain, his blood congealed to gore in puckered orbits on hands and feet. Arms outstretched to . . . to what? Absolve, condemn? He is a wooden man, spindly, grotesque, a mahogany Pinocchio with no strings to hold him down. He dominates the room, his eyes following Patty around, seeming to say: murderer. She takes a seat toward the back, away from the altar and the towering Jesus, but on the aisle close to the exit.

Funereal black is a lifesaver. She is bulked up: three jumpers, jacket and then a black suit. Huge and baggy without the padding, but with it . . . grieving fat woman. The ensemble is topped off with a black hat and veil from Cat Rescue. Patty had hoped the body would be on show—she had wanted to see his face one last time but this is no open-casket freak show.

Slowly, a trickle of people arrive and the chairs start to fill. She holds firm to the aisle seat and moves aside so people can squeeze past her intimidating bulk. The room is full by the time the vicar enters, and even then, as the organ strikes up "Nearer My God to thee," there is another wave of mourners who have to stand along the walls and at the back. There are at least two hundred people in the room before the service begins.

Finally, two women enter, arm-in-arm, both tall and slim— widow and daughter. The older woman walks fully erect, her chin hyper-extended to show she is bowed by nothing. The younger is slightly curved and leans a little into her mother. Both are dressed in elegant black dresses. The two women process down the aisle and take their places center stage, below the all-encompassing Jesus.

"What is a man . . ." the priest begins and Patty shifts her atten- tion to the other mourners. She has never been a fan of organized religion, always thought it destroyed the questioning mind. Her eyes scan the room and her blood turns cold. There is the policeman who tried to question her in the hospital, but he isn't in uniform. He is looking straight at her: their eyes latch, she holds her breath. Finally, his gaze moves on. He seems to be scanning the congreg- ation, is he searching for a killer there? Patty feels herself shake, though it's not her illness, merely the shudder of blood unfreezing and starting to pump again. She has no idea if her disguise held up to scrutiny. He certainly didn't seem to register any recognition and yet policeman are also actors, trained to morph into friend and confidant of the criminal, to blur the distinction between good, bad and ugly.

For a second she wishes Jim were there with her—then feels

guilty for that thought. It was bad enough that she got him into trouble this far; she cannot endanger him any more. "Shit." She suddenly realizes everybody is standing except for her. She blushes and, with some difficulty, pulls herself up for a hymn.

God sent His Son, they called Him Jesus; He came to love, heal, and forgive.

Patty moves her mouth a little, to look as if she's singing. She cranes forward, trying to see the widow, is she singing? She can't tell. The hymn finally ends and everyone sits again. Now the vicar begins to recount a litany of charity work done by Duncan Cobhurn. A long list of young people's charities, homeless and drug-addicted teens mostly. Around Patty, men and women nod their heads, many shed tears and some hold hands; some of these mourners are the drug-addicted teens, now grown up and made good: Duncan Cobhurn helped save them. Patty feels her stomach lurch. He sounds like a saint.

"Here you go," a whisper comes from beside her. A hand is flapping a tissue, she realizes she's crying.

"Thanks." Patty dabs away her Judas tears.

Lorraine, his daughter, rises to read from his favorite book. She makes it through ten lines of *Watership Down* before tears make it impossible for her to continue. Patty gets it though: poor bunnies, life sucks. Then a favorite song: "Lola" by the Kinks. The congregation is told it was playing on the radio when Duncan met Audrey, his wife of more than forty years. At this the widow's head sags and she leans into her daughter, both heads touch and seem to merge into one conjoined grief.

Patty's throat is dry and mouth sour like that little taste of reflux sick. She cannot see the widow's face or look into her eyes and yet knows what is written there. She sees that her need for revenge has sliced love from this poor woman's heart, destroyed her life as callously and as starkly as Dani's murder ruined Patty's. She should stand and announce her guilt, let Audrey Cobhurn have the satisfaction of seeing her ripped to shreds like an exhausted fox set upon by hounds. She should . . . but is too afraid. Patty is disgusted with her own cowardice. Two more songs, then a last reading and it's the final hymn.

The vibrato of the organ hangs in the air as the final words die away and the funeral is over. The widow and her daughter walk hand-in-hand up the aisle. The older woman is still bent into her daughter, deflated like a burst balloon. As they pass she reaches out and touches Audrey's arm, then widow and daughter are gone. Patty can't breathe. She needs to get out. She makes for the door: one step, two, three, four . . . Hand outstretched . . . and is through. She staggers over to the teeth of headstones, leans on one . . . the world is smeary with snotty tears and her chest heaves, she has to breathe or will blac—

"Where—why am I facedown in grass?" Patty asks herself, not sure where she is or . . . the funeral. It leaps back at her. "Crap." Her knee hurts, she puts the slightest pressure on it and it burns— maybe twisted, definitely swollen. Her chin is wet, maybe with blood. She fishes around in her pocket and finds a tissue; she wipes at her chin and it comes away with only tears and mucus. She has no idea how long she's been down here—seconds or minutes or hours? She gets up, slowly, supporting her knee, holding on to a headstone. Died 1824—they won't mind then. Her hat is crushed, she leaves it where it is. Most cars have gone but a couple remain—

she prays the policeman isn't still here. But why pray when she plans to confess?

She can see her little car and slowly walks toward it. She is almost there when somebody comes out of the church. Patty turns—force of habit—and looks directly into the eyes of Audrey Cobhurn. A sign. It's time to confess. She walks over to her.

"You don't know me, Mrs. Cobhurn . . ."

"I bloody do." The widow's face turns quickly from puzzlement through recognition to fury. She pulls her arm free from her daughter.

"She knows me, my God, she knows who I am and what I have done," thinks Patty, incredulous—but then all thought is stripped away as Audrey Cobhurn slaps Patty, who staggers back under the onslaught.

Patty is dazed by the ferocity—her ears ring and cheeks flare. Audrey's hands strike Patty's chest, sinking into the woolen blubber of the disguise—she looks at Patty with wonder. Then lashes out again.

"I buried my fucking husband here today. You have no right, no right."

The punches start to lessen and then die away as the demon departs her. Her daughter manages to grab her arms as she falls forward, clutching at Patty, oozing into the padding as her rage is replaced by the utter desolation of loss. She falls to her knees, still grabbing Patty's body—sliding down her. She looks up as she drops, her face a mass of streaming colors and all she can do is mouth . . .

"You shouldn't have come here. I did what I had to do for . . ." and there is nothing except streaming tears. Patty kneels down and takes the widow in her arms, they hold each other and together they sob. Patty sobs for Dani and Jim. Audrey wails for her Duncan.

Lorraine gently grasps her mother's shoulders and pulls her away from Patty. Her own face is a flood, all has been washed away. She turns her mother around and slowly walks her toward their car. Patty stays on her knees, watching the two women walk toward their car. Suddenly she is bombarded by questions: "How did Audrey Cobhurn know who I was? Why did she have such an angry reaction? Does she know I killed her husband? If she does— then why not call the police? What just happened?"

She sees Lorraine put her mother in the car, say a few words, then she turns once more and walks toward Patty. When she reaches her, Lorraine does not meet Patty's eyes.

"I didn't come here to cause you pain. Not you or your mother."

Lorraine nods.

"I don't know why I came really . . . I just . . ." Patty trails off— she has no idea how to end that sentence.

"We can't cope with you too," Lorraine says almost inaudibly, still looking down at the ground between them.

In the distance a new group of black cars drives through the gate and down to the church—black suits emerge. Next funeral . . . death goes on. Lorraine watches them arrive and forces herself to continue: "What we did to you, what Mum did—all that time ago. It's never left us. I think it cursed us. Dad has tried to pay it back; he tried to make good. I . . . am . . . sorry! I know we all need to bury our dead."

Patty can't breathe.

"Please don't hate us." She pulls her bag open and fishes in it, finding a card and a pen. She scribbles something and then hands it to Patty. It's a business card, LORRAINE SUMMERS DESIGNS, and then a mobile number scrawled on the back. She hands the pen and a blank card to Patty who, with numb fingers, writes her own mobile number on it.

"I can't talk now, Mum needs me. Please call tomorrow and we can meet."

She smiles at Patty, a conciliatory smile.

"Maybe it has been a good thing that you came today. Maybe you can forgive us after all these years, Mrs. Lancing," and she turns and walks back to her mother.

Patty cannot move: she has looked into the heart of Sodom, like Lot's wife, and been turned into a pillar of salt. The cold suddenly blows up and she is dissipated into the air.

THIRTY-FOUR

Tuesday, December 28, 2010

Jim feels anxious. He's been pacing around the house ever since he kissed Patty goodbye that morning. He looks at his watch again—the funeral was supposed to have started ten minutes ago. Christ, what will she do? She had held his hand and kissed him so tenderly, like a permanent farewell. He had asked to go with her, but she had held firm.

"I have to go alone."

"I don't understand why you have to go at all."

"I'll be back this evening."

"Promise?"

"Scout's honor."

He knew she was telling him what he wanted to hear. It was more likely that she would see the weeping widow and then find the nearest policeman to confess to. In many ways he admired that, admired her. But what consolation was that? Admiration—he'd had twenty years of admiration and it didn't fill his empty heart. He feels so alone. Where was Dani? Was he going to lose them both?

Suddenly the phone rings, he snatches it up.

"Patty?"

There is no answer, just a faraway sound of breath.

"Who is this?"

"James Lancing?" It's a voice Jim doesn't know.

"Who is this?" Jim asks.

"A friend, Mr. Lancing. I have some information for you. For you and your wife. Could you meet me?"

"I have not seen my wife in—"

"Please don't bother lying to me, Mr. Lancing. You have been with her for the last few days."

Jim feels sick. He lets the information sit there for a few seconds before he can speak again.

"When do you want to meet?"

"Now. Now would be good."

"My wife isn't here, we can't both meet you."

"You alone will be fine, Mr. Lancing."

Jim is silent for a few moments. "Where?"

"The birthplace of time?"

"When?"

"How about twenty minutes?"

There is a click and the call is ended. It takes Jim just a few minutes to get ready. He stands in the hall looking at the door. His stomach is full of moths. He's scared. He heads out into the cold.

❄

"There he goes." Grant Ronson pulls the binoculars from his eyes and slips them into his pocket. He bloody loves this. He grabs the bag and makes for the door, shouting back as he heads out, "You were brilliant—bloody Blofeld. We have information, Meester Bond—classic."

"Remember what we are looking for, Mr. Ronson."

"Mr. Ronson—classic."

"A small leather book—not a regular published book, the spine will almost certainly be blank."

"Got it, Ernst Stavro." And he is out of the door and gone.

Marcus Keyson watches him go. An idiot. But loyal and good in a scrap—that was Keyson's assessment of his employee. But it was the "idiot" bit that worried him at the moment. The last time he had asked Ronson to break into a house to recover something, he had taken far longer than he should, as he'd been raiding the wife's lingerie drawer and leaving her a "present." They had an hour maximum. They had to be quick.

Jim was only at the end of the road when he realized he didn't have his phone. Patty might need him. He turned and rushed back to the house. He knew exactly where it was. He would grab it and still be at the Royal Observatory in time to meet the mystery voice.

As soon as he opened the front door he knew something was wrong. It wasn't any kind of sixth sense. Someone was upstairs, opening drawers, moving furniture and whistling *The Dam Busters* theme very loudly. What should he do? Not confront the man—he should back out and call the police—but his phone was just inside the kitchen. He could get it in a few steps, then get out and call the police. The intruder upstairs was making too much noise to hear him. He couldn't see a second man. Jim moved as slowly as possible. It was twenty paces to the kitchen. He got the phone in his hand, flipped it open—dialed 99 . . .

Jim crumples from the blow to the top of his head. The phone spills onto the floor. Keyson retrieves it and turns it off. He looks down at the unconscious man.

"I am very sorry, Mr. Lancing. This shouldn't have occurred." He steps over the body. "Ronson, you idiot," he screams up the stairs.

He feels his head move—not that he did it himself. No, someone is holding it and . . . "Shit. Shit. Shit." A finger pokes into his skull and everything explodes. Sticky and wet. Jim feels sticky and wet.

"Jim. Jim."

There is a voice from somewhere. Jim tries to open his eyes but . . .

"Too hard."

"Jim. Here."

Something pressed to his lips. Water. At least he thinks it's water. He manages a sip.

"Need sleep." Jim starts to slip away again.

"Jim!"

Water hits his face.

"Try and talk," the voice says again. Jim attempts to open his eyes to see who's talking. He thinks it may be God or an angel.

"Jim," God says with a slap to his face.

"You are an angry god," Jim croaks.

"Jim, you've been cracked on the head. There's a lot of blood but I don't think it's serious."

You don't expect that sort of talk from God.

"Jim. Can you understand me?"

"Who are you?" Jim asks, beginning to think it isn't God.

"Jim, it's Tom. Tom Bevans. We need to talk."

Jim forces his eyes to focus. "Tom. It's good to see you. I might pass out again."

"No, you don't. Come on, walk around—have you got any painkillers?"

"Kitchen." Tom helps him to his feet and walks him into the

kitchen. Jim sits at the table—pointing to the drawer with pain-killers. Tom finds them and gets a glass of water.

"Thanks." Jim takes the ibuprofen and swallows them down. "What time is it?"

Tom looks at his watch. "Eight o'clock. When were you hit?"

"Erm . . . one-ish. I think." It all seems very hazy. Jim opens his eyes to see he is in the living room but the room has been demolished.

"Patty." Jim suddenly starts to panic. "Where's Patty?"

"You've got a few texts." Tom hands over Jim's phone. "I hope you don't mind—I read them. Patty's fine but she isn't coming home tonight. She says she's got a hotel room—there are things she needs to think about. But . . ." Tom pauses. "She isn't going to confess, she says. What do you think she means, Jim?"

Jim looks into Tom's face. He has not seen the younger man for a few years. He tries to keep his expression neutral. "I have no idea, Tom."

Tom sighs. "Oh, Jim. I know all about Duncan Cobhurn."

Jim looks Tom in the eye—but he doesn't feel scared.

Tom sighs again and holds his hands palms up. "Patty is safe from me. I'm not here as a policeman, but I don't know how safe she actually is. She's in trouble, Jim."

"Why?"

"She's got involved with a nasty piece of work. Do you know who hit you?"

"Didn't see him. Someone was upstairs, pulling things apart and whistling *The Dam Busters*."

"That'll be the charming Grant Ronson."

"Who?"

"He's listed as a private detective, but really he's an errand boy used for your more unpleasant jobs. He's been most recently in the employ of Dr. Marcus Keyson."

"Hang on . . ." Jim fights the swirling broken thoughts in his head and tries to piece his memory back together. "Patty saw him—he's a pathologist."

"He's a psychopath."

"She hired him—he was helping her."

"Helping himself, more likely. Look, he and I have some history and, take it from me: he is not a good guy."

"And that's who could be trouble for Patty?"

"He's trouble for all of us."

"So why was he ransacking the place here?"

"I think he wanted something you had."

"Had?"

"I assume he found it."

"What?"

Tom hesitates; his eyes fall away from Jim's gaze. "Dani's diary."

"There are lots of diaries, she always kept a . . ." Jim trails off. "You mean her university diary?"

Tom nods.

"But, how did he know about it? You told me you'd wiped all trace of it from the files." Jim starts to panic.

"I did. The investigating officers never saw it but . . . I missed something. I never changed the evidence sheet from the crime scene. I mean, nobody ever goes back and looks at those."

"But this Keyson obviously did."

"He has the entire file. I don't know how he got it, but he has. He's got the original log. All you have to do is compare the two and see the diary was logged in at the crime scene but never made it to the evidence list."

Jim closes his eyes and desperately thinks back. That day at the morgue, Tom had disappeared to do some paperwork with a hatchet-faced officer. Afterward, they'd waved something in his face to sign. Later Tom gave him a small bag.

"Here. Don't look now, just take it home. We can't leave it here for the investigation."

Jim hadn't realized what he had at the time. It was only when they were back in London that he looked. There, in the bag, were two small diaries. He'd been excited at first, hoped it might tell him something—even have clues as to who had killed Dani. But of course there was nothing. The diaries only reached the end of that first miserable year. Nothing to do with her death but told of that dreadful time with . . .

"So he knows all about Seb Merchant?"

Tom nods.

"Has he told Patty?" Jim asks, worried.

"I have no idea."

"Hell," Jim feels a sharp pain cycle round his head. He tries hard to concentrate again. "So who is this Keyson? What does he want?"

Tom looks across at the older man; he's worried about his head wound.

"First, let's give that head some attention. We can talk while I clean it. Do you have iodine?"

"Bathroom—under the sink."

Tom nods and walks away. He returns shaking his head. "This stuff is five years past its sell-by-date."

"Wouldn't worry."

Tom takes a small cloth and tips the iodine into it and then dabs at Jim's bloody head. Jim winces but says nothing.

"Marcus Keyson—he worked with us—he was the pathologist allocated to Operation Ares."

"I don't know what that means."

"Sorry, Jim. I forget you aren't a copper. Operation Ares is a special task force, a unit within the Serious Crime Division. I head it up—we investigate sexual murder where we think there are multiple victims or there's some unusual element to the case."

Jim nods slowly. It was a bigger memorial to Dani than he could imagine.

"You save lives? Punish the wicked?" Jim asks.

"We try." Tom sees Sarah Penn's face. The photo from Ibiza and her dead face morph together. Three years dead. She's waiting for him in the dark somewhere with the others, needing his attention and help. "I try."

"So he worked with you?" Jim tries to get Tom back on track.

"Yeah . . . Keyson was our pathologist—a brilliant man. Quite honestly there are two murderers—at least—who we would not have caught without him."

"So why did he hit me over the head if he's a good guy?"

"Oh, I don't think Marcus Keyson's a good guy. But I didn't think he was a bad guy either." Tom stops to concentrate as he cleans into the deepest part of the wound. "He was kicked off the force. Dishonorable discharge, no pension, no consultancy, no references—nothing. He was lucky he wasn't arrested; they just kicked everything under the carpet."

"What did he do?" Jim asks.

"He took bribes to tamper with evidence. Not on any of our cases, but others he worked on. There were two cases in particular. In the first he was caught changing drug results on a hit-and-run drink-drive. They found Keyson was sleeping with the wife and daughter in payment to get the father acquitted. There was another big case: a woman was driving over the limit—she plowed into three children on the pavement. Two dead, one in a wheelchair for life. He purposefully contaminated the evidence against the driver—at trial it all fell apart and she walked away scot-free."

"But I don't understand what this has to do with us."

"I . . ." Tom looks ashamed. "I'm the reason he was investigated. He was my friend. I was at his house one night after work. I dropped by with a bottle, out of the blue. The wife of the defendant was there and I recognized her. I called the DPS. I sold him out and got him kicked off the force."

"So he hates you."

"Pretty much. He certainly blames me for everything that's gone wrong for him."

"But why was he at my house?"

Tom hesitates.

"I told him about Dani—years back, when we were still friends. Told him she was murdered and I loved her. Then, a couple of months ago, Patty went to see him to ask him to investigate Dani's death. It was a freak coincidence that she found him. She mentioned me and he saw it as a way to get his revenge, to hurt me."

"How, how could he hurt you?"

Tom's eyes flash for second. "He knows I . . . he knows I withheld evidence from the reports on Dani."

"I see. He got kicked off the force for tampering with evidence and he wants you to get the same treatment."

Tom nods. "But . . . there's something else."

"Something to do with Dani's death."

"Something I did that I'm ashamed of. If he makes it public it will ruin me, my work, the team will be disbanded. Those girls . . . they need to be remembered."

Jim nods. "I need to get to Patty." He tries to take a step but is still woozy. He staggers and Tom catches hold of him.

"I'll drive," Tom tells him. "It's a while since I've been to Durham." He almost smiles.

The front door slams into place as they leave. As Jim walks away from the house he thinks he sees a slight shape inside. He holds his hand up and waves awkwardly. Dani waves back; his chest flares, he is so happy to see her again. He puts his lips to his mouth and blows her a kiss. He needs her to know she is loved.

"Jim?" Tom is at the car. He turns, unsure of what Jim is doing.

"Coming, Tom."

From inside, Dani watches the two men get into the car and drive off. Tears trickle down her cheeks. She didn't know a ghost could cry before this. She does now.

She is scared for them. And for herself. Slowly her pale face fades from the room until she is gone.

THIRTY-FIVE

Tuesday, December 28, 2010

The widow is alone. After the morning's funeral Lorraine brought her home. She would not go to bed and so her daughter made a daybed for her in the sitting room. On the table there is a sandwich, untouched. Cold tea sits there too, a scum formed on the top. Audrey had tried to lie down but she felt nauseous and sat up. For a long time she has just stared out of the window, but she feels a need for . . . Lorraine has gone through the room removing anything and everything she thought might trigger her mother's grief. Normally the room is awash with family photographs—but now they are all packed away somewhere. Audrey feels a deep desire to see his face again.

She opens the door slowly, quietly. From the kitchen she can hear sounds of life—Lorraine is washing up. Audrey walks carefully through the downstairs and into the room at the back. Duncan's home office. There on the corner of a filing cabinet is a silver-framed photo. Her Duncan grins out from it looking relaxed and happy. He wears black tie. He still has hair and is thinner than he has been over the last few years; it must be at least fifteen years ago. She takes the photograph back to the lounge and sits on the sofa with her Duncan one more time. Earlier in the day, seeing the photo might have tipped her back into the overwhelming grief that had gripped her after the funeral, but since returning home she has self-medicated for the pain; V&V—vodka and Valium. Everything is hazy and colors seem muted. She cannot tell when her eyes are open or closed as pictures still play across her vision. There seems to be no way of telling the past from the present, except he can't be here in the present, can he? But she sees him open the door . . . young, he is amazingly young. That first day.

He opens the door; she catches a glimpse of him in her peripheral vision, a breeze of color. All is in slow motion as she turns and . . . The spotlight of that smile is turned on her, dazzling her senses. The smile blots out everything else. Then slowly she sees how his eyes twinkle . . . oh boy, is he trouble.

He opens the cafe door where Audrey Hall works as a waitress. She is seventeen and has worked there for two years after leaving school with no qualifications.

She turns as he enters; he smiles and her heart slows—like now with the pills. She starts to drool . . . He sits down at one of her tables. She can barely catch her breath then . . . or now. She wants it to stop, she cannot see him like that, young and beautiful.

She has the pill bottle. The doctor said if she needed a quicker relief she should chew so she grinds each pill to powder with her teeth and knocks them back with vodka. It's not part of the pre-scription but the pain is too much to bear alone.

He smiles. "Egg and chips, please, love, and a big mug of tea."

The cafe is gone and she is dressed in white, in a church. Today it was black, now it is white. He kisses her.

"I love you," he says.

"And you loved her too. Didn't you?"

Duncan Cobhurn smiles at his wife and shrugs his shoulders. "All too long ago, darling. All too long ago."

From somewhere far-off there is the sound of a bell. Audrey Cobhurn half registers it, and then hears raised voices from the hallway. She pulls herself up off the sofa . . . immediately her knees begin to buckle but she steadies herself. The room shifts like at a funfair, lines seem to curve in a way that physics should not allow. But she manages to get to the door and open it. A man stands there, seeming to argue with her daughter. When he sees Audrey he pushes himself into the hall, muscling Lorraine to one side so he can talk directly to her mother.

"I am so sorry for your loss, Mrs. Cobhurn." He holds out a wallet. She doesn't understand.

"Detective Superintendent Tom Bevans. I really need to ask you a couple of questions."

"Mum, he can come back tomorrow," Lorraine says, trying to lever him out the door, but he won't budge.

The widow smiles, not really sure what is being asked of her, the pills and vodka swimming in her stomach and her brain, but she likes the look of him. Tall and young, with sandy-blond hair and eyebrows so blond they are almost white.

"Please, you can see the state she's in. Come back tomorrow," Lorraine asks.

But the man doesn't reply. Instead he pulls out a photograph— carefully, almost like a conjuror drawing you into his sleight of hand. The widow looks at it bemused. How odd, she thinks. It's the same photo from his office, the one she has been staring at for so long. Why does this policeman hav—

Then the man takes the photo and opens it. His copy was folded in half. He opens it to reveal . . . drum roll: Dani Lancing. Dani Lancing in a gorgeous silver dress, and she is holding on to Duncan's arm.

Audrey Cobhurn is unconscious before she hits the floor.

PART SEVEN

THE DIARY OF DANIELLE LANCING

Private

Monday, September 29, 1986

So let's start as I mean to go on—with a lie. It's actually Tuesday, technically, as it's three in the morning. I've just got home and I promised I would start this diary thing again so . . . University: day one, Monday, September 29, 1986.

God, Mum has such a stick up her arse. Dad was his usual quiet, great self. Tom . . . oh what about Tom? Tom needs to meet someone—he should have gone to uni, and I don't understand why he didn't. He's so clever but so stupid. And then there's Seb. Wow!

He's not a student—well, he was but he left the course he was on. The philosophy of economics—something weird like that. He came out of nowhere after Mum and Dad left and we started talk-ing and we just talked and talked. We walked over to the cathed-ral and sat on the grass outside by some graves. It was cool. He rolled a joint—it was mild but I got a bit spacey. We kissed, but he was a real gentleman. He walked me home. I'm meeting him tomorrow. Good night, diary.

PS: Just found box from Mum in bed—a bloody letter. She saw me all day, and hardly said a word. She goes on about not saying what she means so she writes—crap. Communication is communication.

Tuesday, September 30, 1986

Met Seb for a drink in C1 bar. After he came back to the dorm and I gave him a shoulder rub and a little bit more. Nikki came back early, so we couldn't do too much, but I am really looking forward to seeing him again.

Monday, October 6, 1986

What an amazing weekend. Went with Seb to a party on Saturday, at a student house in Walltown. Philosophy and ex-philosophy students talking death, the afterlife and Hitchhiker's Guide to the Galaxy. Then a whole crowd of drama students started acting out Monty Python sketches as if they were performed by Neil and Vivien from The Young Ones. I wet myself. It was pretty druggy too, not just joints. There was a room where someone was cooking up heroin. Seb said we should watch—like we were anthropologists studying a tribe recently discovered in the Amazon. I couldn't look when they actually injected themselves. For a few minutes after they talked just like before, then they got all smiley and floppy—they looked like they were having the biggest orgasms and sagged down onto the floor. Three of them, out cold, but looking like they didn't have a care in the world. Seb said a lot of crap gets talked about drugs because the authorities are too frightened of how it liberates young people. So many of our greatest poets and thinkers took drugs to free their imaginations—but governments don't want you knowing that.

Wednesday, October 22, 1986

Should have been at a lecture this morning but too hungover. Went to Seb's last night and stayed over. He had some new weed and rolled a joint that was almost hallucinogenic. An old friend of his was over—a girl I hadn't seen before, Lucy; she had some really big tattoos, the best was a rose with a dagger through it that said Mum. We played truth or dare—Seb dared me to snog Lucy. I did. I quite liked it. Maybe I'll be bi.

Tuesday, November 4, 1986

Not written for over a week, not sure what to say. Seb and I went to a party on Saturday—before last. It was at the same place we'd gone once before, in Walltown. It was pretty fun—I had a joint and then Seb took me upstairs. Some of his friends were shooting heroin. We watched them once before but this time Seb said he wanted to join in. It was safe and we shouldn't be cowed by all the stupid taboos society laid on us. I wasn't sure—but for him I said yes. It was amazing. Everyone should try it. You don't realize how small the world is until you do. And then when you come down off it—it's really disappointing. It's like going on an amazing holiday to the sun—where all the colors are really amazing and the weather is just the best and you come back to dingy England. We did it again this Saturday and last night. Was fantastic again—even better. This time Lucy was there and we got off with each other while we took the stuff. Incredible.

Friday, November 14, 1986

Money is such a mind-fuck. Seb seems to be rolling in it—I don't know where he gets it from. Last night we were gonna shoot some stuff but he said I needed to pay for it this time. I wasn't thinking about money—he always took care of it—but he said he needed £500. I mean that's a lot of money. He said I should call my dad. I said it was okay I just won't have any.

Monday, November 17, 1986

Fucking Seb. I didn't see him all weekend. I really miss him. I hurt. Why has he done this? I called Dad and told him I need some money. Afterward I went to the cathedral and sat for a while. It was calming and quiet. I prayed—Mum would have a fit, but it felt pretty good.

Friday, November 21, 1986

Finally. Finally he comes over. I am like sweating, even though it's so cold out. I give him the money and we go out for a curry but I can't eat. I keep telling him I need the stuff. After the starters he takes me into the toilets and gets me to suck him off before he gives me a tiny little bit of smack. I am so fucking grateful. I think I need some help. I went back to the cathedral and sat in my pew. Stupid—I think of it as mine. There were lots of tourists, and they can be a pain but I sat through a service and even sang a hymn. I kneeled down on a cushion that had been made for the Corona-tion—crazy. I took a pen and wrote my name right at the bottom. Maybe in another thousand years someone will wonder who I was.

Sunday, November 23, 1986

Seb is just the sweetest boyfriend. He turned up with flowers yes-terday and took me out for lunch at this really nice place. Then later we went back to his place and shot the best stuff I have ever had. Today he is taking me out again—he said he'd be here by noon. Should be here soon.

Monday, November 24, 1986

He never fucking came. I waited and waited. He called at seven. Said he was caught up—I could hear music and laughing in the background. He wouldn't tell me where he was—I told him I needed him. That junk on Saturday had been perfect—we should do that again. That shit didn't come cheap, he said—told me I needed to find one thousand pounds. What am I going to do? I sat in my pew again and I must have a looked a right wreck because someone came over, a priest or something, and asked if I was all right. I wanted to tell him. But I ran.

Thursday, November 27, 1986

The money from Nan has gone. I've even sold my coat. What do I do? I'm missing too many lectures and they're starting to ask questions. I can't let them know—I can't let anyone know.

Friday, November 28, 1986

I saw Lucy this morning. I thought Seb might be there—I had been looking everywhere for him. She told me all about his lies. The prison stretch, how the uni had expelled him for drug dealing. No wonder he's got money. Oh shit.

Thursday, December 4, 1986

I called Dad an hour ago. He's coming to get me. He's taking me somewhere for a week or two before I go home—can't do this with Mum looking at me with those judgmental eyes. Oh Christ, I am so fucking dumb. I am going to stop writing this after today but—future Dani: don't do this anymore. Remember yesterday and the shame.

In the weekend, Seb had come round with some shit on Saturday morning and we had got high. Then went to some friends in the evening, four of them. His friends, he said, but they didn't look like his kind at all. Merchant bankers, Midas-rich and mean with it. We went somewhere expensive—Seb had asked me to dress up all fancy. There was champagne with dinner but I didn't drink any. Afterward we all went back to a hotel room—a suite. Seb and two of them went off into the toilet. I was left with the other two—they looked at me like I was meat. I knew Seb was selling them drugs in the loo and I was a sweetener—he was giving them me as well. When the drooling pair went into the toilet too, I ran. I was not going to be his whore. Seb caught up with me when I was almost home. He kicked me. Called me . . . called me something I would never even write down.

On Sunday he brought flowers round. I wouldn't let him in. He called Monday and Tuesday. I didn't want to let him in but . . . I needed the stuff. Being without it burned. I let him in yesterday. He started out all sweet then got mean. Told me if I wanted him to keep me in the manner to which I had become accustomed then I needed to be nicer to him and nicer to his friends. Then he dragged me out of the halls and up to the cathedral. He remembered that I loved to sit in the cathedral library. It is the most amazing room I have ever been in—spiritual but you can feel the centuries of learning, of truth seekers searching through the books. It's tangible, right in the fabric of the building. Whenever I sit there I am filled with awe. The ancient wood that holds the room together is steeped in knowledge—the carvings and ornate stone hold so much pure love of learning. In one room is humanity's striving to learn and grow—a thousand years of human endeavour. And I can never go back. He defiled the place for me, defiled me in there. He pulled me to the back of the study room, behind a bookcase and made me kneel down and suck him, there in the library. At one point a nun walked by and he groaned so that she would see us—see me. I saw her shock and pity. He laughed. I am so dirty. I don't know how I will ever be clean again.

It is the final entry. Marcus Keyson closes the book.

THIRTY-SIX

Thursday, February 9, 1989

Heavy doors swing open. Jim stares into a room and feels his stomach clench. It is the final stop after a maze of corridors that have led down and down and down—into the bowels of the hospital. The morgue. Steel, steel, porcelain and more steel—all scrubbed down and smelling faintly of bleach. In the center of the room is a table. A blue sheet covers it, though it's not flat. Of course it's not, there's a body under it. Alongside Jim is a middle-aged woman with a kind face. She is his guide into the underworld to find Persephone.

"Do you need a minute?" she asks.

He looks at her blankly, not understanding the question. "To do what?" he asks. She smiles and waits. "Oh. I see." She means a minute to brace himself. "No. No, I'm fine."

He's been told he doesn't need to do this. Tom had tried to get him to stay in London, near to Patty. Dani's flatmate was called out and has positively identified the body, so there is no need for Jim to make an identification—not legally, anyway.

"Don't go, Jim." Tom's voice is soft and kind.

"I need to see her." Tom stares off into space for a moment and then nods. Of course Jim needs to go—they both know why. Jim opened his heart to the young man on that dreadful day he brought the news that Dani was dead. He had held it inside for so long he thought he might explode if he didn't share it, so he had told Tom all about Seb Merchant. The drugs and the lies, the shame and that terrible call he got from her begging him to help. How he'd rushed to Durham and took her away from there, from that awful situation. How he found her a clinic and took her there. How he'd hidden it all from Patty and how he had been scared for his daughter ever since.

Tom heard his confession without a word and at the end he said he would accompany Jim to the morgue in Durham.

"Such a kindness," thought Jim.

Jim's guide moves over to the body and pulls the sheet back to reveal a dead face.

"Oh, sweetheart," he whispers, then hides for a moment in a memory.

"This is stupid." Dani calls out. Jim walks into the living room to find her scowling at the radio. She's about nine years old.

"What's stupid?"

"This song."

Jim listens. It's Donovan.

"First there is a mountain, then there is no mountain, then there is—that's stupid. Mountains are big, they don't walk away to have their tea some place."

"You're right."

"So what is he saying?"

"It's very complicated . . ." Jim begins.

Dani scowls at her father.

"It's Zen, I think. One can get over-analytical in this world . . ."

"What?" she asks, getting annoyed.

"Okay," he sits down next to her. "You can look at stuff so

hard—like a jigsaw puzzle—trying to work out what it is, what it does—that you forget it's just a simple piece of cardboard. It's a song about just accepting the world as it is and not looking for anything deeper."

"You have no idea, do you?" she frowns in concentration. "Is it about aliens taking mountains away?"

"Maybe." He shrugs. "Maybe there never was a mountain."

She nods. "That's probably the answer."

"That's my daughter," Jim tells the kind guide.

She takes a notebook from her pocket and writes down the time of his formal identification.

"Could I have a moment alone with her?"

She shakes her head. "I'm sorry."

"PC Bevans will be here. I won't touch her." Tom looked into the rules and told Jim that would be allowable, though not encouraged. If she knew Tom and Dani's history she would definitely say no. But . . .

"Of course." She nods slowly and carefully. "I'll be in the waiting room, take as long as you like and come out when you're ready." She smiles and holds out her hand—one human being to another. Jim takes it and feels a little squeeze. A mother to a father.

"Thank you."

She goes to the door and beckons Tom inside. She whispers something to him and then leaves.

"Jim," Tom hisses.

"Please stay by the door, Tom—this will just take a second."

Jim moves until he stands over her, his face cranes down to just above hers; it's pale, and the tiny traceries of veins can be clearly seen through the papery skin. Not at all like her glowing skin in life. He knows she is not merely asleep and yet . . . he slides his arm under the sheet and holds her hand. It's cold.

"Warm me up, Daddy," she says from far-off. He squeezes her hand but nothing can warm it now.

"Goodbye, pumpkin." He gives her the gentlest of kisses on her pale lips.

"And I am so sorry to do this." He pulls back the sheet. She has been shaved for the autopsy and he's shocked by the nakedness between her legs.

"Please forgive this intrusion, Dani," he asks her.

She is covered in bruises, all over her breasts, thighs and where they have shaved her. Her right hip looks terribly swollen. Her ankles and wrists are sliced where she was tied. Tom had told him that the blood settles, making the skin look worse, the marks more livid—but . . . but this is his girl. With all the strength he can muster, he takes her arm and holds it up. He's looking for something, something he prays he will not find. Tom has walked over to his side and together they see that all over the inner arm there are puncture wounds, track marks.

"My darling, darling girl," Jim whispers to her.

He places her arm back down and takes the sheet, pulling it up over her body, leaving just her head exposed. He leans forward and kisses her one final time.

❄

The kind-faced guide is there as he exits. She has been talking to another police officer, a hatchet-faced man with a pencil moustache who disappears once Jim walks over.

"A tea perhaps?" she asks Jim.

"A coffee would be really . . ." Tears come and he can't fight them. He goes and sits, his head down. After a minute or two some-one brings him a coffee. All sounds seem to come from underwater. Her arms . . .

The coffee is almost cold when Jim is finally able to lift his head. In the corner Tom is making the arrangements for the body to be sent to London once the coroner releases it. Jim watches him—he is so thankful to the young man. He is so grateful to him for help-ing. But now what? How did she lose her way again? Did the drugs make her a target? Is that why she was killed?

"Jim."

Jim doesn't hear Tom, he's so lost.

"Jim." Tom shakes him by the shoulder—softly.

"Miles away. Sorry."

All Jim wants is to get home and get into bed with Patty. She's still sedated, a nurse is with her. She has been drugged to the eye-balls for almost two days now and Jim is terrified that Patty may be lost to him too.

"We should go. All the arrangements are made but you need to sign something. Come here and meet one of the senior officers."

Tom leads him over to the hatchet-faced DI. The three men talk, there's a document signed. Then Tom guides Jim out of the underworld and back up to the land of the living.

They walk—heading to the station but in a meandering way.

"Do I smell?" Jim asks. He hasn't washed or shaved in two days, can't remember cleaning his teeth either.

"No," Tom answers too quickly. "A little . . . you could brush your teeth."

They stop at a pharmacy and buy a toothbrush, toothpaste and mouthwash. At the station, Jim goes into the toilets and cleans his teeth. He also washes his face and, as no one else is there, takes off his shirt and cleans under his arms.

On the platform, Tom is in the waiting room. There are twenty minutes until the London train.

"Thank you, Tom," Jim says, handing him a bar of Fruit and Nut he just bought from a machine.

Tom nods his head—his own graying head. He hasn't shaved today either and the whiskers are starting to poke through the skin; each one is white.

"She should be in London in a couple of days," Tom says, chewing a cube of slightly stale chocolate.

Jim doesn't know who he means for a second—then realizes he means Dani. Dani's body. The two of them sit quietly for a few minutes, then Tom breaks the silence.

"There will be an inquest, maybe next week . . ." He pauses. "Certain things will be excluded from the coroner's report and missing from the inquest."

"What do you mean?"

"The drug use—it isn't relevant to the case."

"Surely the police need . . ."

"Nothing will damage the police investigation. I just think there are certain things we don't need made public. Patty needn't know."

"Is that possible?"

Tom nods solemnly. "Dani was a wonderful girl, a model student who met a tragic end."

"That newspaper story?"

"Jim, don't worry. Ben Bradman retracted that piece of filth and won't repeat the allegation. Don't worry. Trust me. And here." Tom gives Jim a small bag. Jim looks inside—Dani's diaries.

Jim nods, immensely grateful. Then he slides back into the mire of his thoughts while they wait for the train.

THIRTY-SEVEN

Wednesday, December 29, 2010

Audrey Cobhurn is sober now. She was pretty sober before she took the silver photo frame from Duncan's office, undid the small black metal clasps and slid out the photo and mount. The mount had been glued and when she pulled it away, it took small scabs of the photograph with it. Below the mount she could see that the picture had been cut—but she could still see that resting on his arm was a hand, with long fingers that said: "He's mine." It was Dani Lancing's hand.

It's a little after midnight. All good children should be in their beds. She walks slowly through the dark house. It had been a family home just a fortnight ago, everyone looking forward to Christmas. Now it's a mausoleum. She reaches the front door and turns to the coat rack. Lorraine's jacket is there. Audrey pats it until she finds a lumpy pocket. Inside is her daughter's phone and a small card; she slips both into her own pocket. Taking extra care to be silent, she opens the front door and takes a step outside. It's a chill night; she wasn't thinking. She grabs a big duffel coat from beside the door and puts it on. It's too big—was Duncan's—still smells of him. She breathes deeply.

"Careful . . ." a voice from a long way off—was that him?

She wraps her arms tightly around herself—she's about to pull the door shut but remembers something. She goes back inside and pats at another of Lorraine's pockets. Inside is a packet of cigarettes. She takes them and then shuts the door.

She hurries off, not wanting Lorraine to follow if the door woke her. When she's turned a left and a right she slows down to a normal pace. She pulls out the packet of cigarettes and looks inside. Three left, plus a slim lighter. She takes one and lights it. She sucks the smoke deep down. It's the first one she's had in more than ten years. She'd given up for Duncan.

"Those things'll kill ya," he'd said.

He gave them up one day, just like that. He didn't preach at her, but you could see he didn't like her smoking. She'd carried on about nine months after him and then stopped. But her stopping required patches, gum and a mink coat from Harrods. Even then she fell off the wagon a few times. But now, what's the point? Who wants to live forever?

She smokes it right down to the butt, maybe even a little beyond. Then she takes the little card and taps the number into Lorraine's phone. She dials. It takes at least twenty rings but finally it's answered.

"Patricia Lancing," a sleepy voice answers.

"It's Audrey Cobhurn. I realize this is late, but I hoped we could meet."

Patty rushes, the little heels of her black shoes typewriter-clacking on the paving stones as she heads through the empty marketplace, up to the cathedral and Audrey Cobhurn. Patty steals a glance at a clock on a small church—it's just before 1 a.m. She puts on a further burst of speed. The path is steep and twists; she has to be careful. She wishes she'd brought her running shoes with her—anything other than funeral clothes. To her left are the gates to Dani's college. If she goes up to them she could probably see Dani's dorm room where they delivered her all those years ago. All . . . she stops as her stomach twists and sends pain up her back and down her legs. She's eaten nothing since she left Jim that morning—yesterday morning now. Nothing, except about a dozen assorted pills. She remembers that day so clearly. Freshers' week 1986. Patty had never been to Durham before Dani applied. She immediately saw how beautiful it was—Dani's school at the top of the city, nestled in the bosom of the cathedral like Mount Olympus. But she remembers feeling unease—were these children the new gods? They seemed to think they were with ramrod straight backs, ultra white teeth and confidence oozing from every pore of their perfect skin. It was the kind of privilege she had so often complained about . . . and there was Dani inside it all.

"I'm not just some young version of you, Mum. Your values make me sick. Physically fucking sick." The words echo through Patty's head all this time later.

Patty runs on, turns a corner and suddenly it's there. The claustrophobic feel of the twisting streets breaks into the magnificence of the Cathedral Square dominated by the grandeur of the building itself. It takes Patty's breath away. Directly in front of the edifice is a rectangular lawn. To the side is an ancient burial ground, stones toppled like steed fallen in battle. Surrounding the lawn, the ground is cobbled, undulated like strafed soil. It's freezing. Patty can see the breath roll from her mouth and float upward, disappearing into the night. Patty doesn't trust the cobbles, and walks onto the grass—heading straight to the maw of the cathedral.

"I'm not just some young version of you, Mum. Your values make me sick. Physically fucking sick." The same words again. Patty remembers them so clearly: she said them to her mother on the day she left for university. And she never went home again. Did she deserve them—her poor mother? Patty doesn't really remember. But what is a mother for—to keep you safe and protect you—isn't that what a mother should do? Her own couldn't. So Patty never went home again. And Dani?

"Here." A voice calls out from the shadows.

Patty can just make her out—standing before huge oak doors, almost close enough to touch sanctuary. Yesterday she reminded Patty of a swan—elegant and long but bowed. Grief piled on her head and shoulders and yet she carried it with a great dignity. But in this moonless half-light, Patty's impression is of a hawk. Her head is hooded yet her eyes sparkle from the shadows, her talons ready to strike. This does not seem the same woman.

Patty walks to her, like a fly approaching a spider. Audrey stands there, in the shadow of the cathedral. Patty can't see her face, but can see that her arms shake.

"You asked me to come," Patty calls out.

"Did you kill my husband?" Audrey Cobhurn steps forward, out of the gloom. She is completely altered—her face twitches, writhes as if worms tunnel beneath a mask. She looks as if she is consumed by the hunger to know the truth. Patty knows that look, has seen it on a hundred women at Lost Souls, and on her own face for so many years. She feels sick. This is it: she cannot run, would not want to.

Patty feels herself slice into the hand of Duncan Cobhurn.

"I . . . cut him."

All she needed was a few drops of blood. Instead, she cut a river into his hand, through muscle and tendons—down to bone. She caused pain, damage, took revenge; tortured an innocent man. Tears stream down her face. All over, all gone. She thinks of Jim. All she wants now is to hold Jim's hand, to walk with him down to the river, kiss him and tell him that she loves him. She wants to live again. But it's too late.

"Please," Audrey Cobhurn says in a small voice. "Tell me the truth."

Patty breathes. So many images flash through her mind. Dani's face on the missing poster, Jim's tears when he thought he couldn't be seen, Tom's face cracking open with grief, and her own face palsied by loss. The faces of all those students—children really—hundreds of them, saying how they loved and missed Dani. Each one thanking God it wasn't them. Patty feels the shame and guilt of the countless hours she had wished each and every one of them had been raped and murdered, so long as it hadn't happened to Dani. Blame and shame and guilt. Blame and shame and guilt. She wouldn't wish that on anyone—not if she could save them.

"Yes. I killed your husband."

"I so wish you hadn't said that," says Jim-in-her-head.

She sighs, knowing she has lost him now, lost all the love she had known those last wonderful few days.

"I had to, Jim," she tells the man in her head. "She needs peace. I can't let her suffer like we have, not knowing. I couldn't do that to another human being. And the truth is that I killed him."

"You killed him accidentally."

"No, I didn't. I took revenge . . . I killed him. Please, Jim, let me go. I need to take my medicine."

Patty closes her eyes, expecting the world to end. Either Audrey will pull out a phone and call 999—come and arrest a murderer—or she will take a carving knife from her pocket and run Patty through. She waits, prepared for either. For what seems like an eternity there is nothing—Audrey Cobhurn merely watching her husband's killer—but she does not move or make a sound. Then she pulls something from her pocket.

"Here it comes . . . here it comes . . . Be brave," thinks Patty.

"Look," Audrey says, her voice cracking with emotion. She holds something. Patty stays bowed.

"Look, damn you!" she screams, crossing the distance between them until they are almost nose to nose. Patty opens her eyes, and sees that Audrey holds a photo.

"Dani?"

Audrey drops the photo, it spins to earth—Patty instinctively moves to catch it, like a leaf spilling from a tree in autumn. It lands face up in her hands and she cups it.

"I've never seen this picture . . ." she whispers, more to herself. She does not remember Dani ever being so glamorous, ever looking so grown up and happy.

"Where did you get this?" Patty asks the widow.

With a cruel smile, Audrey produces another picture . . . no, the same picture, the other half of the same picture. She holds it just by the corner—as if it might burst into flame.

"My husband," she says, like an introduction at a party.

Twenty years younger, but him. Patty recognizes the man she killed. Audrey hands the two pieces to Patty who puts them together. They fit perfectly.

"I don't understand."

"Forgive me," the widow says.

"What? Why?" Patty's head is spinning.

"I didn't mean it to happen, I just couldn't lose him—I loved him so much, he was my world. I told Lorraine—but she already knew—knew her from university. Knew your daughter, had seen them together."

"What do you mean, together?" Patty asks but Audrey Cobhurn doesn't hear the question. She sees the young beautiful woman again. Sees Dani Lancing, who has listened to all Audrey has to say—all she has to offer and then . . .

"I don't want your money—you can't buy me. I'm not a whore." Dani's voice cuts through her—then she laughs, deep and throaty— it makes Audrey Cobhurn spasm.

"I had begged Lorraine to tell me where to find her so I could talk to her. I had to make her see what she was doing to me, to us—to his family. I went to see her—offered her money, anything to leave him alone."

Patty can't feel her arms or legs—totally numb.

"I couldn't believe he'd want her—she was a kid, the same age as our Lorraine. I gave him everything, you know. He owed me— we were a team. Then this snot of a girl came in and threatened to ruin it, destroy it. I knew it wouldn't last, he'd have realized he loved me, but then she tricked him. Dug her claws into him with the oldest trick in the book . . ."

Patty feels bile rise in her throat.

"She got pregnant."

Patty's hand drops to her stomach unbidden, some physical memory hardwired into her. In a rush she is back at Christmas with Dani. That final Christmas, with Dani so moody, so fractious. So plump. So pregnant.

"Oh, Christ." How had she not seen it?

Audrey Cobhurn reaches out with her hand, lays it on Patty's arm and grips her hard.

"I was at the end of my rope. I didn't want her hurt . . ." Audrey Cobhurn breaks down, tears stream down her face. "My brother knew some men. I asked for them to frighten her, scare her off so we could get back to how it was, the three of us."

"Oh my God . . ." Patty tries to pull away from her, but

Audrey holds on—Patty twists her body—but Audrey won't let go. She needs Patty to listen; she needs her to know—to hear her confession.

"They went to see her, those men my brother got me, and they told her to leave us alone—leave Duncan alone. She wouldn't listen, threatened to call the police and so they grabbed her. Things got out of hand."

THIRTY-EIGHT

Monday, January 9, 1989

He checks the notes and signs the box to start his rounds. It is 2 p.m. He walks onto the ward and goes to the young woman's bed. She has been there for two days. She has barely spoken in all that time, first name but no address. She has one question, which everyone has avoided answering.

The doctor dreads sitting down with her. Her bruises are healing well. She has three cracked ribs but they'll soon knit and begin to mend. She has lost two teeth, but not at the front; so long as she doesn't smile she looks fine. Smiles are probably not on the agenda for a while anyway. On the ward everyone else is at least fifty and most are sixty plus—that is the normal age for women to have hysterectomies. Of course he has, sometimes, dealt with younger women, those with ovarian cancer generally, never someone who has been kicked repeatedly and savagely in the stomach. It had been a matter of life and death when she'd been brought in, and while she may know that—understand the truth of it . . .

"Will I be able to have a child in the future?" she asks him the question.

He cannot say the words to her. All he can do is shake his head. He avoids her eyes and their hope for another answer.

"The pain . . ."

"Of course."

He writes a note for extra medication. He can see how tight her jaw is, how she grits her teeth when it gets bad. He leaves quickly, writes that a counselor should see her tomorrow or the next day, then continues his rounds.

A nurse sits on her bed a short while later and washes her, helping her to move as the pain tramps around her, making her woozy and weak.

"Is there no one to come see ya, pet?"

"No. No one." She wants Duncan, but she can't tell him what has happened. It is all such a mess. She grits her teeth, more at the thought of telling him, than the pain flecking her abdomen.

"I'll get ya some morphine, love." And the angel rises and leaves.

Later, as evening draws in around her, she remembers how she felt when she had her abortion. How stupid she had been to let it happen, and with that bloody art student who was such a shit. How could she ever have been interested in him? Back then she had told herself that she wasn't killing anything, she was just postponing the moment when she met her child and held it. That was what she told herself then. Now, she will never hold a child from her own womb. Life plays such awful tricks.

"Happy birthday to me. Happy birthday to me. Happy . . ." She is twenty-one. In Greenwich she knows her Mum and Dad will be worried—they have never missed seeing her on her birthday. Birth-day . . .

When the nurse returns she will call Duncan. She needs him.

Duncan sits in the dark. Waiting for Audrey. A bag lies by his feet, packed.

Finally, there is a scratch at the lock and the front door opens.

"Lorraine, why are you here, pet?" Audrey calls out as she arrives—knowing someone is in the house. "You'll not guess where I've been," she calls out excitedly, glad to have someone to share the gossip with. She'd been to a salon—exclusive. Had her hair done, her nails as well—feet and hands—plus a wax. Downstairs. It feels really odd. All part of her plan to get him excited in her again.

"Aud."

She almost jumps out of her skin. She flicks on the light and sees him at the table. She knows it's awful news. His skin is chalk, his eyes bloodshot and his cheeks are streaked with tears. But it is the bag that tells the story.

"I love you, Audrey, but . . . she needs me."

There was no need to reveal her name. Duncan knows his affair is an open secret.

"No!" she moans.

"Don't make this harder than it has to be. I owed it to you to tell you face to face. But I'm going."

"You can't, Dunc. We're your family."

"You will always have everything you need."

"Lorraine . . ."

"She's grown, Aud—she doesn't need me and neither do you."

"We do!" she is on his lap in a second, wrapping her arms around his neck. Trying to kiss him.

"Don't, Audrey. Have some dignity."

He pushes her off his lap and she lands on the floor.

"Do you want me to beg? Look, I'll beg." She is on her knees, shuffling forward, arms outstretched. "Please, Duncan. Don't do this to me, to us."

"I'm sorry, Audrey. Christ, I shouldn't have come home." He goes to walk around her but she grabs his leg.

"No, No. No!" she screams.

He tries to shake her off but she won't budge. "Audrey, don't. Christ, sweetheart, don't make this worse."

"It can't be worse. You can't leave."

"She needs me."

"I need you!" Audrey screams.

"She lost a baby. She lost my baby." He is all tears now, they stream out of him, snot too. "Someone beat her to a pulp—almost killed her. They killed my baby."

Audrey lets go, and slides to the floor. He walks around her.

THIRTY-NINE

Wednesday, December 29, 2010

"He left," Audrey Cobhurn continues as Patty tries to reel her mind back into her body.

"I lay there on the kitchen floor, shocked. I'd called my brother. He said it all went fine and she wouldn't be troubling me again. He said nothing about the violence—I found that out later. They'd beaten her badly. She'd been lippy and they were the type of men who liked hitting woman and . . . I hadn't told them she was pregnant."

The cold bites at the two women.

"I lay there all night, praying, cursing . . . then, at dawn, the front door opened. He was back. He didn't say a word. Just came in and unpacked his bag. Showered and went to bed. I didn't know what to think, didn't know what happened—but he stopped with us. I thought they must have had a fight, him and your daughter. Or he realized it was just the baby that had brought them together. We never talked about it and then a few weeks later we saw her photo in the papers. She was missing."

Patty remembers how she and Jim had finally driven up to Durham. She had been so angry with Dani. Starting with that stupid Christmas visit—how the hell could she give up on her education when she was so close to finishing? Then keeping quiet on her birthday, her twenty-first. She had seen how all this had hurt Jim. He kept asking Patty to get in touch with Dani, but she refused. Then they had a letter from the university, asking if Dani was deferring her final year or had dropped out. They had to speak to her. They called and called, but no reply. They decided to drive there.

When they arrived there was no one there. They let themselves in, they had a key, and waited. After a few hours the flatmate came back, very surprised to see them. She hadn't seen Dani since before Christmas.

"I knew she'd gone home to tell you she didn't want to do her final terms. I think she was going to defer them but . . . I thought she was with you. There's a pile of post . . ."

Jim went through the stack of mail for any clue to where she might be. Nothing. Patty sat on the sofa. She already felt something awful had happened. That evening they went to the police and reported her missing.

Audrey continued. "Duncan was beside himself. He was out every night—I think he was searching for her. He didn't talk to me, or Lorraine. Didn't go to work—left his assistant to run the business. Almost ran it into the ground. Duncan was in the same house with me but wasn't my husband anymore. I know that if he'd have found her, he would have left me. Just know it. I prayed she'd stay gone—forever. And then . . . then she was dead."

Patty sees Tom's mouth move but she doesn't understand. The drugs have slowed everything, disengaged her eyes from her ears.

The words make no sense. Then she looks to Jim and she knows what Tom is saying. Jim's face says it all.

Patty closes her eyes and her heart.

❋

"I never said anything to Duncan about what I'd done. But in those early days I saw what it did to him. He thought he'd let her die and it was killing him. That's when the charity work started: young offenders, drug addicts. I helped him with it and we slowly became a team again."

For a few seconds Audrey Cobhurn is lost in her thoughts, memories of the two of them fighting the system, the dynamic duo. Then she is back in the cold reality.

"I thought he'd forgotten her. That it was all over. Then he dies, my poor lovely man. And you show up at his funeral. I hadn't even put him in the ground and you were there. Of course I recognized you right away—knew you were her mum. Then the policeman comes and shows me the photo—this photo." She holds up the picture of Dani and Duncan.

"Now I don't think he ever got over her. I think he loved her for twenty years."

She looks lost, caught in a maelstrom of memories—reaching out to touch them and judge if they're real. Remembering each kiss and thinking—did he mean that for me or for her? Suddenly her face changes—pain streaks it.

"The policeman told me you killed Duncan." Her eyes flash naked hatred for a second, directly at Patty.

Patty closes her eyes. "I thought your husband killed Dani, all those years ago. I kidnapped him to force him to tell me and . . . I killed him. I didn't mean to. I didn't—" but her words sound empty. Patty knows she wanted him dead.

The widow sighs and folds into the earth, whispering softly, "I might as well have killed them both."

The two women are quiet, both locked in their own grief. Until something in Patty's brain switches on. She suddenly feels a chill in her chest, realizing the importance of something Audrey had said.

"What policeman?"

Audrey Cobhurn says nothing, lost, dancing somewhere far away with her Duncan.

Patty grabs at her coat and pulls her up. "What policeman?" She feels something under her hand. She pulls at the coat and jumper; there's a box tucked into Audrey's waistband—a wire runs out of it to a microphone taped to her chest.

Patty panics, she pushes Audrey away from her, and she staggers but doesn't fall.

"That policeman." Audrey points to a figure on the other side of the Cathedral Square, walking toward them.

"He told me you did it, killed Duncan, but he was wrong . . . it was me. I killed him—all those years ago. Killed the baby, killed our love and then killed him."

Patty is superglued to the spot—watching the figure get closer and closer—until . . .

"He isn't a policeman," she calls out to Audrey. She knows him. This is all wrong. She backs away, her eyes searching for an escape.

"Don't run, Mrs. Lancing," Marcus Keyson calls out as he walks closer. He waves a box in his hand. "I have you on tape, confessing to the murder of Duncan Cobhurn. Stay right there."

He is almost on her. She can't run anyway, not in these stupid shoes. She pulls her leg back . . .

Keyson calls. "There's nowhere to—"

Patty lashes her leg out with all the speed and agility she has.

The shoe flies off her foot, streaking like a bullet and slams into Marcus Keyson's face.

"Hell." He staggers and drops to his knees. Patty kicks the second shoe off and runs as fast as she can. She can see, by the side of the graveyard, there's a path that leads back down into town. She goes hell-for-leather toward it.

Marcus Keyson feels his nose. It's tender but not broken. There's a dull ache and he will have quite a bruise there tomorrow, but he doesn't care. He watches Patty run to the side of the graveyard and drop out of view. He could probably catch her, she's in her sixties and he's twenty-five years younger, but it doesn't seem worth it. He's got what he needs. The thought makes him all warm inside. He walks over to the other woman, kneeling on the cobbles.

"Hello, Audrey, thanks for finding Patricia for me. I have her confession on tape, well not tape, of course, all digital now—but you get my point. You should be happy."

He smiles. Audrey curls into herself a little more, wanting him to go away.

"I do have a teensy confession to make though. Patricia was right: I'm not an actual policeman. Sorry. I really wanted her confession—and as a bonus, I got you too, ouch nasty. Having a young woman almost beaten to death and her pregnant. Not good, really. Not something we want in the papers, is it—and they would love it, I'm telling you." He laughs. "It's been a bad Christmas for you, hasn't it?"

Patty runs as fast as she can, on cobbles that threaten to tip her over and break an ankle at every step. She almost falls as she reaches the Market Square. If she can only . . .

"I see her," a shout comes from somewhere to her left. She veers away from the voice, toward the little church at the end of the square. To the left, in the shadows, is the entrance to the indoor market.

"Where is she, Ronson?" Keyson calls out from somewhere behind.

She slams into the wooden door—it's chained and padlocked. The wall curves into a black corner—a dead end, she can't go that way.

"No!" She slams the heel of her hand into the gate. A slat gives ever so slightly. She pushes at it, and a tiny gap appears; barely wide enough for a child to crawl through. Patty scrapes through it, and tumbles into the dark of the market hall.

She lies where she's fallen; her hands are scraped but there's nothing more serious. Her eyes strain into the dark, trying to see something, anything, of her surroundings. She can see nothing. The only sound she can hear is the pounding of her own heart. Suddenly she is hit again by the awful knowledge that Dani was pregnant—it folds her into a ball, clawing her stomach. She wants to scream, howl, but she can't. She needs to get away first, that is the priority. Any thought of confessing to the police for the murder of Duncan Cobhurn has evaporated, this is survival now. She wants to live and she wants to be free. She wants Jim.

With a supreme effort of will, she pushes herself onto her hands and knees. Grief can wait. The drumming of her heart begins to lessen and she listens. To her right she hears footsteps—they're so close, but they're on the other side of the fence. Slowly her eyes adjust to the darkness and she can see she's in some sort of walkway between stalls. She can just about see a large pile of secondhand books and a tray of CDs and DVDs. It will be difficult to get past them without making any noise—and she will need to be totally silent as the men chasing her are so close. From behind her she hears the slam of boots on the gate into the market, testing it to find a way in, just like she had done.

"Where the hell is she?" a voice she doesn't recognize calls out.

"She can't have gone far—keep looking," Keyson yells back.

She can't stay in there, they'll find the way in soon and then she'll be trapped. She crawls on, through a mass of dropped clothes hangers and past a stall smelling of fish. Up ahead she can see a light, spilling through from somewhere. It may be a streetlight. She can . . .

Her phone rings. "Oh shit." She rolls onto her side and scrambles in her pocket, desperate to extinguish the sound as quickly as possible.

"I hear something, boss," the unknown man shouts. "She's in the market. How the hell did she get in there?" He starts thumping on the fence, hard and loud.

The phone screen shows Lorraine Cobhurn's number.

Patty answers in a whisper. "What?"

"I asked you to forgive me," Audrey Cobhurn's voice sounds far-off, barely audible above the wind and sounds of traffic.

"I heard you," Patty answers in as low a voice as possible. "I can't forgive you."

"I didn't really expect you to. I wouldn't if I were in your shoes. And I don't forgive you either—for Duncan. I just don't blame you. I can't imagine twenty years of feeling like this."

Patty could say it gets better. But it doesn't, time heals nothing.

"I . . . I am sorry. For your loss, I—" Patty falters.

"Don't, you cannot have the right to apologize. There is only one thing you could do to make it up to me."

"What?"

"Kill yourself. That would do it. I think you should kill yourself, really I do, and I think it would make you happier."

"You're crazy." Deep down Patty knows it's her grief talking and she understands the urge to make the pain stop.

"Maybe I am crazy, honestly I could be," Audrey tells her. "But it seems very clear to me that I cannot live like this and I'm pretty sure you can't either. How you have coped for twenty years I can't imagine. So I think we should die together. A pact."

"Audrey, don't be an idiot."

"I think it's the best way for both of us, but if you won't then you have to live with what you've done—to Duncan and Lorraine and me. If you can live with it, then great. I know I can't live without Duncan, not now I know that I'm to blame."

"Audrey—what are you saying?" Patty hisses. Scared to be too loud.

"Will you do something for me?" the widow asks.

"Audrey, think straight—Lorraine—"

"Say goodbye to her. Tell her I love her."

"Audrey!" Patty shouts, forgetting the two men hunting for her.

"Goodbye."

Suddenly the noise of the wind screeches in the phone, then a blare of an airhorn as a truck bellows into the night—a scream of brakes and a sickening thud as the truck strikes Audrey Cobhurn's body. There is an explosion of sound and the phone goes dead.

Simultaneously, from outside the market, somewhere on the ring road behind the cathedral, Patty can hear an enormous crushing sound of metal on concrete; almost immediately followed by a cacophony of car horns and car alarms. Patty's hands start to shake.

"She's right here, I heard her," shouts the unknown man. Then there is the crash as a part of the fence gives way under the crunch of his boot.

"I'm in," he yells.

"Oh my God. Oh my God." Patty starts to crawl again toward the light. Fighting to put thoughts of Audrey's death out of her head and concentrate on getting away. The floor is gritty and she feels pieces of glass cut into her left palm, her knees feel shredded. She will have to stand but then she'll lose the cover.

"Come out, my little piggy." The unknown man laughs and then starts to hit the plastic tubs.

Patty almost screams. She feels the blood soak into her trousers as her knees are cut. She needs to get up and . . . there's a doorway up ahead. She can make out a blob of light that spears through it. It looks like it leads to an outside area and maybe to freedom. If she can only . . . there is a crash to her left, as she sends a tray of CDs spinning to the floor.

"There you are." The unknown man screams and heads toward the sound—crashing into a stall himself and sending it flying. Suddenly a line of light shoots out—he's got a torch. He catches her in the arc of light and her eyes widen in fear.

"Got you." He whoops in delight and lunges forward, grabbing at her arm . . . but the stalls are in the way and she is just out of his reach. He grunts in frustration, bats aside a pile of clothes and forces his way into the aisle directly behind Patty. She had been frozen for a second but now the spell is broken and she runs forward at full pelt.

There are stairs to her left. She bolts up them, trying to stay out of the beam of light that tries to track her like a searchlight. She has to keep moving. Below her, on the other side, there is another crash as part of the fence falls into the market and Keyson steps inside.

"Ronson!" Keyson yells. "Where is she?"

"Up the stairs, she's gone up to the second level."

"Go up after her. I'll look for another staircase."

Patty hears Ronson start to head up the stairs. It's too dark up here for her to blindly stagger about, but she knows that as soon as he gets up with the torch, she'll be a sitting duck. There is only one thing to do. She rolls to the top of the stairs and flattens herself as low as she can get. Then as Ronson's head gets level with her foot, she lashes out, kicking him in the side of the head.

"Christ . . ." He flails, trying to grab at her leg as he starts to topple backward. He touches her heel, tries desperately to get a hold on her as he falls back, but he can't keep his footing and he crashes backward down the stairs, head over heels into a crumpled heap at the bottom. Patty is up and after him, running down and jumping over his body.

She hopes he's unconscious but with a roar of anger he is up and on his feet in seconds. She runs as fast as she can, hoping the path ahead is clear. She can see a rectangle of light further on; it must be a door—but where to? She prays it leads outside. She reaches it and—yes, she can see through the gloom to the end of a storage area and there's a fence she could scale that leads to the open world. She could escape. She takes a breath to ready herself for a sprint and jump, her adrenaline spiking. She can do this. She leaps forward, accelerating as quickly as possible—sees the gap with the fence beyond—seconds away, she speeds up and—

"Got you." From nowhere an arm shoots out and grabs her. She tries to spin sideways but it grips on tight, pulling her into a bear hug.

"You've been a bit naughty, ain't ya." Grant Ronson laughs. His other arm pulls her around and his hand clamps a cloth over her face. She twists and kicks like a mule, tries to pull her face away, breathe clean air, but his hand stays firmly around her nose and mouth. Slowly her energy begins to wane as the chloroform starts to take effect.

"Time to sleep," he says as she turns to deadweight. He swings her onto his shoulder like a sack of potatoes. She drops her phone but he bends down and retrieves it. Then, whistling the theme to *The Dam Busters*, he carries her outside.

It's colder out in the open. Wisps of mist have started to trail through the Market Square. Keyson stands under a streetlamp, a sodium-orange pallor making the bruise above his nose look quite nasty. He stamps his feet, partly due to the cold, partly in annoyance.

"Here we go, guv." Ronson gives his boss a broad smile.

"Phone?"

He hands Patty's phone to Keyson, who nods and scrolls through the address book. He finds the name he wants and hits dial. It rings only once.

"Patty. Thank God, I was so worried about you!" Jim's voice blasts from the phone. Keyson pulls it back from his ear a little.

"You will never guess what just happened—a woman jumped off a bridge and landed just in front of us, we had to swerve but a truck hit her. Christ, it was awful. Patty? Patty?"

Keyson smiles. "Hello, Jim, hope your head's feeling better."

In the car, Jim digs his fingernails into the seat, digging small ovals into the leather. He looks across to Tom and whispers, "It's Keyson."

"Oh hell." Tom feels a little sick. He looks out of the windscreen at the anarchy in front of him. Two cars have crashed into the middle barrier. One is crushed into the tunnel support, closing the entrance. A trail of blood is smeared from the tunnel at least twenty yards to where the truck dragged the body; the body itself lies like a battered rag doll, its stuffing pulled from it and smeared all around.

"Where's my wife?" Jim asks coldly.

"Wife? Haven't you been separated for years?"

"She is still my wife. Where is she, Keyson?"

"Okay, let's not split hairs, Mr. Lancing. Your wife is safe. No one is getting hurt, I am not that kind of man."

"Oh, I've heard exactly what kind of man you are, Dr. Keyson."

"From who?"

"Detective Superintendent Tom Bevans."

"Oh, Jim. Honestly, I would take anything he tells you with a pinch of salt. He's not your friend."

"And you are?"

"Me? No, 'friend' is too strong a word—but I am going to tell you some truths, including a particularly juicy one. I am going to tell you who killed your daughter."

From somewhere the sound of sirens begins to wail, getting closer. He turns to see the flashing lights—red and white, rotating—making the blood on the road shine like a trail of bright red breadcrumbs leading to hell. In the mirror, just for a split second, Jim thinks he sees Dani frozen in the red stroboscopic light from an ambulance. She waves solemnly, then she is gone.

Jim strains into the darkness, hoping to catch another glimpse of her but . . .

Whack! The truck driver slams into the car.

"Jesus!" Jim jumps.

The driver is in complete shock, staggering around in a circle. Jim sees a medic jump out of an ambulance and run toward him.

"Are you still there, Jim?" Keyson's voice calls from the phone.

"Yes. Yes, I'm here. Patty was in Durham, are you still there?" Jim asks Keyson.

"Yes, old Durham town," Keyson replies. "Don't tell me you're here too."

"Yes."

"How wonderful. Let's meet and have a lovely chat about abduction and murder."

"Where?" Jim asks coldly, not wanting to get drawn into anger by Keyson's levity.

"How about the cathedral. Lovely spot. Begun in 1093 and is in the Norman style with some beautiful Gothic flourishes. I've got a pile of guidebooks if you'd like one?"

Jim looks out of the side window and up to the heavens. He can see the cathedral above them, dominating the skyline of the town.

"I can be there in fifteen minutes," Jim tells him.

"Alone?"

"I may have DS Bevans with me."

"Oh, Jim. That would be perfect. Please bring him."

But Jim's no longer listening. He unclips his seat belt and opens the door.

"Jim, Jim, where are you going?" Tom asks, but gets no reply. Instead he watches his friend dart across the blocked carriageway and start to climb the hill that leads up to the cathedral.

"Shit!"

Tom slides out of the car and slams the door, pocketing the keys as he does so. He looks around wildly for a second. All is pandemonium as more and more emergency vehicles arrive, each one adding another flashing light and wailing siren. He should help out, move the car to the side, but Jim is getting away from him and he can't let him meet Keyson alone. He looks around. The truck driver is being helped and it is going to take a lot of time to remove the dead woman from the roadway. There is nothing he can do.

"Damn." He runs after Jim.

FORTY

Above them, at the top of the city, Keyson holds Patty, still unconscious, in his arms and watches Ronson work on opening the cathedral door. It is huge, solid oak reinforced by thick slats and possibly metal rods. Keyson doubts it can be breached but he's seen Ronson perform some remarkable feats and Ronson has told him he will get them inside. Keyson presses himself against the door, deep into the shadows, and waits. There is a sudden snap and the door shudders on its hinges and arcs forward.

Ronson catches it as it moves. "There you go," Ronson says with pride as it swings, wobbling on a shattered hinge. "No alarms, and I can't see any CCTV neither." Ronson grins and holds the door for his boss to walk through.

Keyson enters the enormous structure, looking up, as he does so, to see a parade of saints glowering down at him. Each is suffused with moonlight and looking furious at this intrusion.

"Gentlemen." Keyson waves cheerily to them. He walks to the baptismal font and places Patty's limp body on the cold stone. Then, switching on a torch, he begins to explore. There is something he desperately wants to find. He locates the rose window, an enormous wall of stained glass in the shape of a flower. It orients him to the correct set of pews and he kneels down in the central isle and shines his torch into the rows—examining each pew until he finds what he wants. In the faintest of writing he sees her name.

DANIELLE LANCING. 1986.

He sits in the pew trying to imagine her there. It is uncomfortable and drafty sitting, so he kneels and uses a cushion embroidered in 1952 for the Coronation.

"The Lord is my Shepherd I shall not . . ." he begins to intone . . . but there is nothing. Nothing of her to feel. Nothing of anyone to reach out to, in the drafty ancient room. He gets up and walks further into the belly of the cathedral. Now he can give the place his attention. It is magnificent, vaulted ceilings with fingers of wood that worm through stone to hold up the sky. The great rose of stained glass dominating the center of the cathedral. During the day it blazes with light but in the darkness it seems somewhat sinister, a shadow-play of pain and anguish. Keyson likes it.

❄

Jim walks up the final slope toward the cathedral, his legs like pistons—his eyes ahead. In his chest the feeling of panic is slowly being replaced by the fizzing of anger. Behind him Tom follows, not knowing what to do. His professional wisdom says: stop and call for backup—but this is not professional, it's personal. He pulls out his phone, sees the time is 3 a.m. He punches in a number and listens to it ring. An answer phone picks up—his own voice.

"You've reached Tom Bevans. Sorry I'm not here at the moment but please leave a message and I'll get back to you. Thanks." Tom smarts a little at the message. Plain Tom Bevans, no DS—in case a woman he lied to is calling.

"I need to get a life once this is over," he tells himself.

The phone beeps once.

"It's three a.m. Wednesday, December 29, 2010. I am approaching Durham Cathedral in pursuit of Dr. Marcus Keyson and Grant Ronson, who I believe have abducted Patricia Lancing for the purpose of extortion. I am following her husband, James Lancing, to the ransom drop-off point. If for some reason I . . ." He stops for a second. "Jane, just get the bastard."

He flicks the phone closed and hurries off after Jim. Tom catches up with him just as he is crossing the central lawn that leads directly to the main cathedral door, which stands massive and black in the night. Hung in its center is the sanctuary knocker—a blazing metal sun behind a face with soulless dark eyes. By royal decree those who use it to call for the door to be opened can ask for sanctuary. It was granted even to the guiltiest of souls. Tom reaches his fingers out to touch it.

"Oh please, sanctuary—for you?" Keyson appears from the shadows.

"It isn't even the real thing, it's a fake," Tom says a little sadly.

"Nowhere is safe for a murderer nowadays. Isn't that right, Tom?" Keyson asks with a smile.

"Hello, Marcus." Tom attempts to smile back, but in his tired face it looks forced.

"Please." Keyson motions for them to enter as he pushes the door open.

"Into the cathedral?" Jim asks.

"Pretty please."

They enter and Keyson closes the door behind them.

Inside it's mostly dark except for rectangles of moonlight that spill across the floor. The light from the stained glass seems alive, dancing across the flagstones—deep purple, bloodred and undersea blue. Jim looks up and sees the parade of saints who smile down on him.

"Your daughter loved it in this cathedral, she came often. I think it fitting that this is where we all finally meet to unravel this mystery." Keyson smiles but both Jim and Tom feel goose bumps spread over their flesh.

Keyson takes a slim book from his pocket and offers it to Jim. "I do apologize for the way I borrowed this."

Jim snatches Dani's diary back. "Where is my wife?"

"Toward the back, she's perfectly safe—Mr. Ronson is with her."

Jim gives Keyson a filthy look and leaves the two men. He walks quickly, almost running, though he has to take care; the flagstones are smooth like ice, and he can't see where they dip and bow from a thousand years of wear. His head is full of the rushing of his blood as he fights the panic that threatens to overwhelm him. Ahead of him the room stretches forever—the size of a football pitch at least. Jim's footsteps echo throughout, filling the air like a million insects scuttling through the house of God. As he rushes forward, toward the enormous rose of stained glass that beckons him on, for a second he sees Dani sitting in a pew, her hands linked together in prayer. She turns to look at him; her face is so pained, and then she is gone. Ahead he sees an area fully lit, a room off the main throughway—a chapel. He heads to it.

He steps inside, amazed to see it isn't electric light that illuminates the room but more than a hundred small votive candles, which have been lit around a massive sculpture carved from driftwood. It is of a woman who seems to be cut more from pure pain than wood. Her face is long, her lips pursed and her eyes weep. The wood itself seems weathered by a thousand years of sun and sea and salt; the form appears to bear the scars of humanity. At the woman's feet lies a man, twisted, half on his side; he looks emaciated—stripped of hope and life. Mary, the mother, and Jesus, her murdered child. Jim does not appreciate the theatricality of all this. He walks up to the figures until he stands by Jesus' head and the mother towers over him, almost double his height. Then he sees her. With her hands tied and mouth taped, sitting directly before the mother and child, is Patty. Grant Ronson stands beside her like some cut-price nightclub bouncer, his hands cupped in front of him. Jim moves to untie her, but Ronson pushes him back.

"It's fine, Mr. Ronson. Let him untie her," Keyson calls out as he and Tom step inside the chapel.

Ronson steps aside and Jim scrambles forward. He quickly gets the rope undone and pulls the tape off her mouth.

"Patty. Oh Christ, Patty, I am so glad to see you. I was so worried." He hugs her and she holds on to him tightly.

"Jim, I am so sorry to drag you into all this mess."

"I don't care. Just as long as you're safe and we're together."

She pulls him into her so tight they become a single entity for a moment.

She buries her head in his neck. "I'm not confessing—I'm not giving in, I want to be with you."

"You will be," he tells her.

"I told his wife—she needed to know and I had to tell her."

"Of course you did."

"Keyson taped it . . . me admitting to killing Duncan Cobhurn."

Jim feels all the blood drain from his face.

"And she told me—oh Christ, she told me something, Jim. She told me something awful and then. Oh God, she killed herself."

"His wife?" Jim asks.

"She jumped in front of traffic or something—I could hear the truck."

Both Jim and Patty heard the death of Audrey Cobhurn and Jim saw her body fall. The sight will haunt him for the rest of his life.

"They were lovers—Dani and Duncan Cobhurn. And she was pregnant, Jim. Dani was going to have a baby. That Christmas she was pregnant and I screamed at her, told her she was wasting her life, but I didn't know. Jim, I didn't know she was carrying our grandchild." Patty has tears streaming down her face.

Jim grips her tight, his throat closing up as he thinks of Dani that last time he saw her—the rounded tummy he thought was too many chips.

"Audrey found out and confronted Dani, telling her to leave him alone, and when she wouldn't . . . when she wouldn't . . ." Patty dissolves in tears.

Keyson kneels down next to Jim. "Audrey Cobhurn had your daughter beaten until she miscarried. I wouldn't waste a tear on Mrs. Cobhurn if I were you." Keyson then removes the final pieces of rope from Patty and helps her and Jim up, before dropping a hand onto his shoulder.

"There we go. I am sorry for the inconvenience. Don't worry that you missed Audrey's revelation, Mr. Lancing, there are many more to come."

Keyson walks across to Ronson and whispers in his ear. Keyson gives him the recording machine from his pocket and Ronson walks off.

"Mrs. Lancing, I apologize. You are my employer after all and I really have acted badly—but I think ultimately you will thank me."

"I can't see that happening, Dr. Keyson," Patty says, trying to keep her voice level.

"We shall see, because I am about to tell you who killed your daughter."

Despite herself, Patty feels her heart stop for a second.

Tom steps forward with his arm outstretched and places his hand on Keyson's chest, his back to Patty and Jim.

"Marcus, I think this has gone on long enough."

"Mr. and Mrs. Lancing . . ." Keyson begins, ignoring Tom.

"Don't, Marcus." Tom is insistent.

" . . . your daughter, Danielle, was murdered . . ."

"Please, Marcus," Tom says in a whisper, pleading with his old friend.

" . . . by Police Constable Tom Bevans." Keyson steps back. "Now Detective Superintendent Tom Bevans, of course."

"Tom?" Jim shakes his head. It is unthinkable.

"Tom?" Patty barely manages to get the word out, her face contorting with effort.

From the shadows Dani walks forward and circles Keyson, until she can see into the face of her best friend.

"Tom?" she breathes.

Tom Bevans looks through Dani, and slowly turns to face the parents of the woman he has loved almost his whole life. Tears coat his face. Dani walks over to stand between her parents. The Lancing family waits.

"Did you?" Patty asks.

Tom cannot speak. He nods slowly.

Dani seems to crack, like fine porcelain in a fire—hairline cracks that twist throughout her entire form.

"Oh my God." Jim steps back, lurching sideways. He walks away, into the shadows and sits on the floor, lost in thought. He recalls the look on Tom's face when he saw him that morning, over twenty years ago. The look of total distress as they faced each other on the street—how is it possible that he . . . that he . . .

"Dani." Jim holds his head in his hands. He can't bear it.

Patty watches Tom's face, sees the tears and the pain that eats him. It's genuine—she knows the purity of his anguish; he is, after all, the Sad Man. He was transformed by Dani's death but for the first time she wonders what caused that pain? Is it something more than grief? Is it guilt? Her face hardens—like her heart. Her eyes are ice.

Keyson watches her and licks his lips. From his pocket Keyson takes a knife, sharp like the blade Patty used on Duncan Cobhurn. He walks over to her and bends his lips to her ear and whispers, "Twenty lost years. A life snuffed out. Jim lost to you—your whole life ruined, and you yourself turned into a murderer. Responsible not only for the death of Duncan Cobhurn but Audrey Cobhurn too. And the broken heart of Lorraine Cobhurn. Tom Bevans has done that to you. He made you trust him, he wormed his way into your family and then . . ." He takes her hands and uncurls the fingers, wrapping them around the knife handle. "He kills the thing you hold most dear, he killed your daughter, Dani."

Keyson takes a step back. Patty stands there holding the knife before her. Keyson moves to her side and takes her softly and walks her forward.

"He said he loved her but he killed her and left you in anguish for more than twenty years." Keyson's voice is seductive as he leads Patty, knife in hand, to face Tom.

"Is it true, Tom? Did you kill her?"

Tom stands his ground, his eyes red and his mouth in constant motion, yet no words come.

"Tell me, Tom!" she hisses at him.

He closes his eyes and breathes. "I did."

Patty's jaw clenches; it looks like it could shatter. She steps forward to bring the knife up to his chest, level with his heart. The tip cuts into his clothing and, through them, to his skin. He cries in pain but does not move.

"Do it, Patricia. Do it," Keyson urges.

"You killed Dani?"

Tom doesn't answer. His head is bowed to the floor.

"Jesus, Tom." She pushes forward, feels flesh split, and sees red pool on the knife and start to soak into the cloth. Tom sobs with pain. She moves a hand up to his chin and forces his head up; she wants to see his eyes. The blood pools on the hilt and three drops of blood fall to the ground. Patty looks into his eyes and yells into his face—the sound of deep pain.

Jim looks up, hearing his wife's anguish, his own pain broken for a second as he watches her hold a knife to the heart of the man who killed their daughter.

Jim sees Dani walk forward. She seems to flare bright like the sun, filling the chapel with daylight. Tears drop from her cheeks, three perfect teardrops that fade into nothing before they hit the stone ground.

"No, Mum," she whispers, and her light seems to shimmer around Patty for a second.

Patty howls, and throws the knife away. It bounces on the hard stone and skittles along the floor, coming to rest by stone steps close to Jim.

"You didn't kill her."

Patty wraps her arms around him and he sags into her—his sobs loud like screams. "Tom, Tom . . . poor pup." She strokes his hair.

Dani turns and walks away, the brightness fading once again until she is normal. Normal for a ghost.

Keyson looks like he will spit blood. "What the— You stupid woman. He killed your daughter. What the hell is wrong with you—what are you?"

Patty looks up at Keyson. "A parent. That's all." She turns back to Tom, who has calmed a little. "Tom, tell the truth. What happened?"

He whispers so softly that only Patty can hear him.

"I wish you had done it, Patty." He kisses her lightly on the cheek. Then he begins.

"Dani was pregnant with Duncan Cobhurn's child. She told me and Izzy that Christmas she came home. She said she couldn't tell you, didn't know how you'd react as he was married."

Patty nods her head, knowing she would have exploded.

"She planned to take a year out—have the baby and then go back to uni. They were going to live together, he was leaving his wife and everything. I couldn't . . ." Tom closes his eyes and lets the memories flood back.

❄

Duncan Cobhurn hurries, his heart beats fast, she is not chasing him—that's good. It's hard to rush with the case. He feels so ashamed. Telling Audrey was the hardest thing he has ever done. He loves Dani, will do anything to be with her—but . . . no, he has made his choices. Audrey will find it tough but eventually she'll get over it. It will work out for the best, he knows it will. He just needs to get to Danielle, hold her and tell her it will be all right. They can have another baby.

Up ahead in the shadows there is a movement. A policeman who . . .

"Mr. Cobhurn, Duncan Cobhurn?" He steps directly in Duncan's way, stopping him dead.

"Yes, that's me. Do I know you, Officer? How do you know my name?"

"Duncan Cobhurn. Husband of Audrey and father of Lorraine."

Duncan feels something's wrong. "I'm on my way to something important, if you'd just let me pass." He tries to get past the policeman, but he bars his way.

"Sweet kid, your Lorraine. Awful if something happened to her."

"What the hell are you—"

Tom is quick, he swings his arm and from nowhere a truncheon slides into it. He catches Duncan Cobhurn on the leg just below the knee. An inch higher and the blow would have shattered his kneecap.

"Christ." Cobhurn falls, grabbing at his leg and rolling on the ground in pain.

"This is no idle threat, Duncan. You are not going to see Dani Lancing again. You are going back to your wife and daughter and you're going to keep your dick in your pants. If you don't, Lorraine is going to get a visit from some lads I know and they will fuck her up—do you understand what I'm saying? She will wish they'd killed her by the time they finish."

Duncan grabs at Tom, but he's quicker. The truncheon catches him hard on the shoulder.

"Jesus. Why are you doing this?"

"Because Dani Lancing is owned by someone else and they will destroy anyone who hurts her."

"I love her."

"You have caused her nothing but pain. Leave her alone, you bastard. In fact—"

Tom grabs him by the collar and pulls him up on his injured leg—Duncan screams with the pain.

"Come here." Tom drags him toward a phone box close by and throws him inside. "Where are you meeting her?"

"Her home. She's going there by cab . . ."

Tom dials the number. "You are gonna tell her you're finished with her, that she means nothing to you. That you can't imagine having a baby with her—she's just a kid."

Tom pushes the swing and sees the child flash in the air—weeeee-eeeee it cries. Dani waves at them both. "I don't care that he isn't mine—I will love you both forever," he hears himself say. *This is my family.*

"The baby . . . she lost the baby."

"You fucker." Tom's truncheon is in his hand again and he smashes into Duncan's thigh. The older man screams and drops to the bottom of the phone box.

"You will never see Dani again."

"Please, no . . ."

"Say it or your wife and daughter will wish they were dead."

Tom hands him the phone.

In the cathedral, Patty and Jim feel their hearts break. For Dani, for Tom, for the baby . . . even for Duncan Cobhurn. And in the shadows Dani remembers the emptiness—the pain rushes back into her. She remembers the pit opening inside her soul when she heard Duncan on the phone that night.

"I hate you. You won't trap me again with your brat—I'm glad it's dead," he had told her. Tom had made him say that—how could he? He was supposed to be her friend—he had been her protector and confidant. How could he? And Duncan, her poor Duncan.

She looks to Tom. His head is bowed. She fades from where she is and reappears, floating in mid-air below him, looking directly into his face. Tears drop from his cheek and fall toward her . . . flaring slightly as they pass through before striking the flagstones. She sees his pain and yet cannot understand how the gentle boy she once knew beat a man and left him broken in the bottom of a phone box. Forced him to break a woman's heart. How can this man be her Tom?

"Tom?" she whispers.

He looks right through her—there are no answers from him. He stands up and looks back to Patty.

"My plan had been to make him dump her on the phone and then I'd turn up an hour later. I had a cake and flowers. It was just gonna be by chance—on her birthday . . ."

Dani understands.

" . . . and she'd be all sad from Cobhurn—but all happy to see me. She'd fall into my arms and realize we were meant to be together. I just wanted her to love me like I loved her. I even wanted to . . . I thought we could raise the baby. Our baby. I didn't care that it was his."

"But?" Patty asks.

"When I heard she had lost the baby I thought she'd need time. I decided to wait for twenty-four hours. Go back the next day. I still thought she'd be so happy to see me that . . ."

"Tom, I loved you but I was never in love with you," Dani tells the air.

"I just loved her so much," Tom repeats.

"I know you did, Tom. I know you did," Patty says in a tired voice.

"But when I got to her flat the next day—the . . . the door was open. The place was empty. I sat down and waited. I stayed in her flat all that day and night but she never came back. She never came back. I killed her, Patty. I killed her because I couldn't let her be with him."

Patty takes his hand. "Christ, what a mess."

"Oh Jesus, this is desperate," sneers Keyson. "Then what are you telling us? That while she was walking around she was taken by a gang and killed a month later? Is that the shit you're pedaling?"

"No. No, you aren't saying that are you, Tom?" Jim asks. He has walked out of the shadows. "She went back to him, didn't she?"

"Who?" asks Patty.

"Seb Merchant." Jim looks at his wife with, sad, soulful eyes. "In that first year at university, she got involved with drugs. Merchant was the bastard who dragged her into it. She kicked it, though, she was so strong—and I was so proud of her. She promised me she would never go back to him—she promised me."

"Dad, I am so sorry," Dani calls to him.

Patty shakes her head. "But Seb Merchant wasn't in the country when Dani went missing—he'd gone to Australia months before. I found him when he came back to England. I interviewed him and he wasn't involved."

Tom shakes his head. "It wasn't Seb Merchant; I wish it had been. I looked for her for days after that night, but there was no trace. I thought she'd just gone away to think, I was sure she'd call me or Izzy soon. Come home and cry on our shoulders . . . but nothing. I didn't know about the trouble she'd been in that first year, she never told me. I kept waiting to hear . . . then you reported her missing and I just couldn't believe it."

"No." Dani feels so cold.

"I went straight round to you but you didn't know anything. I couldn't tell you what I'd done—couldn't tell anyone. So I carried on searching, kept calling the Durham police—drove up there any time I had off work. Then Ben Bradman's piece came out in the *News of the World*—I was so angry I had to confront him. He told me he'd heard rumors about Dani from a jazz musician but he had no name. It took days to track him down."

Tom finds him in a rehearsal room, alone. Trumpet player, big with a thick neck that oozed gold chains and an enormous crucifix that hung over his heart and danced as he played. In his mid-thirties, shaved head—a large man, but slow, no muscle. Clyde Trent.

Tom pulls the heavy door closed as he goes through. The room had once been an old bank vault, now it's used for cheap bands to rehearse and make tinny recordings. Dead acoustics.

"I done nothing . . ." are his first words as soon as he sees the uniform.

Tom pulls Dani's photo out from his jacket and he holds it out with one hand. In his pocket his other hand slips inside his knuckleduster. Violence is coming so easily to him now.

"Dani Lancing. Remember her? You told a reporter that you knew her, that she was involved with drugs in a big way."

"Oh Christ, man." He makes a break for the door to the outside, but Tom is quicker and bars the way.

"I need to know just what you told him."

"You got the wrong m—"

"Bradman was very clear. Now we can do this messily, which ends badly for you, or you can tell me what you know and I leave you alone and go back to London. That way nobody but you and me know we had this conversation. Which option do you like?"

Clyde is impassive, but Tom can see that inside the large man the cogs are starting to shift.

"The newspaper paid me," he says finally.

"Lucky you. I hope you got at least thirty pieces of silver. I am offering you something far more rewarding than money."

"Shiiiit . . ." He grinds his teeth and shakes his head. "These are bad men."

"Then help me save her from them."

Clyde looks incredulous for a second and then laughs a deep braying laugh. "She don't want no saving. Man, she chose the gig."

"What?"

"I know her a while back. She was with some small-time pusher, worked the university—some spliff then on to H, but she could afford it. She didn't turn no trick. Not then."

Tom begins to feel everything start to unravel. "Now?"

Clyde hesitates, before he leans forward and speaks softly. "A few weeks back I were at a party, she came looking for her ex but no one seen him. She seem desperate for somewhere to crash and get lost, she make an offer. She was pretty, so she got owned," he shrugs. "She knew what she were doing."

Tom feels bile rise in his throat. "Owned," he repeats slowly. He knows what that means. He thinks of the branded girl at Franco's.

"One man?"

"A gang."

Tom wants to be sick but has to keep it all inside. "I need a name."

"Come on, I can't . . ."

"If you don't, I will list you as an informant and have it leaked to every scumbag in this city. They will nail you to a fucking cross."

Clyde shakes his head. Tom feels his fingers tighten inside the cold metal in his pocket. He has come too far, he will do anything now.

Clyde is quiet for quite some time, before he finally speaks. "Jackson. They known as the Jackson Five. Big joke."

"Address?"

"Ain't got."

Tom nods, he can see the big man has given him all he knows.

"Thank you," he says in what must sound so hollow to the other man—then he's gone.

Tom runs back into the early evening gloom and heads toward the center of town. He finds a phone box and places a call to Franco. It takes some time to make his way through the entourage surrounding him, but finally he gets to speak to the man himself and ask his favor. Franco listens to Tom's story.

"I see how you love this girl, Mr. Policeman. I hope there is a sweet outcome here . . . so I will help, but you owe me. You owe me personally, and you owe me big. I will collect on this debt, you can be sure of that. One day you will return these favors."

"I will, Franco. You have my word."

"Your word is your heart and your soul, PC Bevans. You understand that?"

"I do."

He pauses for a moment. "Okay, give me an hour."

It takes twenty minutes. Twenty minutes where Tom stands in the phone box and tries to keep all thoughts out of his head, all thoughts of what *being owned* by a gang might mean. But that is impossible as the image of the beautiful girl in the sarong forces itself into his mind. She was owned, kept junked up, oblivious to the world and whatever she was trying to escape from. And in return she was used whenever the gang wanted, for whatever the gang wanted. He sees again the carved F on her shoulder, her brand.

"Dani," he moans.

Two people come to use the phone box but he makes them move on, growling at them like he's a madman.

After twenty minutes the phone rings and he rips it from its cradle.

Franco has an address in the Gilesgate district.

"This is a heavy scene here, PC Romeo. I tell you this not so you can call in a raid but go there yourself. You okay with that?"

"Fine, Franco."

Tom pulls out his Durham A to Z and finds the address. Not too far. He starts to run. It takes maybe fifteen minutes; he runs like a fox chased down by hounds. He has no plan, he just wants to find her—he'll threaten, barter and pay for her release from them. Anything. He will sell his soul to the devil to get her back.

"Even if she goes straight back to Duncan Cobhurn?" The devil hisses in his ear.

FORTY-ONE

Wednesday, December 29, 2010

In the guttering candlelight of the cathedral, Tom sways, his face drained of all color; contrasted to the bloom of blood on his shirt he looks like a dead man.

"I found her. Patty, I found her and—"

He sees her again, as she was that night. Lying naked, alone . . . already dead.

He finds it; a squalid house in a dirty street of student digs and squats. Its windows have boards nailed across them, the small front garden a tumble of weeds with the detritus of a washing machine lying tangled and twisted across the path leading to the door. Inside, the house seems dark and noiseless.

Tom strides up to the front door and hammers with authority, an authority he no longer feels. There is no answer. He drags a large piece of metal over to the window and stands on it, trying to look inside, but he can see nothing. He makes his way around to the back door. Again it's locked. He lifts some metal, a battering ram of sorts, and begins to swing. It takes seven attempts to shatter the wood and push it through into the kitchen. Then he climbs through the hole he's made, and falls into the darkness. He takes a torch from his belt and . . .

"Christ."

In the beam a sea of cockroaches scuttle away. The smell of rotting food takes his breath away. The floor is sticky, there are empty take-away boxes everywhere, and they undulate with the movement of small insects. Tom pushes on, torch shining the way. He checks the downstairs and then up, up . . .

The first two rooms are empty, abandoned in a hurry. Tom shines his torch around and can see powder residue and empty phials. This had been a factory for the gang—probably where they cut the pure drugs for sale on the street. But they'd moved on—and in a hurry. Tom feels anxiety building in him as he goes room to room. Finally there is only one room left on the second floor. The moment he opens the door he knows something is wrong; an overpowering smell of bleach hits him. He shines the torch inside and it catches the edge of a mattress in the center of the room. He walks in, his boots crunching on shattered glass, bleach lies pooled at the base of the mattress. And there lies Dani.

She is naked—more than naked, if there can be such a thing. And she is dead. A syringe sticks out of her arm. Pushed in but never pulled out. Her hair is greasy, there is semen in it. The mattress is stained with sick and blood. Her legs and arms are heavily bruised, the paleness of the body makes them all the more livid as the blood has settled. Her hip looks swollen.

On her shoulder there is a dark scrawl that looks like a marker pen—but he knows is a primitive tattoo—a brand: J5. He touches her, she is a little stiff with rigor that is fading. Two days—probably two days dead. If only he could have . . . but what is the use of thinking like that? The room is cold, that has kept her looking fresher, but he knows that within a day or two she will start to bloat and insects will come. The bleach has been splashed around to keep anything off of her for a while. He is grateful for that, at least.

Tom kneels down to her and strokes her arm, up to her shoulder and then her hair. He sits there looking at her in the harsh light of his torch beam until he cannot bear it and turns it off. In the dark he does something he has not done since primary school. He prays.

In the cathedral the memories scorch his eyes from the inside.

"They just left her there; they just left her there with the cockroaches," he howls like a wild animal.

Jim looks across from Tom, to his daughter as she stands tall, listening to the story of her own death. He cannot tell what she feels, or if she knows this part of the story at all. Maybe she had watched Tom find her that day, and sit with her lifeless form. Jim feels such sorrow for her.

Tom snorts away tears and snot before he continues.

"I didn't have any plan. There was no power in the house but I found a candle and lit that. She looked so . . . I ran a bath and washed her. She was stiff, hard to maneuver at first but it was lessening and the bath helped. She looked so beautiful when I'd cleaned her up. I cut her nails and her hair a little. Then I wrapped her in a sheet I found—it wasn't totally clean but it was better than nothing."

Tom closes his eyes and remembers how she looked as she lay before him that night so long ago—pale but radiant in death. That night he cradled her head in his arms and spoke to her, told her all the things he'd always wanted to say but was too shy. He told her how much he loved her. He remembers kissing her one last time.

"As I sat there with her I realized I couldn't let anyone else see her and think she'd chosen that awful death. I thought about taking her body away and burying her—but I knew I couldn't do that to you two." He looks to Jim and Patty. "I had to let her be found, but not like that. I knew there was no way I could fool any pathologist or coroner; toxicology reports would show she was a chronic user and . . . and that would have been it. I didn't know what to do but knew I couldn't let the world think she—" He can't finish the sentence.

"What did you do?" Jim asks.

"I made her comfortable and then I left her—just for a little while. I called Franco again. I told him what I'd found."

"I am so profoundly sorry, my friend," Franco had said, then he paused. Possibly realizing he had used the word "friend." "You are a worry to me."

"I can't let her be seen like that, Franco. I can't let the world know her like that."

"You want history to remember her as a victim?"

"I want . . . those who loved her to remember the wonderful woman she would have become. Not the girl who lost her way and couldn't get back."

"You love her?"

"With all my heart."

Franco had sighed. "This all very *Romeo and Juliet*. You are lucky I am a big romantic. Go back to your sweetheart and sit with her for a while. A man will be with you soon. Do as he tells you."

"Thank you, Franco."

"I am not doing this for you, Policeman," Franco tells him and then rings off.

Tom goes back to the house and sits with Dani.

"I'm sorry," he tells her, stroking her face.

Then he begins to recite poetry to her. He had spent hours learning dozens of love poems for her—for the night he hoped they would be lovers. This is the closest he will ever come.

❄

Finally, at around 10:30 p.m., there is a pummeling on the door and Tom goes down to answer it. Before him stands a tall, thin man with a long face. He has a pencil moustache that sits on his upper lip as if it's been inked there. He's dressed in the uniform of a detective inspector.

"You PC Fucking Romeo?" he asks.

Tom can only nod slowly.

"DI Dent." He pushes inside. "Where's Juliet?"

Tom treads up the stairs with Dent following, into the room with Dani.

When he sees her Dent gives a little wolf whistle. "She's a looker." He moves her head from side to side. "Dead thirty-six to forty-eight hours." He touches her shoulder. "Branded—she was their Snow White, for any hardworking dwarf that wanted his wick dipped."

Tom feels bile rise.

Dent touches her leg and swollen hip.

"And they fucked her bandy."

Tom screams and swings a punch at Dent—but the older man is pistol quick. He feints to the side and drops Tom with a fist into the kidney. Tom falls and Dent grabs his arm and twists. Tom yells in pain.

"This is no fucking pantomime, you idiot. If you want your girlfriend to come out of this without looking like a whore you need to think like the shits that put her here. We need to lose the

brand—the hip works for us. Makes it look like she was forced."
He lets Tom go.

"How do we lose the brand?"

"We cut it or burn—"

"No!"

"She's dead. The dead don't feel pain."

With a look of contempt, Dent walks out the door and down the stairs. Tom sits there, at Dani's feet, lost.

"Are you fucking coming?" Dent calls up the stairs. With a last look at Dani, Tom leaves and heads down. The front door is open. Through it Tom can just about see the disappearing form of DI Dent. Tom bounds after him, catching up with him as he climbs into a squad car.

"Where are we going?"

Dent looks up at him from the driver's seat.

"Just get in the fucking car, lover boy."

Tom holds his anger in check and gets into the passenger seat. Dent pulls away from the curb. Tom turns to see the house disappear from view.

"Can you—" Tom starts.

"Button it. Look I don't know how but you've got some seriously fucking important friends and I have been told to do whatever I can to make your lady friend smell sweet as a newborn."

"I—"

"I said, button it. I don't want to hear your stories. We need two things to make this work. Number one—we need some clean samples. Blood sample, piss and cotton swabs from a clean mouth."

They drive in silence for another ten minutes and pull up in front of a regular residential house.

"Come on."

Dent gets out and walks up to the house, Tom follows. Dent pulls keys out of his pocket and opens the door. Tom stops on the threshold.

"Is this your house?"

"Yes—get in."

Dent walks in and heads upstairs, turning the lights on as he goes. Inside the house is really nice. Tom can see the quality of the carpets and the wallpaper. All the way up the stairs are paintings.

"Is that a—"

"Francis Bacon. Just a little one, for me old age," Dent winks. At the top of the stairs he walks into the bathroom and opens a cabinet, taking out a sponge bag. Then he goes back onto the landing and knocks on one of the doors.

"Julie." He waits a moment. "Julie."

"I heard ya."

A minute or so later the door opens. Standing there, in a stripey nightgown is a girl, maybe thirteen or fourteen. Blonde and thin, her skin a little acned.

"Dad."

He stretches out a hand and gives her a test tube, a small pot and a bag of swabs.

"Not again, Dad."

"Come on, darling. I'll buy you something nice."

"You bloody better," she says and walks into the bathroom, closing the door behind her.

Tom feels like he's in a dream. "Is that your . . . ?"

"Eldest. She's a good girl."

They stand in silence for a while and then the door reopens and Julie steps out. She hands the samples back to her dad.

"Thanks, darling."

"Nice, you promised."

"Got it, love."

"Expensive, too?"

"Within reason. Good night, sweetheart." He kisses her and she goes back to bed.

"Romeo—you need to get out of that uniform." He leads Tom into a bedroom. It's stylish, like a fancy hotel. Dent opens a drawer and pulls out jeans and a fisherman's sweater. He throws them at Tom. "Change—then come down. I'll find a holdall for the uniform."

Dent heads back downstairs. Tom puts on the change of clothes, then heads down. The front door is open and Dent is outside smoking. He hands a bag to Tom.

"How did you get here?" Dent asks him.

"What do you mean?"

"From London—I mean, you are from fucking London, aren't you?"

"Yes."

"So?"

"Train."

"Well, it's too late for that now. I'm gonna drop you at an all-night cafe—there you can cadge a ride with a truck. There's loads heading down at this time of night."

"I need to go back to the house."

"No, you don't. You need to get the fuck out of Dodge."

"I have to say goodbye."

"Who . . ." Dent looks lost for a second—then he understands. "To your girlfriend."

"Dani."

"She's fucking dead."

"She—"

"Christ, Romeo, let me tell you how this works. You are gonna get a truck down south. If you're lucky you won't have to suck his cock for the ride. Before you leave you are gonna make a phone call from a public phone to say the police will find Dani Lancing at that house and that she was abducted. Abducted. That will get them looking for signs of a struggle and of forced captivity. You understand?"

"Yes." Though Tom doesn't sound sure.

"That house is a known drugs den. If you just call in a tip-off they will send a drugs team in. That isn't what we want—we need a serious crime team to be called in."

"Why?"

"Cos it'll be my fucking team, that's why." Dent shakes his head. "They'll take photos and collect samples—clean samples, from my fucking pocket."

Tom nods. "The samples from Julie."

"A prize to the shithead for getting it right. My team will write the report up as abduction and multiple rape. Then the body will get transferred to the morgue—and the coroner."

"But he won't—"

"That's the second thing to do. Remember I said there were two things we had to do to make this right?"

"Bribe the coroner."

"Are you fucked? Coroners make too much bloody money and they think they're above all this shit—like they're doctors or something. No, we don't bribe him."

"Then what?"

"Blackmail the fucker."

"How?"

Dent sucks the last of the cigarette into his lungs and flicks the butt into the darkness.

"His son." He walks quickly to the car, Tom follows. They get in the car and Dent drives.

"What's the son done?"

"Took his dad's car when he was fourteen. Thought he was Sterling fucking Moss. Did a shitload of damage and put two people in hospital. One was serious—the kid begged us to hush it up. He's eighteen now—university boy whose life would be totally fucked by this. Pretty sure the old man doesn't know. Well, he will tonight."

"And he'll alter his report."

"Oh yeah—I'll make sure he does. He doesn't want his son going down. He's far too pretty to do well inside. The coroner's a family man."

"So his report won't mention drugs in Dani's system."

"Nothing." Dent pulls onto a stretch of motorway. The car moves through dark to sodium orange and back to dark. Ahead is a transport cafe. Dent pulls into it and up to a phone box. They sit in silence.

"You are gonna get a ride set up for about an hour and make that call just before you leave. That will give me plenty of time."

"You don't want me back at the house."

"You know what I'm gonna do."

"The brand, you'll remove it."

"Yes. And then I am gonna take your girlfriend's hand and scratch the wall. I'm gonna make twenty-one lines on the floor and then the words 'Help me!' Then I'll tie her wrists and ankles together."

Tom nods his head with the smallest of gestures. He realizes what must be done—is even grateful in a way to be saved from seeing that room again.

"Then I'm gonna go and visit the coroner."

FORTY-TWO

Some of the candles have already burned themselves out, leaving the driftwood sculptures darkened in places. The chapel is quiet and cold while everyone takes in what Tom has told them. Suddenly Tom snorts with nervous laughter.

"Then a couple of days later, when we went to see her, you and me," he looks directly at Jim, "I thought the game would be up. The report said no drugs—but you had to look at her arms because you knew about Seb Merchant. I thought I was going to die. I thought you were going to be the one to question why it was a murder inquiry, ask about the drugs . . . but you didn't." Tom stops for a second. "I thought someone, somewhere, would work out what had happened—the coroner would stand up to Dent. But no." Tom looks directly at Patty "I thought you would sink it—make the house of cards tumble down with your questions . . . but it didn't. Everybody assumed she'd been killed. You were looking for a killer, Patty—but there wasn't one to find. There wasn't a murder, but a dead girl. Just a dead girl."

"Tom," Patty's voice is barely audible. Her eyes closed. "Was it an accident?"

Dani hits her head with her palm. Jim hears it but nobody else. He sees the pain in his daughter's face.

Tom shakes his head. "There was no note."

It is not an answer to the question.

Jim remembers the church packed full of people on the day of her funeral, so much love for Dani, for the good girl who had been taken from them. How different would it have been if the truth were known?

Patty nods. "I unders—"

"Bastard." A fist lands on Tom's chin and sends him sprawling. Marcus Keyson stands there glowering, shaking with anger. "You fucking hypocrite. You sad little man. All you've done, lives ruined by you and because of you. Yet you swan around like a saint, dishing out your moral code and judging others like an Old Testament, petty god. You don't have the right."

"Marcus, I—"

"Don't you dare act like we're friends. You let that animal Dent loose on a kind and great man."

Tom is lost for a second and then—the pieces tumble into place; he understands Keyson's anger. "The coroner?"

"Gerald Spurling was his name. He was the greatest man I knew—the smartest man I will ever know. He was like a father to me and . . ." He chokes on the words, a tear falls.

"Marcus."

"For the sake of your fucking dead girlfriend's reputation—you destroyed him."

"I did nothing—"

"Your weapon of destruction—DI Dent. He went to an honorable man and he stuck the knife into his guts and twisted it until he broke."

"I didn't ask him to . . ."

"Oh, Tom, take some fucking responsibility. Whatever it took to make your girl look clean. You ruined Ben Bradman's life and you let Dent pressure an old man into fabricating a report."

"It was only changing evidence."

"Only." Keyson's eyes flash violence. "Only. What the hell did I lose my career for? Lose my reputation for?"

"That was different."

"How different? You made a man who was proud of a lifetime of honesty and service to this country lie—and you did it by threatening his family and his way of life. Do you know, he was so ashamed of what he'd done he took an overdose—it didn't kill him, probably would have been better if it had—it gave him a massive stroke. He took more than ten years to die—ten years of misery. His son, Paul, nursed him all those years. He felt so guilty that a reckless moment as a teenager had been used to destroy his father. When Gerald finally died do you . . ." Keyson closes his eyes, unable to go on for a second. "Paul hanged himself. Both gone, what a fucking waste."

"Marcus, I had no idea—"

"No, of course you didn't. You high and mighty bastard. You use people. Knock down anyone that gets in your way and don't care what happens to them."

"Back then—"

"But if anyone else deviates, even slightly from the Bevans code, then you judge them. You are judge, jury and executioner—you judged me and had me thrown out with the rubbish. Yet you—"

"You're right. I have done awful things, I should pay for it all and I've tried. For twenty years I've tried to pay for what I did, tried to do right by women like Dani."

"Like Dani . . . like Dani."

"Damn you, Marcus."

"You already have—you damned me. You sold me out."

"You slept with women and took bribes to change evidence."

"No. No, I did not. People came to me to help right wrongs,

men and women who were being failed by the system. I altered evidence to highlight the truth—show it had been presented by liars
and cheats. Men with ulterior motives, men like you and DI Dent.
I was wronged, I am the victim."

"Oh, come on. I saw your bank records—I saw the women vis-
iting you."

"They wanted to say thank you. Who was I to deny them that?
It was never about the money—I accepted their gratitude as I had
saved them from wrong."

"You are crazy."

"And you, DS Bevans, are ruthless. You know nothing about
true friendship or real loyalty. You would betray everyone for the
sake of the memory of a long-dead girl. How do you sleep at night?"

"Me? What about you, Marcus—you're here to blackmail us."

"Blackmail?" Keyson spits. "I need money to keep fighting for
truth and justice, to protect society from men like you. You don't
keep the girls safe."

"That's not true," Tom says sadly.

"Oh, my melancholy friend—you need to learn a lesson. I don't
want money anymore. You have destroyed so many lives. I am
going to destroy yours." He turns to Patty. "And you, Mrs. Lancing. Mr. Cobhurn was weak, his wife vicious, but you cannot take
the law into your own hands. You can't take a life—you are not
God. I've asked Mr. Ronson to deliver your confession to someone
who can make good use of it." Keyson stands above them all—
looking down with triumph.

"I deserve it." Patty starts to shake. The end will be soon.

Tom puts his hand on her shoulder softly, kindly. "There's no
need to bring Patty into it. She didn't kill Duncan Cobhurn. I did."

"What?" Patty feels everything shift below her, she almost falls.

"And it's your fault, Marcus. You came to see me too soon after

Patty hired you." Tom turns to Patty now. "He'd already talked to the journalist who wrote the *News of the World* piece all those years ago, Ben Bradman, and had sniffed out where I'd altered evidence. He had the case notes from that first night—showed them to you. Even though Dent was good, there were inconsistencies. I knew he could find the truth—that didn't worry me so much as you digging deeper. I . . ." He snorts back some tears. "I didn't want you to know about her death, or my lies. I'm sorry . . . that's why I wanted it to be me that told you about the case review. I hoped I could do it in such a way that you wouldn't get worked up about it . . ." He smiles a tight smile. "Fat chance of that happening. You immediately got roused, a dog with a bone. I could see it that day." He looks directly into Patty's eyes. "Then, after Keyson came to see me, I knew you'd have to follow it up and that Cobhurn was at some kind of risk. I put him on an alert, you and Jim too. Then I decided to visit you again and this time I intended to tell you the whole truth. But, as I got there you came out—in disguise. I followed you to a Heathrow hotel."

"That was a reconnaissance trip." Patty sighed.

"When Duncan Cobhurn went missing I guessed what had happened and figured out why you'd gone to the hotel before. So I went to the same hotel; I thought I would find you there with him. Instead, I found him trussed up—he was unconscious, but alive. There was a syringe on a table with phials of Ketamine. I saw red. I remembered what he'd done to Dani. Got her pregnant and . . . I pumped him up with another two phials, enough to kill him, and then I left."

"Oh, Tom."

"I would never have let you take the blame. I tried to find you after—but you just disappeared."

She nods.

"He destroyed Dani—he should have loved her enough to stand up to me. He should have loved her as much as I did. I would never really have hurt his wife or daughter, it was just a threat, but he didn't love her enough."

"Tom." Patty folds over and begins to sob and sob with relief. The pressure of believing herself to be a killer had been too much. She had been so close to the edge.

"Oh thank God. I didn't . . . thank you thank you."

Jim watches his wife cry tears of happiness—joy that she isn't a murderer, and then looks to Tom. Jim sees the lie. He didn't find Cobhurn—he is taking Patty's crime onto his own shoulders. He can cope with it, whereas it would crush Patty eventually. In that moment Jim loves Tom, sees the hero in him. Not the villain.

❄

Tom looks up to Keyson. "Marcus, stop torturing us, turn me in. For everything—for the cover-up of Dani's death, for Spurling and his son, for Cobhurn, for you. End all this."

Keyson grins. "Tom. It will be a pleasure."

Jim watches Keyson open his phone and start to dial.

"Dad." Dani's voice is all around him. With a smile he looks into her beautiful face again.

"Oh, sweetheart, I am so sorry."

"You need to help me, I can't do it alone," she pleads.

"Anything."

She takes his hand in hers—and for the first time he can feel something, a real physical presence. He stands up and she leads him over to the wall. By the steps is the knife Patty almost killed Tom with.

"Pick it up, Dad."

He does so, and she points to a brass censer tied to the wall.

"Cut it for me, please."

He cuts the censer free from the wall. It is made of brass and incredibly heavy. It hangs from one end of a very long leather strap that extends down, out of the gloom above them. As soon as he cuts it free, it begins to arc into the center of the room and he grabs at it to keep it steady.

"Hold it for me, Dad." She slowly rotates her hands, showing him how to aim it.

Keyson stands with his telephone in hand.

"What service do you require?" The 999 operator asks him.

"Police." Keyson smiles.

"Thank you," Dani says to her father as he holds the brass globe. She moves her hand close to it, as if she could almost touch it herself.

"You can let go now," she tells him and he opens his hands. It swings—a pendulum building up speed as it flies through the air.

"I love you, Dad." She vanishes and appears next to her mother. "I love you, Mum." She blows a kiss to Patty, who for a second feels a shiver deep in her heart. Then she is next to Tom.

"My white knight, be safe," she tells him.

Dani waves to Jim. He watches her float up from them, into the shadows above their heads. Gone.

The sound is like a watermelon hit with a hammer, brass on skull. Keyson's eyes flare as his brain shifts to the left and countless blood vessels burst. His right eye pools with blood and he falls to the ground.

"What?" Tom is up first. He thinks Keyson has been shot, it was so quick.

"The censer." Jim points to it as it sways on the rope like a punch-drunk boxer. There is a slight dent on one side.

"How the hell did that happen?" Tom asks.

Jim would like to tell but . . . what would he say?

"The phone," hisses Patty and she drops down to it. From a long way off she hears: " . . . do you need emergency assistance?"

"Help me," Patty croaks into the phone, then kicks it a long way.

"They'll trace it," Tom warns.

"He needs help."

"What about the other man?" Jim asks.

"Ronson. He probably ran." Tom indicates the prone form of Keyson. "Is he alive?"

Patty reaches out to his neck and lays her fingers over his throat. It's barely there—but there is a pulse.

"Yes, just," she tells him.

Tom looks helpless. A part of him wants to finish Keyson off. Patty sees that run through his mind.

"There's been enough killing, Tom. Enough people hurt. Let's go."

"The knife." Jim goes and picks up the knife.

"Try and clean anything you might have touched. Use a sleeve," Tom warns.

The three of them retrace their steps, picking up anything they see—wiping and cleaning as they go. They walk away from the driftwood Mary and Jesus. Now the ancient woman of wood has two sons at her feet. Cain and Abel?

There is no sign of any other living soul as they leave the cathedral. It is still night but from somewhere they hear the bark of a dog. They pull their coats up to cover their faces and run to the path down by the graveyard.

As they get to the main road, they see their little car is still there. The accident has still not been cleaned up, the police barrier still in place—no vehicle has moved. The three of them get into the car, Tom in the driver's seat and Jim and Patty in the back. Each is silent as the events of the night rerun in their heads. Patty looks out and sees Audrey Cobhurn's blood shine in the light of the emergency vehicle's headlights.

Jim feels Patty place her head in his lap and he strokes her hair as she falls asleep. He looks out of the window and wonders where Dani is. Is she released from her stay on earth?

He wants to call to her—he feels an ache in his heart already. But he looks down and nestled in his lap is his wife who is asleep. That feels like a miracle to him.

Together the two men and sleeping woman wait in the car, to be released. From somewhere far-off they hear a siren. Maybe heading to the cathedral to find Marcus Keyson. Maybe.

As the first light of dawn strikes the city—the emergency vehicles are finally done, and the cars and truck in front of them start to move, limping away from the scene of such awful events. They all have stories to tell. Tom drives them all the way round the ring road, and then second star on the right and straight on till London.

EPILOGUE

Monday, February 7, 2011

The three of them meet at 11 a.m. They go to the garden of remembrance where Jim and Tom have gone, both together and alone for so many years. This is Patty's first visit. Together they read the words on the plaque: DANI, LOVED DEARLY AND MISSED DEEPLY. They lay flowers alongside and Tom reads from Keats.

Then the three of them go to Patty's place of remembrance, the park by the hospital where she planted a tree for Dani. They even go into the supermarket and stand in the deli aisle, on the spot where Dani was born. They all agree it's too cold to stay long. They buy a bottle of champagne and some cheese and bread. They go back to the park and open the fizz. They've forgotten cups so they drink from the bottle, like students.

They toast Dani. She has been dead longer than she lived, but each of them still loves her so fiercely. They toast Jim and Patty—about to renew their vows once again. Tom's phone beeps. He looks at the message and his face clouds over.

"What?" Both Jim and Patty ask.

"It's Keyson. He just woke up from his coma."

Dani stands and watches the watery sun ebb away. Behind her, in a shadowy corner of the room, the young woman sobs quietly. Dani would love to help her, but how—it's impossible.

"Please stop crying, Sarah. It doesn't help."

But the tears continue. Dani sighs. She knows what Sarah Penn needs—to tell her story to the Sad Man. That's what the three of them need, because somehow they know there will be another victim. Soon. But what can she do, apart from listen to the tears fall?

"I'm sorry, Sarah. It's lonely being dead."

ACKNOWLEDGMENTS

I owe a great debt of gratitude to many people who helped me in the planning and writing of this book. My biggest thanks goes to Catherine Smith who pushed me right at the start and nurtured the first shoots of the story. Sophie Hannah gave me support and advice at a crucial time and connected me with my agent, Simon Trewin, who helped me to craft all those pages into something that felt like a book. I am also incredibly lucky to have Gillian Green and Zachary Wagman, two wonderfully creative editors, and Justine Taylor, my copy editor. Plus everyone at WME, Ebury and Crown—what a team.

I also want to thank for their insight and advice on technical aspects of this novel—Durham Coroner Andrew Tweddle and DI Vicki Harris. For medical expertise—Kellie and Kim Cronin. Thanks also to Dominic Parker for his knowledge of Durham.

Many people read early drafts and gave me wonderful feedback and support. I especially want to thank Rebecca Ball, Sylvia Cooke, Rachel Donoughue, Annie Fletcher, Melanie Green, Vikki Logan, Lynne Murphy, Mark Slater, Sam Shorter, Charlie Turner, Jools Wood, Jane Viner, Michael Viner and all at CCE.

And for inspiring me—Arden Murphy-Viner.

ABOUT THE AUTHOR

P. D. Viner is an award-winning filmmaker and creator of the highly successful SmartPass audio guides. He's married to an American doctor of linguistics and, along with their five-year-old daughter, he is her test-subject. He has lived abroad for ten years, working and studying in the USA, New Zealand and Russia, and has been a pretty bad stand-up comedian, produced mime shows for Japanese TV and written theater for the Shakespeare festival produced in London and Verona.

This is his first murder.